Bewitched

Jack sat bolt upright and looked at the clock. Barely after dawn. The cat must have gotten into some—

He stopped. He sniffed. The bacon smell was still there, permeating the apartment. And so were other smells, just as wonderful. Jack had the bizarre notion that the cat had learned to cook. Hadn't he had some sort of weird dream about the cat and some woman with the same green eyes. . . .

—from "Saving Sirena" by Susan Krinard

Bewitched

Susan Krinard

Maggie Shayne

Lisa Higdon

Amy Elizabeth Saunders

JOVE BOOKS, NEW YORK

"Saving Sirena" by Susan Krinard copyright © 1997 by Susan Krinard.
"Everything She Does Is Magick" by Maggie Shayne
copyright © 1997 by Margaret Benson.
"To Mend a Spell" by Lisa Higdon copyright © 1997 by Lisa Higdon.
"A Spell of Mist and Roses" by Amy Elizabeth Saunders
copyright © 1997 by Amy Tucker.

BEWITCHED

A Jove Book / published by arrangement with
the authors

PRINTING HISTORY
Jove edition / October 1997

ISBN: 0-515-12157-6

A JOVE BOOK®
Jove Books are published by The Berkley Publishing Group,
a member of Penguin Putnam Inc.,
200 Madison Avenue, New York, New York 10016.
JOVE and the "J" design are trademarks
belonging to Jove Publications, Inc.

PRINTED IN THE UNITED STATES OF AMERICA

10 9 8 7 6 5 4 3 2 1

Contents

Bewitched

Saving Sirena

Susan Krinard

Prologue

"She's almost out of time."

The Council of Three, West Coast Region, gazed down at Demosthenes with widely varying expressions. The Maiden, as always, looked severe, the Mother sympathetic, and the Crone thoughtful.

Not one of them appeared ready to revoke the curse.

"You realize," the Maiden said, "that she has but one life remaining. If she loses this last chance—"

Demosthenes knew all too well. He twitched his nose and summoned up all his courage for another try.

"Only look at her," he said. "Please."

They looked. The scrying pool shimmered into focus again. The Crone leaned closer, squinting. "She looks pathetic, all right," she commented. "Waste of talent."

"She earned this punishment," the Maiden said. "She misused her power over mortals one too many times. She was warned."

"Poor child," the Mother crooned. "Why did she find it necessary to use spells at all? She was so attractive. Any mortal man would have fallen in love with her just as she is."

"*Was,*" the Crone corrected.

"It wasn't about love," the Maiden said. "It was all a game to her."

"But none of her mortal lovers truly suffered," the Mother protested.

"I believe it was an addiction with her," the Crone remarked. "Similar to Wilhelmina's kleptomania—"

"Wilhelmina stole *things*, not hearts," the Maiden snapped. "Sirena stole the free will of the men she seduced. She was without compassion. Without compassion, Magick becomes a tool of darkness."

Demosthenes scurried forward. "I beg to differ. She has a very large heart—"

"*Had* a very large heart," the Crone said.

"—but you have taken away any hope that the curse can be broken," he finished in a rush. "She is on her last life. If someone doesn't rescue her soon . . ."

Ripples disturbed the clear water of the scrying pool. The image within it shuddered. Demosthenes shivered in sympathy. Cold, and wet, and hopeless—he had come to know how terrible that felt.

"I've never seen a mouse with so much sympathy for a cat," the Mother said. "It does you great credit, Demosthenes."

"Ha," the Maiden scoffed. "He knows if Sirena pays in full for her crimes, he'll have to find himself another patron."

"But he's stayed close to her, in spite of her loss of memory," the Mother said gently. "To act against the Laws of Nature with such courage—"

"It's not the Laws of Nature we're discussing," the Maiden said. "Or Demosthenes. Sirena must complete her trial. If a mortal does not choose to take her in—of his own free will, and in spite of her nature and appearance—before her ninth life is up, she will die as a cat. Are we in agreement?"

The Mother sighed and the Crone pursed her lips, but when the Maiden extended her hand the others placed theirs upon it, sealing the judgment to which there was no appeal.

Demosthenes closed his eyes and tucked his tail close to

his side. It had been a forlorn hope, but one he'd had to try. It was hard watching over a mistress who kept trying to eat you. Even though that was hardly Sirena's fault. She didn't remember she'd ever been anything but a cat.

And she never would, unless a miracle occurred. . . .

The Council members were rising, preparing to depart the Chamber of Judgment on the astral plane and return to their mortal lives. Demosthenes was bound for the same— for the dark, cold alley and puddles of black water and whatever shelter he could find on this bleak October night.

Poor Sirena.

He glanced again at the scrying pool. The view had expanded beyond the alley, taking in the buildings and the street and a man walking, his raincoat pulled high around his ears and his head down under the driving rain.

A miracle. That was what Sirena needed. Demosthenes twitched his whiskers and recited the incantation that would take him home.

Maybe it was time for a mouse to become a miracle worker.

One

Jack turned the collar of his raincoat higher around his ears and wondered why he bothered. He was already soaked to the skin, and it wasn't as if he had any reason to rush home.

Tonight's clinic had been particularly difficult. Oh, not for himself, but for all the people he had so little power to help in the ways that mattered most. The free legal aid he gave them seldom completely solved their problems. He'd seen only a fraction of this suffering when he'd been a county prosecutor.

Law and order. That had always been his mantra. He'd learned in the past eight months how blurry the line could get between right and wrong, justice and injustice. And how necessary *pro bono* work was. And how hard it could be to make ends meet on temporary day-job wages when no one would hire him for what he was trained to do. No one wanted a prosecutor whose blunder had let a con man walk. Especially when half the town of Vinatera had been bilked by the bastard.

Jack slowed as he passed Walter's hardware store and stared into the dark, rain-streaked window. *Ditch the self-pity, Danner. You can keep going as long as it takes. Until someone's willing to overlook the past.*

Sheer stubbornness had kept him in town when he could

have gone someplace where they wouldn't know or wouldn't care about his slipup. He could have found work in another county, or a big city like San Francisco, or even L.A.

But he'd grown up in Vinatera. Here he'd earned the money to work his way through law school. This was home. He had to prove he wasn't the fool the whole county thought he was. Somehow.

He was turning for home again when someone cried for help.

It was a very faint voice, almost childlike. It was coming from the alley next to Walter's. Jack didn't stop to analyze it further; he stepped into the alley.

Something small and white ran between his feet. He jumped. Only a damn mouse, but he didn't have much use for rodents. He waited for the voice again, but it didn't come.

He took another step into the alley, peering into the gloom. No one. Nothing human, anyway. Only the mouse and something else moving under the dubious shelter of a stack of crates. Something black and soaking wet, with wide green eyes that blinked at him fearfully.

A cat. Jack straightened and passed his hand over his face, wringing off the wet. He needed to have his hearing checked. The poor beast looked miserable enough, but he didn't think cats had learned how to talk.

But if they could . . . if they could, this one might have quite a tale to tell. It was small and scrawny, with its fur plastered against a half-starved body. Its eyes were the only feature remotely attractive about it, and they were fixed on him as if he were a judge about to hand down a life sentence.

Jack crouched. "Here, kitty kitty."

The cat arched its back and tried to make its wet hair stand on end, none too successfully. Jack gave it a lopsided grin.

"Scared, huh? You look as crummy as I feel. How long you been out here?"

Disdaining to answer, the cat scrunched farther back into its corner. The rain pursued it mercilessly.

Damn. Jack stood, glancing over his shoulder. What could he do? Pretty obvious the cat wouldn't let itself be caught. But it wasn't right leaving an abandoned creature out in weather like this.

He had to try. He'd come into the alley thinking he'd heard a cry for help. Maybe that part had been his imagination, but he knew when something needed him.

Something he could save.

"Okay, kitty. Your luck is about to change." He noted the length of the alley, the high chain-link fence at the back. The cat probably couldn't climb it. He had a suspicion that it would have run if it could.

After a moment's deliberation he shrugged out of his coat. The inside was fairly dry, and warm with his body heat. He tucked it over his arm. Cold rain sluiced down his shirt.

"Nice kitty," he said, stalking forward. "I won't hurt you. I've got some milk at home—"

The cat hissed and streaked from its hiding place to the back of the alley. There it huddled, ears against its head. As Jack drew closer it seemed to press flatter and flatter to the ground. He thought it was too scared to fight. He *hoped* it was.

Just a few more feet. Jack crouched again and gingerly held out his hand. "That's right. Just relax—"

A black paw shot out. Jack gave a startled yelp. He looked at the neat parallel scratches on his finger. They hurt like hell. The cat followed up with a hiss that made its opinion of him very clear.

"Okay, kitty. If that's how you feel . . ." He stood up. The cat tried to squeeze through the chain-link fence. Almost skinny enough to do it, too. Jack muttered and imagined a nice cup of coffee and a sandwich and a late movie—thoroughly escapist fare that had nothing to do with rain, dark alleys, and ungrateful felines.

He was turning to go when the cat whimpered. Not a mew, or a purr, but a whimper.

Oh, hell. Jack stopped with his coat half on and the rain plastering his hair to his forehead. He couldn't leave her. He didn't know what had put the idea into his head, but suddenly he was sure the cat was a *she*. Even if females were a load of trouble in general, he couldn't abandon the cat to an undoubtedly grim fate.

He took off his coat again. Time to attack the problem from a different angle. And make sure the cat had no more chances to attack *him*.

She hadn't moved when he turned back to her. He would have sworn the light was fading from her green eyes, her body going limp and melting into the puddle that gathered at her paws.

"I'm going to save you, kitty," he said, "whether you like it or not." And he spread his coat wide between his hands and cast it like a net.

He moved very fast and gathered the bundle of struggling feline in his arms. Her outraged yowls were faint and muffled further by the coat. After a few moments she went completely still.

In alarm he checked beneath the coat. She was staring at him, eyes slitted, exhausted but alive. He felt a surge of triumph.

"Let's get out of this rain, kitty." He frowned. "I'm going to have to come up with a better name for you. 'Kitty' doesn't cut it. What's a good name for a nasty, bad-tempered, scrawny, ungrateful cat?"

The animal in question gave him a look of utmost disdain and sneezed in his face.

Jack covered her up again, tucked her under his arm and walked the remaining blocks home without further speculation about his unwilling guest's obstinate nature. The apartment building looked even more run-down than usual in the rain. He managed to get his key out of his pocket one-handed and checked his mailbox on the way upstairs.

He knew before he flipped awkwardly through the envelopes what he wouldn't find: a response to his résumé. Not that he hadn't hoped. After eight months he still hoped.

"How do you like that, kitty? Am I a fool?"

The cat shivered, and he remembered that there were a lot of folks much worse off than he was. At least he had a roof over his head—even if it was probably leaking.

But the place was warm and out of the rain. He got the door open and carried the cat inside, catching the light switch with his elbow. He looked around the small living room, considering the best place to put her. He didn't have a cage, and somehow it seemed wrong to lock her up after what she'd been through. Even if she decided to claw his furniture, it wouldn't be much of a loss.

"Listen up, kitty. I'm going to let you loose. I hope you have the sense to make the most of this. I think I have a can of tuna left, and it's all yours."

He set his bundle on the ugly green sofa. The coat rippled and rocked, and then the cat's head emerged. He left her to her exploration and went into the kitchen to check the cupboards.

He found the tuna. The rest of the cupboard was depressingly bare. But he did have milk—enough for him and the cat. He poured a cupful of milk into a pan and set it on the stove to heat.

When he got back to the living room his coat was empty and the cat was nowhere to be seen. Hiding, undoubtedly, until she had a chance to check the place out. He didn't blame her.

He set the warm milk and tuna down where she could reach it and sighed. He'd lost his desire for the sandwich and late show; better turn in. Tomorrow he'd have to pound the pavement for another temporary job—whatever he could find to keep body and soul together. And provide for his new roommate.

It might not be so bad, at that. At least he'd have nonjudgmental company. The cat wouldn't care if he'd screwed up.

Maybe he and the cat needed each other.

"Make yourself comfortable," he said to the room at large. "We'll get better acquainted in the morning."

The cat chose not to answer. Jack shrugged and removed his shirt and tie, leaving them draped over the permanently listing recliner. He had to remember to get to the Laundromat tomorrow. . . .

On his way to the bedroom he nearly tripped over a tiny scurrying form. Another mouse, for God's sake. They seemed to have it in for him. At least the cat might be good for keeping them away.

Pleased at the notion, Jack settled into his lumpy double bed. For once he went to sleep quickly; his last drowsy thought was that the apartment had become a little less lonely than it had been this morning.

The next thing he was aware of was the incredible smell of frying bacon. Hot, sizzling bacon, burnt crisp just the way he liked it.

He rolled over with a groan, flinging his arm across his face, and tried to hang onto the dream. Groggily he tried to remember the last time he'd had bacon. He couldn't cook worth a damn—he'd eaten most meals out when he'd been working for the D.A.

But this was heavenly. He might have gone right back to sleep except for the rather loud clang from the vicinity of the kitchen.

Jack sat bolt upright and looked at the clock. Barely after dawn. The cat must have gotten into some—

He stopped. He sniffed. The bacon smell was still there, permeating the apartment. And so were other smells, just as wonderful. Jack had the bizarre notion that the cat had learned to cook. Hadn't he had some sort of weird dream about the cat and some woman with the same green eyes. . . .

Who in hell was cooking in his apartment?

He swung his legs over the bed, grabbed hastily for his frayed terry-cloth robe and jogged down the short hall. A quick glance into the living room brought no sight of the cat. And in the kitchen . . .

In the kitchen stood a woman. A petite woman with tumbled dark hair cascading down her back. A woman with shapely legs visible to upper thigh, the rest of her barely covered by the shirt he'd left over the chair last night.

"Man, oh man," Jack muttered.

She turned. The shirt was unbuttoned to the deep vee between a pair of very nice . . . He jerked his gaze up to her face.

Green eyes. They were the second attribute he noticed. Brilliant green eyes, slanted like a cat's, shadowed by equally slanted dark brows that gave the woman a permanently mischievous look. Her nose had a Mediterranean cast, her lips were full, her chin pointed. And she was grinning at him as if she'd just won the lottery and he was the guy with the check.

But that was only the half of it.

Jack felt behind him for the wall. For a moment he was too stunned to do anything but stare. Between him and the woman was spread, on a huge table he'd never seen in his life, a breakfast banquet of epic proportions. The bacon was only a small part of it. He counted at least three kinds of eggs, each on its own silver plate; pancakes heaped nearly to the ceiling; bowls and plates of exotic fruits; lobster and roast beef; and a half-dozen other items he didn't immediately recognize.

His stomach rumbled loudly. He disregarded it and met the woman's laughing gaze.

"What the hell are you doing in my—"

He didn't get a chance to finish. He didn't even realize what she intended until, having somehow circumvented the table in a matter of seconds, she was on him. *On* him, her arms locked around his neck, her breasts against his chest, her mouth fitted to his.

The kiss was spectacular. It held a quality Jack didn't think he'd ever experienced in a kiss before—unmitigated joy, a blending of sophistication and innocence that bypassed all the nice civilized controls of logic and reason. Jack found himself responding, his arms closing around her, his tongue touching hers.

And then his brain kicked in. He pushed her away—not without effort, since she seemed determined to attach herself to him permanently.

He caught his breath, dizzy with the most immediate and

potent desire he'd ever experienced in his life. "Who," he croaked, "who the hell are you?"

She laughed. "Don't you know?" She spun around in a circle, hugging herself, and the tail of his shirt lifted to reveal the sleek curve of one hip.

Jack beat down his body's instant reaction. "I don't have the slightest idea who you are," he said stiffly, "or how all this food got in here, but I think you'd better leave."

"Oh, Jack." She glided back to him. "You are my savior, and you must let me thank you." She placed one delicate finger on his lower lip. "Don't you like my gratitude?"

Okay. She was obviously disturbed. Someone off the streets, maybe—except he was sure he'd locked the door. And it didn't explain where all this food had come from. Or how in hell she knew his name.

Or why he could stand here wanting a total stranger after what had happened last time.

"How did you get in here?" he demanded.

"Why, you brought me," she said. She all but danced to the couch in the living room and picked up his coat, wrapping it around her shoulders. "Don't you remember?"

He shook his head. No, dammit—*no*. He hadn't been drunk last night. He hadn't taken a drink since the mistake that had cost him his job. He wouldn't have brought a woman home after that. He *hadn't*. In eight months the only female he'd had any dealings with, outside the clinic, was the cat from the alley.

The cat. He looked to the place where he'd left the milk and tuna. Both bowls were empty.

Suddenly—he didn't know why and didn't question the impulse—it seemed vitally important to find the cat. Ignoring his unwelcome guest, he began to search. Under the sofa, under the recliner, in the closet, everywhere a cat could conceivably hide.

"She's right under your nose," the woman said, clearly amused. "Oh, you mortals can be *so* shortsighted."

He straightened from his crouch beside the chair. "What?"

The way she moved was mesmerizing. One moment she was across the room and the next kneeling beside him, rubbing against his shoulder and jaw with a mass of slightly damp and curly hair.

" 'Here, kitty kitty,' " she purred. "Does that ring a bell?"

Good Lord. He scrambled to his feet. "How did you know that? Did you follow me?"

She stood and placed her hands on her hips. "Can't all this wait until after breakfast? I spent the past two hours conjuring it up for you." She plucked her lower lip. "I *am* a bit out of practice."

Jack wondered if he'd heard her right. Conjuring? Was everything she said crazy, or was it him? "Look," he said calmly. "Whoever you are, I think—" He stopped as she moved closer, fingering the button of the shirt she wore— the button closest to the shadow of her cleavage. "Uh, where are your clothes?"

She stretched, arching her back in a way that came dangerously close to popping the button. "Oh, I haven't had any in ages. What would you like me to wear?"

He clenched his teeth, trying to think with something above his belt. His lapse in judgment had been what got him into trouble before, and he knew less about this woman than he had about Bagley's ex-wife.

He wasn't like those guys who'd jump into the sack with anything in skirts. Or, in this case, shirts. Not even when they turned up in his apartment with a full-course breakfast.

"Well?" she said, tossing her luxurious hair over her shoulders. "Perhaps you'd rather I wore nothing at all?"

He blinked. When he looked at her again she was wearing . . . nothing. He spun away before he'd had more than a glimpse, fiery heat washing his face.

"I think you'd better go," he choked.

"You wouldn't throw me out when you just took me in," she said behind him, her voice a throaty whisper. "You aren't the type of man who'd do that. You're far too kind." Her hands settled on his shoulders, fingers curving in, massaging his rigid muscles. "Don't you even want to know my name?"

"Uh . . ."

"It's Sirena." She put her lips to his ear. "Sirena. And you saved my life, Jack Danner. You saved it when you rescued that scrawny, ungrateful black cat from the alley. Of course—" Her lips brushed his neck above the collar of his robe. "I do think I look much better now, don't you?"

The touch of her mouth on his skin was making his pulse do cartwheels. "You—the cat—"

"That's right, silly. But I'd rather not talk about it. There are so many better ways of . . . spending our time."

The primitive part of Jack agreed completely. His brain was still trying to make sense of what she'd just said, and coming up with utter nonsense.

"You, uh—were in the alley with the cat?" he asked blankly.

She sighed, and he felt the thump of her forehead against his back. "Jack, Jack, Jack. I *am* the cat."

"You *are* the—"

"Come on, before it all gets cold." She took his hand and tugged him toward the kitchen. At least she was dressed again—more or less—but that was little comfort. Jack dug his feet into the worn carpet, freeing himself from her tenacious hold.

"Hold it. Did you just say you *are* the cat?"

The woman's—Sirena's—full lips were curved, her eyes sparkling. She clapped her hands. "I knew you'd understand. Now, would you rather have orange juice . . ." She eased up against him, working her hand beneath the collar of his robe. ". . . or something a little more exotic?"

Her innuendo raised the temperature in the room by another ten degrees. With a supreme effort Jack shook off his befuddlement and took her by the shoulders, holding her away.

"Listen," he said carefully. "Maybe you should go lie down. You're not . . . well."

She rolled her eyes. "I summon you as witness, Demosthenes. I've been totally honest with this man." Her attention seemed focused on an invisible object. "Oh, very well. If you think it will make a difference."

Oh, brother. Now she was talking to invisible Greek orators. Jack wondered if she'd escaped from some kind of institution. Except there wasn't one here in Vinatera. The nearest hospital was—

"Come along, Jack," she said, grabbing him by the hand again. It was only a few steps to the kitchen. The incredible smells hadn't dissipated; in fact, they were more overwhelming than ever. Sirena let him go and walked, hips swaying, to the other side of the laden table.

"Now watch carefully," she said. "I've never shown this to a mortal before. But Teeny is right. I do owe you my life." She grinned. "It might even be fun."

With a dramatic flourish she lifted her hands and closed her eyes. Her lips moved. The air over the table seemed to shimmer like a country road on a hot summer's day.

And then the table . . . wasn't there anymore. Or the plates and bowls and silver. Or the food. A faint scent of bacon lingered in the air, and then that too was gone.

Jack laughed. He coughed. He passed his hand over his eyes and pinched himself. When he was perfectly certain he was awake and hadn't lost his mind, he met Sirena's triumphant gaze.

"Would you mind telling me . . . how you did that?"

Sirena brushed her fingers through her hair. "The technicalities, you mean? It's all so boring. Esmeralda could have explained—Yes, Teeny, I know she's Crone now. But she was always so . . . *logical*."

Jack didn't ask who "Teeny" was. "Is this some kind of illusion?"

She walked across the room to him and draped her arms over his shoulders. "Of course not. It's magic."

Okay. He'd go along. It was hard to concentrate when her lips were inches from his. "And you're a magician?"

Her laugh was sparkling. "How funny you are, Jack. I do like you. And I know I can trust you." She leaned closer still. "Haven't you guessed by now? I'm a witch."

Two

Sirena didn't know quite what to expect. After all, she hadn't told any of her previous mortal lovers what she really was. And it *was* frowned upon by the Council.

Not that that would have stopped her. But revealing her true nature did make matters unnecessarily complicated when all she—and for that matter, her mortal lovers—wanted was a bit of fun. *Those* men hadn't needed to know what she was to enjoy what she had to offer.

Jack was different. It wasn't only that he'd broken the curse. There'd been his gentleness, of course, in the way he'd handled a thoroughly nasty cat. Not that she'd meant to be nasty. That had been part of the curse as well, to make sure a mortal would have to work to save her.

But it was more than his gentleness, or his generosity in saving her. More than his clean-cut but eminently masculine good looks and auburn hair and deep brown eyes. He was intriguing, especially because he could resist her.

She wasn't used to men resisting her. But it had been so long since she'd been with a man at all. Her memory of years spent as a cat was blessedly foggy, but she remembered loneliness, and helplessness, and fear. Feelings she didn't like.

Now that was over, thanks to Jack. Sirena was grateful.

Deeply grateful. And she intended to show her rescuer in ways he'd never forget.

Oh, yes. This *would* be fun.

"You're a what?" Jack asked, breaking into her pleasant reverie.

"A witch." She searched his eyes. He wasn't taking this as well as she'd hoped. "Oh, I always forget. You mortals always have to have proof, don't you? I suppose once isn't enough."

She glanced over her shoulder and reversed the spell. The table and its burden reappeared. Jack flinched.

At least he was fairly pliable in his amazement. She laced her fingers through his and led him to the table. "Go ahead. Taste it."

He barely resisted, thank Diana. He went for the bacon first. He gave a startled oath when it burned his fingers. He sniffed and studied it from every angle.

Sirena thought how easy it would be to cast a tiny little suggestion spell and make him believe. Easy, but annoyingly impossible considering the circumstances. Thanks to those stick-in-the-mud Puritans who ran the Council. . . .

She was wondering just how much she *could* get away with when Jack finally dared to sample the bacon. He bit down—and his face took on an amazed expression that swiftly turned to sheer bliss.

"You like it!" Sirena exclaimed happily.

Jack dropped the remaining bacon and stared at her. "It's real," he said.

"It's the best," she corrected. "My hero deserves only the best." She looked over the table. "Is there something I've forgotten? Maybe—"

But he wasn't listening. He was on the way out of the kitchen, hitting the doorframe hard with his shoulder as he walked into the living room. Sirena left the food where it was and followed.

"I hope you're not one of those people who thinks witches have warts and hooked noses," she said, kneeling before him as he sat on the hideous green sofa. "I just can't do that to myself." His knees felt firm and masculine as she touched him. Oh, *how* she'd missed men. "But there's so much more I can give you, Jack. Whatever you could possibly desire."

There was a brief flicker of response in his gaze, intriguing and too quickly gone. "Why?" he asked bluntly.

"Because you broke the curse. The one that turned me into a cat until someone—" She slid her hands under the hem of his robe. "Until *you* rescued me."

Jack stared at the slow but steady progress of her hands. "Curse?" he muttered.

Teeny had recommended honesty—insisted on it, in fact—but honesty was useful only to a certain point. She'd admit to a curse, but not the reason for it. That was all in the past, anyway.

"It doesn't matter now. What matters is you saved me, and I'm so . . . very grateful."

Her fingers brushed the muscle of his upper thigh. He all but shot off the couch, yanking the sash of the robe tightly about his lean waist as he crossed the room.

By Diana. He was actually blushing. That was certainly not a habit she'd seen in any of her lovers before. They weren't the kind of men who blushed. Any one of them would have been accepting her gratitude with open arms by now.

They also weren't the kind of men who'd save an alley cat during a rainstorm.

Sirena frowned. Jack Danner was a bigger puzzle than she'd first imagined. He might even take a little more effort than she was used to expending. But his reluctance wasn't, *couldn't* be because she was forbidden to use the glamour. She didn't need spells to win any man she chose. The Council might believe it, but she knew better.

Jack Danner would be proof of that. Repaying him was not her only motive. Now she had something to prove. He was a challenge . . . and such a thoroughly delicious one.

By the time she was finished, he wasn't going to be the least bit shy about accepting his reward.

She jumped to her feet. "Well? Where shall I begin?"

Jack's straight brows were drawn in a look as severe as

any Council member had ever bestowed on her. "Begin what?"

"Giving you whatever you desire, of course." She looked around the apartment and clucked sympathetically. She could certainly begin with this.

Chanting softly, she began to circle the room, touching the hideous worn furniture and noting every bare shelf. No, this wouldn't do at all. Her Jack should be living in luxury.

With an appropriate image fully formed in her mind, she built the proper spell around it. After the morning's work with the breakfast she was just a little tired, but seeing Jack's face when she was finished would be more than worth the sacrifice.

She knelt in the center of the room and traced a circle in the matted carpet with a fingernail, silently requesting Teeny's aid to focus her power. Jack stared at her as if she'd lost her mind, but she didn't let herself be distracted. Not until the transformation began.

When it was finished she laughed and clapped her hands. Perfect. Where there had been ugly secondhand furniture was now the best designer models, rich leather upholstery, and the finest walnut cabinets. The carpet had been replaced by priceless Persian area rugs. She did have excellent taste, if she did say so herself.

"Now, Jack," she said. "What do you think of that?"

All the color had left his face. He opened his mouth and closed it again. It was obvious that she'd overwhelmed him with her skill. Possibly she'd been just a little impulsive. . . .

"Put it back," he croaked.

"But—" She stared at him. "But Jack, this is only—"

"Put it back. Please."

She couldn't deny his request, incomprehensible as it was. She nullified the spell. The apartment returned to its dingy, dismal origins. Jack closed his eyes and slumped against the nearest wall.

Sirena tugged her left earlobe. Where had she gone wrong? It was obvious how much Jack needed her assistance, as little as she knew about him. "You didn't like it? I can make it any way you want."

He met her gaze with a level, unblinking stare. "You said you can give me anything I ask for?"

This was more like it. "Anything."

"Then I'd really appreciate it if you'd just go away."

She laughed at his absurdity. "Go away?"

"Go—wherever you like. If I broke your curse, you're free. You don't owe me." He strode to the door and opened it. "You can . . . certainly take care of yourself."

He was serious. Sirena blinked. He could have whatever he desired, and *her*, and he asked her to leave. There was no such mortal on earth.

"You don't mean that, Jack," she said, swaying toward him.

"I do. Look, I've got . . . important business to take care of this morning. If you need money, I can lend you some."

As absurd as it was, he *did* mean it. He didn't want all the gifts she could give him. He didn't find her desirable. His expression was locked in rigid lines that showed no signs of softening. His brown eyes were focused on some point above her head, refusing to acknowledge her beauty.

And Sirena knew, from a century's experience with mortalkind, that she would lose him before she could make him see how wrong he was. If she gave him what he asked and walked out that door, she might not get another chance.

Panic was not an emotion she was used to. Or rejection. Or the real, burning certainty that she could not be separated from Jack Danner until—until . . .

"I can't go," she whispered, and buckled dramatically to the floor.

At once Jack was at her side, hovering, almost touching but not knowing where to put his hands. After a moment he tugged her shirt down around her hips and cupped his fingers under her neck.

"Are you all right?"

"Oh, Jack," she said faintly, fluttering her eyes. "I can't leave. It's part of the curse. If my rescuer refuses to keep me for . . ." She calculated quickly. "For three days—until midnight on Halloween—the curse will recommence. I'll become a cat again—forever.''

It was quite satisfying to watch his face. He didn't want to believe, but he hadn't wanted to believe the rest, either. Sirena knew how persuasive she could be. Unless she'd been completely wrong about Jack Danner, he wasn't going to kick her out with such a threat hanging over her head.

He was too . . . decent. Yes, that was the word. He practically exuded decency. And honesty. He'd no more abandon her than he'd abandon the cat she'd been.

''Oh, man,'' he muttered. ''This is insane.''

''This is witchcraft,'' she said, making a valiant attempt to rise.

''Stay right there. Do, uh, witches—do you need some aspirin or something?''

''We eat and drink and do everything much as mortals do. Only better.'' She laced her arms around his neck. ''I'll be all right if you'll just hold me, Jack.'' She gave a little shuddering sob. ''It was so awful being a cat, with no one to care for me, all alone in that alley.'' A tear trickled down her cheek. ''No one wanted me. Oh, Jack, you can't imagine.''

Strangely enough, the look he gave her suggested he might imagine more than she expected. He glanced around the room as if checking for invisible observers and slowly, reluctantly gathered her against him. His arms were strong and capable and wonderful. Sirena sighed and melted into him.

This was much better than merely fun. Now she simply had to loosen him up.

His heart was beating very fast. He was far from indifferent to her, no matter how much he pretended otherwise. She sniffled for effect and snuggled closer.

''I knew you were a good man,'' she murmured. Her lips found the bare vee of his chest where the robe didn't quite cover.

He stiffened. ''If you're all right now, I . . . need a little fresh air.''

Her protest was ignored. He eased her down gently and

retreated into the bedroom as if a thousand demons were at his heels. Sirena folded her arms indignantly. He couldn't have seen through her. Mortals just weren't that perceptive.

But when he emerged he was fully dressed, hastily knotting his tie. "You just . . . stay put, okay?" he said, not meeting her gaze.

"Then you'll let me stay?"

His muffled curse was mild but ardent. "For now. Just don't . . . *do* anything while I'm gone. Don't replace my furniture—or anything else." He finally looked at her. "Promise me."

"I promise," she said solemnly. "If that's what you want—"

"I want. And could you get dressed?"

She plucked at her borrowed shirt. "What would you like me to wear?"

"Something"—he cleared his throat—"a little less revealing."

That didn't sound at all fun. But she had three days, at least—three days to make him fall for her like all the others. And prove to the Council she didn't need spells on him or a glamour on herself to do it.

Wouldn't that prune-faced Maiden be annoyed.

Jack gave her one last, uneasy look before he went out the door. Sirena sat on the carpet, legs crossed, and pursed her lips.

"Come on out, Teeny. He's gone."

The mouse emerged from behind the dusty particle-board television stand. "I wish you wouldn't call me that, Sirena," he complained. "It's not dignified."

"Demosthenes," she said, pronouncing each syllable with mocking precision, "is such a stuffy name."

He sat on his hindquarters, whiskers twitching disapproval. "You'd better start getting stuffier yourself if you expect to stay human. You're already flirting with danger, casting spells left and right—"

"But only the safe kind," she retorted. "The curse didn't forbid me from using Magick, only from bending the will of mortals or making myself irresistible. I don't need spells to do that."

Teeny covered his face with his paws. "I don't like the sound of this," he groaned. "You're going to step over the line, Sirena. I know you. You can't resist temptation. Let's just get out of here while he's gone, and we'll go somewhere nice and quiet—"

She rolled onto her back and kicked up her legs. "Quiet? After years as a cat, that's the last thing I need." She frowned. "It *was* years, wasn't it? I lost track of time."

"Five," Teeny said. "And you used up all but your ninth life, too."

"Poor Teeny. It must have been so hard for you. Did I try to eat you?"

"More than once."

"I'm sorry for that." She held out her hand, and Teeny came to her. She stroked his soft fur and suffered a jarring flash of guilt. When had she last felt guilty? "You shouldn't have suffered because of me. You could have found another patron—"

"Then who'd look after you?" He fixed her with his beady stare. "You can't stay here, Sirena. This man saved you. He doesn't deserve what you'll do to him."

"Do to him? I only want to help him."

"And what if he doesn't want your help?"

"He will. I'll make—" She stopped herself. "I'll convince him. When he sees what I can do for him . . ."

"You know nothing about him."

"I'll learn."

"You never bothered to learn about your previous conquests."

Her skin was oddly warm. "Jack's different. Can't you feel it?"

"All the more reason to leave him alone."

"I can't."

He looked at her narrowly. "What is it, Sirena? There's a change in you. Have you finally learned your lesson?"

"Maybe I have," she said. For a moment she relived the moment when Jack had held her. She couldn't remember the last time she'd felt so . . . safe. Protected. She, a witch, who'd never deprived herself of anything she desired. Who'd never needed anything from mortal men but amusement and an escape from boredom.

Until she'd needed a man to rescue her from the curse.

That train of thought disturbed her. Much too serious. She winked broadly at Teeny. "Stop worrying. When I'm through with Jack, he'll know that rescuing me was the best good deed he's ever done. You wait and see."

Teeny rolled over on his side and played dead. Sirena tickled his tummy and left him writhing while she began a more thorough exploration of Jack's little apartment.

The mouse was right. She didn't know nearly enough about Jack Danner . . . or what it would take to break down his resistance.

His bedroom seemed the place to start looking. It was very neat in spite of the sparse furniture and modest possessions. An old scratched desk stood against one wall; Sirena ran her hand idly over the books lined up in a row on the meticulously neat surface. She paused at the spine of a battered textbook that had obviously seen heavy use.

Ah. Yes. She closed her eyes, cleared her mind, and left herself open to the images that came to her.

The dorm room is quiet and dark. Jack's roommate is out partying, confident of passing the test. Jack doesn't have that luxury. His day job leaves him with only the nights to study, and he must pass this exam. No, he has to do more than pass—he has to do well, to prove to everyone who didn't believe in him that he can succeed, that he's more than the kid from the wrong side of the tracks who won't ever amount to anything.

He pushes away those dark reflections and concentrates on the book. Let the others party. He knows what's really important.

Sirena withdrew her hand and grimaced. Jack had been much younger in that image, but he was already serious, determined . . . driven. While his friends were out having fun, he could think only of studying for some awful test.

What mortals did to themselves!

She continued to survey the desk, discovering a pile of dog-eared notebooks, each crammed to the margins with notes in bold but precise handwriting. She opened a notebook at random and laid her palm flat against a page.

The book-filled room is dark save for a single light on the table beside him. He closes one massive legal text and moves to the next, searching for the precedent he needs. The coming trial is his big break; he has to plan this perfectly, leave no loopholes for Bagley to weasel out of his just punishment.

Jack glances at the clock on the wall. Past two A.M. He won't sleep tonight. He'll have to cancel lunch with Bartlett tomorrow. He feels a twinge of regret and crushes it. Sacrifices are necessary. He's not lonely. He's too busy to be lonely.

Sirena shut the notebook, shaking her head. Oh, this was worse than she'd expected. A lawyer, no less! Almost as bad as a Puritan!

She glanced around the room and wandered to the closet. A mortal's clothes said so much about his personality. Jack's wardrobe was filled with dull suits and conservative ties. She reached in to finger the wool of a very proper gray suit jacket, and the next image came.

The courtroom is crowded. He's standing before the defendant, confronting the con man with sharp and merciless questions. Bagley's counsel objects and the judge overrules him. It's all going Jack's way. He'll get this guy, make him pay for all the wrongs he's done innocent people in town. When Bagley's ex-wife testifies for the prosecution, it'll be in the can.

And when Jack's won this trial, nothing can stop him. All the years of putting himself through school, of fighting every step of the way to make something of himself, will have been worth it. He'll make a career of putting criminals behind bars where they belong, of standing up for justice and law and order. . . .

Jack wasn't merely a lawyer—he was a prosecutor. Sirena gave a delicate shudder. What would Jack think of *her*

Magickal "crimes"? No, she wasn't about to tell him more about the curse.

But what was a lawyer doing living like this?

Poor Jack! He was in desperate need of rescue from the dull life he'd made for himself. Sirena released the jacket and folded her arms, frowning in concentration. Clearly he *needed* her help. She could loosen him up and teach him to enjoy life—whether he realized he wanted it or not.

But she would have to be creative. Sirena jumped onto Jack's bed and performed a pirouette on the pillows. Creative was exactly what she was good at. Jack's most secret fantasies were not exactly obvious, but . . .

On a burst of inspiration she returned to the closet and initiated a search spell. It led her to a dusty box shoved far into the corner—a box packed with books. Not legal tomes or textbooks but paperbacks: fiction, novels of adventure, derring-do, romance. Books Jack hadn't touched in a very long time.

Sirena rocked back on her heels and banished the dust on her hands with a light cleaning spell. Now she had something to go on.

The living room was depressingly dark and quiet. She brightened it with a flood of candlelight and sat cross-legged in front of the television set. A little more inspiration from that technological altar to mortal amusement wouldn't come amiss.

There was no telling when Jack would return, but return he would—and when he did, she'd be ready.

Her savior was in for the most wonderful surprise of his life.

Three

Jack paused on the sidewalk outside his apartment and jammed his hands into his pockets. A cold gust of damp evening wind pressed his jacket to his body, reminding him how much warmer it would be inside.

And what else waited for him.

He had no more excuses to put off returning home. He'd spent the day dutifully searching for another temporary job, without success—but at least it had kept him away from Sirena.

Sirena. Good Lord, what had he gotten himself into? *A witch?* If anyone else had told him this story he'd have been sure they were crazy.

He, however, was fully convinced of his own sanity. And somehow or other he'd become the guardian of a cat who'd turned into a wild, voluptuous, seductive woman. A woman who seemed intent on turning his already complicated life upside-down.

And she was waiting. Waiting to tempt him again, he was sure. She wouldn't have to try very hard to make him want her. And the temptation went further than that. The grilled cheese sandwich that had been his sole meal of the day was pretty pathetic compared to the breakfast he'd passed up this morning.

Sirena claimed she could give him *anything*.

Like a new job. Like a second chance. The things that mattered most to him.

Jack scowled and kicked a pile of withered fallen leaves out of his path. Forget that. He wasn't going to start taking favors from anyone now, not after he'd earned all he had— his own way. The hard way, perhaps, but still *his* way.

And that way didn't leave any room for a crazy witch and her reckless, frivolous, and possibly illegal spell-casting.

If only she weren't so damned attractive, so . . . full of life, of high spirits that touched some part of him he'd left behind the day he swore to prove everyone wrong about Bad Boy Jack Danner. He'd succeeded, too—until he'd erased years of work with one night's indiscretion and a bad decision.

He squared his shoulders and marched up the stairs to his apartment. He'd simply have to lay down the law, make clear what he expected of Sirena as long as she was his "guest." And after those three days were up . . .

The doorknob turned easily in his hand. Sirena hadn't locked it. Maybe she'd left. He sucked in a breath, wondering why the idea didn't make him feel better.

He pushed the door open. And stared.

Oh, the hideous green couch was still there—and so was the rest of the furniture, wildly incongruous in the place his apartment had become. Every wall surface seemed covered in red velvet that clashed miserably with his couch. A chandelier hung overhead. A long, mirrored bar lined one wall, neatly incorporating his bookshelves and TV. A tinny piano sounded from somewhere out of sight.

It took him a moment to recognize what he was seeing. He glanced around, half expecting a gunslinger to plop down at the bar and demand a drink. But there was no bartender. No rough men in leather vests and ten-gallon hats playing cards at the single table in the center of the room. The saloon was a movie set waiting for the actors to walk on.

Only he was the sole actor, and he sure as hell didn't

know his part. In a moment the director would arrive, and he'd have a word or two with—

"Well, Jack," a rich, throaty voice said. "We wondered when you'd be back in town. I've been saving up a special welcome for you."

The woman who approached him was Sirena—more or less. She had the same lush shape and the same slanted eyes. But those eyes were now blue and set under pale brows. Her hair was blonde, piled up on her head in an old-fashioned style formed from masses of curls.

The long, brilliant red, bustled dress she wore hugged her figure and squeezed her breasts over the top of a low-cut bodice. Her skirts swept the floor as she swayed toward him.

"Miss Kitty, I presume?" he asked hoarsely.

She gave a husky laugh. "Call me whatever you like, Jack darlin'. It hasn't been the same with you gone. I have a special room upstairs, reserved just for us."

He folded his arms, unable to choose between amazement and alarm. Her rounded posterior swung from side to side as she moved to the bar and poured a drink from a tinted bottle into a crystal tumbler. "You must want a drink after such a long, dusty ride," she said. "I'll have a bath drawn just as soon as we've exchanged a proper greeting." She strolled back to him and pushed a glass into his hand. It smelled of whiskey.

Jack was very tempted to take that drink. He knew he should be angry and outraged and more than a little uneasy at his own surprising calm. She'd done it again—taken over his home without so much as a by-your-leave.

And made him feel—an emotion he didn't entirely understand. He shifted his stance and felt an unexpected weight on his hip. A quick glance confirmed the transformation that had crept up on him with no warning at all. The gun in its holster was ivory handled, hung from a tooled leather belt. He wore scuffed leather riding boots. And on his head . . .

He removed the hat and studied it. It looked real. It felt

real. When he was a boy he would have given almost anything for a real cowboy hat like this one.

"Where," he said, clearing his throat, "where did all this come from, Sirena?"

She leaned back against the bar, displaying her impressive feminine attributes. "Here and there," she said. "What does it matter?"

He slapped the hat against his jeans-clad thigh. "It doesn't feel like an illusion."

"What's illusion, Jack?" She set down her drink and circled him, drawing a finger up his arm and down his shoulder blade. "This is all for you. You can be whoever you wish in my world. And I can be whatever you wish me to be."

Jack shivered. He closed his eyes and smelled leather and dust and horses, lingering on his clothes and in the air from a prairie town. Her perfume was subtle, working on him like an intoxicant.

Sirena was in front of him again, playing with the tin star pinned to his vest. "You brought the Willis boys in, Jack. The whole town is grateful. You deserve a little rest and recreation."

So she expected him to play along. Be town sheriff to her saloon madam. Figured he'd fall for this setup like a kid who's just been transported into his favorite western.

Only no kid would put a woman like Sirena in his fantasy. Especially not when she was leaning into him, her breasts against his chest, invitation in her eyes. "Come on upstairs, Jack. Let me wash off all that dust." She loosened the shoestring tie around his neck. "A nice hot soak—"

He broke away and put his glass down on the bar, none too gently. The bath Sirena promised him was tempting. She'd probably have it rigged to perfection. He had no doubt that she'd be an expert at making a man very relaxed and very . . . taut at the same time. She'd already accomplished the latter as far as he was concerned.

"No, Sirena," he said.

"No?" There was genuine puzzlement in her voice. "No, what? Don't you like what I've done for you?"

Done for him. Where'd she found the idea for this get-up, anyway? Was she still trying to thank him for rescuing her?

"It isn't necessary," he said. "However you came up with all this—"

She joined him at the bar, gazing into his face with a quizzical frown. After a moment she brightened, and her eyes were suddenly green again.

"I know," she said. "It isn't exotic enough, is it? I thought I should start simply, but—" She grinned and snapped her fingers. "I have it."

Jack had about two seconds to hear the warning bells go off in his brain before everything changed and Sirena vanished.

The red velvet walls and the chandelier and the pock-marked wooden bar were gone. Instead, striped sheets of silk billowed overhead, and diffuse light came from brass braziers placed in the corners of the . . .

Tent. That was what it was, Jack recognized belatedly. A tent heaped with pillows and carpeted with intricately knotted Persian rugs. His green couch was almost unidentifiable beneath thick tasseled cushions. His television served as a stand for a silver tray of exotic delicacies.

Exotic was a tame word for what Sirena had done to his clothes. Jack winced as he sifted the loose silk robes through his fingers. If he'd had a mirror he knew what he'd see: a crazy takeoff of Rudolph Valentino in *The Sheik*.

A sheik who lived in the lap of luxury. His coffee table was spread with a feast to put Sirena's breakfast banquet to shame. Jack didn't need to recognize the dishes to know how good they would taste. The scents were spicy and evoked blue desert skies and tree-lined oases and the strains of beautiful, alien music.

Music. No, that wasn't his imagination, either. Bells, and drums, and a flute, and some stringed instrument played by invisible musicians. The sinuous melody promised sensual pleasures beyond the dreams of ordinary men.

At the moment Jack was thinking more of the food and how long it had been since he'd eaten. Sirena was bound to turn up any moment; he should stay on his guard. But it wouldn't hurt to taste the stuff, would it? The bacon this morning had been real.

He looked around for a place to sit and pulled a pillow up to the coffee table. His robes billowed and settled about him. They were unexpectedly comfortable. He selected a piece of tender meat on a skewer. It tasted as good as it smelled. He hesitated on the second bite. Should he really be encouraging Sirena by going along with her?

He set down the skewer, planted his elbows on the edge of the table, and rested his chin on his fists. Sirena hadn't exactly been forthcoming when he'd asked her where she got all this stuff. How did magic work, anyway? Did she conjure this stuff out of thin air—or move it from somewhere else? The latter might possibly be construed as theft, though he doubted too many witches had been prosecuted for it lately.

The situation was bad enough without his becoming an accessory to some form of supernatural larceny. He was debating what to do about the problem when the background music doubled in volume with a thunder of drums.

The dancer swept into the tent on a cloud of multicolored silken veils that obscured all but her slanted dark eyes, a few stray wisps of red hair, and bare, beringed feet and fingers. Jack sat frozen as Sirena—he knew her, changed as she was—began to undulate to the music.

She was an expert dancer. Jack hadn't seen too many harem girls in his life, but he was beginning to see why that old cliché of a hundred cheesy desert movies was so durable. Sirena made it look far from cheesy. There was something deeply erotic in the filmy layers of silk that seemed to hide and reveal simultaneously. She was doing incredible things with her body . . . and *to* his.

He was so fascinated by her graceful, hypnotic moves that it took him a moment to realize that she was shedding veils. The first four or five lay at her feet. The rest of them were peeling off one by one, and Jack could see the pale flash of Sirena's limbs more clearly with every sway of her hips. She twitched one way, and he found himself staring at the brown peaks of breasts barely covered by a single sheer layer. She swayed in the opposite direction and lost a whole section of her skirt. She had great legs. Great everything, for that matter. He couldn't take his eyes from her. In another second she was going to lose the veil that covered her—

Jack shot to his feet. "I, uh—Sirena—"

She didn't stop. She came closer, red lips parted behind one of the few veils she had left. She reached out to him with beckoning fingers. The scent of her was a thousand times more erotic than any perfume.

Desert robes were definitely not designed for hasty retreats. Jack stumbled and nearly fell before he caught his balance and realized he was losing what dignity he had left. Hell, this was *his* apartment, whatever it looked like at the moment.

"Sirena," he said in his most intimidating courtroom voice, "That's enough. I'm tired, I want some peace and quiet, and I'm going to bed."

A little firmness did the trick. The music came to a clashing stop, Sirena paused in the act of removing her second-to-last veil, and the tent began to dissolve around them.

The next moment Jack was standing in the middle of his apartment, wearing his regular clothes. The coffee table was bare of food, and the hideous green couch bare of any ameliorating camouflage.

It all looked strangely empty.

"Sirena?" Jack said.

Not so much as a giggle answered him. *Good going, Jack*, he thought. He'd probably hurt her feelings.

He sat down on the couch, wincing as the broken springs gave under his weight. Hurt her feelings? He couldn't even tell if she had feelings like a . . . regular person. And wasn't that what he wanted, anyway? To be rid of her?

A weak laugh escaped him. He seriously doubted he'd be that lucky. She was undoubtedly off thinking up another scheme to—what? Seduce him? He was probably the only guy in the world who wouldn't be glad to take her up on it.

He pushed to his feet and made his way toward the bedroom. He couldn't think clearly. A good night's sleep would bring a solution. Maybe he needed to get to the library and do some research on witches.

Maybe he *was* losing his mind.

On that happy prospect he walked into the bedroom. He stopped at the threshold and leaned against the doorframe, gathering all his resolution to meet the vision that greeted him.

Sirena was waiting for him beside the bed. Only it wasn't *his* bed. It wasn't his room. She'd changed it into something medieval, with heavy tapestries lining vast stone walls and flickering candles on massive wooden chests. A steaming tub of water stood beside a blazing fire. The bed itself boasted an immense wooden frame carved with fantastical beasts, and the mattress was heaped with furs.

Sirena herself was modestly dressed—more modestly than he'd ever seen her. She wore some kind of nightgown that reached from her throat to her ankles, a simple white shift that should have been chaste compared to her previous wardrobe.

She even looked like herself. Almost. Her dark hair hung in braids down her back, and her slanted eyes were green again. If that *was* their true color. She stood very still, lips curved in a slight smile of welcome. There was nothing remotely blatant about her.

But that was the real illusion. Just standing there, Sirena managed to be more seductive than any ten other women dancing naked on tabletops. He was hardening even as he told his body in no uncertain terms to ignore the blandishments of his overactive imagination.

"Welcome, my lord," Sirena said. "I have been longing for your return."

Jack swallowed, shifted and bumped his sword—yes, a real sword, by the weight of it—against the stone of the doorway. He looked from his mailed arm to the blue-and-gold surcoat and heavy boots on his feet. So now it was Knights in Shining Armor, and the knight was home from slaying dragons to claim his reward.

He'd played such games as a kid, and with considerable gusto. But back then he hadn't envisioned what came after the adventure was over.

The bath was incredibly tempting. The mail was heavy on his shoulders, and he could swear he'd been wearing it through several nonexistent battles. Sirena would undoubtedly be an expert at massaging away the aches in his arms and neck.

It would be so easy to give in. This wasn't like what had happened with Bagley's ex-wife. No one in Vinatera seemed to care whether he lived or died, let alone what was happening with his love life. Whatever Sirena's motives, he couldn't see any reason she'd be trying to entrap him.

But he couldn't give in. He hardly knew Sirena; he certainly couldn't trust her, and there was such a thing as values. The old-fashioned kind that said you didn't sleep with a woman you'd just met because your libido was jumping off the scale. Especially not the kind of woman who made valuable objects appear and disappear and had been punished with a curse for some unknown transgression.

For all he knew he'd been aiding and abetting a criminal from the moment he'd rescued the cat in the alley. But he couldn't convince himself that it was wrong. And he couldn't pretend he didn't desire her. All he could do was try to keep his distance.

Sirena wasn't going to make it easy. After he refused to go to her, she came to him. "Let me help you with this, my lord," she said, and proceeded to unbuckle the studded leather belt that supported his sword. There was an uncomfortable intimacy in the gesture. She laid the sword on a carved wooden chest and returned to take his hand.

He should have stopped it then and there. Instead he let her lead him to a U-shaped chair and sat down as she silently urged him. Then she knelt at his feet.

"Hey. Don't do that—"

But she was already working at his boots, sliding them off one at a time. Her braids swung against his shins. She removed his stockings and laid her hands on his bare feet.

Oh, man. He hadn't anticipated how incredible it felt to

have a woman—*this* woman—rub his feet. He hadn't realized how much they hurt after days, weeks, months of pounding the pavement. She knew just how to touch him. His bones were beginning to melt. The tub was starting to look irresistible, and the bed like paradise. Paradise complete with Sirena wrapped around him . . .

"No, Sirena," he said. He caught her shoulders and pushed her away, smiling crookedly to ease the rejection. "I'm not that kind of guy."

She gazed up at him, her lower lip caught between even, white teeth. "But my lord—"

"The name's Jack," he said, getting to his feet. "Plain, boring Jack Danner, with a hopeless attachment to the real world. If you wouldn't mind bringing it back . . ."

She did it where she was, with no more than a gesture. His bedroom materialized around him. Plain, boring, colorless. Sirena was still wearing the shift, but she wasn't trying to touch him. She wasn't looking at him at all.

Why was he suddenly feeling guilty, like a dyed-in-the-wool bastard who'd just stolen candy from a baby?

Hell. Sirena was no baby. Anything but. But her lower lip was trembling, and he remembered when he'd held her this morning, tried to comfort her when she'd told him how awful the curse had been. This was another of those moments. She had wildly divergent effects on him, and he was beginning to wonder if he could stand the strain for the full three days.

"Sirena," he said. "We need to have a serious talk."

She sniffed audibly. "You don't like me."

He reached up to loosen his tie and realized it had somehow been removed during the course of Sirena's theatricals. "Of course I . . . like you."

"But you want me to leave," she said in a small voice.

"No. It's just that—"

Long, dark lashes shielded her eyes as she looked up at him. "Don't you find me pleasing?"

He groaned.

"If you don't like the way I look, I can change," she said.

As she'd changed three times tonight, from blonde to redhead to her original dark coloring, becoming three different women. She'd dug up a handful of what she guessed were male fantasies and made them real, all in an effort to please him.

How many other men had she done this for? He clearly wasn't the first. Perhaps her "gratitude" to him wasn't all that unique.

The disquieting thought lodged in his brain, and he swallowed back the unexpected flare of irrational jealousy.

"You're beautiful, Sirena," he said stiffly. "But we've barely met. I don't know you. You don't know *me*—" Another unwelcome thought occurred to him. "Unless you can . . . You can't read my mind, can you?"

She shook her head.

Thank God for that. "Then it only makes sense that people get to know each other before . . . before they—"

She gazed at him with that startling combination of sensuality and innocence that made him weak in the knees. "Do people have to know each other to enjoy each other?" she asked.

Jack groped for the edge of the bed and sat down. He had the blinding insight that mature adult reasoning wasn't going to cut it with Sirena. She needed a firm hand . . . He quickly changed that mental image. Obviously she hadn't come up against resistance before. What she needed was someone to point out to her that there were limits, boundaries that had to be observed.

Or else you pay the consequences.

"They should," he said, more harshly than he'd intended. "It's just too easy these days. People do things without considering the consequences. Right and wrong still exist." He stood again and began to pace the room, back and forth, as he'd once done in court. "Sirena, why were you cursed?"

Her silence was significant. When he looked at her she was staring at the carpet, drawing circles in the matted pile with one finger.

"Someone must make the rules that govern what you

do,'' he pressed, ''the same way we have laws that tell us right from wrong. Did you break some kind of . . . magical law? Did someone sentence you to serve your time as a cat?''

He'd spent too much time observing the guilty to doubt that he'd struck a nerve. She flinched and covered the reaction with a toss of her head. ''It doesn't matter now.''

Oh, but it does, Sirena. Mistakes always follow you. He stared at her grimly, wondering how far he ought to push. ''Very well, then. What are your plans?''

Her glance was utterly ingenuous. ''Plans?''

''When the three days are up. When you leave here. What do you *do*, when you're not casting spells?''

She jumped to her feet and did a little one-woman polka, as if she hadn't a worry in the world. ''I have fun.''

''Fun? Is that your purpose in life?''

''Yours is to have no fun at all,'' she retorted, running her fingers dismissively along the spines of his secondhand legal books.

''Not if it means sacrificing my principles,'' he snapped.

Right, Jack. Those precious principles you gave up so easily when your friend below the belt started talking.

He made himself stand still and folded his hands behind his back. ''Sometimes we have to draw the line, Sirena. That's what comes with being mortal. You have incredible powers, but the rest of us have to do things the hard way. The real world may not be much fun, but it's what we mortals have to live with every day.''

Her little dance came to a halt and she faced him, the teasing light gone from her eyes. ''Your real world is a cruel place.''

Had he underestimated her? There was a gravity in the words he'd not thought her capable of—after all, he had no way of knowing what she'd been through before he found her in that alley.

''I know,'' he admitted. ''But if I had powers like yours, I'd try to use them for good. The things someone like you could do—'' *The things you'd be tempted to do, Jack, would send you right over that line you've been lecturing her about.* "Look, Sirena, whatever brought on this curse, you have a chance to start over. Make the most of it."

"Does that mean I'm allowed to help people, Jack?"

"Well—of course."

"How?"

"I can't tell you that, Sirena."

"But how do *you* help them?"

He stared at the dingy beige wall. "I try to work for justice," he said.

"And you always know what 'justice' is."

How could he answer that question? He had a hunch that she'd have him over a barrel if he let this conversation go on much longer. At least he'd managed to distract her from her seduction, and that was good enough. For now.

He yawned broadly behind his hand. "I really need some sleep. Let's continue our philosophical discussion tomorrow."

During the last exchange she'd managed to work her way close to him again. "I'd like that."

They were both standing next to the bed. Sirena's hair had come out of its braids and framed her face in lush curls. His heart began to hammer, his breath to come short. He all but leaped away, gaining the safety of the door.

"You can have the bed, Sirena. I'll take the couch tonight."

He didn't hang around to hear her opinion of his offer. The couch, with its broken springs and too-short length, was a welcome refuge. He waited for Sirena to follow, and breathed a deep sigh of relief when she didn't.

With any luck he'd gotten through to her, just a little. Maybe he'd survive the next couple of days after all.

Four

Sirena heard the front door close—very softly, as if he believed she wouldn't notice.

She sat up in Jack's bed, stretching from toes to fingertips. Demosthenes scrambled from his nest at the edge of her pillow, and she scooped him up with a sleepy apology.

"What am I doing wrong, Teeny?" she said.

He nestled in the warm crook of her shoulder, his tail looped halfway around her neck. "You don't need me to tell you that. Mr. Danner did a pretty good job of explaining, I think."

"Whose side are you on, anyway?" she complained. But she was remembering Jack's words last night, and the way they'd made her feel emotions she hadn't felt before.

Like shame. And regret. And the sense that she should be questioning everything she'd ever done in her life—or everything she *hadn't* done. Even what she *was*.

No man had ever managed that before. None of them had made her think about herself that way. And not one of her erstwhile mortal lovers had inspired her to wonder about the life he lived before she met him, or what he did after she left.

Jack was different. She found herself needing to know about him—all about him, every dream and hope and fear.

There was so much she didn't understand, and that bothered her. It bothered her deeply. She couldn't remember ever being quite so bewildered.

If this was what mortals had to put up with all the time, she was glad she'd been born a witch. But even that wasn't much fun anymore.

It had all become so terribly *serious.*

"Why do I bother?" she asked crossly. "He doesn't appreciate what I can do for him."

"Because he really doesn't want what you're offering."

As much as his words stung, she knew that the mouse might have a point. Obviously Jack had much more demanding tastes than the mortal men she'd known in the past.

Sirena curled her toes and fell back against the pillow. "What am I missing?" she muttered. "I should be able to read Jack like a book—"

"When did you ever sit down and read a book?" Demosthenes interjected.

She swatted at him with a fingertip. "I'm starting to think the Maiden's been coaching you on how to scold someone to death," she said. "Maybe you should have joined her team."

Demosthenes made a rude sound. "Don't insult me." After a moment his small paws patted her cheek. "I'm your friend, Sirena. If you get into trouble again . . ."

"I won't. But I can't leave here—" She stopped, amazed at how unpleasant it was even to think of leaving. Very odd. "I can't leave here until I've repaid Jack." She transferred Demosthenes back to the pillow and scooted to the edge of the bed. "I should have followed him today."

"Not a good idea."

"No. I suppose not, since I told him I couldn't leave."

"You lied to him, Sirena."

"So? I didn't hurt anyone." But her own voice sounded strange to her, strained and too indifferent. Why did she feel as if she'd dabbled in Black Magick when all she'd done was try to make someone happy and grab a little fun for herself?

"Jack's so purposeful," she said to Teeny's silence. "So . . . upright."

"Some mortals consider that admirable," Teeny said dryly.

"But he doesn't know how to enjoy life. There's no such thing as a perfect mortal. He must have some weakness."

"And you *have* to find it. Oh, Sirena—"

But she wasn't listening. She whispered a quick spell and clothed herself in a thick velvet robe that took the chill from her bones. She'd sought answers about Jack in this room before. Obviously she hadn't looked deep enough.

She returned to the closet where she'd found the books and sat cross-legged on the floor. Jack Danner's serious, handsome face rose in her mind, and she fixed it there.

> *"Soul of earth and soul of air*
> *Water, fire, and spirits fair*
> *By the seas and by the skies*
> *Show me where his weakness lies."*

The spell was makeshift but efficient. It led her to the very back of the closet, and a battered leather briefcase. She pulled it out, sneezing at the dust stirred up by the motion.

No sooner did she have the briefcase in her hands than the first image came.

Jack has never done anything so impulsive since he was a kid from the wrong side of the tracks.

The woman sits beside him in the car, gorgeous and sophisticated, murmuring seductive words in a heated voice. He can barely keep his concentration on the road as he heads for home. Her fingers slide along his thighs, coming dangerously close to the taut fabric over his crotch.

He thinks he must be out of his mind. He doesn't know her. He picked her up in a bar, for pity's sake. But when he saw her at The Gavel and she came over to him, talked to him, he stopped thinking about the case and how much rides on it. For a while he was just a man enjoying the company of a woman, and nothing else mattered.

She listened to him—really listened, even though he couldn't talk about the case. And he hasn't been with a woman since he doesn't know when.

Hell, he's lonely. He'd like to be close to someone, even for only a night—to feel someone's arms around him. He wants her, and she wants him. What other reason do they need? He'll be responsible about this.

Just one night. What could it hurt?

Sirena shoved the briefcase away furiously. Another woman! And she was beautiful—for a mortal. Jack's eyes had shown that clearly enough. Red hair, lush figure, tall. Was that the kind of woman Jack liked?

With an effort she forced herself to take the briefcase in hand again. If this woman was her rival, she had to know more about her. Much more.

But the woman's image did not reappear. Instead, Sirena picked up a jumble of confused pictures laced with equally tangled sensations. And then another scene resolved itself within her mind's eye.

The stern, middle-aged man behind the wide, polished desk is staring at Jack, disgust plain on his face. "Thanks to your bad judgment, Bagley's getting off. You just had to have a little fling with his ex and let her convince you that she'd be the perfect witness for us. Oh, she hated him, all right. All that dirt on her husband she was going to spill at the trial—and she lied." He throws up his hand sharply. "One hell of a mess, Danner. Maybe Bagley will fall on some other charge, eventually—but your 'star witness' really screwed us over. She played you for an idiot, and everyone else paid."

The man circles the desk, slamming his hand on the surface as he does so. Jack stares blindly at the framed diplomas and certificates on the wall and watches his career crash and burn before his eyes.

"This isn't going to make you the most popular man in the county," his boss snarls. "It's made me look bad enough, appointing you in the first place. You had your chance, and you blew it. I think you'd better start looking for another job, Danner."

The image ended with a slam of a door as final as the sound of the last nail being driven into a coffin. Then came another chaos of pictures: endless walking and interviewing, accusing words and faces, piles of bills to be paid, the nice apartment given up for this one at the edge of town, a string of temporary jobs that led nowhere.

And always, always the knowledge that he had failed.

Sirena sat back, shaking with the depth of her emotions. The emotions she'd shared with Jack.

Shame. Self-disgust. Despair.

That *woman* wasn't in Jack's life. Not anymore. She'd had something to do with making him lose his job—a job that had mattered deeply to him. A job that defined who he was, the payoff for years of struggle and sacrifice.

She pushed the briefcase back into the closet. No wonder he didn't like women! She couldn't blame him. She had gone about this all the wrong way. Jack wouldn't like her until she proved that she could help him as much as that other woman had harmed him. Until she showed him that she understood the things that were truly important to a mortal.

"I know what I have to do now, Teeny," she announced, jumping to her feet.

The mouse gazed at her from the foot of the bed, whiskers twitching madly. "Sirena, I think you'd better—"

"This time Jack will realize how much he really needs me." She spun in a joyful circle, hugging herself. "You just wait and see."

"Diana spare me," Demosthenes groaned.

It was only midafternoon when Jack went home. His hunt for a new temporary job hadn't been any more successful, but all day long he'd been haunted by images of Sirena: visions of each of the fantastic incarnations she'd assumed last night—and uneasy speculation about what she was concocting while he was out of the apartment.

He'd hoped it might clear his head to leave before she woke. So much for that theory. He'd hardly slept last night as it was; he hadn't been able to keep his thoughts away from her since.

So here he was, standing before his apartment door, bracing himself for what waited inside. His feelings should have been simple and straightforward. Instead they were thoroughly messed up, and he didn't know why. It wasn't merely a matter of lust. He'd proven he could stand firm against that.

No. Jack took a deep breath and swung open the door. Whatever challenge Sirena presented, he could handle it. Only the rest of today and tomorrow to get through.

His living room was . . . normal. No fantastic draperies or exotic props. He exhaled slowly and closed his eyes. Maybe she'd listened to him.

"Mr. Danner?"

He opened his eyes. The Sirena who stood before him was unlike any he'd met before. She was almost unrecognizable, though she'd done nothing to her hair color or eyes, and wore thoroughly modern, respectable clothing.

Unbelievably respectable, in fact. Her gray suit had a skirt that came well below her knees. The fitted jacket was boxy and masculine. She even wore a neat little tie at the collar of her pristine white blouse. Green eyes were shielded by too-large glasses, and her hair was pulled back in a severe, no-nonsense knot.

"I hope you're ready to get to work, sir," she said, her voice brisk and exuding competence. "I've assembled a list of prospects for you. If you'll kindly look them over—"

She gestured him toward the couch, relieving him of his briefcase as she did so. Dazed by the change in her, he didn't even put up a fight. When he'd settled, he saw what she'd done to the coffee table.

It was covered with brochures, financial reports, pamphlets, and folders, laid out in attractive and efficient patterns. He picked one up at random. It was a financial report from one of the major law firms in San Francisco—one that he strongly suspected was not meant for the eyes of the general public.

Not all the documents were from prestigious law firms. Many were from major companies in various fields, and there were a few reports from the district attorneys' offices of the biggest West Coast counties.

Jack dropped the file from the Los Angeles County D.A.'s office and looked up at Sirena.

"Where did you get all this, Sirena?" he asked.

She tilted her glasses on her nose and peered over them. "The usual way, Mr. Danner. Now, shall we proceed?"

"Proceed with what? Sirena, whatever you're—"

"I've assembled the most promising job prospects on the West Coast. Of course I can investigate the rest of the country if you prefer, but I thought this was a good place to start." She pointed to one end of the table. "These are the top law firms. In the middle are well-established, prosperous companies that require good lawyers. And here are the district attorneys' offices that have the best positions available for prosecutors. I'm sure that among all these you can find exactly what you're looking for."

A shiver of alarm raced up Jack's spine. Oh, yeah, he could find the perfect job among all these prospects. Sirena might have read his mind. But she'd claimed she couldn't do that. And he hadn't so much as hinted that he was out of work.

"Sirena," he said flatly, "how did you know I needed a job?"

"I did a little research, sir."

Research, my foot. "Did you follow me?" he demanded.

"No!" Her mask of professional reserve slipped a little. "I never left this house, Mr. Danner. I simply . . . looked in on your past."

Magically, no doubt. Jack rubbed his aching forehead. This was not getting any better. "How much of my past, Sirena?"

"Enough to know that your previous employer made a serious mistake in letting you go. They didn't deserve you, Mr. Danner. We'll find an establishment that will truly appreciate your talents. All you need do is choose."

"I see." He wanted to stand up and pace furiously across the room, but his legs wouldn't support him. He could see exactly where this was going—he'd briefly, and dishonorably, entertained a few daydreams about it himself.

"Are you telling me I can have any job?" he prodded.

"Precisely, sir."

"And how exactly will that happen, Sirena?"

Her glasses seemed to grow just a little more opaque. "You don't have to worry about that. Simply tell me where you'd like to work, and I'll—"

"Create an opening? Use your witchcraft to make them give me a job?"

She folded her arms across her chest. "It's really not at all difficult, Mr. Danner. Any of them would be grateful to have you."

Right. Just like all the places I've interviewed with over the past eight months. He wondered how far Sirena would go to make this happen. Have someone fired? Take over someone's mind—hell, he wouldn't put it past her, after the marvels she'd been able to perform.

The worst of it was that he was tempted. So very tempted.

Any job. He could show all of them—the people who'd said he couldn't make it, his old boss, everyone in Vinatera who hadn't forgiven him for his one stupid mistake.

Sickened by his own weakness, Jack managed to stand. He strode away from the table and leaned against the wall by the door.

"No," he said harshly. "I can't do it, Sirena. And neither can you. It's out of the question."

"But isn't this what you want more than anything in the world?"

So she'd figured that out. He felt vaguely violated, and that, along with his own shame, fed his anger. "Not at the price you'd charge for the favor."

"But I wouldn't charge you, Jack." She came toward him, hands clasped as if in supplication. "I know what that other woman did to you. I can make up for it."

Worse and worse. She knew about Bagley's ex-wife. And if she knew that . . .

"You can't help me," he grated.

"But last night, you told me I could use my magic to make things better for people."

Jack massaged the fierce ache between his brows. Yes,

he had implied something like that. Damned stupid when he didn't know diddly-squat about magic—hadn't even believed it existed until he'd met Sirena. And now she was trying to follow his guidance.

"I'm sorry, Sirena," he said. "You can't interfere with people's lives this way. It's wrong."

She gazed at him through those ridiculous glasses, green eyes filled with bewilderment. He didn't think he was up to tutoring her in the ethics of magic. Probably an impossible task, in any case.

"I have to go out, Sirena," he said, remembering the clinic with relief. "I'll be back later tonight, and I'd appreciate it if you'd return all this to wherever it came from."

"You're afraid," she said, pulling off her glasses. "You won't accept help from anyone. Are you punishing yourself, Jack Danner, because you made a mistake?"

Her question hit him in the gut like a well-placed punch. Did she know everything about him? "I don't need *your* kind of help," he snapped. He retrieved his briefcase from the couch and strode to the door. "Maybe if you tried to be an ordinary woman for once, I might be more inclined to trust you. But you could never give up your powers, could you?"

Her voice followed him as he walked out. "You're wrong, Jack. I *can* be an ordinary woman. I'll prove it to you—"

The closing door cut her off. Jack hunched his shoulders against the late October chill. The clinic would take his mind off problems he didn't want to think about.

And there was only one more day to get through; tomorrow was Halloween. How very appropriate.

Jack wondered why the thought of Sirena's leaving brought so little satisfaction.

The first thing he noticed when he walked through the door six hours later was the distinct smell of burning. The second was the unwelcome glimpse of a mouse running under his feet.

He hopped out of the way, scowling. Damn it, he'd have to report this to the manager. Not that *he'd* do anything about it, considering the run-down state of this heap.

And what the hell was that burning smell, anyway? It was coming from the kitchen. A fog of smoke hung near the ceiling. In a minute it would set off his smoke alarm—if the batteries were still working.

He strode to the kitchen, waving away the haze that stung his eyes. Sure enough, there was Sirena at the very center of it. A Sirena he recognized no more than her other, more exotic incarnations.

She was standing in front of the oven, removing a pan with Jack's worn potholders. A plume of smoke drifted out, and she coughed. She plunked the pot down on the stove and backed away, giving Jack a good view of the blackened roast.

But he was much more interested in the would-be cook. Sirena's dark hair was snarled and limp about her shoulders, all the curl leached out of it. She was wearing one of his old T-shirts, the one he used for working out, and a grossly oversized pair of jeans rolled up several inches at her ankles and cinched at her hips with his brown leather belt. She looked ordinary and artless and . . . vulnerable. A lump formed in his throat as she pushed her hair from her forehead and bent over the stove in a posture of utter defeat.

"Sirena," he said softly.

She turned. Her face was pale except for the dark smudges on her chin and nose. Her mouth was turned down, and there were hollows beneath her eyes. But those eyes brightened as they met Jack's, and the corners of her lips twitched in a hesitant smile.

"I did it, Jack," she said. "I did things the way an ordinary woman would, just as you told me." She gestured at the table. A pile of singed and lumpy biscuits sat on a cracked plate, and a collection of ragged greens that might have been a salad filled a beige plastic bowl Sirena must have dug out of one of his cupboards.

"I had to borrow some of your money to have the food delivered from the store," she went on uncertainly, "but

I'll repay you. I wanted to make you dinner, but—'' She looked at the burnt roast and blinked rapidly. ''I don't think I was very successful.''

Her voice was so forlorn that Jack's heart did a quick meltdown. She probably hadn't cooked a meal in her entire life, and he knew all about being completely inept in the kitchen. ''It all looks ... wonderful, Sirena,'' he said. ''Thank you.''

She stared at him, lower lip trembling in spite of her smile. ''I know you're just saying that. You're so kind.''

Kind, hell. Jack was suddenly bitterly ashamed of himself. He'd been a total creep, treating Sirena the way he had. Here she'd tried to do as he asked, given up her magic, while he hadn't been willing to sacrifice his pride for even a moment.

''Are you very angry with me?'' she asked. ''I made a terrible mess, I know. But I didn't use magic, Jack. I *didn't*.''

''Sirena, I—''

''Not even a little,'' she hurried on, as if he didn't believe her. ''Not even when the meat burned. . . .'' Her brave expression crumpled. ''But I couldn't do it. I just couldn't do it.'' She covered her face with her hands. Little hiccuping sobs escaped between her fingers.

Jack didn't think. He went to her and put his arms around her, drawing her close. Her body was slight and fragile. She held herself still and withdrawn, face turned away.

''I'm nothing without magic,'' she whispered brokenly. ''I'm not good enough.''

''Sirena,'' he murmured, stroking her hair. ''Don't talk that way.''

She shook her head against his chest. ''I'm not beautiful or interesting. You'll never like me.''

Oh, God. ''You're wrong. Of course I like you.''

''But whenever I try to ... do a favor for you—'' She sniffed and Jack fumbled in his coat pocket for a handkerchief. She took it and blew her nose. ''You shouldn't have rescued me. I should have ... stayed a cat.''

Her tears got to him more surely than any magical strategy she'd tried. "No. No, Sirena." He cupped her chin and pulled her head up. "I'm glad I was able to rescue you. And you *are* interesting. And beautiful. Just as you are now."

"I am?"

She looked up, hope in her gaze, and he decided she was beautiful with her hair tousled and her eyes red and her face streaked with tears.

He didn't know quite what came over him then. One moment he was looking into her eyes, and the next he was lowering his mouth to hers. Her answer was tentative, but before he could think better of his impulse she'd wound her arms around his neck and was returning the kiss with interest.

It was very different from the last one. Then he hadn't known Sirena at all, and she'd given him no warning. This time he'd started it. And he craved it. He reveled in the sweet curves of her body against his, the breathless and yet somehow innocent passion of her response.

Oh, he wanted her. He'd wanted her from the moment he'd laid eyes on her wearing only his shirt and doing her best to express her gratitude. But there was more to it now. She needed him in a way he only sensed, a way beyond logic or all the mundane rules of an ordinary life.

And he needed *her*. They were both adults. She couldn't hurt him.

Even if she could, he didn't care. He deepened the kiss and kept it going as he swept her up into his arms. She clung to him, trembling, eyes closed. When he laid her on his bed, she looked up at him like a virgin on her wedding night—no fear, only sweet anticipation and humbling trust.

"I've never . . . done it like this, Jack," she said.

He didn't ask her what she meant. It didn't matter. Instead he gazed at her, wondering why he hadn't seen her this way before. Wondering why she hadn't let him. This was no witch, but a woman. A woman no more perfect than he was.

She reached up, and he came down beside her. He kissed the hollow of her throat and pushed the hem of the T-shirt up over her ribs. She giggled and squirmed to assist him while he struggled to pull it over her shoulders. His suit jacket and shoes had already gone by the wayside; Sirena was making quick work of eliminating his tie. He sucked in his breath at the sight of her firm, exquisite breasts—or perhaps it was because of the way her fingers caressed his chest as she unbuttoned his shirt.

He stopped her with a hand over hers. "Uh, Sirena—wait a minute. We need protection. I think I still have a few—"

"You don't have to worry about that, Jack," she said, stroking his hot cheek. "Not with me. Magic *is* good for some things."

Then his shirt was off, and they were lying side by side. Jack touched her almost reverently—the soft skin of her shoulders, the swell of her breasts. She gasped and murmured and touched him in return. There was nothing false or counterfeit or theatrical in any of it, only the quiet joy of discovery.

"Oh, Jack," she sighed. "How I've waited for this."

He was about to show her how thoroughly he shared that sentiment when he caught movement out of the corner of his eye.

A mouse—the same damned mouse he'd nearly tripped over when he'd walked in the door—was sitting, bold as brass, at the foot of the bed. Staring at them both with its beady little eyes. If Jack hadn't known better, he'd have sworn the beast had a look of stony disapproval on its pointed face.

"Great," he muttered. "A voyeuristic mouse." He glanced around and grabbed the nearest missile he could find. The pillow flew at the mouse, which squeaked in outrage and scrambled out of sight. Far out of sight, Jack hoped. He wasn't keen on being interrupted again.

Beside him, Sirena made a muffled sound that might have been laughter. "Ha," he said, looking into her shining eyes. "You think it's funny? I think I'm going to have to get a cat after—" He caught himself and closed his mouth.

But Sirena wasn't offended. She laughed, aloud this time, and shook her head.

"Don't worry, Jack. I have a hunch that mouse won't bother us again." And she pulled him down with surprising strength, driving all thoughts of annoying vermin from his mind.

But as he turned back to the pleasures at hand, he almost imagined that he heard the distant sound of a small voice launching into a good, thorough scold.

Then the voice faded away, and there were no more distractions.

Five

Sirena slept, tangled up in the sheets Jack had just abandoned. She didn't wake as he moved quietly about the room to dress, or when he paused by the bed again to cover her with the thin wool blanket.

She slept like a woman deeply contented after a night of lovemaking, and Jack wished that he could be there beside her, blissfully lost to reality.

But he'd been lying awake the past two hours, waiting for the dawn and any revelations that might come with it. Because after their last loving, he'd come to a very uncomfortable conclusion.

Something was happening to him. Something that had no relationship to logic or clear thinking or right or wrong. Something all his professional training hadn't given him the means to fight.

He sat down at his desk and touched his old legal textbook from college. He'd bought it third- or fourth-hand, and it had become as dog-eared and worn out as he felt. Once, the book and other volumes like it had been his closest companions—solid, safe, reliable. But it wasn't going to do him any good now.

As much as he tried to marshal his best arguments, analyze the situation from top to bottom, he was left only with more questions. Questions that made him feel like a defendant with ineffectual and incompetent counsel.

Jack planted his elbows on the desk and rested his head in his hands. After last night he should be on top of the world. It had been good. More than good. Shorn of her tricks, Sirena had been a sweet and generous lover. More, she'd let him be generous as well, had shown such unaffected delight in his lovemaking that he'd become the last of the red-hot lovers. No woman had ever done that to him before.

That was the scary part. Why did it seem as if his whole life had undergone a drastic and irrevocable change in the past two days? Why was it getting harder and harder to imagine Sirena leaving when her time with him was up? Today was the last day she'd asked for.

And today was Halloween. If that wasn't a good joke, he didn't know what was. He'd be spending an otherwise lonely kid's holiday with a genuine witch.

Jack scooted his chair around to gaze at Sirena. Out like a light, as if nothing had ever troubled her conscience. She could be totally amoral, could have committed a thousand misdeeds with her talents, and yet all he saw when he looked at her was a beautiful, giving, life-loving woman who made him feel wonderful.

No. That wasn't right. *Wonderful* wasn't quite the word. Confused, terrified, angry, yearning. Those were better descriptions. And running through all that was one unifying emotion. The one he didn't dare look at too closely. The one he hoped wasn't what he was afraid it was.

He still didn't know how it had happened. Or when. There was no good reason for it that he could see. She'd turned his life upside-down, and he'd known her for a little over forty-eight hours.

Jack jumped to his feet and strode across the room until he reached the wall, laying his forehead against the cold surface. Forget it. He was definitely crazy to even *think* such a thing. Stuff like that only happened in fairy tales or romance novels. You didn't fall in . . . you just didn't get so deeply involved with someone this fast.

Unless . . . He froze, transfixed by a sudden and terrible suspicion.

Unless that someone was a witch. A witch capable of seeing into your past and creating incredible illusions. A witch who might be able to cast a certain kind of spell, the kind that had an old and well-known tradition in folklore.

He laughed silently. That was even *more* crazy. Sirena, cast a love spell on him? Hell, if he was that much of an easy mark, he'd probably be working in some convenience store right now, with no law degree and no prospects.

You were an easy mark for Bagley's ex-wife, he thought. *And your current prospects aren't so hot.* What made him think he would be invulnerable to Sirena if she decided to put him under some kind of enchantment?

How would he even know if she had?

Coldness washed over him. He shivered and put his back to the wall. Last night—even last night might not have been real, if it came to that. Maybe her remorse and vulnerability had been an act. He thought he'd finally seen the real Sirena, but couldn't that be wishful thinking?

Man, oh man. He was in deep trouble if he couldn't be sure whether or not his mind—and his heart—were his own.

On the bed Sirena stirred, flinging an arm up over her head. The motion revealed a flash of breast, and Jack caught his breath. He almost didn't give a damn if she'd bespelled him.

Almost.

The cold, hard fact was that he couldn't trust her.

Jack went to the closet and thumbed through his jackets. If he got out of here, kept his distance from Sirena for the rest of the day, he might begin to figure this out.

Or he was just being a coward. But the alternative was to have it out with her here and now, and he couldn't do it. He'd end up in bed with her again. He'd let himself be sucked in by these feelings that might or might not be real, and lose whatever sanity he had left.

What am I going to do with you, Sirena? What am I going to do with myself?

The closest thing to an answer came, not from the heavens, but from the faint ring of the phone in the living room. Jack glanced at the clock. Later than he'd realized . . . nearly nine. There weren't many people who'd call him at any time of day.

Sirena stirred again, and he jogged from the room to answer the phone. It would be best if Sirena didn't wake up before he was gone.

And if that made him a coward, he'd have to live with it.

"Mr. Fontino," Jack said, surprise in his voice. "Good morning. No, no, it's not too early . . . by all means."

Sirena listened from just inside the bedroom door, putting the final touches on a temporary invisibility spell. After a night—a wonderful, marvelous night—of no Magick at all, her abilities were at their fullest.

Better still, it was Samhain—Halloween—and she was both joyous and strong. It took only a little additional effort to extend her hearing to pick up not only Jack's low voice but the one on the other end of the line—another man, brusque and clipped of speech. Older than Jack, she guessed. And right now he was saying something about a job.

"I know we said initially that you wouldn't suit our needs, but I'll be frank. I've been disappointed in the other candidates for the position, and if you're still interested . . ."

"I am, Mr. Fontino." Jack sat down on the couch and raked a hand through his hair; the gesture belied the calmness of his words. "I've been impressed with the work your firm is doing."

"And if you've done your research, you know we aren't going to make you wealthy, Mr. Danner. We're a small firm, and some people would say we're behind the times because we work for the little guy, not the big corporations. Ordinarily I wouldn't consider a prosecutor, but I know about the work you've been doing at the free legal clinic. That stands in your favor." There was a moment of silence.

"Do you think you can come in for an interview at—say—two o'clock this afternoon? It's short notice, but I'd like to get this wrapped up."

"I think I have an opening at two," Jack said. "Yes. I'll be happy to come in then."

"Good. We have your résumé. Be prepared to field some tough questions, Mr. Danner. We hire only the best."

"Thank you, Mr. Fontino. I'll be there."

Jack hung up the phone, stood very still, and broke into a brief but energetic dance of celebration. "All *right*," he exclaimed in slightly less than a shout, and then glanced quickly at the bedroom door.

He looked right through Sirena, of course—to the bed where her temporary simulacrum lay in her place. Even when he crept into the bedroom he didn't detect her spell.

"This is it, Sirena," he whispered to the figure on the bed. "My big chance. I didn't need your help after all."

Sirena winced. Strange how much simple words could hurt. She couldn't remember when they'd bothered her before.

A lot of things had been affecting her in ways they hadn't before she met Jack Danner. Last night, when he'd come home to find her in the midst of disaster, she'd felt like a failure. A sham.

But failing Jack had been the worst. She hadn't repaid him for saving her, hadn't made him happy, hadn't made him like her. And just when matters had been at their blackest, when she'd known there was no hope, he'd taken her in his arms.

And the loving, afterward . . . had been like nothing she'd experienced. She hadn't been in control. She hadn't used her powers to make herself into someone more beautiful, more alluring. There'd been only a soul-deep honesty between her and Jack, and instead of exposing her weakness it had made her strong.

Strong enough to know what must be done.

Jack had a chance to get a job that meant the world to him. She would simply make sure that chance was magnified to its fullest.

Not Magickally, of course. Jack had made his opinions clear on that. But she wouldn't have to use Magick. Jack might be a particularly tough case, but he was not the average man. This Mr. Fontino would succumb to her charm, and she'd make him see that Jack was the perfect, the *only* candidate for the job.

Sirena tugged at her lower lip. The interview was at two o'clock. Plenty of time to get to Fontino first. Jack was getting ready to go out, and she had her own preparations to make.

She slipped back into the bed, banishing the simulacrum, and stretched sleepily. "Jack, is that you?"

He froze in the act of putting on his suit jacket and cast a wary glance in her direction. "You're awake?"

"Not really." She stretched again and snuggled deeper under the covers. "I think I'll sleep for a little while longer."

"You do that. I have some stuff to take care of. I'll be back late this afternoon." He hesitated, as if weighing a question in his mind, and came to stand over her. He laid his hand on her hair, stroking it with the lightest of touches. "Thank you for last night, Sirena."

She all but purred at his caress. "It was wonderful, Jack. Let's do it again."

The gentle weight of his hand lifted. "Go back to sleep. I'll see you later."

"Hmmm." She closed her eyes and waited until she heard the door close. A tickling on her cheek reminded her that she wasn't entirely alone.

"I know you're up to something, Sirena," a mousy voice hissed in her ear. "If you're thinking what I think you're thinking—"

"Oh, Teeny. I'd blush if you could read my mind." She sat up, dislodging Demosthenes from his perch on the pillow. "You weren't watching last night, were you?"

The mouse drew himself up, front paws clutched to his chest. "Sirena! How could you even think it!"

"Well, you were giving me that look—"

"Because I know you."

"Do you?" She sat on the edge of the bed, shaking out her hair. "I'll bet you didn't think I could give up Magick."

"But for how long? Sirena—" He wrung his paws anxiously. "You can still leave before this goes any further. You got what you wanted."

She knew exactly what he meant. Yes, she "got" Jack, after she'd lost her last hope of bringing him around. Once, the victory would have been enough. But there was still a hollowness inside her, and she wouldn't be satisfied until it was filled.

"No, Teeny," she said, getting up and making the bed with an easy housekeeping spell. "There's something I still need to do for Jack."

The drone of Demosthenes' warnings was background accompaniment to her preparations. First she conjured up an outfit that was perfectly poised between seductive and businesslike, with an above-the-knee skirt and fitted jacket and midheel shoes. She gave her hair a style that hinted at abandon just barely in restraint, with a few artful curls loose about her face. Her makeup was subtle, and she completed the image with a pair of modest but fashionable glasses.

"There," she said, studying herself in an ornate mirror better suited to a palace than to Jack's bedroom. "Perfect."

"For what? Sirena, think about this before—"

"I'm beginning to agree with the witch who said that familiars should be seen and not heard," she grumbled. "Cool it, Teeny. I have everything in control."

She didn't listen to his final admonishment. A quick stop by the kitchen disposed of last night's mess—which Jack had already made a start on, having stacked the dirty plates in the sink and discarded the burned roast and biscuits. Sirena wrinkled her nose in disgust, glad to leave behind all memories of her dismal failure at mortality.

Only certain victory was ahead of her now.

The day was cold and brisk, with yellow and brown and the occasional orange leaf skirring in the wind. A perfect Halloween. Tonight there would be every reason for celebration—the best Samhain of all. Sirena could hardly wait.

• • •

"Mr. Danner! Come on in. Good to see you."

Fontino grabbed Jack's hand in a crushingly enthusiastic grip and ushered him into the office. "I've been looking forward to this interview," he continued jovially. "Seems you're better qualified for this job than I'd expected."

More than a little bewildered, Jack took the offered seat in front of the desk and set down his briefcase. "I'm glad you think so, Mr. Fontino. I've come with a few additional documents I'd like to . . ."

"No, no. No need to bother with that. I've made my decision."

"You have? But the interview—"

Fontino laughed. "It's people we hire here, not résumés. Are you complaining, Jack?" He sat down, sweeping a stack of briefs out of his way. "You don't mind if I call you Jack, since we'll be working together? I feel as if I know you already."

Jack cleared his throat. What was going on? He hadn't spoken to Fontino since this morning, and the man had made it clear that he intended to grill Jack thoroughly. Now he was offering Jack the job on a silver platter, no questions asked.

"Have you, uh, been talking to Ms. Panati at the clinic?"

"Good gracious, no. It's that young lady of yours. She's a real charmer, Jack. Don't let that one out of the net. If I were twenty years younger—" He laughed again. "The stories she told! To think you actually . . ."

Jack didn't hear the rest of Fontino's monologue. He was thinking hard, and the suspicion that came to mind wasn't a pretty one. A knot of almost physical sickness twisted in his stomach.

He'd told her she couldn't *do* this. To think she'd turned around and disregarded him so completely . . . But maybe he was wrong. Maybe he'd misunderstood Fontino.

"Your Sirena is quite a woman," the older man finished. "She convinced me you're the man we need. Too bad she's not in law herself, or I'd snap her up in a moment. She'd be one hell of an attorney. I suggest you don't wait too long to tie the knot yourself, Jack.''

Tie the knot. Jack found himself getting to his feet, though his legs were shaking badly.

"Thank you for seeing me, Mr. Fontino," he said, amazed at the steadiness of his voice. "I'm afraid I can't accept the job."

Fontino stared at him as if he'd lost his mind. "What?"

If you only knew, Jack thought grimly. "Under the circumstances," he said, "I'm afraid it just won't work out." He didn't extend his hand, afraid it might reveal his inward agitation. Instead he gave Fontino a brusque nod and strode for the door. "Good afternoon, sir."

Fontino made some protest and might even have followed him, but Jack was too numb to care. He walked past the curious receptionist and out into the wan October sunshine.

Sirena was waiting for him outside. He wasn't surprised. It seemed she was always waiting, ready with some new and unwelcome surprise. *Not always unwelcome*, he thought, remembering last night. But last night had been an aberration. Sirena would never give up using witchcraft to make things go her way. She simply wasn't capable of it.

"Did you take the job, Jack?" she cried, grinning from ear to ear. "Oh, I'm so happy for you."

She flung her arms around him, just as she'd done that very first morning. Then he'd responded instinctively; now he peeled her away with arms as heavy and cold as lead weights.

"How did you know I'd get it, Sirena?" he asked hoarsely. "Why are you here?"

A flicker of apprehension crossed her face. "Well, I . . . overheard you talking about the interview. I had to see . . ." She gave him a less confident smile. "I just knew you'd get it, and it was so important to you—"

"What have you done?"

She took a step back. "It isn't what you thi—"

"I didn't take the job," he interrupted. He barked a laugh. "Fontino didn't even interview me. Instead he talked about you.'' Jack felt that sinking feeling in his belly and knew there were worse ordeals than being fired. Worse than knowing you were capable of stupid mistakes—not once, but twice. ''You *made* him decide to hire me, didn't you? What was it, some kind of spell? Did you do something to his mind?''

''No, Jack,'' she protested, voice shaking. ''It wasn't like that at all. I only—''

He cut her off with a slashing motion of his hand. ''Forget it. This time you've gone too far, Sirena. I told you that you couldn't get what you want by manipulating people with magic.''

''But it *wasn't*—''

He didn't wait to hear her explanations. ''Did you think I'd accept some job you . . . handed to me and be grateful for it?''

''Jack—''

''You think you can work people like puppets, as if they don't have any will or awareness.'' He hooked his finger in the knot of his tie and loosened it with a jerk. ''If this is what your kind is like, I think I understand where the folks in Salem were coming from.''

The look on her face almost stopped him, almost made him listen to the small part of himself that said he was missing some vital piece of evidence. He'd seen that look on the faces of witnesses before—witnesses he'd hammered until he got what he needed to convict the malefactor.

But then he'd always been sure he was right. Now he wasn't sure of anything. And he needed to be. He *had* to be.

''I thought you said you couldn't leave the house before midnight tonight without setting off the curse.'' He went on relentlessly, ''You didn't lie to me about that, did you, Sirena?''

She stared at the pavement, twisting her hands together at her waist. ''The curse would come back only if you . . . made me leave,'' she whispered.

''Then you don't have to worry,'' he said. ''I keep my

promises. You can stay until midnight, and then you're free to find someone else to 'help.' '' He started toward home, shoving his hands into his pockets as if warming his fingers could thaw the ice in his heart as well.

Sirena didn't answer. She trailed him silently all the way back to the apartment. He couldn't have spoken again even if he'd wanted to; his throat was closed up as tight as a rich man's fist.

Damn it, he'd be glad when the clock struck midnight and everything went back to normal. Without Sirena around, life would be . . .

He couldn't even complete the sentence. He tried to shut Sirena out of his mind as he walked through the door.

But such an easy escape wasn't in the cards. She'd decorated the place—not as a harem or medieval bedchamber or cowboy saloon, but with the festive colors of black and orange, streamers and balloons, and cheerful ghosts hanging from the ceiling and every piece of furniture.

''Happy Samhain,'' Sirena said behind him.

Six

Jack didn't tell her to remove it all. He couldn't. He threw his jacket and briefcase on the sofa and went into the kitchen to look for a beer. No, no beer; it was Halloween, and kids would be coming by as soon as dark hit.

Kids. Jack ran his hand through his hair and groaned. He'd forgotten the candy. Well, it wasn't too late to walk to the store and buy some. There were a few hours left. . . .

A strange urge to laugh came over him. He was probably being overly optimistic to think any kids would come anyway, not in this day and age. He didn't have lots of friends in town who'd send their children.

Funny; he hadn't realized until now how much he'd been looking forward to seeing some young, friendly, decorated faces at his door. When he was a boy he'd loved Halloween—you didn't have to be rich or come from a happy family to enjoy it. You could forget who you were for a little while.

There were a lot of things he wished he could forget at the moment.

He wandered back into the living room, wondering how he'd deal with Sirena until midnight came. She could make it very difficult for him if she chose.

She sat quietly on the sofa, wearing his old jeans and

T-shirt as she'd done last night. Before her on the coffee table were bowls of candy—ten or twelve different kinds, the deliciously unhealthy sort he'd adored as a kid.

"Is it all right, Jack?" she asked, almost meekly. "I couldn't find any in the house. It's for the children. . . ."

So Sirena liked children. He hadn't thought to ask before. One of a million things he didn't know about her. How deep had he looked beneath the frivolous, irresponsible surface by which he'd so quickly judged her?

And yet there'd always been that generosity, that desire to give pleasure. He found himself staring at her, remembering. Only three days, and it seemed like years. As if she'd been bewitching and exasperating him for an eternity.

As if he'd wanted her forever.

He leaned against the doorframe, safely distant. "Samhain," he said. "That's what you called tonight. Is it important to witches?"

"It's one of our great holidays," she said, looking at her hands. "A time of celebration. Not of evil, as mortals believe, but of light and life."

Light and life. The quiet earnestness in her voice held him rapt. "And what would you usually be doing tonight, Sirena?"

"I've always loved seeing the children. Sometimes . . ." She hesitated, glancing up as if she expected to find him mocking her. "Sometimes I'd go to places where the children didn't have any Samhain treats. I'd leave them little presents, and watch to see—" She shook her head, flushing behind a curtain of dark hair.

"Sirena Claus," he said. That damned lump was back in his throat again. "I hope you're not disappointed. We may not get too many kids here."

She smiled sadly, and his heart turned over. "They'll come, Jack. Don't worry—I won't have to cast a single spell. There's magic in the air tonight, all around us. They'll come."

He only shook his head. An awkward silence fell between them; Jack's stomach rumbled, and he faced a mo-

ment of weakness when he wished Sirena could conjure up
a big, juicy steak and a baked potato.

But no. That was the problem, wasn't it? He could never
trust Sirena, or trust himself with her. He'd never know
what was real. Every hour with her would be a surprise, a
challenge, a tangle of uncertainty and discovery. He could
never be sure of her.

A moot point, all of it. In less than eight hours she'd be
gone.

"I have some work to do," he muttered, and made a
retreat into the bedroom. He spent the hours until sunset
doodling on a blank sheet on his legal pad. When the doorbell rang just after six-thirty, he saw what he'd drawn.

Eyes. Sirena's eyes, wide and brilliant and laughing.

He tore the sheet from the pad and crumpled it into a
ball. At least one kid had shown up; that was something.
He pushed away from the desk and marched back into the
living room, where Sirena stood in the doorway, chuckling
as she passed a handful of treats to the small group of
costumed children.

She looked at him as she closed the door. "Weren't they
adorable?"

"Yes," he said thickly. But it wasn't the kids he was
thinking of. Sirena filled his vision: Sirena the woman,
whom he'd held in his arms last night. Sirena and her
eyes—eyes that held his gaze without a hint of deception.

The doorbell rang again, saving him. After that there
wasn't much opportunity to brood over his precarious state
of susceptibility.

Because, as Sirena had predicted, the children came.
They came in droves, in herds, escorted by parents and
older friends, their bright voices filling the crisp night air
with joy. Jack hung in the background at first, letting Sirena
pass out the treats. She sparkled, radiating her own light
that drew the children to her.

It drew him as well. He went to stand beside her and
handed out candy, grinning like a kid himself, joking with
the older children and exclaiming over the little ones. He
saw faces of parents, people who wouldn't have given him

the time of day a few hours ago; they were as caught up in the holiday spirit as he was.

Sirena made it happen. For a few enchanting hours it didn't matter how. She spread a cloak of wonder over the world, and it cradled Jack's heart in its warm, all-encompassing folds.

Only afterward, when the last child was long gone, did Jack think to look at the clock on the wall. The stark gray hands seemed to reach out, yanking him back to reality.

Halloween wasn't over, but that was a mere technicality. Two hours remained until midnight.

Jack's unreasoning happiness fled. The house was still festive with decorations, but the mood was gone. He looked at the now-empty bowls lined up on the coffee table. Fitting symbolism. He felt rather like those bowls—temporarily used to hold something magical, now asked to return to mundane kitchen duties.

"Jack."

He turned, bracing himself to face the woman who owned that warm, seductive voice. He and Sirena were alone again, and there was no way out of it.

"Jack," she repeated, injecting a world of promise and beguilement and hope into that single, simple, unremarkable name. She held out her arms. He wanted to tumble into them, let her pull him down, a willing victim, under her spell. He wanted to laugh like a kid again, embrace all the joy he'd seen in Sirena's eyes.

But what he felt now could be a lie. If she could make old Fontino fall, how much easier *he* would be, having shared her bed and her company. His only advantage was that he knew the danger he was in. She might claim to have used no enchantments on the trick-or-treaters, but he'd learned his lesson.

Damn it, Jack. You have *learned it, haven't you?*

He backed away, watched Sirena's arms fall to her sides again. "Thanks, Sirena," he said. "You did a great job tonight. Those kids were . . . crazy about you."

"But not you," she said. "Never you, Jack."

His shoulder hit the wall as he fumbled his way into the kitchen. Sirena didn't try to follow.

Man, oh man. That beer was still waiting, and did he ever need it.

"I was afraid of this," Demosthenes muttered.

Sirena sat cross-legged on the apartment's narrow balcony, gazing up at the stars as they slipped in and out among the clouds like air sprites at a game of tag. It should have been a glorious night, the best night of the year. For a while it *had* been, but now she was left with only a desperate sadness that weighed her down like the stones once used to test a woman for the evil of witchcraft.

She almost envied her more unfortunate ancestors that decisive fate. "What's happened to me, Teeny?" she asked. "What's *wrong* with me?"

"Exactly what I could see coming a mile away," the mouse said. He hopped onto her knee and looked up, his whiskers drooping forlornly. "I tried to warn you. I tried to tell you to leave before your heart was broken. . . ."

"My heart?" She stared at him. "What does my heart have to do with it? I've failed. For the first time in my life, I can't make a man *like* me—"

"Diana preserve us," Demosthenes said. "Do you still think that's all this is, Sirena? And I thought *mortals* were blind."

She clenched her teeth. "All right, O Wise Mouse. Tell me. Just what am I missing?"

"You'd know if you weren't afraid," he said, holding her stare. "If you looked into your heart instead of pretending you don't have one."

A hot retort came to her lips and died there. Afraid? She'd never been afraid—well, except when she was a cat. She'd do anything to avoid that. She *had* avoided it, by obeying the letter of the Council's law.

"You should be satisfied," she said. "I didn't make Jack fall in love with me."

"Because your tricks didn't work, Sirena. You pushed

right to the limit of what was allowed, but Jack didn't fall for it. And that hurt.''

She looked away. ''But you just said I didn't have a heart.''

''No, Sirena. You have one. A bigger one than anyone knows. And it's aching right now, isn't it?''

Aching. Sirena pressed her palm to her chest. Her heart hadn't really changed. It beat in the same rhythm, pumped blood—so much like mortal blood—through the same veins and arteries.

But Teeny was right. There was something wrong with it. Something dreadfully wrong.

''Yes,'' she whispered. ''It aches. And I don't know how to fix it.''

''Because you didn't understand what love was. You imagined that what those men gave you was love, but it was all one-way. You had your fun. Now you're on the other end, Sirena.''

''What?''

''You've fallen in love with Jack Danner.''

''I've . . .'' She repeated the phrase silently to herself. Fallen in love? Was Teeny right? Was this what it was, to want someone so badly, to believe you would die without him, that he filled some kind of empty space inside you that no one else could?

To know he not only belonged to you, but you belonged to him?

The realization swept over her with the irresistible force of truth. ''You're right, Teeny,'' she said in wonder. ''I love him.'' She stood up and walked to the edge of the balcony, clutching the cement wall as if she could crush it in her fists. ''But there's a problem. Jack—'' She swallowed miserably. ''Jack doesn't love me.''

Teeny levitated himself to the top of the wall. ''Mortal love—the *real* kind—isn't easy, Sirena. I've watched it for a thousand years. You can't make it happen. You can't force it.''

You can't force it. What he meant was that you couldn't

get a man like Jack to love you by giving him whatever he wanted. Or making yourself beautiful and irresistible, or fulfilling his every fantasy.

He didn't love her, and she couldn't imagine leaving him tonight, never seeing him again, never feeling his strong arms around her, anchoring her as she'd never been anchored before. Making her feel real and important—for *herself*, not for what she could make herself become, or what she could create by Magick.

The mere idea of leaving him terrified her. And she couldn't stay as things remained.

There was still one way. . . .

No, Sirena. But even as half of her recoiled in horror at the madness of it, the risk of terrible consequences, the other half was prepared to gamble her very fate on the chance it would work.

On the chance it would make Jack love her. It wasn't as if she couldn't lift the love spell once she had him. And he wouldn't know. He'd be happy . . . she'd make sure of that.

Her conscience lost the brief debate. Time was of the essence. At midnight she'd be at her most powerful; all the forces of the elements would be at her command.

She looked up. The roof of the building was but a brief levitation overhead. No one would see her perform the spell.

"I know what I have to do. Don't try to interfere, Demosthenes," she said firmly, and summoned a binding spell as extra insurance. It wouldn't stop him, but it would slow him down, keep him from levitating to follow her before she'd had a chance to complete the spell. Ordinarily she'd use him as a focus for such an important task, but he'd only be a hindrance now. Tonight she was on her own.

His squeaking protest followed her as she drifted upward, arms spread to catch the starlight and the nascent strength of the new moon. The flat, empty roof was perfect. Before she could entertain second thoughts she began the chant, kneeling and drawing an invisible circle with her fingertip.

> *"Love, whose name is e'er threefold*
> *Passion's tale that's oft retold*
> *Let thy secrets now unfold. . . ."*

In the dim light of ancient stars the air itself began to dance.

Where was she?

Jack finished his second search of the bedroom and charged back through the living room.

All right. It wasn't quite midnight yet. Had she already left? That would be typical of her, to thwart him at the very last minute by doing what he least expected.

"Sirena," he muttered, cursing the weakness that had led him to down two beers in rapid succession and left him woolgathering at the kitchen table for a good hour and forty-five minutes.

The beer hadn't helped. He was in a far from good mood, and wholly, painfully sober. So what was he forgetting?

The balcony. Of course. He seldom used it, but Sirena might have gone out for some fresh air. He had just flung open the sliding glass door when something small and all too familiar skittered across the floor.

"Damn! It's that mouse again!"

As if it heard him, the beast froze and looked up with an almost eerie intensity. Jack had just enough presence of mind to grab the old plastic bucket he kept on the balcony. He upended it over the mouse before it had the sense to run again.

"Ha. Got you now, you rodent. No more sneaking around this apartment." Not that he had any idea what to do with the pest, but he couldn't worry about it now. "I guess you'll get a reprieve from sentencing, mouse, because there's someone I've got to find—"

"If you're looking for Sirena," a tiny, tinny voice said from under the bucket, "I know where she is. Let me out of here!"

After a moment Jack picked himself off the floor. "Uh, who said that?"

"Lift this bucket, you fool mortal, and you'll find out! That is unless you want Sirena to suffer for your idiocy."

In a daze Jack lifted the edge of the bucket. A narrow nose thrust out the crack, twitching furiously. A mouthful of rodent teeth flashed at him. "Satisfied?" the mouth said distinctly.

Good God. The mouse—the mouse he'd been seeing ever since he'd discovered a certain black cat in an alley.

"What in hell are you?" he rasped.

"Sirena's friend. And if you're her friend you'll stop delaying me. At this very moment she's up on your roof, about to call the wrath of the Council down on her head. If she isn't stopped, there'll be no hope."

Jack took a deep breath. Okay, he was talking to a mouse. Fair enough. Weirder things had happened in the past few days. The beast's peculiar urgency cut through his fog of amazement.

"Sirena's in trouble?"

"Brilliant deduction. And it's all because of you. I told her not to fall in love with you, but she wouldn't—"

"What?"

"You heard me." With a remarkably strong heave for such a tiny creature, the mouse pushed the bucket up and darted out. It perched on its haunches a few inches from Jack's foot, positively glaring. "Sirena had the great unwisdom to love you, for all the appreciation you've shown her. All she's had from you is rejection. Now she thinks she can't live without you, and that the only way to win your love is to risk destroying herself."

"Destroying—"

"Listen to me, human. She's about to make a terrible mistake. The Witches' Council cursed her before because she'd misused her magic to make mortal men fall in love with her." The mouse flung up one paw in an imperious gesture. "And before you go judging her, human, she never did it to hurt anyone. She only wanted love—and now that she's found it, it's brought her to terrible danger."

This obviously wasn't the time to examine the fine nuances of the animal's revelations. "How is she in danger?" Jack demanded.

"If she goes through with what she's planning, if she casts a love spell to *make* you love her—the Council will reinstate the curse permanently. She'll live out the rest of her single remaining life as a cat, and no one will be able to save her again. I've got to stop her."

Jack hadn't thought so fast or so clearly in all his life. Along with the clarity of thought was an odd giddiness, as if he were Superman and nothing in the world could stand in his way. He scooped the mouse up in his hand, barely shuddering at the touch of feathery little paws and a naked tail. "Let's go."

He ran. He dashed down the hall, climbed the back stairs and reached the door to the roof in less than a minute. It was jammed. He began to yank and hammer, pounding as he did so. "Sirena!"

"Wait!" The mouse raced up his shoulder and crouched by his ear. "It's all right! She stopped—I can feel it. She didn't go through with the spell." The animal sighed, a faint and gusty breath on Jack's neck. "She's safe now. They can't do any—"

The mouse's words were lost in a sudden, violent gust of wind that nearly knocked Jack from the top step and blew the door open with a bang. The roof lay before them, awash in light that blinded Jack and drew a moan from his rodent companion.

Four figures—that much Jack could make out behind the glare. One stood apart, a small and slender form bent low in a posture of utter despair.

"Sirena!" Jack tried to walk toward the ghostly apparitions and found himself locked in place. A whirlpool of wind, like a miniature tornado, began to form about the figures. They were caught in it like autumn leaves, rising with it, higher and higher until they merged into a blur of light, a shooting star that flashed across the sky and winked out of existence.

"Sirena!" Jack fell to his knees, drained of strength. "Oh, God. Where did she go?"

"They took her." The mouse slumped on his shoulder,

limp as a rag. "The Maiden was always a high stickler. They must have decided . . ."

"You mean . . ." Jack stood so quickly that he almost shook his passenger from his mooring. "No. There must be a way to stop this. I won't let her be turned back into a cat." He grabbed the mouse as gently as urgency would allow and pointed the animal's face to his. "What can we do? Tell me!"

"All right. There still may be a chance—if you're willing to take it."

"I'll do anything to save her. Anything."

The mouse stared at him like the meanest, most cantankerous judge in the county. "I think I believe you, mortal. But you'll have to go to a place out of time itself, a place where no mortal belongs. I've never transported one of your kind before. I may not be strong enough. You could be lost in limbo forever."

"So what's new?" Jack said with a devil-may-care laugh.

"And that's not all. The Council may resent your interference. If you're lucky, they may ignore you. Or they may decide to curse you as well. You might not come back—as a human."

Jack shrugged with his best imitation of fearlessness. "They sound like a tough bunch, all right. But I've never faced a judge I couldn't handle."

"Tricky words won't work with them, Jack Danner. I hope you find what will before we're all lost."

Jack stared up at the cloud-mottled sky. "You know, mouse, I think that just maybe I have."

"Then hang on, and don't let go of me no matter what happens." The mouse closed its eyes, muttered under its breath, and opened them again. "By the way, the name's Demosthenes."

Seven

"Are you prepared to face your fate, Sirena?"

She looked up at the three women who were about to carry out the sentence. It seemed an eternity since she'd last stood here in the Chamber of Judgment, awaiting a similar doom.

Only this time the punishment would be permanent, and there would be no rescue. She wanted none.

"I am," she said calmly. The transformation wouldn't hurt, of course. Nothing so blatantly cruel. There would be a moment or two of disorientation, and her body would shift like the formless mists surrounding them. They would leave her in a place on earth where she had a moderate chance of survival—as a cat.

Sirena didn't particularly care what they did.

"Make your peace, then," the Mother said.

She closed her eyes and prepared herself. There wasn't much she regretted leaving behind. Jack had made her see how empty her life had been before she'd met him. And without him. . . .

Good-bye, Demosthenes, she thought. *You were a loyal friend, but you're better off without me. Some other lucky witch will snap you up.*

The second silent farewell was one she had already made again and again.

All blessings go with you, Jack. I wish I'd been able to earn your love, but I could never steal it from you. Forgive me.

I love you.

She opened her eyes and met the Maiden's unyielding stare. "I'm ready."

The Maiden, the Mother, and the Crone joined hands. A white mist began to gather about them, a tangible symbol of the Magickal energies they invoked. They began to chant—softly and then with greater and greater force.

The first tingling portent of the coming transformation had begun at the tips of Sirena's fingers when a great roar, like a clap of thunder, brought everything to a crashing halt.

A window appeared in the wall of vapor beside her. The Council of Three turned to stare as a tall, solid shape stumbled through, sending eddies of disruption through the ether and breaking the unfinished spell.

"Hold it right there!" a deep, masculine voice commanded.

"Jack," Sirena whispered.

He staggered before he found his footing, which made his unexpected entrance only slightly less impressive. His glance swept the ethereal arena, took in the Council on the podium, and came at last to rest on Sirena with warmth enough to banish the last chill from her bones.

"I'm here, Sirena," he said. "You're safe now."

Demosthenes—dear, loyal Teeny—scrambled up Jack's arm and hissed into his ear. Jack nodded and turned to face the Council, shoulders squared.

"Your Honors," he began, "I—"

The Maiden shot to her feet. "How dare you bring a mortal here, Demosthenes?"

"Fascinating. How did the familiar manage it?" the Crone asked the air, stroking her shriveled chin.

"Your Honors," Jack repeated. "I know what you're about to do, and I can't permit it."

"Can't permit it?" the Maiden repeated with an incredulous gasp.

"I will not allow a gross miscarriage of justice to occur in this courtroom."

The Maiden seemed at a loss for words. The Crone leaned forward, and the Mother settled back in her chair, a faint smile on her plump face.

Jack paced the length of the podium and back again. "I have reason to believe you haven't given the defendant a fair trial," he said.

"What do you know of it?" the Maiden snapped, finding her voice again.

"A fair trial?" the Crone repeated. "But the sentence has already been passed."

"Without benefit of all the evidence," Jack said. "It so happens that I—"

"We aren't mortals to go by mortal ways," the Maiden said. "We had enough of your trials in Salem. Now, I suggest you leave, human, before we decide to—"

The Mother raised her hand. "Let him speak," she said. "What harm can it do?"

She spoke seldom, but when she did the others always heeded her. Three sets of eyes focused on Jack.

"Do you understand the charges against Sirena?" the Crone asked.

"I do."

"And what can you possibly offer in her defense, when you were the injured party?"

Jack glanced at Sirena as if to send her a dose of courage. "In what way was I injured, Your Honors?"

"The love spell," the Maiden said impatiently. "She intended to make you enamored of her."

"Ah. *Intended* is the key word. But did she complete the spell for which she's being punished?"

The Council members looked at each other. "She'd already begun it," the Maiden said.

"But we did not wait for the end before we took her," the Mother temporized.

Jack raised his hand. "I'll make this brief. I present as

witness Demosthenes, familiar to the defendant, who will testify that Sirena did not complete the spell in question, but voluntarily broke it off free of outside influence.''

''A familiar's word is always acceptable,'' the Mother said. ''Do you so swear, Demosthenes?''

The mouse sat erect on Jack's shoulder. ''I do. I felt her end the spell.''

''If this is so,'' the Crone said, glancing at Sirena, ''why didn't she speak up in her own defense when we came for her?''

Overwhelmed and humbled, Sirena struggled to find her voice. ''I . . . I—''

''It isn't enough,'' the Maiden said. ''Her purpose was plain. She knew the penalty. She intended to steal this mortal's will and make him love her—''

''Impossible, Your Honors,'' Jack said. ''She could not have succeeded.''

The Council fell silent. The tentative, yearning hope drained from Sirena's heart. He had come to save her out of a sense of duty, no more. If not for her worry about the terrible risk he'd run coming to defy the Council, she would have begged them to end it here and now. *Oh, Jack. . . .*

''She could not have succeeded,'' Jack continued slowly, turning to gaze at Sirena, ''because I was already in love with her.''

The nonexistent floor seemed to drop out from underneath Sirena's feet.

''What?'' the Maiden said.

''I believe I fell in love with her the morning I found her in my kitchen,'' he said. ''Before I knew what she was. And even after I knew, it didn't change.''

He turned his back on the Council, unafraid, as if only he and Sirena existed in the Chamber. ''At first I couldn't admit it. It scared me. Loving you went against everything I thought I believed in. And when I realized I loved you, I was afraid you might already have used your magic to make me feel that way.''

''A-ha!'' the Maiden exclaimed.

''But,'' Jack said, facing the Council again, ''when I

heard that you'd taken Sirena away, I didn't care how it happened. I still don't. It's real, and that's all that matters.''

"Did she know of your feelings?" the Crone asked.

"No."

"And it doesn't matter to you that she was casting a spell to compel your love?"

"What matters is that she stopped." His gaze washed over Sirena, caressed her like a wind from heaven itself. "She didn't go through with it."

"Do you know about Sirena's past, mortal?" the Maiden demanded. "Do you know how many hearts she's broken, how many lives of men like you she's disrupted by misusing her—"

The Mother raised a plump hand and looked to Sirena. "Child, answer truly. When we found you, had you completed the spell?"

"No." Sirena held Jack's gaze. "I couldn't."

"Then why did you let us believe you had?"

"Because—" She swallowed, fighting the tears she wasn't ready to let fall. "Because I thought I'd lost Jack. I tried to give him things, change myself to make him love me, and nothing worked. He made me see how—meaningless my life was." She smiled hesitantly at Jack, begging him to understand. "Without him, without his love, I didn't care if I became a cat again. At least that way I could forget."

"And why did you stop, Sirena, if this man's love was so important to you?"

She had never felt a greater love for Jack than she did then, knowing that the Council might still refuse to listen. They didn't matter. She had to explain to *him*, so he'd know, no matter what became of her.

"I couldn't, Jack," she said. "I couldn't go through with it. I knew it was wrong, and I realized . . . I realized I loved you too much to do that to you. That I'd rather have you free and not loving me, than *with* me bespelled. You taught me that, Jack."

"Sirena," he said thickly, starting toward her.

"Hold, mortal," the Crone said. "Sisters, we must discuss what we have just witnessed."

"Do whatever you wish to me," Sirena said, "but don't punish Jack for coming here. He was the one who saved me. He's noble and good and courageous, and you can't blame him just because he—"

But the Council was no longer listening. They had retreated behind a cocoon spun of vapor, faint blurred shapes veiled in ominous secrecy.

Jack came to Sirena, arms outstretched. Without a word he pulled her close, kissing the top of her head and all but crushing the breath out of her.

"Thank God I was in time," he murmured.

"Excuse me," Demosthenes protested, working out from between them and finding a new perch on the top of Jack's head. "It isn't over yet."

But Sirena didn't care. Jack loved her. He loved her, and that was miracle enough to fill whatever time they had left, be it minutes or an eternity.

"Jack," she sighed. "You really love me?"

"Crazy, isn't it?" He cupped her cheeks in his hands. "No, not so crazy at all. You brought magic into my life, Sirena—the kind of magic two people make when they're meant to be together. And . . . you made me see how bleak and empty my life had become. I'd forgotten how to live— you told me that. And you were right."

"But I was the one who did wrong, didn't care who I hurt—"

"We all make mistakes. I made my share. I had to realize that I wasn't perfect, and that imperfection wasn't such a terrible failure. That I didn't have to do everything alone and the hard way just to prove I could. We both have a lot to learn, but it's hardly hopeless." He chuckled. "You can teach me how to have fun, and I'll teach you some good old-fashioned mortal rules. Sound fair?"

"What are you saying, Jack?" she asked, half afraid she wasn't hearing right.

He took her hands in his. "It was Fontino who put the idea into my head," he said. "He was pretty impressed with you, Sirena. Said he'd hire you if he could. He was insistent that I shouldn't let you go—''

But he didn't finish the sentence. The cocoon of mist behind the podium dissolved, and Sirena looked up to see the Council waiting in portentous silence. Jack squeezed her hand and turned to face them, while Teeny clutched his hair for dear life.

"Our deliberations are complete," the Crone said. "We have reached a verdict."

Sirena expected the Maiden to make the pronouncement—she was always the one with the most to say, and that was usually disagreeable. But it was the Mother who spoke, her gaze fixed on Sirena with benevolent satisfaction.

"You have discovered something we never expected to see in you, Sirena," she said. "You've not only learned your lesson . . . you've learned how to love. Not every witch is so blessed." She glanced at Jack. "Because this mortal chose to risk all to intercede on your behalf—because he dared to defy us and declare his love—you are saved. Love has saved you, Sirena."

Jack closed his eyes. Sirena's knees begin to buckle. Saved . . .

"But there is still a price to be paid by you both." The Mother's face grew solemn, though her eyes continued to twinkle. "Hear our sentence, child. You shall be released into the custody of the mortal Jack Danner, to remain in said custody for the rest of your natural life. That life will be but the short span of years allotted to mortals, no more. Your Magickal powers shall be bound away from your use for the years remaining to you."

The shock Sirena felt staggered her anew. She looked at Jack, who gazed steadily at the Council, erect and attentive.

"Jack Danner shall guide you in mortal ways and watch over you," the Mother went on. "In return, you must cleave only unto him. Will you abide by this decree, Sirena? Are you prepared to live a mortal life?"

This wasn't how it was meant to be. The tears escaped Sirena's eyes, free of her control. It wasn't the loss of her Magick; that she would give up gladly for Jack's sake.

But Jack was not supposed to be punished, forced to take her on for the rest of his life without any say in it at all. It was wrong. She knew how wrong it was.

"No," she said, stepping forward. "Don't do this to him. You can't make him—"

"And you, Jack Danner," the Mother continued, ignoring her, "do you agree to abide by this binding? To watch over her, and guide her in the ways of right?"

"I do," he said. "To the very best of my ability. But only on one condition."

Sirena and the entire Council held their collective breaths.

"Only," he said, "if you don't take Sirena's magic away." He looked at each of the Council members in turn. "There's a lot I don't know about this stuff, but I understand this much. It's a part of her. It's what she is. It's in her soul, and you can't separate her from it without destroying her." He lifted his hands in a gesture of entreaty. "Maybe she didn't always use it the right way, but she can learn. And so can I."

The Maiden scowled, the Crone looked thoughtful, and the Mother nodded. "Do you know what you're getting yourself into, young man?" the Mother asked.

"Yes. A lifetime of surprises." He flashed a tender smile at Sirena. "And love."

"Then—" The Mother consulted her Sisters with a glance. "Then so mote it be. Judgment is given. It only remains that the bargain be sealed—with a kiss."

Jack didn't hesitate for as much as an instant. He spun and swept Sirena up, kissing her with an enthusiasm Sirena could not possibly mistake. Joy bubbled over within her, coursed through their joining like an elixir made of starlight and dreams.

"Jack," she gasped when she could speak again, "are you sure?"

In answer he kissed her again, until the Maiden cleared her throat with a stentorian rumble.

"This session is ended," she declared. "Sirena, take

your foolish mortal home. And don't ever let us see you here again!''

With a *whoosh* of air the Council members vanished one by one, the Mother last of all. She winked at Sirena and sketched a sign of blessing that lingered in the mist long after she was gone.

"You heard the lady," Jack said. "Take us home, Sirena."

"That includes me, I hope," Demosthenes interjected from the vicinity of Jack's temple.

"I guess I'm going to have to live with vermin in the house," Jack said, winking at Sirena. "Thank God your familiar wasn't a cockroach."

"Vermin!" Demosthenes sniffed. "That's gratitude for you."

But he only snuggled deeper into Jack's hair as Sirena chanted the spell that took them back to the mortal sphere. And when they were safe in Jack's apartment again—his dull, ordinary, wonderful apartment—Teeny made himself scarce as the pair of lovers cuddled on the hideous green couch and waited in sweet oblivion for the coming of dawn.

"I never got to finish what I was trying to tell you—back there," Jack said, nuzzling Sirena's neck.

"Tell me what?" she murmured.

"That I'm going to marry you."

She sat up abruptly. "You don't have to do that, Jack. They didn't expect—"

"*I* expect. You're stuck with me, Sirena, but not as a parole officer." He searched her eyes. "Unless you . . . don't want to?"

"Want to?" She shrieked and flung her arms around him. "Oh, it'll be so much fun. A mortal wedding with *all* the trimmings—"

"Sirena—"

She laughed. "Don't worry, Jack. I know you'll keep me in line." But a certain nagging concern intruded on her happiness. One she'd been putting off mentioning. She braced herself and took Jack's hand, facing him squarely.

If there was to be complete honesty between them, it had to begin now.

"Jack," she said with a quiver in her voice. "What about the job?"

His mouth twitched. "You know, I've been thinking about that, Sirena."

"I really didn't use Magick. Truly. I—"

"I believe you," he said, folding her fingers within his. "But it's still something I need to do on my own. I've decided to swallow my pride and go hat in hand back to Fontino. See if he'll still hire me." He pulled her against him, kissing her ear. "It's a job worth fighting for. The firm actually helps people, and I've come to realize that's what I want to do, not just prosecuting the bad guys."

Sirena caught his shirt collar in both hands. "Me, too. You'll show me how to help people the right way, won't you? Teach me the rules?"

"To the very best of my flawed mortal ability," he promised.

"Then let's seal it with a kiss," Sirena purred.

And they did.

"Humans!" Teeny snorted from the foot of the couch, and scampered away as if a legion of cats were on his tail.

Everything She Does Is Magick

Maggie Shayne

Prologue

Midnight, October 31, 1970

A little Witch is born.

"Her name will be Aurora," Merriwether said firmly, staring down at the cradle she'd bought for her brand-new charge. The baby's mother, Merriwether's niece, had never embraced the secret ways of the Sortilege women. She'd rejected her heritage, turned her back on the ways of magick. Even claimed she didn't believe in it. Then she'd run away with a leather-bearing beast on a motorbike, shouting over her shoulder that her three aunts were completely insane, and ought to be committed because everyone knew there were no such things as Witches. Almost as an afterthought, she'd added that her aunts had best not be casting any spells to make her come back, or she'd hate them forever.

Nine months later, Melinda had the good sense to send her newborn daughter home to her three aunts, delivered to the front door by a social worker with the message that Melinda was "just not mother material."

Merriwether had known the child would end up in her care. She hadn't known *how* it would happen, but she'd never doubted it would, because she'd seen it in the stars. Aurora Sortilege was a special child, a child of destiny. And her aunts were here to see that she fulfilled it.

"Oh, yes, Aurora. It's perfect!" Fauna clapped her plump hands together near her rounded middle and gave a good belly laugh. Her face quivered with mirth, and her outrageous orange hair—frizzed from too many colorings and permanents—bobbed and bounced as if it were laughing, too. "It brings our little fairy tale full circle, don't you think?" she asked, still grinning.

"Our dear mother knew what she was doing when she named us after three benevolent—if fictional—fairies who care for a special little girl," Merriwether said, and she frowned a little at her younger sister's laughter. This was a serious matter—a great responsibility had been entrusted to them. But as she glanced at the child again, even her own stern expression softened. "Mother truly was gifted at divination."

Fauna smiled, and it dimpled her cheeks. "And so are we," she declared with a slap of her hand against one ample thigh. "Our Aurora will be blessed with an abundance of magick."

"Magick even more powerful than our own," Flora added in her gentle, timid voice. Her tiny frame bent over the cradle, she was tickling Aurora's chubby chin and eliciting a smile. "And a healing gift beyond measure."

"Oh, yes, indeed," Merriwether agreed. "But even then, it won't be as powerful as *her* daughter's will be."

"Only if we're successful." Flora frowned then, small face puckering, and paced away from the cradle in small, agitated steps. Leaning over the round pedestal table nearby, she peered into the misty depths of a crystal ball that reflected her face and snowy white puffs of hair. "Oh, so much hinges on this. What if we fail?"

"We won't," Merri assured her youngest sister in her firmest take-charge tone. "We can't. We all saw the prophecy at the same time. You in the crystal, I in the stars, and Fauna in the cards of the sacred Tarot. We've been entrusted by our ancestors with a great responsibility, sisters, and we cannot fail.'' She was putting on her drill-sergeant persona, and it fit, she knew, with her regal stature and steely gray hair. Her sisters called her imposing. But always with love in their voices. And *someone* had to be in charge, after all. As the oldest, it had simply always been her.

But when she looked down at the baby, she deliberately gentled her tone. ''Aurora is going to become the mother of the greatest Witch our family has ever produced. But it can only happen if we follow the instructions we've been given to the letter.''

''Yes,'' Fauna said. She, too, had come to the table, and she'd already begun shuffling her Tarot cards. She did that when she was nervous. Shuffled and shuffled. ''The child has to be fathered by little Nathan McBride, Daniel's boy, from Mulberry Street. And you're a lucky one, little Aurora, 'cause that boy's gonna grow up to be a looker.'' She shook her head and stifled a chuckle. Then she frowned. ''How we'll arrange that, I'll never know. Merciful Goddess, the McBrides don't even know about the traditional magick of their ancestors, or the power of their bloodlines. They don't practice the ancient ways. They live like . . . like *normal* folk.'' She grimaced after she said it, as if the words left a bad taste in her mouth.

''Not only that,'' Flora said, taking a hanky as snowy white as her hair from her pocket to polish her spot- less crystal ball. ''But he has to be a—a—a *virgin* when they . . . you know.'' She lowered her eyes and her cheeks flushed pink.

''We're all well aware of *that*, Flora,'' Merri said. ''But there's just no help for it. We have to see to it that every- thing happens as it should.'' She glanced out the window above the baby's bed at the formation of the stars on this crystal-clear night, and frowned. ''I've decided we should do this subtly, not come right out and tell Aurora the plan.'' She turned to the baby again. ''Because if she's even half as rebellious as her mother . . . well, she'll be determined to do exactly the opposite of what we ask.''

''You're right,'' Flora said, nodding slowly. ''Though it's a shame we can't tell her the truth about her destiny.''

She blinked up at Merri. "But we will tell her the truth, eventually, won't we?" Merri nodded, and the worry in Flora's face eased.

"What I want to know is how we're supposed to keep that McBride boy from . . . er . . ." Fauna grinned, dimples deepening. "Expending his affections on some other girl?" She blew a carrot-colored curl off her forehead and kept on shuffling.

"Thunderbolts, Fauna, he's only two years old!" Merri glared at her.

The shuffling stopped. "Oh, but have you seen him? The lad's going to grow, and with those dark brown eyes and thick lashes, and those raven's-wing curls of his . . . well, let's just see what the cards say." She fanned the deck and pulled one card. "Knight of Swords."

"Oh, my," the other two said in unison.

"I think we'll have our work cut out for us, sisters," Flora said.

Merri sighed and shook her head. "Don't be ridiculous. Nathan McBride, even if he's the reincarnation of Don Juan himself, still won't stand a chance against three Sortilege Witches."

"So it's decided," Fauna said, nodding hard. "We keep him pure . . ." she grinned, "even if it kills him. For our Aurora."

The three Witches smiled knowingly, while the baby looked on with what seemed to be a worried frown creasing her forehead.

October 31, 1973

Little Nathan McBride scowled at the dark-haired toddler. He was already in kindergarten and he couldn't *wait* to learn how to read. He loved books and it frustrated him to no end that he couldn't decipher the words inside.

And now, here were those very weird old ladies from Raven Street, with their little kid who couldn't be more than three years old, and the brat was *reading*. Not whole sentences, of course. But words. That tall, mean-looking aunt of hers with the steel-gray hair would hold up a flash card with letters on it, and the kid would say "Cat!" or "Dog!" or "Bird!" And then everyone at the neighborhood Halloween party would burst into applause. Like she was some kinda genius or something.

Aurora. Whoever heard of a girl named Aurora, anyway?

Everyone was so busy fussing over her that they'd barely noticed the Batman costume he'd spent so much time picking out. Nope, they only had eyes for the brat-kid with the strange black eyes.

Nathan *hated* Aurora Sortilege. And he vowed he always would.

October 31, 1980

It was Halloween. And more than that, it was Aurora's tenth birthday. And more than that—*this!* She could hardly believe it.

"Mr. McBride has invited you to go trick-or-treating with Nathan tonight," Aunt Merri said. And her words made Aurora's belly clench with excitement. Even *Aunt Merriwether* seemed excited. All of them did. "Do you think you'd like to accept?"

"Oh, yes! Yes!"

She hopped up and down, and could barely stand still while her three aunts helped her fuss with her Egyptian princess costume until she looked just perfect.

She'd had a wild crush on Nathan McBride for *weeks* now. But he was older, and he barely seemed to notice her. Tonight, he would, though. Maybe he liked her, too! Why else ask her along on tonight of all nights?

Tonight of all nights. . . . She blinked up at Aunt Merri. "I don't want to miss our Samhain celebration, Auntie."

"You'll be back in time, sweetheart. We'll wait for you. You just go and have a good time with young Nathan."

"If you're sure it's okay."

Aunt Merriwether nodded. "It's okay."

And so she went. She skipped all the way down Raven Street, turned right at the corner onto Mulberry, and only slowed down and felt her nervousness return when his house loomed just ahead of her. It was a nice house. Newer than her own. Hers was *ancient* in comparison. And Nathan's father was pretty important in this little town. He owned the drugstore, and a couple in other nearby towns, too. And she was just . . . just Aurora. She bit her lip.

Swallowing hard and whispering a tiny little invocation for courage, she marched up the walk and rang the front doorbell.

Nathan opened it. He was wearing blue jeans and a sweatshirt. His dark hair was long. He liked wearing it long because the big kids wore it that way. Aurora liked it, too. It was curly and soft-looking. She thought Nathan was the handsomest boy in the whole town.

"Where's your costume?" she asked him.

"Very funny. I'm almost thirteen, you know."

"You're not dressing up?"

"Course not, 'Rora."

She wished *she* hadn't dressed up. Suddenly she felt like a big baby in her beautiful princess outfit. "But how can you trick-or-treat without a costume?"

He shook his head, and stepped outside, pushing the door closed behind him. "I'm not trick-or-treating. I'm babysitting you while *you* trick-or-treat."

Her heart felt as if something sharp had just pierced it. "B-babysitting . . . ?"

"Hey, it wasn't my idea. Something those wacky aunts of yours cooked up with my dad. So are they really Witches like everyone says?"

She opened her mouth, but she couldn't seem to say anything to him. She was so shocked and so hurt she could barely breathe, let alone talk.

"Are you one, too?" Nathan gave her Egyptian princess gown a teasing tug. "So how come you didn't wear a pointy hat and carry a broom then? Do you think you'll get warts on your nose when you grow up? I heard all Witches get big ugly ones, sooner or later. And that they—"

She whirled and ran from him, tears burning paths down her cheeks.

"Hey! 'Rora, wait up! I was just kidding around."

"I hate you, Nathan McBride!" She never slowed her pace until she got back to her house. And she managed to wipe the tears away before she faced her aunts. She lied to them for the fist time in her life that night. Told them she was too sick to stay out. And that year she skipped Samhain, as well.

October 31, 1986

It was Aurora Sortilege's sixteenth birthday, and her crazy aunts were having a Sweet Sixteen party for her. Up there at that crazy excuse for a house. The big old Gothic was older than this entire town, or so people said.

Nathan and Aurora had never gotten along. They tended to avoid each other like the plague. At school, if they were forced into it, they'd say hello and not much else. He didn't really care. He had a crowd of friends. She didn't have many at all. It was partly because everyone knew her aunts thought of themselves as Witches, and that made a lot of the parents nervous—some because they figured the three ladies must be nuts, and others because they figured the three ladies sacrificed children in naked moonlight rituals and worshipped demons.

Nathan had done a little reading on the subject. Just out of curiosity, of course. So he knew that none of that was true. And he really didn't believe in any of that Witch stuff anyway. But he still didn't like her.

The Witch thing was only part of the reason Aurora wasn't very popular. Mostly it was just because she was such a brainiac. Nathan was graduating this year. So was Aurora, two years ahead of schedule. And then he was heading off to college and she'd be shipping out to premed. She wanted to be a doctor. She'd make a good one, too. He remembered a time two years ago, when a great big red-winged hawk had swooped down in front of his car, right after he'd gotten his license. It crashed into the windshield and then rolled to the ground.

Aurora had been out walking and she'd seen the whole thing. Of course, she'd stomped over to the car screaming at him for being careless and stupid and a hundred other things. But then she'd knelt down on the road, and there had been actual *tears* in her eyes as she touched the unmoving bird. He'd walked over there to see if he could help. But he'd ended up just standing still and watching her as she'd started running her hands over the hawk, real slow, and talking under her breath. Her eyes were closed, he remembered that. All the sudden, the bird twitched. Then it came to flapping, shrieking life, and hauled tail out of there.

It didn't go far, he recalled. It landed heavily in a tree along the roadside, and it looked back at him and Aurora, and then it let out a piercing cry.

"You're welcome," Aurora had whispered. Man, he'd never forget that. He'd thought then she must be totally bonkers. Nathan had ignored her bright smile, and her whispered, *"I did it."* He'd told himself the bird was probably just stunned. He didn't believe all that Witch crap for a minute. And if Aurora was as smart as everyone thought, she wouldn't either.

Anyway, she'd had a nice touch with that bird, even if it had only been stunned. And she couldn't stand to see *anyone* hurting. So he thought she'd make a pretty decent doctor. Not that he cared. Hell, he wouldn't even be going to this birthday party except that . . . well, word around school was that no one else was going to show. And he kind of felt sorry for her. So he'd bought her a pair of fairly expensive earrings with emeralds on them. Tiny emeralds, but heck, he was making only three-fifty an hour part-time at the greasy spoon in town. And he was going over there to that house on Raven Street. He'd grit his teeth and ignore the way she always managed to irritate the hell out of him, and he'd wish her a happy birthday.

When he got there, though, and saw her sitting on the front steps crying her eyes out, something happened to him.

He went all soft inside for some reason. He walked up the steps and sat there beside her.

"What's the matter, Aurora?"

She lifted her head, looking straight into his eyes with her black, shiny, wet ones. "You know. I can see that you know."

He shook his head in denial.

"No one's coming, that's what's the matter. And you knew it, Nathan. Why didn't you tell me?"

He blinked in surprise and glanced at his watch. It was still ten minutes before party time. How could she know already? Unless someone had said something. "It's early yet," he told her. "What makes you think . . . ?"

She sent him a look of exasperation. "I *know* things, Nathan. And I know this. And I know that you knew and you didn't tell me."

He lowered his head, unsure of what to say. Maybe she really did have some kind of . . . Nah. But when he looked up at her again, he noticed for the first time that Aurora was turning into one drop-dead beautiful girl. And he wondered why he had never noticed it before. She'd never cut her hair, so far as he knew. It hung to her waist like a black satin flag, smooth and shining. And her eyes had a very slight tilt to them that made them exotic, entrancing. And since they were as black as her hair, you couldn't tell the irises from the pupils. Just big black marbles. Onyx eyes. Deeper than just about any eyes he'd ever seen. Lashes like sable paintbrushes. Lips that used to seem too plump when she was little, now looked like they belonged on a cover model.

It surprised the heck out of him. But he suddenly realized that this girl, whom he'd spent most of his life disliking, was incredible. And unusual—and he supposed he found that just as attractive as everything else about her.

Did he . . . actually . . . *like* her?

He got to thinking about the possibility that maybe he did. Maybe he *more than* just *liked* her; the more he thought, the more he realized that it was true. He lifted his chin and looked at her, sitting there beside him on the top step, so heartbroken. He was going to do it. He was going to ask the little Witch for a date. He could hardly believe it.

He smiled to himself, because he sort of knew she'd always had a crush on him. It would make her day. Make up for the birthday party not happening and her favorite holiday being a wash, and everything else.

She got to her feet slowly while he was still thinking. "I can't believe I got all dressed up for nothing."

And she had gotten all dressed up. But not for nothing. She looked great in her denim skirt and silky sleeveless blouse. Pretty. Feminine. Delicate.

"Maybe not for nothing," he said.

She looked down at him, and for the first time, he saw hope in her eyes. "Why?" she asked. "Have you heard something?"

Heard something? He just shrugged. "What if some good looking senior came over here and asked you to go to the drive-in with him?" he said, as suavely as he could manage. And then he waited for her eyes to light up.

And they did. Widened and lit and shone, and she started to smile.

"You *have* heard something, haven't you? Is it him? Is it Bobby Ridgeway? Is he really going to ask me out? I had a feeling he was, but I didn't trust my own . . . oh my Goddess, here he *comes!*"

Nathan stood there feeling as if he'd just been dropped into a play where he didn't know the lines, while Bobby Ridgeway, the biggest jock in school, and until this very second one of Nathan's best buds, pulled up in his dad's station wagon and blew the horn.

"Hi, Bobby!" Aurora waved so hard that Nathan thought her hand would fall off, and went running down the steps to the car.

Nathan couldn't hear what they were saying after that. Just Bobby revving the Ford's motor once in a while and Aurora's deep, soft laughter. She didn't giggle. He'd never once heard Aurora giggle. A minute later she got in the passenger side and the wagon roared away.

Bobby Ridgeway was no dummy. Apparently he, too, had noticed that there was more to Aurora Sortilege than an overdeveloped brain and an Addams Family upbringing. Only *he'd* noticed a lot quicker than Nathan had.

The front door opened and Aurora's Aunt Fauna, five feet tall and three feet wide with blazing orange hair, stepped out looking heartbroken. "Oh, Nathan," she said— as if she knew. "I'm so sorry."

He wiped the stricken expression off his face and got up. "Hey, sorry for what? You oughta be happy. That niece of yours finally got a date. I was beginning to think it'd never happen." He turned to go, then turned back again and thrust the small, clumsily wrapped box into the woman's pudgy hand. "Give this to her when she gets back, will ya?"

"Of course I will. Thank you, Nathan. That was so thoughtful."

He shrugged and turned to leave. Thoughtful, heck. It was a pity gift, just like it would have been a pity date. He didn't even *like* Aurora. Never had.

Never would.

June 1987

Aurora was valedictorian of the graduating class. She could have felt a little bad about that. Probably should have. After all, she was only sixteen, and was graduating early, and most of the other seniors thought one of them should have won the honor—that she should have been disqualified because she didn't really belong.

She'd never really belonged.

But she refused to feel guilty. Because the salutatorian— the sap who would have made valedictorian if not for Aurora—was none other than Nathan McBride. And he'd been a lousy jerk to her all year long. Sure, they'd never really gotten along, but he'd been worse than ever this year. It seemed to Aurora that it had begun about the time she'd started dating Bobby Ridgeway.

And she used to think Bobby and Nathan were friends!

Well, apparently not. But she didn't see why Nathan was taking it out on her. It had ended with Bobby, anyway. He'd pulled a hamstring at football practice in the middle of the season, and was going to have to miss an important game. So, being bound by oath and ancestral blood to help others whenever possible, Aurora had offered to work a healing for him.

He'd acted as if she'd claimed to have two heads. Said he didn't think all the talk about her being a Witch was anything more than gossip, or he'd have never asked her out. He called her a psycho and a weirdo and a dozen other names, and dumped her like a carton of sour milk. And as if that weren't bad enough, he went around telling everyone at school that Aurora really believed she was a Witch. As if it were impossible, for goodness' sake!

And then Mindy had tried to help. She really had. It wasn't her fault it backfired. Mindy had moved into town only last year, and she'd felt like an outsider too, at first. Aurora, being who and what she was, had tried to make her feel welcome when everyone else had just ignored her. They'd become friends, and even when Mindy started hearing the gossip, she'd stuck by Aurora.

One day, Mindy heard some of the jerks scoffing about the Wallingford High Witch, and she jumped in their faces. Told them how Aurora had sped up the healing on her broken leg earlier that year, and how she'd been able to play soccer again before the end of the season, against the doctor's predictions and everyone's expectations.

But instead of helping, it only made matters worse. Everyone knew about her leg, and the unusually speedy recovery. But until then, no one knew the rest. And until then, everyone had ribbed and teased Aurora about the whole Witch thing, but no one had really believed it.

Now they did. And everything changed after that. When Aurora walked down the hall, conversations would stop, and wary eyes would watch her. Students, and even a few of the teachers, would step well out of her path to give her a wide berth. It was as if they were afraid of her.

Except for Mindy, of course.

And lousy rotten old Nathan McBride. *He* wasn't afraid of her, didn't believe in magick anyway, and probably wouldn't have been afraid of her even if he had. He laughed at the kids who acted skittish around Aurora and kept right on teasing her just the way he always had. "Hey, Broom-Hilda," he'd yell, because he was too dense to know the name was Brynhild and that she was a Valkyrie, not a Witch. "Get your broom outta your locker and fly it over here, will ya? I spilled something." Or " 'Rora, you'd best get your butt into that science lab and turn the eighth period class back into humans again before somebody dissects them!"

She *hated* that boy.

He'd always follow up by thumbing his nose at her, turning to his pale and wide-eyed companions, and saying, "See? I'm still in one piece. No warts, no locusts. I told you nothing would happen."

She figured he was probably tormenting her to prove she wasn't a Witch at all. Just a crazy teenager with delusions. And if she hadn't had the Witches' Rede drilled into her for most of her life, she might just have supplied him with whatever proof he required, the more painful the better.

But she couldn't do that. Wouldn't do it. She was a healer. She was going to medical school to become an even better one. If she went around causing harm, she might just lose the healing gift she'd been born with, and that would break her heart.

At the graduation ceremony, she delivered a short speech no one really wanted to hear, about kindness and tolerance and open-mindedness and freedom. And she wore a tiny pair of emerald earrings.

And when it was over, and everyone threw their hats in the air, someone turned to hug her impulsively, and she impulsively hugged back. And then she realized it was Nathan, and backed away with a gasp.

He blinked and looked as surprised as she was. Then his gaze shifted downward just slightly, and he smiled. "You wore them," he said.

The crowds surged around them, tugging them apart. She was surrounded by her loving aunts, and he was being slapped on the back by his father and a bunch of relatives from out of town.

And that was the last time she saw Nathan McBride for a very long time.

One

October 1997

Nathan McBride stared across the fancy restaurant's most secluded table into Elsie Kincaid's big blue eyes. The taper candle set her blonde hair alight with its golden gleam, and cast dark shadows into the depths of her cleavage. And he did mean *depths*. It was like Davy Jones's Locker down there, and he was more than ready to go diving. The way she kept leaning over the table suggested she was ready, too.

And so what if those baby blues were a little vacant? It wasn't as if he were looking for a prospective brain surgeon here. He simply wanted to get laid. Period.

He felt a little guilty for that rather unenlightened thought, but damn, frustration would turn a red-blooded man into a chauvinistic beast pretty fast. He ought to know. He'd been frustrated for well over a decade now.

He pushed his plate aside, reached across the table, took her hand in both of his. "You ready to order dessert?" he asked her softly.

"Oh, Nate, I think you *know* what I'd like for dessert."

He gritted his teeth and managed not to grimace when she called him "Nate," which he detested. It wasn't hard to ignore that minor irritant when her foot, minus its spike-heeled shoe, began running up the inside of his leg under the table.

Hot damn, this is it.

"So, um, can I take you back to my . . ." He bit his lip. "Your place?" No more taking chances by bringing a woman back to his place. He was beginning to think it was haunted. There was the night with that blue-eyed blonde, Suzanne, when the heating ducts decided to spew black smoke. And the time with that other blue-eyed blonde, Rebecca, when the air conditioner mysteriously caught fire. And don't forget the blue-eyed blonde, Anne Marie, and the SWAT team with the wrong address.

Nope. Not with . . . er . . . Elsie. Yeah. Elsie. With a chest to match the name, he thought. Then he realized he was turning into a real pig.

"Sure," she said. "My place is great." She slinked out of the chair and across the floor for his viewing pleasure, pausing at the exit to send a wink over her shoulder at him. She was very good at slinking. He fumbled for his wallet, dropped it twice, and fished out a handful of bills to pay for their meal. Then he got up and wandered out after her.

And the whole time, he was feeling very nervous. Glancing over his shoulder. Wondering what could possibly go wrong *this* time.

She sat behind the wheel of his car, the Jag he'd spent a small fortune on because no man could drive a Jag and not have constant bouts of wild sex, right?

Wrong, as it turned out, but it had been worth a shot.

Elsie called out the window to him. "Can I drive it, Nate, sweetie? I'd be soooo grateful."

"Oh, yeah," he said, and stopped near the door to hand her the keys. She started the engine, and it gave its distinctive Jaguar roar when she revved it. Nathan smiled, about to turn and walk around to the passenger side.

He only vaguely heard the change in the engine's sound when she slipped the shift into gear. The way the tires spun when she popped the clutch was a whole lot louder, causing him to spin around in surprise. And of course, he was paying complete attention when the sideview mirror of his car plowed into him like a wrecking ball intent on castration.

Elsie screamed before Nathan ever hit the pavement. Then he landed like a ton of bricks. He heard those heels clicking toward him, heard her babbling about her foot slipping, saw her cleavage in his face as she bent over him and figured that was about as close as he'd ever get to it. He was going to die a virgin.

Then he passed out.

"Ooops!" Fauna said.

She and her sisters stood around the crystal ball, looking on, wide-eyed.

"Oh dear!" gasped Flora. "Did we kill him?"

"No, but we might have damaged something vital!" Fauna shouted. "Did you see where that bubblehead hit him?"

"He'll be all right." Merriwether stroked the crystal ball with her palm. "Aurora is on E. R. duty tonight. Now that she's finally come home, it's high time we see to the business of getting those two together."

"And not a moment too soon. I'm exhausted." Fauna fanned herself. "I vow, Merriwether, I've never seen a man so determined to get—"

"*Fauna!*" Flora's shocked voice and red cheeks stopped her sister's descriptive sentence.

Merri simply shook her head at the both of them. "You're overstating it, Fauna. Any man would be acting just the same."

"But he tries every night!"

"And every night we have to bring disaster crashing down on his head. You'd think he'd give up after a while, wouldn't you?" Flora asked softly, shaking her head and looking truly sorry for all the havoc they'd been forced to wreak on Nathan McBride's life.

"He isn't thinking with his brain, sisters," Fauna quipped with an impish grin.

"He just doesn't realize that he's been waiting for her all along. Er, with a little help from us. But once he does . . ." Flora's clasped hands pressed to her cheek, her lashes fluttering. "Oh, I wish I could be there to see it when their eyes meet across the room for the first time, and Cupid's arrow hits them right in their tender little hearts."

Fauna stifled a laugh, and snorted. "I'll admit it would be good to see that man hit with *something* besides his own car!" She and Flora burst into laughter at that, and while Merri sniffed indignantly at their irreverence, she had to battle a grin herself.

"Dr. Sortilege to E. R." the hushed voice on the P. A. system repeated. Aurora hurriedly gulped the rest of her herbal tea and got up from the first break she'd had all night to rush down the hall to the emergency room, her senses pricking to full alertness and telling her all she needed to know.

It was not a life-threatening injury coming in. It was minor, but pretty painful to the victim. Her brain told her those things before she ever set foot inside the treatment room, just as it told her when things were not so good. It was nice, this gift she'd inherited from her ancestors. It gave her time to prepare, and more often than not, helped her make her patients well again.

She'd had the powers for too long to consider them odd. They were just a gift of heredity, like her jet-black hair and ebony eyes. Then again, she didn't broadcast the fact that she was a Witch, either. While she was at work, the gold Pentacle rested *under* her white coat. But it didn't matter. Everyone in this town knew about those strange Sortilege women in the old house on the hill. She'd thought they might have forgotten while she'd been away, but no such luck. But for some reason, the whispers and gossip no longer bothered her. Maybe because she was an adult now, sure of herself, who she was *and* what she was. Confident and proud of both. And maybe because of that change in attitude—or maybe because they'd done some growing up, too—the gossips were not as malicious or mean-spirited as they had been in high school.

Some of the locals looked at her oddly. Some were nervous around her, and simply avoided her. Some came to her asking for love potions or lottery numbers. But most of the longtime residents just shrugged off her family's weirdness. They'd had generations to get used to it, after all.

She stepped into the treatment room, quickly scanning the chart the nurse handed her. "Hello, Mr. . . . ." Her eyes found the name. "McBride?"

She blinked, and lifted her gaze to the man on the bed.

His eyes were closed as he lay there, hurting pretty badly, not looking back at her. But it was him. And she felt something. Some jolt. A psychic buzz. She swallowed hard and shook herself.

"Call me Nathan," he told her through gritted teeth. He turned his head toward her and opened his eyes, but they focused on the front of her lab coat instead of her face. His eyes widened with interest then, and his gaze slid down her body, over her legs to her toes, and back up again. "Call me anything you want, as a matter of fact."

"Nathan McBride?" She lifted her brows. "You're just as sleazy as you always were, I see."

He frowned, bringing his eyes up to meet hers at last. And then she saw the recognition in them. He glanced at the name tag pinned to her white coat. "Dr. Sortilege. Holy crap, Broom-Hilda's back."

"That's right," she said, and she lifted her chin and forced a smile. If no one else's opinions mattered to her anymore, then why did his lighthearted barb sting? "The little girl who used to play tag-a-long. You must remember. You said I was a pest, and that my aunts were weirdos and that I would probably grow up with warts on my nose."

Her patient's face went a shade whiter, and he licked his lips nervously. "You . . . have a real good memory, Aurora." He tried for a smile. "Do you hold a grudge as long?"

"Of course not," she said with a sweet smile, and then turned to a stainless steel tray full of instruments at the ready, picked up the longest, sharpest scalpel on it, and tested its edge with her thumb. "Nurse, bring in the cranial drill, will you?"

"Hey, wait a min—"

She looked at her patient and winked. The nurse, Meg, a friend of hers, burst out laughing while Nathan McBride, former jerk of the universe, sat in the bed staring from one of them to the other. "You ladies are brutal."

"No more than you were ten years ago," Aurora quipped. She handed the scalpel to Meg. "Get this sterilized, will you?"

Meg nodded and left the room. Aurora managed to stop smiling and leaned over the bed. "I guess you're hurting enough right now without me adding to it."

"Does it show?" he asked wryly. "And here I'm trying to impress you by being too manly to let a little pain bother me."

"You can't hide it from me, anyway, so don't waste the effort."

"Yeah, I forgot. You're a Witch."

"And a doctor," she reminded him, lest he forget.

"A Witch doctor? God help me."

"Watch yourself, Nathan, or you'll be sitting on a lily pad eating flies."

"Very funny." He lay back on the pillow, then eyed her. "You *were* kidding, right?"

" 'An it harm none, do what ye will,' " she quoted. "The most important line in the Witches' Rede."

"Lucky for me."

"You're damn right, it is."

He frowned at her, but she didn't elaborate. "So let's see if I have this straight," she went on. "Your date backed your Jaguar into your groin, is that about right?" She leaned over him and lifted his shirt away from his belly. He hadn't gone to pot. He had washboard abs that sent little tingles of awareness up into her fingers when she touched him there. Ignoring the shivers, she probed his abdomen gently. "Is this tender?"

"Yeah. A little bit."

She took her hand away, and held it, palm down, a fraction of an inch above his groin, and she closed her eyes.

"You preparing to grab me?" He sounded a little nervous.

She smiled slightly. "Shhhhh. Relax for a second."

He did. She felt the pain, the bruising, but nodded, reassured that the damage wasn't serious. She'd confirm her diagnosis in a more scientific manner, of course. But she always felt better knowing as soon as possible.

Opening her eyes again, she asked, "You hit your head when you landed?"

He nodded.

Aurora pushed his dark hair aside and looked at the bump on his head. She held her receptive hand over it and knew it was throbbing, but not dangerous. Mild concussion at the worst. She'd confirm that, as well, with a precautionary X ray. "You can feel better knowing there's nothing seriously wrong," she said. "Let's just be as thorough as possible, though. Don't want you suing me." And she pulled on a pair of latex gloves, then slipped her fingers inside the waistband of his jeans and began undoing them.

His hand landed atop hers instantly. "Hold on a minute!"

She couldn't pull her hand away, so she left it there. "Problem?"

"Yeah, there's a problem. What do you think you're doing?"

She smiled. "I always heard that men who drive Jaguars are trying to make up for having small genitals," she said sweetly. "I just wanted to check." His jaw dropped. She shook her head and rolled her eyes. "I'm examining you. I'm a doctor, Nathan. What do you *think* I'm doing?"

"I *think* I'd like a doctor with a little less sarcasm, and a little more testosterone. A *male* doctor, if you don't mind. And could you make him a few years older than Doogie Hauser?"

She lifted her brows. "So it *is* true? About the small—"

"Dammit, Aurora, get me a male doctor or I'm outta here."

"You're as big a jerk now as you were ten years ago,

McBride,'' she snapped. ''And I hope your balls swell up and fall off.''

''What happened to your phony line about harming none, *Endora?*''

She smirked at his name-calling. ''Hey, I didn't say I'd cause it, just that I'd *like* it.'' She peeled off her latex gloves and tossed them onto his chest. ''And before I go, I'll tell you what Dr. Stewart is going to tell you after a thorough exam and a few hundred dollars' worth of X rays. You probably have a mild concussion, which is amazing considering how hard that rock you call a head must be. Your family jewels will be sore for a day or so, but no damage was done. And you have a big purple bruise on your right elbow. That's going to bother you more than anything else, because you'll wince every time you bend the arm.'' She spun on her heel to head out the door, then stopped in her tracks and turned to face him again. ''And one more thing—something Dr. Stewart *won't* tell you. You're still a virgin.''

He gasped. He sputtered. He stared at her as if she'd grown another head.

''Remember all this next time you feel like calling my abilities as a doctor—or as a Witch—into question, Nathan McBride.''

Dr. Stewart examined him thoroughly and ordered a complete set of X rays. When all was said and done, he told Nathan that he had a mild concussion. That his groin was going to be sore but no serious damage had been done. And that the bruise to his right elbow would probably give him more trouble than any of the other injuries.

He *didn't* tell him that he was still a virgin, but Nathan didn't figure that sort of thing showed up in an X ray.

But Aurora had known. And how the hell did a skeptic like him explain that? How could she know something he'd never told another living soul?

Damn.

He felt invaded. Embarrassed. As if he had to explain or defend himself to her. It insulted his pride that she knew, that she must be thinking what she . . . must be thinking. And for God's sake, when had he ever given a damn *what* Aurora thought? Besides, it wasn't as if he'd *chosen* to be celibate. It was just that every time he got anywhere near scoring with a woman, some sort of disaster happened. It had been this way since college, and he was beginning to think it would stay this way for his entire life.

Hell, maybe he ought to join the priesthood.

It was as if he were cursed.

Cursed?

What if . . . She'd always hated his guts. So suppose she'd . . .

Nah.

He sighed and fell back on the bed. Dr. Stewart came in with release forms for him to sign, and Nathan took the pen and scratched his name across the bottom. "Tell me something, Doc, do you believe in curses?"

Dr. Stewart smiled. "I know you made her mad, son, but Aurora Sortilege would never go putting any curse on anybody. Wouldn't hurt a fly, that one. Don't be listening to gossip."

"That's easy for you to say." He shook his head. What he was thinking was really silly, because he didn't believe in that kind of crap.

"If someone put a hex on you, son, it wasn't Aurora." He winked then. "But I'd bet my last dollar she could help you get rid of it."

Nathan gaped. "You telling me you *believe* in all that . . . that *Witch* stuff?"

Dr. Stewart drew a thoughtful breath, frowning hard. Then he sighed and sat down in the chair beside the bed, crossing one leg over the other. "Yesterday, Aurora and I were sitting in the doctors' lounge having coffee. All of the sudden, for no apparent reason, she dropped her cup on the floor." He shook his head. "Coffee all over the place. She got up and ran out of there like her chair was on fire. Next thing I knew she was pushing a crash cart down the hall. She stopped outside one of the patients' rooms . . . and about a second later, the man inside went into full arrest."

Nathan scanned the doctor's face to see if he was kidding. Didn't look like he was. "Did you ask her about it?"

"She said she heard the alarm going off on the man's heart monitor, but she didn't. There wasn't any alarm. We found out later that one of the nurses had left it unplugged. Damn thing never would have gone off."

Sure, and it's almost Halloween and I'll bet it's this guy's favorite holiday—next to April Fool's Day, that is.

"It wasn't the first time something like that's happened, either."

"Then you *do* believe she's some kind of a Witch?"

"It's uncanny, boy. I'll tell you that much."

The man didn't seem like the practical-joking type. And Nathan got to thinking about some of the uncanny things *he'd* seen Aurora do, from the time she'd been pint-sized to a peanut.

"So . . . so if there *were* some kind of curse on me . . ."

"Or even if it's just bad luck," Dr. Stewart continued, "Aurora would be the person to talk to about it. No doubt in my mind about that."

"Yeah," Nathan said. "Unless she happens to hate my guts." *Or unless she's the one who cursed me in the first place.* The possibility didn't seem quite so farfetched anymore.

Dr. Stewart chuckled deep in his gut as he got up and walked out of the room, shaking his head.

Well, Nathan thought, he really had nothing to lose. If he didn't figure out why the fates seemed to be conspiring to keep him from ever having sex in his life, he was going to lose his mind. And the embarrassing part—the part where he actually had to admit that he was still a virgin at twenty-nine—was already over. Aurora already knew. So maybe he *should* try to get her to help him.

And maybe he should just stick hot needles into his eyes. First he had to decide which would be more unpleasant.

Two

Aurora ducked her head to miss the wind chimes that hung from every possible place on the front porch and kept the house sounding like an ice-waterfall all the time, and headed through the front door.

Aunt Flora looked up from where she'd been concentrating hard on two pink candles with heart shapes carved into their bases and rose petals scattered around them. And her athame was still in her hand.

"Sorry," Aurora whispered, pausing in her tracks. "Am I interrupting a ritual?"

"No!" Aunt Flora said, too quickly. Almost as if she had something to hide.

"Now, Auntie, it looks like a love spell to me." Aurora crooked a brow. "Hey, you aren't trying to conjure up some prince to come steal you away from us, are you?"

"Of course not, dear! Why, I would never. Oh, no, absolutely not, darling." She cleared her throat, muttered a quick, "As I will it, so mote it be," half under her breath, and snuffed her candles.

Aurora got a little queasy feeling in the pit of her stomach, one that told her she was being kept in the dark about something. Before she could question Aunt Flora, however, Aunt Fauna came in from the back door, a basketful of freshly cut herbs and various roots over her arm. "Ohhh, you're home!" she exclaimed. "Merriwether, she's home!"

Aunt Merri's steps came from the second floor as she hurried to the top of the stairs. "Wait until you see what I bought you today, Aurora!" She waved the little box she held in her hand as she trotted down the stairs. Aurora winced, and quickly sent a protective wish out to her, to keep her from falling and breaking something. "I saw it and I just knew—"

"Oh, wait until you see it!"

"You'll never take it off!"

Her aunts were acting decidedly suspicious tonight. Aurora's warning bells were going off. Of course, she loved them with every cell in her body, and knew they'd never dream of harming her. But meddling was certainly not beyond them.

"Thank you, Aunt Merri," she said, taking the box warily and opening the lid. "Oh. My. That *is* beautiful." Aurora lifted the necklace from the box—a gold chain with a rose quartz stone suspended from it, and the Runic symbol for love etched onto the surface. "But, Aunt Merri, why this particular stone?"

"It spoke to me," Merri said. "Just felt right, you know. One of those impulse buys."

Aurora frowned. "You've never done anything impulsive in your live, Aunt Merri. Now why don't you girls tell me just what's going on here? Hmmm?"

They all shook their heads, muttering denials, and averting their eyes. Aurora's sense of foreboding grew stronger.

"Tell us about your day, dear."

"Oh, yes, do! Did you meet anyone interesting today?"

"Anyone new?"

She tilted her head, knew they were changing the subject, and decided to let it slide. For now. "The only new patient wasn't really new. The little brat who used to pick on me when I was younger. He grew into a bigger brat, and a chauvinist pig to boot."

"Why, whoever can you mean?" Flora asked faintly.

"Certainly not that sweet little McBride boy?" Fauna said, as Merri elbowed her in the ribs.

"Now how on earth could you know . . . ?"

"The cards, dear! The cards."

"I didn't know there was a Nathan McBride card in your deck, Aunt Fauna. Unless you're referring to The Fool."

"Oh, dear," Fauna said. "Then you did see the McBride boy today?"

"Only long enough to wish I hadn't," she said. "I swear I've never known a bigger jerk in my life. Demanded a male doctor. Of all the nerve . . ."

"Don't be too hard on him, Aurora," Aunt Merriwether advised. "Maybe he was just embarrassed."

"Or shy," Flora put in.

"Or nervous," Fauna added.

"Or an idiot," Aurora declared. "If I ever see him again, I think I'll . . . What? Why are you all looking at me like that?"

"Like what, dear?"

"Like you've done something I'm going to hate, is like what."

"Well . . . well, you see, we were under the impression that . . ." Fauna began.

"That you and Nathan McBride were old friends," Flora finished for her.

"So when his father called to say he'd heard you were back in town, and to ask how you were doing . . ." Merri's voice faltered. "We . . . well, that is, we . . ."

"You what?"

Merri swallowed, lifted her chin, and said with authority, "Invited him to dinner."

"Nathan and his father, that is," Fauna added quickly. "You know, his father, Daniel, he's always been kind to us. Always willing to order even the most obscure herbs, if we asked, and never once pried into what we could want with them."

"He's retired now, you know. Turned the chain over to Nathan," Flora said.

"Chain?" When Aurora had left, there had only been a handful of small drugstores.

"It's a rather impressive chain of pharmacies now, dear," Aunt Merri clarified. "Nathan has a head for business. And you mustn't be upset about this dinner. We just thought it would be nice to . . ."

"To be sociable," Fauna finished. Then she sighed and wiped her neon hair from her brow as if exhausted.

"When?"

"Why, tomorrow night, dear."

"Fine. I just won't be here then. I'll make something up and . . ."

"Oh, no you won't," Merri said, and for once her voice sounded a bit harsh, and even a little disapproving. "That would be not only deceitful, but rude, and we've raised you better than that."

"Oh, that we have," said the usually timid and soft-spoken Flora, shaking a forefinger. " 'Ever mind the Rule of Three. Three times what thou givest, returns to thee.' "

Aurora pressed her fingertips to her temples and closed her eyes. "All right, all right. I'll suffer through dinner with the idiot. But if you expect me to enjoy it, you'd better think again."

"Oh, darling, that's better. And of course you'll enjoy it. I'm sure Nathan's become a wonderful man." Merri smiled.

"No one's at his best when he ends up in an emergency room," Flora said sympathetically.

"You might be very pleasantly surprised, dear," Fauna put in.

"I'll be surprised if he has the nerve to show up," she retorted; then she made her way upstairs to her own suite of rooms to sit and ponder the possible reasons for such a terrible scourge appearing in her life right now, just when everything had been going so smoothly.

The place scared the living hell out of him.

First, it was old, and creepier than even he remembered. Then again, he'd never come all the way inside before. And the house was older now than it had been last time he'd come over here. But only by a decade.

It was Gothic in style, with tall narrow windows so ancient that the glass was thicker at the bottom of the panes than at the top. The house had been freshly painted, sure, and kept in good repair. But a weed patch that his father assured him was an herb garden took up half of the side lawn, and a dense flower garden, with a path that led to its center and enough trees and shrubs to keep that center hidden, took up most of the back. He'd always wondered what was hiding inside the depths of that garden. Then there were those wall-to-wall wind chimes lining the front porch, tinkling constantly. The place gave him the chills. He kept expecting bats to come flying out of a dormer window.

His dad had come down with a mysterious, hacking cough just before it was time to leave, and insisted it was probably his allergies acting up. He'd said Nathan had to go or the three old ladies would be insulted, and goodness only knew what would happen then.

Nathan didn't particularly want to think about what would happen then. He grinned self-consciously and reminded himself that he didn't believe in that stuff.

He rang the doorbell and it chimed with a deep and resonant tone. He grinned harder as he imagined Lurch coming to answer it. But instead a tall, regal woman with steel-gray hair and piercing black eyes opened the door, and Nathan's smile died. "Hello, Nathan," she greeted him. "You probably don't remember me. I'm Merriwether. Do come in."

"Hello, Nathan," said another voice, this one coming from a body no bigger than a minute. She was four-eleven if he'd ever seen it, and weighed perhaps ninety pounds dripping wet. She had hair as soft and white as cotton, and the face of everybody's cookie-baking grandma. "It's so good to see you again, young man. I'm Flora, remember?"

"And I'm Fauna," called another, this one short as well, but as round as a pumpkin and with hair about the same color. This one he remembered.

"Good to see you again," he managed. "I'm sorry my

father couldn't make it. He said to tell you how badly he feels for missing this.'' As he spoke and listened to their pat replies about being sorry that his father couldn't make it, Nathan looked past them. But *she* was nowhere in sight. There was plenty to look at, though. It smelled fantastic in here, and he spotted the source—incense burning in brass pots that looked Oriental and ancient. There were candles glowing everywhere. Mostly pink and red, he noted, wondering if the colors were significant in any way. Soft music was playing, sounding whimsical and Gaelic to him. Every window had a crystal prism suspended in front of it, and every shelf was lined with other stones—amethyst clusters and giant glittering geodes big enough for a small child to crawl inside. A tiny table sat in the window to the north, and there was a black iron cauldron sitting in its center, and various other items arranged around it: candlesticks, statuettes of mythical figures of some sort, wineglasses, an ornate silver hand mirror.

"And what is it that kept your father away, Nathan?" the tall one—Merriwether, he thought—asked.

"I think it's an allergy or something," he said, still distracted—still searching the place for Aurora, and wondering why he was. He didn't even like her. Didn't even like her type. He liked blue-eyed blondes with more bustline than brain. Not willowy raven-haired Witches with black eyes that could burn holes in solid rock. He still didn't see her. But there was a round table in the room's center with an elaborately decorated deck of oversized cards on it, and what he thought was a crystal ball in the center. Its base looked like pewter, and was made in the shape of a gnarled, clawed hand, long fingers grasping the crystal ball and holding it up.

A cold chill went up his nape.

"Oh, your father's ill?" tiny Flora asked with concern.

"Yes. Just allergies. Nothing serious. He's . . .'' Nathan's voice trailed off. Aurora appeared at the top of the stairs, and he went utterly still. She was . . . man, she was mesmerizing. Okay, so maybe he *did* like dark, spooky women. Maybe he'd just never realized it before. She just . . . she hadn't looked like this at the hospital, in that lab coat with her hair tied back and . . .

But now . . .

She came down the stairs in a black dress that hugged her arms from her wrists to her shoulders, dipped to cling to her breasts and her waist, snugged its way over her hips, and then turned into free-flowing rivers of satin that swayed around her legs when she moved. Her hair was long, very long, and gleaming in the candlelight like magic. And her eyes, they were almond shaped and more exotic than ever, lined and shadowed and as black as polished onyx.

For the life of him, Nathan couldn't figure out why she would take pains to look this good for a man she disliked as much as she disliked him. Why? He wondered if maybe Bobby Ridgeway was coming over later.

Why? For Goddess' sake, why did she go and dress up in her full-moon best for a man she didn't even like?

To punish him, that's why, she thought forcibly. To show him just what he's missing by brushing me off as too weird or too intelligent, too female or too young for his tastes. Let him see what he's missing and live the rest of his life writhing in agony over his foolish pride back at the hospital. And before, when she'd been younger, and he'd shunned her so often.

She told herself it meant nothing, that she had forgotten all about it long ago. But it was a lie. She'd adored him when she'd been a child, and he'd tossed her hero worship back into her face. Well, let him just take a good look now at what he'd rejected back then.

And if that's what she wanted, it was working, because he couldn't seem to take his eyes off her.

"Aurora," he said in a choked voice.

"Hello, Nathan. How is your . . . elbow?"

"Still pretty sore," he said. "But amazingly enough, everything else seems to be back in working order."

"Who could have guessed?" she asked sweetly.

He lowered his head. "You could. And you did, and I was an idiot. Okay?"

She blinked twice, standing at the bottom of the staircase. "Was that an apology?"

"Maybe," he admitted, coming forward, crossing the room until he stood a foot from her, facing her. "Let's not forget, I wasn't the only one who was obnoxious in that emergency room."

"So, you're expecting an apology from me?"

He let his gaze dip lower, slowly, and brought it up to her eyes again. "I'll tell you what, Aurora. That dress is apology enough for me. What do you say we call it even?" He said it softly, for her ears alone.

She felt her face drain of color. "This dress is no apology to you, Nathan. I wore it because I'm too old to stick out my tongue and thumb my nose at you. But you're obviously too dense to get the message."

"The only message I'm getting from that number, honey, is 'come and get it.' "

"The only message this number is sending out, *honey*, is 'you can't have it.' "

"Hey, did I say I wanted it?"

"Your pants said it for you." She sent a meaningful glance at the changing shape behind his zipper and lifted her brows, daring him to deny it. "You were right. Everything seems to be back in working order."

It seemed he'd run out of comebacks.

She smirked, but only for a moment. It was when she saw her three aunts grabbing for their coats, and the little emergency totebag they kept near the door, that she felt her smugness turn to panic.

"Where do you three think you're going?" she asked, trying not to sound desperate.

"To see Daniel, dear," Merri announced calmly.

"Nathan's father, Aurora."

"He's ill. It's the least we can do."

"Yes, I have the best remedies for allergies like this," Flora added, running into the hallway where bundles of herbs hung upside-down to dry, and snatching a sprig of this and a pinch of that to take along.

"But . . . but . . . Aunt Flora, the man *owns* his own drug-stores!"

Aunt Flora put a hand to her mouth and tittered delicately. "You're such a joker, Aurora. As if a drugstore compares to a Witch when it comes to remedies."

Aurora gave her head a shake. "Well then . . . what about dinner?"

"You'll have to play hostess tonight, dear," Aunt Merri chided. "It's your duty. You do right by our guest, and don't embarrass us."

"Everything's ready, Aurora," Fauna called. "It's all on the warming rack. Just take it out and eat."

"Enjoy!" Flora sang out as she headed through the door. And that was that.

"Well," Aurora said, hands on her hips. She stared at the door they'd just exited for a long moment, then turned to face Nathan again. "I hate to tell you this, but I think we're being . . . fixed up."

"I thought my father's cough sounded a little overblown," he said wryly. "He must be in on it with them."

Aurora stared at him, eyes narrowing. "Was this your idea, Nathan McBride?"

"I told you, I like blue-eyed blondes. Glenda the Good Witch is my style. Morticia Addams does nothing for me."

She looked at his crotch. "Oh, I can see that. Shall we put it to the test? You want me to speak French and see what happens?"

"Go ride a broom, why don't you?"

"We don't *ride* our brooms, you idiot."

"Hey, don't tell me what you *do* use them for. I don't think my heart can take it."

"I don't think your zipper can."

He sighed, looked at the floor, and shook his head. "Dammit, Aurora, I can't believe I came here thinking I could ask you for help when you're every bit as defensive and touchy as you ever were."

"You try growing up with half the local ignoramuses thinking you're some kind of satanic nutcase and see how defensive and touchy *you*—" She blinked and stared at him. "What do you mean, you came here to ask for my help?"

"I never, ever thought you were satanic."

"I don't even believe in the devil," she told him.

"Well that's a relief. I was beginning to think you thought I was him."

"The way you teased me, back then . . ." she began. "I thought you were as superstitious and bigoted as . . ." She gave her head a shake and cut herself off.

"I was a kid. Kids are idiots sometimes. Hell, Aurora, I teased *all* my friends." He frowned a little, and tilted his head. "I should have thought harder, though. I guess you took about all the teasing you could handle. My adding to it didn't help a bit, did it?"

"I don't see how anyone could think it would *help* at all." She blew air through her teeth. "Not that it bothered me in the least."

"Only enough so you're still angry about it."

"Do you want to eat, or what?"

"No. I want to tell you something."

She lifted her head, met his eyes, and thought he looked sincere. "What?"

"I think . . . I might have . . ." He closed his eyes briefly and clenched his jaw. "This is going to sound insane."

Frowning, she scanned his face. "Is this something physical? What do you think you have, Nathan?" The doctor in her was at full alert as she searched his face, mentally noting the healthy color of his skin, and the clarity of his eyes. Brown eyes, velvety brown, with darker stripes. Eyes that were looking into hers right now with . . .

She blinked and looked away.

He lowered his head. "Yeah, it's physical all right, but not the way you think. I think I might have some kind of curse clinging to me, Aurora. Does that sound crazy?"

She took a step away from him, watching his face, wary of a trick to make her look foolish. "A curse? I didn't think you believed in that sort of thing."

"I don't . . . do you?"

"Of course."

"So . . . did you?"

She frowned up at him. "Did I wh—" She opened her eyes wider and lifted her brows. "You want to know if I hexed you, Nathan?"

He only nodded.

She closed her eyes to hide the flash of pain she felt. Unexpected, unreasonable, but real. "I always thought . . ." Biting her lip, she shook her head and turned away.

"Aurora?" He touched her shoulder, bringing her gently around to face him again. "You always thought . . . what?"

"That you were the only one who wasn't afraid of me, Nathan. The only one who didn't seem to think that being a Witch made me some kind of monster." She shook her head. "I guess I was wrong."

His brows furrowed when she felt the barest hint of moisture burning in her eyes. He leaned closer, staring at it there, as if he couldn't quite believe it.

"For the record, Nathan, I would cut off my hand before I'd hurt anyone. I don't even kill spiders, for Goddess' sake."

He looked slightly ashamed. But he offered no apology. "Hell, if you had a Witch who hated your guts living around the corner, combined with the kind of luck I've had lately, you'd probably think—"

"I'd think of asking for some help," she said. She walked past him into the dining room and sat down at the little round table with the crystal ball and the cards. "So what makes you think it's a curse? Maybe the things that have been happening to you are for the best, did you ever think of that? A lot of people think they're having bad luck . . . missing planes or appointments or having their cars break down—when in fact, the delays and such are really protecting them from disasters."

"Yeah, well this delay isn't saving me from anything but pleasure."

"Really?" She lifted her brows. "So you really believe it's a curse?"

He came closer, but didn't sit. "The evidence sort of makes it hard not to believe it."

"What evidence?" she asked him.

He sighed and met her eyes. "I can't get laid to save my life."

Aurora bit her lip. She gritted her teeth. She held her breath. Nothing worked. She burst out laughing uncontrollably. And she regretted it instantly when his face darkened with furious anger, and he whirled around and slammed out of the house without a backward glance.

Her laughter died slowly as she stared after him. And then she titled her head to one side, frowning. "My Goddess," she whispered. "He was serious." She went after him, called his name out into the night, but he was already slamming his car door and roaring the engine.

She thought about making it stall so she could go and apologize. But messing with his car wasn't a good idea, and it might be considered manipulative magick, not letting him leave when he clearly wanted to. A Witch mustn't mess with another person's free will. No manipulation. Then again, she wasn't supposed to hurt anyone either. And she had a hollow feeling that maybe she just had . . . badly.

Three

"Aurora Rose Sortilege, what *did* you do?" Aunt Merriwether looked very upset as she stood there with her hands
on her hips, glaring.

"I didn't mean it," she said, and she knew she sounded
like a six-year-old. "He was so obnoxious. He made me
angry, and then he told me something and I thought . . .
well, I didn't think, but I . . . well, I laughed at him." She
drew a breath, cringing beneath the shocked expressions on
her aunts' faces. "I know I shouldn't have done it, but it
just came out. And then I realized he was sincerely asking
for help, but by then it was too late. He was furious, and
stormed out of here like the hotheaded childish brat he is."

"And I can't say that I blame him," Merriwether retorted.

"Oh, Aurora, men have such easily wounded pride, you
know. You shouldn't have laughed." Fauna wrung her
hands as if this were the most horrible of circumstances.

"Look, don't worry about it. I never liked him and he
never liked me and we'll probably never see each other
again, so—"

"I'm afraid that won't do, sweetheart." Flora said sadly.
She looked at the others. "I think it's time we told her."

"I *knew* it! What have you three been keeping from me?"

Tiny, delicate-looking Flora faced her, while the other two waved their hands wildly as if to tell her to keep quiet. "Darling, there's a secret the Sortilege Witches keep—the secret of our powers. The reason our magick is so much stronger than that of most other practitioners of The Craft."

Merriwether and Fauna stopped gesturing and frowned, as if they had no more clue what she was getting at than Aurora did.

"I thought . . ." Aurora said in confusion. "I thought it was just the bloodline. The power of our ancestors, and all that . . ."

"No dear. There's more to it than that. A secret you must vow never to tell . . . unless it becomes absolutely necessary. I never would have told it to you, dear, except perhaps on my deathbed. But now you must know."

Aurora leaned forward, brows lifting high. This sounded so . . . so dire.

"Every Sortilege Witch is destined to lose her powers, her gifts, her magick—on the day she turns twenty-seven, my child."

Aurora drew back as if her petite aunt had slapped her. She'd be twenty-seven in a little over twenty-four hours. At midnight on Halloween! *Tomorrow!* "No!"

"Oh, yes. I'm afraid it's true."

"My . . . my *healing!*"

"Well, you can still practice medicine, dear, but—"

"No. This can't be, Aunt Flora, please!" Panic was making her heart beat wildly in her chest. She couldn't lose her healing gift. Suppose some injured child was brought in, like the one last month with the ruptured spleen, who'd been wheeled past her in the hall after the physician on call had missed the diagnosis. He'd have died if her special sense hadn't told her . . .

"What can I do?" She gripped her aunt's shoulders, and searched her face. "There's something. Yes, there must be! You still have your magick. All of you do!"

She turned to Merriwether and Fauna, but they only

shook their heads and nodded at Flora to go on.

"Yes, child. There's one way you can keep your magick. But I'm afraid you're not going to like it very much."

"I don't care! I'll do anything. Tell me."

Flora cleared her throat. "You have to have . . . er . . . *relations* . . . with a man before your twenty-seventh birthday, dear. And . . . the . . . the man, has to be . . . pure."

"Pure?"

"Unsullied," Fauna said helpfully.

"Oh for heaven's sakes," Merri put in. "A virgin. The man has to be a virgin. *Now* do you understand why we're so upset with you for driving Nathan off the way you did?"

Aurora stood still, gave her head a shake, but they were all still there, still looking at her expectantly.

"That has to be the most ridiculous bunch of . . ." She stared, wide-eyed, from one of them to the other. "But . . . you have to be joking. I mean, it makes no sense. I've never heard of anything so . . . so bizarre!"

"We're not joking, darling," Flora denied gently. "So I suggest you begin making amends with that young man. And the sooner . . . the better."

The reality of it hit her then. They were telling her she had two choices—lose her powers, or sleep with Nathan McBride.

"Wait," she said, racking her brain. "There must be some other male in town who's still a virgin."

"Of course, dear. Over at the high school, perhaps, but they'd arrest you for that."

"*Aunt Merri!* I didn't mean—" She pushed her hands through her hair and began pacing. What was she going to do? What in the world was she going to do? "There has to be another virgin! Anyone but him!"

"Even in our day, we had trouble finding them, child," Merriwether explained. "It's long been tradition for . . . yes, for the older women of the family to see to it that one young man remained . . . chaste, so that when the time came . . ."

Aurora's eyes widened until she felt they would burst. "It was *you?* You three are the ones who hexed Nathan?"

"We didn't *hex* him, dear. We just . . . interfered a bit. A little binding spell. A little spying in the crystal. A little . . ."

"Aunt Merri, you ran him over with his own car! I wouldn't call that little!"

"That was an *accident!* We'd never hurt the boy . . . well, not deliberately."

Aurora pressed her fingers to her temples and closed her eyes. "I'm going to my rooms," she said. "I have to meditate."

"Flora, that was positively ingenious," Merri exclaimed, hugging her small sister hard. "How did you ever come up with it?"

"Well, she was going to blow the whole thing. We couldn't let that happen, could we?"

Fauna shook her head. "It was awfully mean, though. And where did you come up with that deadline? By her birthday?"

"If we don't hurry, that young man will kill himself trying to get past our spells to get . . . well, you know."

"Halloween's a good date anyway," Merri said practically. "It's going to work out perfectly. You picked the one thing she would never risk losing—her healing gift. It was brilliant."

"But poor Aurora. This isn't going to be easy for her. And I hate that we had to lie to her like that," Flora fretted.

"We'll tell her the truth later. She'll understand. And she won't mind, once she falls in love with Nathan."

Fauna, though, was still shaking her head. She paced to the table, picked up her favorite Tarot deck, and drew a single card. "Two of Swords. Ladies, you're forgetting. Our divinations told us Nathan was to be the father of Aurora's little girl. But not that they'd ever fall in love. There's a good chance they won't."

"Not fall in love?" Flora asked in dismay.

"Have a child and not be together?" Merri added.

"It's possible."

Merri wrung her hands and began to pace. "Oh, my. Oh, dear. We *can't* have that."

Aurora didn't sleep all night. She couldn't even lie still. Mostly, she paced as various scenarios played out in her mind. This couldn't be true. It was too ludicrous to be true. Her aunts must be playing some horribly cruel trick on her. But why? They were eccentric, yes. And meddlesome. But this . . .

Maybe this was just a matchmaking scheme gone too far. Maybe they were just trying to set her up with the man they perceived to be perfect for her.

Perfect for her? Nathan McBride?

She groaned softly and paced some more. She supposed it was possible they were matchmaking.

But what if they weren't? What if she really would lose her healing gift?

Closing her eyes, Aurora realized she couldn't risk that. Even sleeping with Nathan would be better than that. And besides, she'd only have to do it once. Right? Just one night with Nathan, and she could relax. She grimaced and shuddered a little. One night with Nathan. Maybe if she got really drunk first . . .

For just a moment, she pictured Nathan trying to rid himself of his virginity all these years, with her aunts constantly interfering. The thought made her smile, and then made her laugh softly. Poor Nathan. No wonder he thought he was cursed.

But this wasn't funny, and her laughter turned sour. She didn't have any choice here. She was going to have to make nice with Nathan. She was going to have to . . . she bit her lip and made a face . . . seduce him. Oh, Goddess, if this did turn out to be a trick she was going to strangle those aunts of hers!

Meanwhile, though, she was just going to have to straighten her spine, grit her teeth, and get through this thing. She was strong. She was a Sortilege Witch, for goodness' sake. She could do it.

Unless, of course, Nathan wasn't willing.

Nathan, twenty-nine and still a virgin. So frustrated he'd actually made himself come to her for help. Mercy, he'd be more than willing.

Four

It was Halloween, and Nathan had decided to take the day off and sleep in for a change. Hell, he'd earned it. Last night's humiliation had taken quite a lot out of him. Not to mention that he was still a bit sore—mostly that elbow, though. The rest of him was already back to normal. Not that it mattered, he supposed. The parts of him that were better would probably never see much use, anyway.

He'd like to strangle Aurora Sortilege. Coldhearted snake of a woman.

He was plodding through the apartment in his boxers, heading for his first cup of coffee, when the doorbell sounded. Pushing both hands through his hair, he stopped in midplod and turned. Probably his father. He'd promised to do some work at the house today, hadn't he? He was going to mow the lawn and take a look at that sticky window in the back.

He strode to the door and yanked it open, only to see Aurora standing on the other side. She looked at him. Huge ebony eyes, wide and a little uncertain. Satiny hair framing her face.

He took a single step backward and started to close the door.

"Hold on! I brought a peace offering!" She held up a

big white bakery box, and he caught a whiff of fresh doughnuts. Blueberry filling, if he wasn't mistaken. His favorite.
He wondered for a minute if she knew that because he'd
told her, or because she'd been reading his mind.

Hell, no. If she could read his mind, she wouldn't be
here without an armed bodyguard.

He pulled the door wider again. "What's this about, Aurora? What are you up to?"

This time her almond gaze slid from his, traveling slowly
downward, and he squirmed a little, realizing he was standing there in nothing but a pair of boxers. Her eyes widened
and she jerked them up again. "Maybe this was a bad
idea." It was her turn to take a step backward.

He reached out fast, not quite sure why he did it, but
sure enough, his hand was wrapped around her wrist and
she was looking slightly alarmed.

He shook his head and let go. "Come on in, Aurora.
Rest assured, if I get the slightest urge to try anything, my
apartment will catch fire. You're perfectly safe with me."

She lowered her gaze quickly. Guiltily? What the
hell . . . ?

Sighing in resignation, she came in. He closed the door.
"There's fresh coffee in the kitchen," he told her as her
eyes once again slipped lower. "I suppose I'd better put
some clothes on. You sure as hell aren't here to see me
naked."

As he turned to go, she muttered something that sounded
like, "A lot you know," and he spun around frowning at
her, and asked, "What's that?"

"Nothing," she told him quickly. "Go ahead. Get
dressed."

There was something different about her, he realized
while he was searching her face. Something more than just
the fact that she seemed nervous and less hostile than usual.
And then it hit him. She was wearing more makeup than
he'd seen her wear before. Subtle, but there, shadowing
those black eyes with mystery. Clusters of silver moons and
golden stars dangled from her ears, and he thought he
caught a whiff of exotic perfume mingling with the coffee

and doughnut aromas. He looked her over more thoroughly than he had before, his curiosity piqued. She wasn't dressed for the hospital. Short black skirt and a semisheer blouse to match. He could see the dark sports bra she wore underneath. The nylons were black, too. And the shoes were open toed, with heels four inches high.

What the hell was she doing here, dressed like that?

He took a step toward her, forgetting for a second that she was the woman he'd been fantasizing about murdering, and entertaining a few more pleasant fantasies instead.

Her eyes met his and widened. "I th-thought you wanted to get dressed," she stammered.

He stopped, the fantasy shattered. Who was he kidding? It wasn't going to happen. Hell, as much as he disliked her, he didn't think he wanted it to. No matter how deprived he was. He shook his head and turned to go into his bedroom.

When he came back, he found her in the kitchen, sitting at his small round table, staring into space with an unfocused look on her face, and stirring her coffee into a small caramel-colored whirlpool. The box of doughnuts sat in the middle of the table, unopened.

Nathan walked past her, poured himself a cup, and sat down opposite her. She seemed to pull herself together, and looked at him. "You didn't shave."

"Didn't know it was required," he responded. "I never shave on my day off."

"Oh."

He ran one hand over his stubble. Hell, some women found the unshaven look sexy. Or . . . so he'd thought. It looked to him like it just made this one nervous. More nervous than she'd already been.

"So are you going to tell me what you're doing here dressed to kill, Aurora, or am I supposed to guess?"

She started, and glanced down at her attire. "What's wrong with the way I'm dressed?"

"Nothing."

"Then why—"

"What are you doing in my kitchen, Aurora?"

She licked her lips. Drew a breath. Stirred faster. "I wanted to apologize. For last night."

Aurora? Apologize? To *him?*

"I shouldn't have laughed at you. I just . . . I didn't realize you were serious, you know? You're always teasing me. I half expected you to follow it up with some lewd proposition or smart remark."

He didn't say anything—just sat there, watching her, waiting for her to cut to the chase.

"I wasn't laughing *at* you, Nathan, I was laughing with you. I thought you were joking—about the curse, not the . . . other thing. I mean, I know you. I figured if you'd been celibate all this time it was because you had a good reason to want to be. I mean, come on. *Look* at you. Any woman would want . . ." She clamped her jaw as if to stop herself, and her eyes widened.

Nathan felt himself smile, just a little. So she did like the unshaven look after all, did she?

"That's not the part I have trouble with." He took a long, slow sip of the hot coffee, then lowered the cup. "Them wanting me, I mean. But something always happens. Just like this last episode with what's-her-name . . ." He stopped talking and shook his head. "Why the hell am I even discussing this with you?"

"Because I can help you," she said. He met her eyes. She looked away, reaching for a doughnut he had a feeling she didn't want.

"I doubt that." He watched her face. "I don't know why I thought of asking you in the first place, Aurora. You know damned well I don't believe in your hocus-pocus bullshit."

Her eyes narrowed, and anger reddened her cheeks. Her head came up fast, and her lips parted to deliver the scathing comeback he fully expected.

But it never came. She caught herself, drew a breath, closed her mouth.

"You can at least let me try."

Nathan leaned back in his chair, frowning at her. Now this was one hell of an interesting turn of events. Since when did she resist an opportunity to slam him? "How?"

"Well . . . this woman who ran over you . . . you don't even remember her name."

"So?" He reached for his coffee, took another sip.

"So . . . have they all been like that? Women you barely knew, just wanted to sleep with?"

He pursed his lips and thought about it. "Yeah, pretty much."

She shrugged, a delicate lift of one shoulder. "So maybe that's the problem. Maybe you're subconsciously sabotaging yourself because you know you don't really want to sleep with a stranger."

His frown grew. "You sound more like a shrink than a Witch."

She tilted her head. "Maybe you'd be okay if your first time could be with someone . . . someone you know. Someone . . . you've known for a long time."

"Yeah, right. Like who?" He took a big gulp of coffee this time. Bitter and black and strong, just the way he liked it.

"Like me."

The coffee spewed from his mouth like a geyser, showering the table, the doughnuts, and the front of that sexy blouse she was wearing. The cup fell to the floor, spilling what was left. And Nathan bent over the table choking on the small amount he'd managed to swallow.

Aurora came around the table to pound on his back, which any doctor should know was totally illogical, but was the instinctive reaction anyway.

He drew a few wheezing breaths and managed to sit up straight again, as he lifted his head and stared into her eyes. She was joking. She must have been joking.

She stared back at him, dead serious.

"Hell, you're not joking, are you?"

"I . . ." She took her hand off his back, and shrugged. "I was just trying to help. If it seems so ludicrous to you, then just forget it."

She turned around and headed for the door.

He leaped out of his chair as what might be his only

chance at sex seemed about to flee. "Wait a minute! Hold
on, for crying out loud."

She stopped, her back to him. And he stopped, too, looking her up and down from behind, liking what he saw, and
shaking his head. This was too strange.

"You took me by surprise, that's all. Look, if you're
willing . . . well, hell, Aurora, I'd be nuts to say no."

He saw her stiffen her back, square her shoulders, and
slowly turn to face him, looking like Joan of Arc turning
to face the stake. "All right then."

"All right then?"

She nodded, her face grim, and lifted trembling hands to
the tiny buttons at the front of her blouse. "Let's get this
over with."

Nathan stood there, feeling as if she'd just dumped ice
water on him. "I can tell you're really looking forward to
this."

"Don't get any ideas, Nathan. This is nothing personal."
She unbuttoned another button. And then another. Crisp
and efficient, she removed the blouse and stood there in a
sports bra and a miniskirt, looking like every man's fantasy.

"So you don't really want me," he said flatly.

"Of course not."

"You're just doing this as a favor."

"Naturally." She reached behind her to unzip the skirt,
pushed it down over her hips, and stepped out of it when
it slid to the floor. The nylons were not panty hose—they
were stockings, black and silky and held up by lacy red
garters. The panties she wore were red, too, and skimpy.
And her belly was smooth and tight, and her breasts round
and firm behind that black scrap of spandex that covered
them. He wished he liked her at least a little bit.

He swallowed hard. It looked as if she'd come here for
the sole purpose of bedding him. It made him nervous as
hell. "And what do you get out of this?"

She shrugged again. "Nothing you need to know about.
Are you going to stand there gawking or get naked?"

Good question. Nathan wasn't sure he wanted a woman

who didn't want him back. But . . . what if she did? "Come here, Aurora."

He saw the alarm flash in her eyes, followed by resignation and stoic resolve. She stepped closer, then still closer, like the village virgin stepping up to the mouth of the volcano.

Nathan slipped his hands around her waist and pulled her against him. She was warm, trembling slightly. He bent his head and touched her lips with his. She gasped and drew away.

He pulled her close again. "Come on, Aurora. If you're afraid to even kiss me, how do you expect to do anything else?"

"I'm . . . n-not afraid."

"No?"

She shook her head.

"Prove it then. Kiss me like you mean it. Maybe even pretend to enjoy it." He didn't give her time to answer. He kissed her again.

It was slow, her reaction. Her lips relaxed bit by bit as he worked them, and even parted a little. Her arms went around him, palms pressed flat to his back, softly. Nathan touched her lips with his tongue, traced their shape lightly, then slid between them.

And she shivered.

A delicious little shiver. It made him shiver a little himself.

He cupped her bottom with his hands and pulled her hard to him, arched his hips so that he pressed tight into her, bent her backward, and proceeded to kiss the living hell out of her.

And surprise of surprises, she started kissing him right back. He felt her hands moving upward, threading into his hair—felt her body press against his. She tipped her head back and opened her mouth to him, and her tongue danced with his and tangled and fought.

He lifted his head slowly, staring down into her face. "I can't believe it," he said softly. Her eyes were glittering, her face flushed, her lips parted as short, shallow little breaths rushed in and out between them. "You want me. You little fraud, you've wanted me all along."

"In your dreams," she whispered in a voice so sexy it sounded like an endearment.

He let his arms fall to his sides and stepped away from her. "You're a liar."

"I—" She followed him with her eyes as he bent to pick up her blouse, then her skirt, and turned to hold them out to her. "What . . . ?"

"Put your clothes on, Aurora. I don't accept pity sex, so if that's what this is, you can forget it." It wasn't, though. He knew damn well it wasn't. He wasn't sure how he felt about that, but he wasn't going to do her unless she admitted it.

"But—"

"But nothing. I know you want me. And if you're honest with yourself, you know it, too. So why don't you just come back when you're ready to admit that, and then we'll see."

Her eyes rounded, gleaming with a slow burning anger and maybe just a hint of the humiliation he'd felt last night when she'd laughed in his face. Good.

"You arrogant, egotistical, *stupid*—"

"Yeah, yeah."

She pulled on her blouse in angry, jerky movements, and yanked the skirt up in much the same way. "You're going to regret this, Nathan McBride!"

She spun and slammed out of the apartment.

"Hell, Aurora," he whispered after she'd gone. "I already do."

Five

Aurora couldn't believe it. She was humiliated. She was disgusted. She was . . .

She was turned on.

By Nathan McBride, for Goddess' sake!

It wasn't as if she were some blushing, clueless virgin being assuaged by unfamiliar urges, either. She'd had men before. In college, in med school. Not many, but enough to know her way around.

So why had a single kiss from the man she'd spent her entire life detesting sent her senses spinning out of control? Why did it feel as if he'd made love to her more thoroughly than any man ever had, when all he'd done was kiss her?

Why had he turned her down?

"I'm pathetic," she whispered.

She'd made a fool of herself with Nathan just now, and she kicked herself for it all the way home. But as she walked up the front steps in the early-morning breeze, she knew that wasn't the worst of it. The worst was that she still had to make him sleep with her. Somehow. She had to. And she had to do it before this day ended. Because today was Halloween. At midnight tonight she turned twenty-seven. There was no getting around it. She had to sleep with him.

But if that meant admitting to the creep that she might have decided it wouldn't be a totally revolting experience, it would never happen. She'd die before she'd do that.

She stood there, not wanting to walk in and face her aunts, debating whether she could get away with sneaking off for the day, when the front door burst open. Aunt Merri stood there, her face chalk-white, her eyes wide.

"Aurora! Thank goodness! We've been calling . . ." Her voice trailed off and she blinked at moisture gathering in her eyes.

Something terrible was happening. She knew it with every cell in her, and not just because of her aunt's stricken face.

Flora. It's Aunt Flora.

"Where is she? What happened?" Aurora followed quickly as Merriwether turned to hurry back inside.

Aunt Flora lay on the sofa, looking for all the world as if she were sound asleep. It was only Aurora's keen healing sense that told her otherwise.

"We can't wake her up," Fauna whispered, looking up into Aurora's eyes, her own red-rimmed and puffy. "She just came in here, lay down, and closed her eyes. And now we can't wake her up."

Aurora stared down at her beloved, fragile aunt, lying so still, and her heart tripped over itself in her chest. Vaguely she heard squealing tires as a car skidded to a stop out front, and then heavy steps thudded into the living room.

"Aurora?"

She turned. Nathan stood braced in the doorway, looking worried. "How did you—" she began.

"I called him, looking for you," Aunt Merri interrupted. "But you'd already left."

"Never mind that," Fauna said, and her voice was a plea. "Aurora, what's wrong with her? What—"

"I don't know." Her hands trembling, Aurora reached to her tiny aunt's throat to feel her pulse, soft and too slow. Her breaths were slow, too. And shallow. Her skin was clammy to the touch. Her Aunt Flora . . . her precious Flora.

So fragile, even in the best of health. "I . . . I can't . . ."
Aurora battled tears, but they came anyway.

And then she felt Nathan's hands on her shoulders, a
gentle squeeze. "Merriwether, call the hospital and tell
them we're bringing her in. Fauna, will you get us a blanket? It's still chilly outside."

The two nodded and scurried to obey the calm orders he
gave. And his hands were still on Aurora's shoulders, so
he must feel her sobs.

"You can help her, Aurora. You're letting your emotions
cloud your judgment."

"What do you know about my emotions, Nathan?"

"Nothing. But I know what I saw when I was sixteen
and hit that red-tailed hawk with my Mustang. You remember?"

She closed her eyes. How could she forget? It had been
the first time she'd actually tapped into this power she'd
been born with. She opened her eyes and looked at Nathan.
"You don't believe in my . . . 'hocus-pocus bullshit.' Isn't
that what you called it?"

"So maybe I lied." He was kneeling now, beside the
sofa, hands still on her shoulders. "And maybe it doesn't
matter what I believe. It's what you believe that counts,
here. So pull yourself together, Aurora. Your aunt needs
you right now."

Something passed into her. Some calming, strengthening
energy flowed, and she was too in touch with the vibrations
around her not to be fully aware of it. The warm force
moved from Nathan's hands, into her body where he
touched her, and it filled her.

His own power. The power he didn't even know he had.
Still alive in his blood and somehow infusing her with courage. She closed her eyes, and he started to move his hands
away from her. But she caught them with her own and held
them to her shoulders, and felt the energy building until she
brimmed with it. She'd drawn in before the powers of
Mother Earth and Father Sky and even the energies of the
moon to empower her magick. But never the essence of
another human being. . . .

She pulled the power into her, centering it, feeling the pulsing golden glow of it in her solar plexus. And then she took Nathan's hands away and turned to her aunt. She lifted her hands, palms down, and moved them slowly, hovering a hair's breadth above Flora's small body, head to toe, feeling her aura, searching for the invader that was making her aunt so ill.

And finding it. A red throb, pulsing against her palm from Flora's left ankle.

Quickly, Aurora grasped Flora's ankle, pushing up the leg of her pants, bending closer.

"Aurora?" Nathan asked.

"Snake bite," she whispered, and she spotted the tiny marks and the red swelling around them.

"But . . . we don't have any venomous snakes around here. Are you sure it's—"

"Rattlers. We have rattlers. Not many, but every once in a while . . ." Her senses told her she was right. "Aunt Merri," she called, louder now, and her aunt poked her head in from the kitchen, the phone still held to her ear. "Tell them to get some antivenin. It was a rattlesnake. And then come to the hospital. We have to hurry." As she spoke she was yanking the silk scarf from Flora's head and twisting it around the leg, above the bite.

"Get her to the car, Nathan," she said softly. "You drive."

He didn't believe it. Okay, he'd told her he did, but he'd only said it . . . hell, he didn't know why he'd said it. To snap her out of her momentary panic, he supposed. To give her some kind of strength so she'd do what needed doing.

And oddly enough, it had worked. When he'd picked up the phone after she'd stormed out of his apartment—when he'd heard her aunt's frightened voice on the other end— he'd had this feeling that he should come over here. That Aurora . . . needed him. Stupid. Ridiculous, really.

But then he'd touched her, and it was almost as if she really had. As if his hands on her shoulders, his being there with her, had helped her somehow. As if she were drawing something from him. . . .

He shook his head and paced the waiting room some more. He'd driven like a maniac to get here while she'd worked on the snake bite in the backseat. He'd slowed down once—only once, and she'd snapped at him for it.

"The light's red, Aurora—I have to—"

She'd glanced over his shoulder, waved a hand toward the light. Green. It had turned red two seconds ago, but when she did—whatever the hell she'd done—it turned green. "Don't worry about the lights," she'd told him. "Just drive."

He hadn't hit another red light all the way to the hospital. Just roared right up to the red ones without even slowing down, and every last one turned green before he got to it.

He frowned slightly, glancing toward the doors to the treatment room where Aurora and her aunt Flora were. "Weird," he muttered.

Merriwether and Fauna came running in, rushing up to him, wide eyes full of questions. He opened his mouth to tell them he didn't know anything yet, wishing he could say something more reassuring, but before he spoke, the doors opened. Aurora stepped out, leaned back against the door she had closed behind her, and met their eyes one by one. She nodded and smiled tiredly to reassure them of dainty Flora's well-being.

God, she looked wiped out.

"She's going to be okay," she said. "You can go in . . ."

She never finished. Her two aunts rushed her, nudging her gently aside and hurrying in to see their sister, the doors banging closed behind them.

Nathan took a step toward Aurora. "What about you?" he asked her gruffly. "You going to be okay?"

She smiled weakly, nodded once, and sank toward the floor as if her legs had just melted beneath her. Nathan lunged, grabbing her before she landed and pulling her into his arms to keep her upright. She only leaned against him as if she were made of water, so he turned her and scooped her up, carried her into the first empty room he came to, and lowered her to the bed there.

She didn't pass out. She was conscious, shaking her head, blinking. "I'm okay. Really, I'm—"

"The hell you are." He kept her from sitting up by gently pressing her down to the pillows. "Just lie down for a minute and tell me what happened."

She did lie down; she closed her eyes, then closed them tighter, and a tear slipped from beneath them to run slowly down her cheek. "I almost lost her. For the love of the Universe, Nathan, I almost lost her."

The tears came then, fast and furious, and she sobbed so hard it broke his heart to see it. He sat on the edge of the bed, gathered her small body close to his, held her hard against him, and felt her trembling in his arms. "But you didn't. She's okay, Aurora. You saved her life. I've never seen anything like what you did today."

Her arms crept around him and she clung there, crying. "But if . . . if I hadn't known what was wrong . . ."

"You did know," he said softly. "I don't know how, but you did. And she's going to be okay now."

"I know," she whispered. "I know, but . . ."

He straightened away from her, but she clung. "Hold me, Nathan. I need you."

He held her. He couldn't believe what she'd just said, but he'd heard it, loud and clear. She needed him. Holy crap. She was so soft, so vulnerable, so tortured right now. And Nathan was overwhelmed with the need to make it better.

God, how had he ever thought he disliked Aurora Sortilege? Right now, he didn't think he'd ever want to hold anyone else.

I need you.

"I'm here for you, then," he told her. "Aurora, I'm right here, okay?" He stroked her hair. "Anything you need, you just say the word and I'll do it."

She sniffed, sat up a little straighter, wiped at her eyes, and stared into his. "I hope you mean that." Her voice was hoarse.

He smiled gently at her, as he reached up to brush his thumb over her tear-stained cheeks. "Hell, Aurora, it surprises me as much as you, but I do. I mean it."

"You don't even like me."

He shrugged. "You were never my number one fan, either, as I recall." She lowered her gaze. He hooked his forefinger under her chin, lifting her head until she looked at him again. "But what if we forget all that?"

She frowned, searching his face. "Can we? Can we really do that?"

"Hell, Aurora, I think we already have." He smoothed her hair away from her face. "I like you now."

She closed her eyes, almost as if she felt guilty. "You saved Aunt Flora's life," she said softly.

"All I did was drive. You're the one who—"

"No." She opened her eyes and looked right into his. "You did it, Nathan. I was standing there falling apart, and you . . . you helped me. You knew it. You felt it, too, didn't you?"

Nathan battled a shiver. "I felt . . . something. I still don't know what it was."

Aurora nodded, but said nothing. After a moment, she pushed herself up straighter. "I should go, see about Aunt Flora, talk to—"

"I want to see you, Aurora." He blurted it without even realizing he was going to. And then he added, "Tonight."

She bit her lower lip. "I don't know . . ."

"Because you still don't like me?" he asked, only half kidding.

"No," she whispered, and she reached out and touched his face. "Because I do."

Six

Aurora paced the house, wringing her hands. This whole thing would have been easier if she'd kept on hating Nathan. But now . . .

Now, she liked him. And maybe she always had. And maybe it was a little more than *like* that she felt for him, and had been all along.

And so she was going to use him. Sleep with him for the sole purpose of preserving her powers. She felt like a slug.

But what choice did she have? Suppose something like this happened after tonight, after she lost the gift? Suppose she was unable to help one of her precious aunts when they needed her? Or one of her patients?

Oh, what was she going to do?

She couldn't eat. Aunt Flora was spending the night in the hospital, just as a precaution. Aunt Merri and Aunt Fauna refused to leave her side. They insisted on spending the night with their youngest sister. Aurora wasn't worried about them, not even Flora. She was fine. The three of them were probably organizing a senior slumber party and ordering pizza by now.

Tonight was Halloween. At midnight she would turn twenty-seven. She had to make a decision, and make it fast.

Looking skyward, Aurora whispered, "I need help. I don't know what to do."

And like the whisper of a breeze, she heard, "Yes, you do."

"Yes," she said softly. "I do."

An hour later, Aurora sat outside bathed in moonlight. The circular spot in the center of her aunts' flower and shrub garden was sacred ground. They'd made it so, and so it was, surrounded by blossoms—this late in the fall, mostly oranges and yellows, sunflowers, marigolds, and daisies. She reclined on the grassy ground in the center, where a large flat stone of dark granite held court. She lit the candles she'd placed on the stone, then the incense. And then she rose and lifted her arms out to the sides, head tipped back. Slowly, she drew her arms in again, crossing them over her chest, lowering her head.

Aurora stood still for a moment, feeling her energies gathering, ready to do her bidding. She opened her palms, cupped in front of her, and visualized a tiny ball of pulsing white light swirling in her hands. A ball of purity and goodness and power. A ball where only positive forces could exist, and where time and space did not. A meeting place between the worlds. When she could *feel* it there, when she could *see* her ball of light, she parted her hands and let it fall to the ground. And when it hit, it exploded. The bubble of white light expanded on impact, filling the tiny spot in the center of the garden, and surrounding Aurora completely. Above and below, continuing beneath the earth's surface. Around and about, creating a place of magick.

This done, Aurora sat down. "And now," she whispered, "Ancient and Shining Ones, tell me what I must do."

Nathan got no answer at the front door. He hadn't really expected to at this time of the night, but he couldn't sleep. He was worried. Not about Flora. That eccentric old Witch would be just fine. He hadn't left the hospital until he'd been assured of that. He wasn't even all that worried about Aurora, though he had been for a short while. Falling apart in his arms wasn't exactly typical behavior on her part. Then again, neither was offering to sleep with him.

Couldn't quite get that part off his mind, could he?

Figured. He was nothing if not obsessed.

Well, he'd tried the door, and she hadn't answered, so either she was sound asleep or she didn't want to see him. He turned to go, then paused as a stray breeze carried a whiff of something smoky and exotic to his nose. He inhaled, frowned. There. A thin tendril of smoke, and it almost seemed to crook like a finger, beckoning him to follow. Dumb idea, of course, but as it receded around the corner of the old house, he followed it anyway.

And then he came to a stop in the backyard. Because there was a glow coming from the hidden center of that mysterious flower garden. A flickering dancing glow, as if of candles . . . and something else.

He walked closer, slowly, and for some reason he couldn't even begin to understand, he followed the path that had frightened him as a kid—followed its twisting, snake-like course, to a place at the center, a clearing amid the greenery, in the shape of a perfect circle. And he stood there, frowning at the sight of Aurora in its center. She wore some sort of robe, hooded and black and gleaming like satin. She'd been sitting when he'd first spotted her, but she was standing now, moving in graceful patterns that seemed almost like a dance. The moonlight beamed down on her. But the light was more than that, as well. It seemed to surround her—a shimmering, surreal kind of opalescence bathing her like the glow of a spotlight. Or was it radiating outward from somewhere inside her?

She went still, head tilted as if she were listening to something. Or someone. And then she turned, and she saw him there.

He held those black eyes of hers, unable to look away. And he could have sworn someone gave him a shove from behind to get his feet moving. He walked up to the very end of the path through the flowers, and stopped at the edge of that circle of light that surrounded her, not quite sure why, not even sure it was real.

She smiled very softly, as if she approved of something he'd done. She didn't say a word, just came forward and knelt down, pointing her finger at the ground near his right foot. She rose, tracing an arch in the air, up one side of him, over his head, and down the other. And damned if it didn't seem to him that the odd glow, the one that couldn't be real, vanished in the spot she'd outlined. It was like a . . . a doorway.

She took a step backward, still not speaking. He swallowed hard, not quite sure what he was getting himself into. A little bit afraid.

This time he was *sure* someone shoved him. A hard hand seemed to slam into his back, and he lurched through the imaginary doorway, swinging his head around to see who was back there. But there was no one. And the hairs on his nape were beginning to stand upright and bristle with electricity.

Aurora seemed unperturbed, though. She moved past him to the spot he'd just come through, knelt again, and drew with her finger . . . a line this time, right to left, along the bottom of that doorway that wasn't really a doorway.

And the glow filled the area once again. Nathan blinked and rubbed at his eyes, but it wasn't going away. This spot, this one circular area, looked different from everything else around it. And it *felt* different, too. Warmer. Even a hint stuffy. Like he was inside instead of out.

Dumb.

"Take off your shoes, Nathan," she whispered, and her voice was soft and deep. "This is sacred ground."

Sacred ground. Right. Okay, he'd definitely entered the Twilight Zone. But he took off the shoes, all the same, and peeled off his socks too, just for good measure. He tossed them without thinking, expecting them to sail right on out of this unearthly glow and into the darkness of the garden beyond. But they didn't. It was as if they hit a wall and bounced back, falling soundlessly to the ground.

He stared at them. But Aurora was moving again, and that drew his attention back to her. And then he was pretty sure that his heart stopped for a second. Because she was slipping that black satin robe down off her shoulders, and it fell to the ground like a pool of black water. And she wasn't wearing a single thing underneath, except for a mystical-looking pendant and a pair of emerald earrings.

The ones he'd given her? He glanced away from her, toward the flat stone, and saw a bit of paper lying there, with the candle flames on either side casting shadows that danced over the crude line drawing of a face. A man's face. Remarkably like his own.

He looked back at her again, a little chill dancing up his spine. "A-a-a-Aurora?"

"I needed you, Nathan," she said softly. "So I brought you to me."

He stared at her, still far too unsettled by the nude work of art standing before him to give his full attention to her words. "Brought me," he parroted.

"Manipulative magick is not something I'd normally use. But I was careful," she said, explaining herself to him as calmly as if every word she said made perfect sense—which, of course, they didn't. "I made sure the words I composed couldn't interfere with your free will," she went on. "I said, 'If he wants me, let him come to me now.' "

"I see." But he didn't. All he saw were a pair of perfect breasts, as round and firm as his fondest fantasy. And a waist he could fit his hands around. And a triangle of curls between her legs that was as shiny black as her hair.

"And you came."

He swallowed hard. Not yet he hadn't. But maybe he would before the night was over. He just hoped there wasn't going to be an earthquake or flash flood within the next hour or so. His gaze slid upward, meeting her eyes, seeing the mystery he'd always noticed there, the darkness, the night itself, glimmering back at him. Okay, then. Make that the next several hours.

She said nothing—just looked back at him, slowly turned, and from the big flat rock in the center, reached for a jeweled dagger that looked as deadly as it did beautiful. Facing him again, she pressed its hilt into his hand, with the blade pointing downward. She squeezed his fist tight around the weapon, then drew his other hand to close on it, as well.

Turning away from him again, she picked up a fat three-legged cauldron of black cast iron. And when she faced him she held it, one palm pressed to either side, arms outstretched as if she were offering it to him.

But she wasn't, because his hands were both occupied with holding the dagger. He didn't know what—

"Your ancestors performed this rite for centuries, Nathan," she whispered. "Close your eyes and open your heart. Listen to the power that still lingers in your blood. The voices of your ancestors. They're here tonight. They live . . . in you."

Something made him close his eyes. And he didn't feel like Nathan McBride, owner of a chain of pharmacies and frustrated sex maniac. He felt . . . different. Liberated. Strong. Fierce. Powerful. Male.

"As the cauldron is to the Goddess," Aurora said softly, "so the athame is to the God." Nathan blinked his eyes open, saw her holding the iron pot up to him, saw the dagger in his own hands, blade pointing down at it. Heard her whisper, "And together, they are one. . . ."

Very slowly, he lowered his arms, gently plunging the dagger into the cauldron, knowing somehow that this was what he was supposed to do. And as he did, Aurora's head tilted backward and her eyes fell closed. There was something . . . some surge of energy shooting through him, into him from where his fists clenched around the dagger's hilt, rushing up his arms and infusing his body until he felt as if he must be glowing.

He lifted the blade again, blinking his eyes open, seeing the stars and the moon above in a way he never had before. They were brighter, clearer. They seemed . . . *alive*.

Aurora gently took the blade from him and replaced the cauldron and knife on the makeshift table. Nathan couldn't take his eyes off her. It was as if he'd wanted her all his life. As if being with her were suddenly a force of nature raging inside him—something that could neither be denied nor controlled.

Aurora faced him, and he saw the same kinds of passions swirling in her eyes. "Now—"

"Now," Nathan said, gripping her shoulders, "this." He pulled her close, bent to kiss her, fed from her mouth, and hungered for more. And he knew this was right. It was right, and perfect, and he couldn't live without it. He adored her. Didn't know why or when it had happened, or what was making him realize it now. But he did. He adored her, and he didn't care if she wouldn't admit she felt the same way. She did. He knew she did.

She kissed him back as if she did.

Her hands threaded into his hair. Her body strained against his, warm and naked and wanting. He moved his hands down her back, tracing the delicate curve of her spine, then filling his palms with the swell of her buttocks and squeezing and lifting.

Her mouth tasted of honey. Her tongue was moist silk, stroking his, tasting him, driving him mad. And then her hands were there between them, working his clothes free, tearing his shirt in her eagerness to rid him of it, yanking with fierce and frightening determination at the button and zipper of his jeans. And before he knew it, he was stepping out of them, kicking his shorts aside, feeling his shirt fall at his feet. Her hands explored now, and he relished every touch, every gentle pinch and tender raking of those nails.

She turned him, and he went. She pushed him and he fell, sitting now, sucking in a quick surprised gasp when his backside came to rest upon the chill of the granite boulder. But her mouth still fed, and her hands still worked, and he couldn't notice the discomfort of the cold on his flesh for more than a moment. He felt her hands again, pressing his chest, and he lay back, and the chill sent shivers up his back as her lips did likewise to his front.

Her hungry little mouth devoured his chest, bit by bit, small white teeth nipping, plump lips working, pointy tongue tormenting. She moved over him, straddled him, leaned down so that her breasts dangled just above his face, and he leaped at them, capturing one with his teeth and torturing her the way she'd done to him. Her hands were in his hair, holding him, soft pleading sounds coming from her throat. He gentled his mouth, sucking at her breast, feeling her relax, and then nipping her again, pinching her nipple gently between his teeth and hearing her moan in anguished pleasure. His hand moved into the warm wetness between her legs, to explore her there as his mouth applied the exquisite torture to her breast. His fingers parted, probed, hunted, and found. Invaded and stroked. And her hips arched to ask for more.

So he gave her more. Taking his hand away, he nestled his hips against hers, and slid himself inside her, as slowly and as reverently as he had lowered the athame into the cauldron. And as he did, she tipped her head back again, closed her eyes, and the sigh that escaped her was one of pure ecstasy as she tilted her hips to slide lower over him. And he wrapped his arms and legs around her, and rolled them both over, pinning her beneath him. Her hands closed on his backside, drawing him closer, pulling him deeper inside her. And he knew he'd never felt anything as intense as this. And likely never would.

He wanted, with everything in him, to take her hard and fast. But he denied those desires, because he wanted to see her face when she came. He wanted to feel her muscles convulse around him in pleasure. So he took his time, moving slowly, withdrawing to the very tip of him before pushing deeper, loving her with long, slow thrusts so exquisitely unbearable that his entire body quaked and shuddered.

Her breaths came faster; her hands slid upward, nails dragging over his back and then suddenly sinking into his shoulders. Her hips snapped up to meet his, faster and more demanding each time, and she breathed his name, again and again.

At her signals he moved faster, ending the tight hold he'd placed on himself, freeing his body to obey its own urges and sending his conscious mind scurrying into oblivion. There was only sensation now. Her body beneath him, her heated flesh surrounding him, holding him, her mouth, her hands, her hair, the sounds she made, the way she smelled.

And then even those things vanished in a haze of pure

feeling because his body was tightening and clenching as he neared the climax he'd been longing for all his life. The one he would share with her. With this woman.

He opened his eyes, determined to know it would be as incredible for her, desperate to see and feel her own release as well as his. And he did. Her eyes met his, and he saw the feelings swirling in the onyx depths. Her jaw worked as she held his gaze and moved with him, and she seemed to know what he wanted. To see when it happened for her. And her gaze never wavered, even when she cried his name in a voice choked with pleasure. Even when her eyes widened, and her hands gripped and her nails sank deeper. Even when he thrust himself harder and faster into the depths of her beautiful body, and exploded inside her, feeling his world shatter around him. Their eyes still held. Even when he whispered, "I love you, Aurora. Dammit, I love you."

She stiffened suddenly, pushing him upward, her palms flat to his chest, and staring up at him in what looked like shock. "You . . . ?"

"Never mind," he told her. "Come here," and he drew her to him again, stroked her hair. "It's after midnight," he whispered. "Happy birthday, Aurora."

Seven

Aurora tried not to think about what he'd said, and focused instead on what he did. On what *they* did. On how he made her feel in a way she'd never felt before, and how no one else could bring her to this point of what felt very much like a melding of two souls. Far more than just sex.

At some point she got up, focused her energies, sat very still with her palms cupped, and willed the magick that formed her circle to shrink and concentrate itself, until it was once again that glowing orb in her hands. A swirling ball of light and energy.

As she stared down at it, she heard Nathan gasp, and glanced up to see him gazing, wide-eyed, into her palms.

"I can't believe this," he muttered.

She frowned. "Do you mean . . . you can see it?"

And it was his turn to frown. "Shouldn't I? I mean . . . you see it, don't you?"

"I see it because I'm a Witch."

But his attention was on the energy sphere again. Tentatively, he reached out with a forefinger and touched the glowing ball she held.

"Hold out your hands, Nathan," she told him. And looking at her a little uncertainly . . . he did.

Gently, Aurora transferred the energy into Nathan's

hands. And he gazed down at it in wonder. "What is it?" he whispered.

"It's magick," she said simply. "The magick you don't believe in. And if you can see it, Nathan, that proves you're just a big fraud."

He shook his head. "I don't understand."

"They say seeing is believing, Nathan, but they have it backward. You have to believe in something first, *before* you can see it." He started to look up at her, but she shook her head. "Concentrate or you'll lose it."

He focused again on the glow in his hands. "W-what do I do with it?"

"I usually give leftover magick back to Mother Earth, for healing."

"How?"

She smiled. He was so wary of the power he didn't even know he had. He was a Witch, too. He just hadn't realized it yet. "Kneel down. Press your palms flat to the ground, and in your mind, see the light sinking into the earth and spreading there, spilling its healing, loving glow all through the planet."

Nathan did as she told him. When he rose again, he was looking at his hands as if he'd never seen them before. "That was incredible." He moved closer to her. "*You* are incredible."

"I'm selfish," she told him. And she meant it. She hated what she'd done to him tonight. Loved it. But hated it. She'd used him. And only when he'd blurted that he loved her had she realized just how deeply all of this might hurt him.

She didn't want to hurt Nathan.

She should tell him the truth. Now, before . . .

Nathan swept her into his arms and kissed her again, scooping her up and carrying her around the house and then inside, straight up the stairs to her bedroom—his lips never leaving hers on the way, his hands never leaving their job of caressing her body to look for a light switch. He was entirely focused, it seemed, on driving her out of her mind with wanting him again, even though she knew it was wrong. She'd done what needed doing. She'd done it in time. She wouldn't lose her powers now.

And yet she wanted him all the same. So when he tumbled with her into her bed, she didn't object. And they were still there when her aunts returned home in the morning.

Nathan saw the panicked expression on her face when the door slammed downstairs and the voices of her aunts came floating up to them. "Oh, no!" She sat up, clutching the sheet, head swinging this way and that frantically as she looked for clothes.

Footsteps pattered up the stairs. Someone called her name. She gripped his shoulder, pointed toward the bathroom door, and hissed, "Hurry!"

"Okay, okay!" Nathan jumped out of the bed, taking the sheet with him, and made it into the bathroom just as he heard a perfunctory tap on her bedroom door, followed by the creak of its hinges.

"Didn't you hear us calling, Aurora? We're home! And oh, so excited over what we found when we arrived!"

"What you—"

"These!" one of the aunts—Merriwether, Nathan thought—announced. And he wondered what prize she was showing off.

He crouched low to peer through the keyhole, first spying Aurora's pale face and stunned expression, then locating her tall, imposing Aunt Merri, arms outstretched and holding a bundle of clothes.

His clothes.

Oh, boy.

"Am I wrong in assuming these belong to Nathan?" the woman asked, while the other two, including Flora, who seemed in perfect health again, stood looking on.

"No, Aunt Merri. But—"

"Then you did it!" She clapped her hands together. "You did it and now you're—"

"Your powers are safe," Aurora's Aunt Fauna interrupted. He glanced toward the bed and saw Aurora frantically waving a hand as if to shut her aunt up. Just as he'd sensed Fauna had jumped in to shut her sister up. Very strange. What wasn't being said here was almost as interesting as what was. But Fauna rushed on. "You slept with a virgin before your twenty-seventh birthday, just as we told you you must. You won't lose your powers after all. And that's all you need to know, for now."

As she spoke, Aurora, clinging to a blanket for cover, lunged from the bed to silence her aunt, but Fauna had finished her little speech before she ever reached her. And Nathan felt as if he'd been hit between the eyes with a mallet.

Aurora went still, halfway between her aunt and the bed. Her head bowed slowly.

Nathan rose, wrapped the sheet around him, knotting it at his hip, and opened the door, more humiliated and angry and . . . and he didn't know what else . . . than he'd ever been in his life.

The three aunts gasped, but Aurora only stood there. She couldn't even look at him.

"Well, at least now I know why."

"Oh, dear," Fauna said in distress. "No, you don't, dear boy, not really. I was only—"

"Please leave," Aurora said, turning to her aunts. And nodding quickly, they did, backing out of the room and muttering apologies all the way. Aurora turned to him and opened her mouth.

"Don't bother," he told her coldly. "Hell, Aurora, I've seen what you can do. I suppose you'd have slept with the devil himself to keep that . . . that whatever it is."

"I don't believe in the devil. And it wasn't why I—"

"Don't lie, okay? At least give me that much." He shook his head, and reached for the clothes Merriwether had dropped on Aurora's bedroom floor. "Man, I made a real fool of myself last night, didn't I? How many times did I tell you I loved you, Aurora? A dozen, at least. What an idiot. All the time I was just part of . . . of one of your *spells.*"

"That's not true. I—"

He shook his head, jeans in place, shirt draped over one

arm. "Save it. I suppose that was the reason for the damn curse, as well, wasn't it? You . . . or those nutty aunts of yours, or all of you together—you made sure you'd have your virgin lover intact when the time came."

"You're right," she admitted. "But their intentions were good, Nathan. They didn't mean to hurt anyone."

He shook his head in disgust. "So am I right in assuming their damned hex has been lifted now that you have what you wanted from me?"

Lowering her eyes, she nodded.

"I don't know how you people sleep at night."

He yanked the door open and slammed out of the room, taking the stairs almost blindly, ignoring the sorry looks the other women threw him as he strode out the front door to walk home, struggling into his shirt on the way.

Aurora was miserable. And she didn't know why. She should be happy. She'd done what was required. She would keep her powers. And yes, she'd hurt Nathan's feelings in the process, but how many times had he hurt her feelings in the past? Their whole lives he'd been hurting her.

"Why do you think that is?" a soft voice asked.

Aurora sat up in her bed, where she'd been spending most of her time. Oh, she went in to the hospital and worked her shifts, but then she came home and returned to this room, and more often than not, she shed a few tears as she tried to make sense of her misery.

Flora stood in the doorway, looking at her sadly.

"Why do I suppose what is?" she asked her aunt.

"Why do you suppose Nathan McBride has hurt you in the past?"

"Because he's a jerk, that's why."

Flora smiled gently and came in to perch on the edge of the bed. "A lot of people are jerks. But they don't hurt you. Because you don't care. No one is capable of hurting you, Aurora darling, not unless you care very deeply about them."

Aurora blinked and sat up straighter. She sniffed twice, swiped her eyes dry, and nodded. "You're right. I know

it. I've known it for a while now. I do care for the idiot."
She closed her eyes. "I care a lot."

"You hurt him," Aunt Flora said softly. "And if you're
capable of hurting him, then . . ." She lifted a hand, palm
up.

"Then he cares, too," Aurora said. "But I knew that,
too. It's past tense, though. He did care. For a while. But
not anymore. Not now that he thinks I only used him."

"He's still hurting, sweetheart. So he must still care."

Aurora lifted her eyes to her aunt's and felt a tiny flutter
of hope try to come to life in her chest. "I love him, Aunt
Flora."

"I know, dear. So tell him. No matter what happens, just
tell him. And when you do, he's going to say, 'I love you,
too, Aurora Sortilege.' "

"I hate you, Aurora Sortilege. Detest you and despise you.
I do not love you. I do not, not, *not* love you. Never have,
never will. And that's final."

Nathan paced the floor of his living room whispering
these reassurances to himself over and over again. Because
he had a pretty little thing named Bobbie Lou or Sally Jo
or something like that, waiting for him to perform, and his
body was utterly unwilling. She'd shown up on his doorstep
an hour ago. A stewardess he'd taken out once before. She
said she remembered how strangely that night had ended
and thought she'd give it another shot, as long as she was
in town. And did he want to take her to dinner. And he
did.

*No, I don't. I don't want to take her anywhere. I want
Aurora.*

Bull. He most definitely wanted the bimbette with the
copper-colored curls.

Or were they brown?

She was in his bathroom now. Freshening up, as she put
it. And as he paced, she called, "If you don't feel like going
out, Nate, honey, we can order in. It would be cozy, don't
you think?"

Why the hell didn't she squelch that ear-splittingly irritating whiny voice so he could think?

"Nate? Sweetie?"

"Don't call me Nate," he snapped.

Her head popped out of the bathroom and she glanced at him questioningly. Copper. The curls were copper. Practically metallic.

"Sorry," he said. She smiled and stepped out farther. And there she was, wearing a skimpy black teddy and looking like a centerfold.

Nathan looked at her. Then he looked down at himself. Nothing was happening. He was having no physical reaction whatsoever. He shook his head. "Sorry, Betty Ray," he said. "But this isn't going to work. Why don't you get dressed and go home?"

Her lower lip thrust out. "It's Becky Lynn. Jerk." She slammed the bathroom door, presumably to dress.

As the door shut, there was a tap at the door behind him, the one that led outside, and he turned just as it opened. And then his heart flipped over. Because Aurora stood there. He felt a thousand pounds float away from his shoulders. He felt as if he could fly. He was stupid. He should be mad as hell.

"You told me the curse was gone now," he muttered. "But you're still messing with my head, you and those nutty aunts of yours. Aren't you, Aurora?"

She pursed her lips. "I didn't come here to fight with you. Or to listen to you rant. I came here to tell you something, and I'd appreciate it if you'd shut up and let me get it said."

He lifted both hands, palms up, and raised his brows, giving her the floor with the gesture.

"Okay," she said. She paced a few steps, pushed a hand through her glorious hair, and faced him again. "Okay. This is it. What happened between us wasn't just because of what you overheard at my house. I mean . . . it started out that way, but then . . ." She closed her eyes and straightened her spine. "Hell, you said it to me, and I can damn well say it to you." Eyes opening wide, she strode right up to him, stared right into his eyes and said, "I am in love with you, Nathan McBride, and I imagine I probably have been for most of my life.'' She drew a deep breath and blew it out. ''There. I said it.''

Nathan gaped. He searched her face and tried to stop his heart from palpitating. She meant it. She actually meant it. He lifted his hands to frame her face. ''Aurora, I—''

''Here,'' Becky Lynn shouted, and flung something at his head. ''Keep that as a souvenir, creep!'' And she stormed out the door.

Aurora backed away suddenly, and as he peeled the thing away from his head, he saw her eyes filling with tears. ''Oh, hell. Aurora, wait. This isn't what you think.''

But she was shaking her head, backing away. ''You . . . and she . . . you . . . after what we . . .''

He reached out for her, belatedly realizing he held a black teddy in his hand. He tossed it to the floor. ''Dammit, Aurora, nothing happened with her. I couldn't—''

''But you wanted to. You were going to. You . . . that's why you said what you did, about the curse, and—'' The tears spilled over and Nathan's heart cracked. ''How could you, Nathan?'' And she turned and ran the same way Becky Lynn had. With one major difference.

When Aurora left, he cared.

Eight

Oh, no. Oh, for crying out loud, he blew it! He had her, right there, knowing damn well that he loved her beyond belief. And she'd stared up at him with those big ebony eyes of hers and told him that she loved him, too.

And he'd blown it all to hell. Why had he even let Becky Lynn in the front door? Why hadn't he borrowed a page from that old antidrug campaign and just said no? He should have realized it wouldn't work, anyway. It never had.

Not until Aurora. And frankly, after that experience, he really didn't think he cared to do any comparison shopping. Nothing could be the way she was. The way they were. And she loved him. And now she was crying because he was an idiot.

Well, he had to find her. He had to fix this. There must be a way.

Okay, he'd grovel. He'd beg if he had to. He'd buy her pretty things and write sonnets and turn handsprings if that's what it took, but he wasn't going to let this incredible woman slip through his fingers. No way in hell.

He had to find her. Yes, and when he did, he'd give her something that would leave her with no doubt in her mind as to just how much she meant to him. Okay. So first, the

jewelry store . . . and maybe the bank. And then he'd track
her down.

Aurora knew he was looking for her. He called so often
there was no doubt, but she wouldn't talk to him. He came
by, but she refused to see him. He'd even shown up at the
hospital a few times this week, whenever his schedule and
hers allowed it. But she'd managed to duck him.

She stopped counting how many days and then weeks it
had been since that magickal night in the circle where
they'd made love. But she never stopped thinking about it.
Remembering. Wishing. Even aching for him.

And then her world fell apart, the afternoon her aunts,
the three of them, came to her in her room and stood around
her looking sheepish and guilty.

"What?" she asked them, her spine tingling with warnings. They were up to something.

"The girls say I'm the one who has to do the talking,
Aurora," Merriwether said strongly. "So I'll just come
right out with it. We lied to you."

Aurora blinked. "You lied to me?" The three nodded.
"About what?"

"About the reason you had to . . . er . . . that is, you and
Nathan . . ."

"The reason I had to have sex with a virgin?" She felt
her eyes widen. Again, the three nodded. And Merriwether
said, "You see, it couldn't have been just any virgin. It had
to be Nathan McBride."

"Yes," Fauna piped in, "and you wouldn't have lost
your powers if you hadn't done it."

Aurora gaped and felt her legs buckle. She sank onto the
bed. "I don't under . . . I can't believe . . ."

"You're going to be upset at first, dear," Flora said
softly, patting Aurora's hand. "But all of this was foretold,
after all. Now I'm sure you'll want to confirm it with a
doctor, but you can take my word for it. You're almost
certainly pregnant with Nathan's child."

"Pregnant? *Pregnant?*" Aurora's head swam. And then

she did something she'd never done before in her life. She fainted.

Nathan was immersed in the stacks of books and photographs and journals he'd hauled out of his father's attic. Aside from this new obsession he'd developed for Aurora, he seemed to have discovered another powerful interest.

His family history.

And it was a rich one. It had been Aurora's words about his ancestors, that night in that magick bubble of light that had made him wonder, and now he understood.

Nathan McBride came from a long, long line of Celtic Witches. And now that he knew it, he felt oddly drawn to his heritage. He wanted to know what it meant . . . to him. He wanted to learn about and study the beliefs of his forebears.

So when he wasn't constantly trying to get a moment alone with Aurora, he was delving into the old diaries and books, and finding a wealth of information he'd been clueless about before. And it was as he was intently reading one such diary that his telephone rang, and an elderly female voice said, "If you hope to run into Aurora, try the drugstore. Not yours, your competitor's. On Main Street." That was it. The caller hung up.

Nathan frowned. Aurora hated him so much that she was shopping at the competition? Or maybe she just wanted to avoid any chance of running into him. But she knew he ran the stores from a corporate office downtown. She knew that, right?

So what was she doing in his rival's store? Hell, who cared what she was doing there? This was his chance to finally make her understand.

He got to his feet, pulled on a jacket, double-checked the pocket for the tiny box he'd been carrying with him everywhere he went, and headed out. Pouring rain. Great. He turned up the collar on the coat and ducked his head.

Aurora hoped no one would recognize her. She was a doctor, for crying out loud. But this wasn't something she dared to do at the hospital. It was too private. Too personal. Too unbelievably stupid.

She was a doctor. A doctor knew better than to get pregnant. What the hell had happened to her that night? Why had she totally neglected to even consider . . .

Oh, hell, if her aunts were telling the truth—and Aurora was fairly certain they were—then she *knew* why. If this was meant to happen, the way they said it was, then all the protection in the world wouldn't have worked, anyway. So why kick herself?

Her eyes felt gritty and hot. She knew they were red and puffy. And she knew her hair was more mussed than combed, and that she probably looked like a drowned rat incognito, skulking through the drugstore aisles in her rain-spotted trench coat with the Druid-like hood pulled up and a pair of great big sunglasses on her nose, despite the gray skies.

She'd cased the aisle three times, and knew exactly where the stupid little home pregnancy test kits were located. She could swoop by and snatch one without anyone knowing the difference. Paying for it was going to be another matter, but she'd just have to do it. Stealing went against her belief system. So she'd muddle through and figure it served her right.

She looked around, saw no one in the aisle, lowered her head, pushed her sunglasses up on her nose, and hurried forward. Her hand flashed out and scooped up the box and she never missed a beat. She kept her quick pace up right to the end of the aisle . . .

. . . where she collided with a broad, strong chest and a familiar scent. A pair of hands she'd missed desperately came up to her shoulders to steady her.

She looked up and shoved the box she'd just grabbed into the deep pocket of her raincoat.

Nathan frowned at her. "Shoplifting, Aurora?"

"Of course not."

His brows rose. "So what is it you're buying that you don't want me to see?"

She licked her lips, took a step backward, and lowered her eyes, no longer able to look into his.

Then she noticed the tiny box that he held in his own hand. Oh, Goddess! It looked like—

He saw her looking at it, and swept it behind his back. Then his free hand came out as he hooked a finger under her chin and tipped her head back so he could stare into her eyes. He grimaced and plucked off the glasses. Then his frown creases deepened. "Aurora, honey, you look terrible."

"Thanks bunches."

"What's the matter?"

"Nothing."

"You've been crying." She turned away. But he caught her and turned her around, very gently. "So maybe it's not too late after all . . . if you still care enough to cry over me."

She swiped self-consciously at her sore eyes. "Don't be so sure it's you I've been crying over."

She meant it as a barb, but worry clouded his eyes so fast it pricked her conscience. "Is something else wrong? Is Aunt Flora—?"

"No, Nathan. Aunt Flora's fine. Really." She realized her voice had softened toward him. But his genuine concern for her aunt touched her—that he could still feel that way after what those three had pulled on him . . . well, that touched her even more.

He sighed in relief, but just as quickly scanned her face with worry in his eyes. "You sure you're okay?" When he said it he touched her face with his palm, and she closed her eyes because it felt so good to feel him again.

She wasn't okay, hadn't been okay since the last time he'd held her in his arms, but she nodded anyway.

"Aurora, let's go somewhere and talk." His voice had softened to a raspy whisper.

She almost nodded, then remembered the pregnancy test kit in her pocket. She couldn't tell him about that, not yet. And she couldn't even think straight until she knew the results. "I can't, Nathan."

He lowered his head. "You're still angry with me . . . about what you thought you saw at my apartment."

That reminder pricked a sore spot, and Aurora bristled. "What I *thought* I saw?"

Nathan nodded. "Yeah. But all you really saw was a perfectly gorgeous woman failing to interest me in the least, no matter how she tried."

Aurora narrowed her eyes and peered up at him.

"I didn't want her. That's why nothing happened, Aurora. I never wanted any of them, not really."

"You didn't?"

He smiled gently and stroked her hair. "No. I'm just beginning to catch on. All this time . . . it wasn't about spells or curses or your three crazy aunts. It was about you, Aurora. I've never been able to settle for any other woman . . . because the only woman I ever wanted is you."

His words took her breath away. Her heart hammered in her chest, and her knees turned to water. She sagged a little, but his strong hands came around her waist, and she clung to his shoulders and managed to remain upright. But there was still too much space between them.

"You told me you loved me, 'Rora. I'm hoping that's still true."

She searched his face, hesitating, and finally, bit her lip and nodded. "I've loved you since second grade," she whispered. "Maybe longer than that."

He smiled, but it was shaky, uncertain. "Then . . ." He let go of her long enough to retrieve the small box from a back pocket, and then he opened the lid. "Then marry me, Aurora."

Aurora caught her breath. The ring was a flawless diamond surrounded by emeralds glittering up at her. Its facets sparkled and shot fire even through the tears that suddenly filled her eyes.

"It will match those earrings I gave you for your sixteenth birthday," he said. "The ones you've kept all this time."

"I . . . I didn't think you remembered."

"I remember everything about you, 'Rora. Everything

about the two of us, and how every time we got close I did something to screw it up. Something to hurt you.''

"It wasn't only you," she argued, but he silenced her with a gentle forefinger to her lips.

"I'm never going to hurt you again, Aurora."

She wanted to speak, but she couldn't. And he lifted a thumb to wipe the tear from her cheek.

"So what do you say, 'Rora? Will you be my wife?''

She wrapped her arms around his neck, and his closed around her waist, but when he pulled her close, the box in her pocket pressed insistently between them, and Aurora remembered that he still didn't know the whole truth.

Stepping slightly away, she sniffed, reached up and stroked his hair. "It depends.''

His eyes looked almost panicked. "On what?''

"How you react to what I have in my pocket.''

He frowned at her, and tilted his head to one side. Then he reached down, dipping his hand into her pocket, closing it around the box. She willed herself not to close her eyes so she could watch his face as he pulled the box out and scanned the label.

Then he stared at her, wide-eyed. "You . . .'' He looked at the box. Looked at her face again. "You think . . . ?''

"I'm almost sure," she said.

"We're having a baby," he whispered, shaking his head in disbelief. And then he smiled and said it again, louder this time. "We're having a baby!'' His arms wound around her waist and he lifted her off her feet, holding her tight to him and spinning her around. And then he lowered her down, and bent to kiss her more tenderly than any man had ever kissed any woman. And without breaking that kiss, he took the ring from the box in his hand and slipped it onto her finger.

A smattering of applause made them draw apart suddenly, only to see that every patron in the drugstore had crowded together at the end of the aisle to watch them. Aurora wiped the tears from her face, too happy to be embarassed. He still wanted to marry her. She stared down at the glittering ring in wonder, then up into Nathan's shining eyes.

He closed his hand around hers. "Come on." As he drew her past the registers, he pulled a twenty from a pocket, tossed it on the counter and said, "Keep the change," and then they ran together out into the pouring rain toward his car.

But before they got to it, he stopped and turned to face her. Rain dripping off his nose, he said, "You didn't say yes."

He seemed so vulnerable right now, all his joy on hold, awaiting her answer, the look in his eyes telling her that his very life depended on it.

She swept one hand through his wet hair and stood on tiptoe to press her lips to his, right there on the sidewalk in the pouring rain. And then she whispered, "Yes."

Epilogue

Nathan paced the living room of his small apartment, and wondered how the hell Aurora could be sitting so calmly on his sofa. He glanced at his watch, then at the clock on the wall, and then at the oven timer clicking madly on the coffee table.

"Is it time yet?" he asked her, for good measure.

She looked up at him, smiled gently, shook her head, and bent again to her perusal of the old books and diaries Nathan had left sitting out. "So are you going to tell me what all this is about?" she asked him.

He frowned at his watch.

"We have time."

He nodded, went to her, sat beside her. "I was curious. About my ancestors and . . . and about Witches in general, I guess."

She smiled. "You are one, you know."

Nathan's brows rose. "No. I couldn't cast a magick circle the way you did that night—wouldn't know where to begin conjuring elemental forces or any of that."

"You *have* been reading, haven't you?"

He gave her a sheepish smile, nodding once.

"But those things aren't what make you a Witch, Nathan. They can be learned. I can teach you. It's the magick that makes you what you are." She reached up to stroke his cheek. "And that's something you're born with. It's inside you. I felt it that night."

"You think so?"

She nodded, and he wondered if she could be right. He'd felt something, too. "That orb of energy would have been invisible to someone void of magick."

Her eyes danced over his face, their touch palpable. And he knew he'd always believe every word she said to him, even if she said the sun would rise at midnight.

"I hope I'm not going to have to sleep with a virgin to keep it," he said with a grin. Her gaze fell, so he leaned forward to kiss her nose. "Hey, that was a joke."

"It was a lie, Nathan. My aunts made it up. I was never really in danger of losing my magick."

"Then why—"

"This baby. They claim it was foretold. They say that you and I are supposed to give birth to—"

"To the most powerful Witch ever," he finished for her. "A little girl."

"How did you know that?"

Nathan gave his head a shake to clear it. This was all a bit too much to believe. But believe it he did. He riffled pages from one book and another until he found the passage he'd read in one of them. "My great-great-grandmother wrote it down, right here. She said that one day a McBride would father the child who would grow to be . . ." He stopped and shrugged, and instead of telling her, pushed the book into her hands so she could read it for herself. He remembered the passage. It had struck him as more moving, more memorable than anything else he'd read. It went on, about the healing gift the girl was to be born with, and how the cures for many of humanity's most dire illnesses would be discovered because of her work and her magick.

The timer pinged. Aurora closed the book, and her eyes met Nathan's. They were dark and wide and half afraid. "It'll be all right," he told her. And he glanced at the testing kit visible in the bathroom from here. "Do you want to look? Or should I?"

"I already know what it's going to say," she whispered.

He went into the bathroom, lifted the stick, and examined the shape clearly defined there. "Aurora?"

She rose and looked at him. Nathan smiled at her, and she ran into his arms. He kissed her mouth, held her close, relished the very fact that she was here with him, like this, and finally, lifted his head. "I hope she looks just like you," he told her tenderly.

To Mend a Spell

Lisa Higdon

To Evan Marshall and Denise Silvestro,
thanks for the wings!

One

"Oh, Mistress Pratt," the magistrate's daughter breathed as she gazed into the full-length mirror, admiring the shimmering material of her bridal gown. "Surely, you *must* have enchanting powers."

Laura Stuart let her scissors clatter to the floor in astonishment, and silence fell over the seamstress shop. Her grandmother shot her a reproachful look, and she dashed to claim the fallen shears. Mortified, the other ladies waiting for their fitting gaped at one another, but Grandmother only smiled at the careless remark and hugged her chagrined patron.

"Only with a needle and thread, my dear," she laughed, putting everyone at ease. "But what dress wouldn't be lovely on you? You'll be the prettiest bride in Massachusetts."

Beaming at the compliment, Charity Wyatt resumed admiring her reflection in the glass, turning this way and that, with a dreamy look in her eyes. "Just wait until William sees me in this."

"He'll be speechless," Grandmother assured her. "Now let's get you out of this. We still have two other gowns for you to try on."

Magistrate Henry Wyatt was finally marrying off the last

of his five daughters, and Hester Pratt had sewn the wedding gown and the trousseau, just as she had four times before.

As her grandmother finished with Charity, Laura busied herself pinning the hemline for the maid of honor's dress and hurried to make the final fitting for the mother of the bride.

"Charity's wedding will be the social event of the year," Mistress Wyatt declared, peering down at Laura. "I only wish William would agree to wait for a spring wedding, but he wants to have their house in order before planting weather."

Laura only nodded, unable to speak with so many pins held tight between her lips. She suspected Charity's haste to marry had more to do with her lack of a waistline than her betrothed's agricultural concerns. Like everyone else, Laura would say nothing and act surprised when the bundle of joy arrived early. She wondered if Mistress Wyatt would excuse the babe's untimely arrival by way of the father's need to have his crops harvested before being distracted by a child.

Mistress Wyatt smiled slightly and added, "Of course, Laura, you and your grandmother will attend the wedding, but I want you to also come to the bridal dance."

Laura's heart skipped a beat. The Wyatts had made a custom of having a grand party for the betrothed couple one week before the wedding. An invitation was highly coveted, even among the social elite, and Laura couldn't prevent the gasp of delight that sent pins scattering onto the floor.

"Pardon me, Mistress Wyatt." Embarrassed, Laura made haste to collect the pins, barely remembering her manners. "I'd be honored to attend the dance. Thank you for inviting me."

Mistress Wyatt smiled knowingly. Of course, the little seamstress would be honored at being included in something so grand, and Laura flinched at her own eager reaction. The magistrate's wife considered her daughter's wedding to be the most important event of the year and envied by everyone.

To her dismay, Laura *did* find herself envying Charity. Not for wealth or prominence, but for the cocoon of security and happiness in which the Wyatt girls had been reared. Laura often wondered what her own life would be if a whim of tragedy had not taken her parents. Shrugging off the moot thought, she returned her attention to the task at hand. Mistress Wyatt's conversation was now directed at her elder daughters, warning them that she had no intention of being late for tea with the minister's wife.

At last the Wyatt ladies left in a cloud of petticoats and chatter, and Laura began sweeping up the bits of material and snips of thread that littered the floor of the shop. Grandmother began sorting through the dresses, putting them in order of task. Laura would do the simple work, hems and tucks, leaving the intricate work to more experienced and skilful hands.

"You'll get better with time," Grandmother had assured her every day since she was twelve years old. "It just takes patience and practice."

Laura doubted she would ever be able to wield a needle and thread with the artistry that made Hester Pratt the most sought-after dressmaker in New England. For ten years, Laura had been an industrious apprentice, eager to please and help the grandmother who'd given her a loving home after her parents were lost at sea.

"Charity isn't too bright, is she?" Laura remarked, sweeping the bits of cloth and thread into the dustpan.

"She's a sweet girl," Grandmother reproached gently, moving to open the door on the iron stove. "You mustn't be unkind."

"Yes, I know," Laura sighed, dumping the contents of the dustpan onto the red-hot coals. " 'Tis thoughtless remarks like hers that keep folks whispering behind our backs."

"Laura Stuart," Grandmother scolded, "surely, you've not been listening to a lot of silly old wives' tales about witchcraft."

"I haven't," she insisted. "But many folks in this town still believe in that nonsense. Just last spring, Abigail Lamb asked me if I knew how to cure warts!"

Grandmother chuckled. "Why didn't you tell her two pence a wart?"

Laura couldn't help but smile. "You're right, Grandmother. I shouldn't wear my heart on my sleeve."

"That's a good girl." The older woman smiled, fetching her cloak from the hook by the door. "Now, if you'll finish tidying up, I'll dash down to the market."

Laura dutifully returned to her sweeping as her grandmother scurried out of the shop. The tiny brass bell tinkled in her wake and a cold gust of autumn air rushed inside to nip at Laura's ankles.

Surely you've been listening to a lot of silly old wives' tales.

That was always Grandmother's way of dismissing the whispers and curious stares that were sometimes directed at them. Refusing to elaborate, she always assured Laura that such tales were nonsense and should be ignored.

Grandmother had tried so hard to make Laura happy after her parents died, and she hadn't the heart to tell the kindly lady how miserable she was in New England. Even now, she missed the warm, sunny climate of Virginia. Her father had been a planter, and her mother, Hester Pratt's only daughter, had followed him to the southern colony where he made his fortune in tobacco and cotton.

The couple had sailed to the islands for a holiday, leaving young Laura behind to study with her tutors. By the time word of the lost ship reached the plantation, Laura was nearly complete with her studies in French and was just beginning Latin. She had even written a welcome-home play for her parents entirely in French.

Whisked away to the home of her only relative, Laura took comfort in knowing that the kindly woman had loved her mother dearly and shared her loss. Life in Salem, however, proved to be an eye-opening experience. Children in New England attended dame school rather than being tutored, and Laura did not fit in at all. Too tall, she didn't know their games or their customs, and she certainly hadn't memorized the Psalms. French was useless, and Latin was only for boys, the teacher huffed, placing Laura with the younger children until she was able to recite the first ten Psalms.

She lived for the moment school was dismissed, and she could escape the taunts of her classmates.

"My grandfather says that your family is filled with witches," one little boy had informed her. The other children giggled and he embellished, "They fly around on broomsticks and consort with the devil when the moon is full."

"Nonsense," Laura had insisted, but the other children eyed her warily. "There are no such things as witches!"

"Witch! Witch!" they had taunted, joining hands and dancing in a circle around her. "Fly, witch, fly!"

The schoolmistress entered the playground just in time to witness the scene and demanded of Laura, "What sort of evil tales have you been telling these children?"

She was made to stand in the corner the rest of the afternoon and ran home, vowing never to return to school.

"Are you liking school?" Grandmother would ask. "Are you making new friends?"

"I try, Grandmother."

The older lady would smile and pat her on the shoulder. "I'm so glad you like it here."

"I do," she would lie, and returned to school the next day, hating it all the more.

Diligently, Laura applied herself to the tasks assigned to her in the seamstress shop. With practice, her stitches grew neater and her seams hung properly, and finally the day came when she was allowed to work in the shop rather than attend school.

Would she ever understand these New Englanders? Laura tossed the last of the sewing scraps into the fire and hung the broom in its place. She began sorting through the various sewing tasks, deciding to surprise Grandmother by having a few remaining jobs finished when she returned. She couldn't do anything with the Wyatt wedding party, but there were several tasks waiting. She scooped up a cloak she was making for the minister's wife and decided to use a better quality of material for the lining. Mistress Finn had always been kind to Laura.

She knew the perfect fabric that would complement the cloak, and she ventured up the narrow stairs to the chilly attic to retrieve it. The lamp she carried scattered the shadows, and she waited until her eyes grew accustomed to the dimness before searching for the material. She sorted through two trunks, unable to find the length of emerald satin she was certain Grandmother had stored away last fall. She searched a wooden barrel and a burlap bag, only to find scraps saved for quilting. Far in the corner she spied a tiny trunk, hidden in the shadows behind a beam. She dragged the chest toward the center of the attic where the lamplight shone the brightest.

The trunk was caked with dust, and the hinges were rusted stiff. Mice had nibbled at the leather lacings, and Laura knew that no one had opened the trunk in years, let alone her grandmother in a recent search for a place to store fabric. Curiosity outweighed her better judgment, and Laura reached for the latch only to find it locked.

She sat back on her heels and studied the ancient chest. Where had it come from and what in the world was locked away inside? Laura absently traced the intricate carvings across the top of the trunk, plowing tiny furrows in the thick coating of dust.

Grandmother had never *forbidden* her from going into the attic for any reason. Indeed, Laura was often asked to fetch something down or store a box away when the older woman's stiff joints made climbing up and down the narrow stairway difficult. Surely there was nothing in the trunk but a few bolts of long-forgotten cloth, rotting away.

Laura's thumb caressed the latch, her curiosity growing stronger along with her grip. She tugged, gently at first and then giving a firm tug. The rusted latch groaned and gave way, snapping off in her hand.

"Laura, dear!" Grandmother's cheery voice called. "Laura?"

Like a marionette being yanked up by a clumsy puppet-master, Laura bolted to her feet, guilt stealing her voice. She slipped the bit of broken metal into her apron pocket and made a hasty attempt to brush the dust from her hands, but the grime clung to her fingers.

Grandmother's voice grew nearer, more concerned. "Laura? Where are you, dear?"

"Up here!" Laura called out with false brightness. She winced and tried to sound normal as she hurried to shove the trunk back into its rightful place and blow out the lamp. "In the attic."

"What are you doing up there?"

Laura descended the stairs to find Grandmother waiting at the bottom, her eyes bright with merriment. "Mercy, child, you're a mess."

Glancing down at her dress, Laura grimaced at the smudges on her white apron and shuddered as Grandmother tugged a mass of cobwebs from her hair. "I was looking for something."

"What did you need that was under so much dust?"

"That length of satin left over from Mistress Tanner's ball gown last spring," Laura answered, hoping to sound earnest. "The emerald piece. I thought it would be nice to line Mistress Finn's cloak."

"Fancy bit of material to be used as a lining," Grandmother clucked but smiled indulgently. "I know you're fond of Mistress Finn, but I'm afraid I used that material to fit a bodice for the deacon's niece visiting from Boston. I'm sorry, dear."

Laura shook her head. " 'Tis no matter."

Turning toward the kitchen, Hester Pratt removed her cloak and hung the garment on a peg on the wall. "The butcher's son asked after you. He always does."

Laura grimaced, not flattered in the least. "Every time you send me to the market he insists on carrying the packages home."

"Well, you're a pretty girl, and I'm certain he's not the only young man in town to notice." Grandmother made her way to the hearth and placed the great iron spider over the coals to heat. "Fetch the lard for me, dear, and we'll have supper quick as you please."

Laura slipped into the pantry and felt her pocket to be sure the broken latch was still there. Guilt outweighed curiosity, and she decided not to ask Grandmother about the trunk. But why should she feel guilty? The trunk was like any other in the attic and there was no reason she shouldn't open it. Laura hefted the lard tin down from the shelf.

"Laura, I don't like you going in the attic when you're here alone." Grandmother spoke loudly to be heard over the tripe hissing and sizzling in the iron skillet. "This house is old and there could be loose boards or rotten wood. You could fall and no one would be here to help."

Laura never looked up from the bowl of potatoes she was mashing. "How old is this house?"

"My goodness, let me see." Grandmother tipped her head to one side and thought long and hard. "Well, I was born here, and my mother used to tell stories about my father building the house before they were married."

"So you've always lived here?" Laura placed the potatoes on the table along with the bread and honey. "Even after you married?"

"Oh, yes. By then my father had died and your grandfather and I took care of my mother."

Grandmother seated herself and motioned for Laura to do the same. The conversation was interrupted long enough for grace to be said and their plates to be filled. Laura's curiosity was piqued, and she asked, "Your mother was also a seamstress, is that right?"

"The finest," Grandmother declared. "Ladies came from as far away as Boston to be fitted for gowns."

"You've done very well yourself, Grandmother. People are always saying how skilled you are."

"When I was younger, there were few who could best me." She sighed and shook her head. "Magistrate Wyatt has kept us in house and home, but now he's fresh out of daughters."

"Come spring, we'll have more work than we can keep up with," Laura assured her as she rearranged the tripe on her plate. "Everyone will want a wedding dress like the one you made for Charity."

"Ah, but these old hands are giving me grief." She held up her fingers, stiff and swollen, her knuckles large. "I dread the day I can't hold a needle."

Laura laid her fork aside, the food forgotten. For the first time she saw worry in Grandmother's eyes. They had always lived comfortably, if not extravagantly, and Laura had never given much thought toward money.

Her father's debts had taken most of her inheritance, and what she had received went to pay for schooling. The seamstress shop provided amply for their needs, but it was Grandmother's skill that drew patrons. What would they do if Grandmother could no longer sew? Laura's skill certainly wouldn't keep a roof over their heads.

"Shame on me for such talk." The older woman shook off her worry like a cumbersome shawl. "There's no cause for concern. Charity's wedding alone will fill the pantry for the winter, and when everyone sees her going-away dress, well—"

"They'll beat a path to our door," Laura concluded.

"All I need is that material from the West Indies, and we'll be set."

The house was silent as Laura made her way down the stairs, and she frowned to herself as she peered into the empty sewing shop. Where had Grandmother gone so early?

In the kitchen, she found a note beside a plate of blueberry muffins. Sampling a muffin, she read aloud, "I've gone to deliver Timothy Hawkins's winter coat."

Guilt knifed through Laura. She should be out making deliveries for her grandmother, not sleeping late and eating muffins. She took stock of the cluttered kitchen and vowed to start taking on more of the workload.

There was always some task needing doing, and Laura was only too happy to let something wait if Grandmother said she may. Even now, there were dishes to wash and linens to iron, and Laura intended to have them done when Grandmother returned.

She rolled up her sleeves and reached for her apron hanging on a peg, tying it about her waist. The smudges across the front reminded her of the locked trunk in the attic, and she felt her pocket for the broken piece of the latch. Now would be the best time to explore the forgotten chest, she rationalized, while Grandmother was out and didn't need her to help in the shop.

Before she could rethink her motives, Laura hurried up the attic stairs. With no windows, the attic was just as dark in the day as it was at night, and she carefully lit the lamp she'd left behind last night. She found the trunk and hurried to resume her inspection of the contents. She grasped the handle and drew a deep breath, lifting the lid with one swift motion, lest she lose her nerve.

At first, she thought the trunk was empty, save for the strong scent of lavender that rose from within. The dim glow from the lamp did little to light the depths of the trunk, outlining only shadows. Cautiously, Laura reached inside and felt a length of cloth. Fabric . . . what else did she really expect to find? She laughed at her foolishness for allowing her imagination to conjure up magic wands and crystal balls.

She lifted the dark material from the trunk and rose to examine the length of fine black woolen with not one rip or fray. Holding the cloth up to the light, she found it to be a cloak of some kind, lined with black satin. A shiver ran through her as she realized that the garment had been locked away in the trunk for a very long time, yet bore no sign of age or wear.

Puzzled, she folded the cloak and bent to replace it in the trunk. Curiosity rose swiftly when she beheld the interior of the trunk, visible with the great black cloak removed, and she knelt to have a better look. In sharp contrast to the old, worn exterior, the inside was lined in a rich satin the color of dark wine, and Laura smoothed her hand over the exquisite material. She had not seen the like of such fabric even in Virginia, and certainly not in Salem. Her fingers skimmed the bottom of the trunk and within lay only one other object: a small leather-bound volume. A diary, perhaps!

Reaching for the book, Laura found that her hands were trembling, and she forced herself not to hurriedly rifle through the journal in search of answers. Lifting the book, she carefully leafed through the first few pages, amazed not to find them yellowed with age. The words, as well, had been spared the ravages of time and she could easily read the flowing script.

"A charm to win another's love," she read aloud and turned the page. "A charm to bind an enemy."

Quickly she closed the book and scanned the cover, finding no inscription. What else could it be but a book of spells? Realization came crashing down around her. Someone in her family *had* dabbled in magic. Despite Grandmother's amused dismissals of local gossip, Laura knew she held the proof in her hand.

She glanced back at the cloak and wondered who had worn it and when. She set the book aside and reached for the garment, examining it with a seamstress's eye. The design was simple and common. Two lengths of black woolen hemmed at the bottom and sewn up the sides and across the top, save for an opening to fit over the head. She tested the seams and found them sturdy. She couldn't imagine fashioning a garment from such exquisite material and adding not one adornment, but the robe held not even a trim of lace.

She let the cloak tumble back into the trunk and took up the book, again scanning the pages for any clue as to the owner.

A knock downstairs at the front door startled her so that she gasped in astonishment and nearly let the book fall to the floor. She tucked the book in her apron pocket and slammed the lid of the trunk. She blew out the lantern and hurried down the stairs as the knock grew insistent.

"Laura! What were you doing?" Prudence Rutherford hurried inside without waiting for an invitation. "I could catch my death of cold standing out there waiting on you."

"I was upstairs." Laura ignored her friend's dramatics as usual and offered to take her wrap. "What brings you out so early?"

"Mother sent me to tell your grandmother that Mistress Tupper has taken ill."

"Not gravely, I hope."

"She has consumption and fever." Prudence followed Laura into the kitchen and helped herself to a muffin. "The doctor has bled her twice, but she seems only worse."

Laura shuddered as she filled the teakettle with water and hung it over the fire to heat. She plucked two mugs from the cupboard and said, "I wouldn't let that old goat put leeches on me."

"Dr. Powell is a fine physician," Prudence insisted. "He studied at Oxford and in Boston. When my sister and I were young we had measles and would have died if not for him."

Laura paused and tried to recall ever having the physician tend her in illness. Grandmother had always looked after her if she became ill. The kettle steamed and Laura filled the waiting mugs while Prudence elaborated on the miseries of childhood illnesses. "I'm thankful for my own good health."

Laura nodded in agreement. "We can only pray that Mistress Tupper will recover. I know Grandmother will appreciate you bringing the news."

"Actually, I insisted that Mother let me be the one to tell you and Mistress Pratt." A mischievous smile crept over Prudence's face. "I was *hoping* I might have a peek at Charity's dress."

"You know the rules," Laura admonished her friend. "Grandmother never allows anyone to see one of her gowns before the lady who'll wear it."

"You see them!"

"That's different. I work in the shop and sew the dresses as well."

"The Wyatts always have the most beautiful weddings," Prudence sighed, absently stirring her tea. "I shall never forget Abigail's gown. She married the year before you came to live here."

"I've heard plenty about it," Laura assured her friend. Setting her tea aside, she raised her hand, as if conducting a choir, and mimicked Mistress Wyatt's singsong voice. "Everything must be perfect. The tiniest detail will not go unnoticed."

Prudence broke into a fit of laughter, and Laura pinned her with a disapproving glare. "Young woman, such behavior is unseemly and shan't be tolerated."

"Oh, Laura," Prudence managed between giggles. "You sound just like her."

Reaching for her cup, Laura only replied, "I ought to as often as I've had to listen to her. You should have heard her yesterday. 'Of course, Laura, you and your grandmother will attend the wedding, but I want you to also attend the bridal dance.' "

"But that's wonderful!" Prudence declared. "Those dances are always so grand."

"I know, but she acts like it's some sort of privilege to be invited." Laura shook her head. "Perhaps I should feel privileged. I haven't exactly been overwhelmed by the kindness of this town."

"You never have learned to like Salem, have you?"

"Perhaps, if I'd come here under different circumstances."

"Well, I'm glad you came here. You're my best friend."

Laura smiled. "For that I'm grateful as well. And I intend to make more of an effort to learn to like Salem. For starters, I'll make a pot of soup to carry to Mistress Tupper."

Prudence slid off the stool. "Good for you."

"Won't you stay and help me?"

"I would, but Mother said for me to hurry home and help her with a batch of bread."

Laura stirred the fragrant broth, quite pleased with her first attempt at preparing chicken soup. She had followed Grandmother's recipe to the letter and the soup had turned out delicious. The entire house bore evidence of her labors. The furniture gleamed with beeswax, the hearth had been swept, and the pewter had been scoured. The sewing room was neat as a pin, with a great stack of completed tasks waiting for delivery.

The soup had only to simmer a bit more and she would allow it to cool slightly before taking the pot to the Tupper home. More than a little pleased with herself, Laura plopped onto a kitchen stool. She slipped the tiny book from her apron pocket and skimmed through the peculiar verses.

"A charm to gain wealth. A charm to keep a cat from straying," she mused, turning a page. "A charm to rid the body of nagging ailments."

Laura glanced at the pot of soup then back at the verse. *"The body must be purged of harmful spirits before healing may begin. Prepare a tea of willow bark or a broth of aromatic vegetables and say these words while stirring the pot counterclockwise."*

Laura closed the book and gazed at the soup kettle. Did she dare? Suddenly, she felt foolish and laughed aloud at herself. Surely, no words murmured to a pot of chicken soup could cause a person to recover from an illness. Still, someone had gone to great lengths to hide the book along with the mysterious cloak, and she suspected that the need for secrecy was just as prevalent today as before.

She flipped the book open again and reread the passage regarding healing the sick. There was certainly nothing evil about wanting a neighbor who was good and kind to regain her health. Rising from the stool, Laura slipped the book into her pocket and approached the hearth. She plucked the wooden spoon from the spoon rest and drew a deep breath, exhaling slowly as she began stirring the soup, counterclockwise.

"Bitter doth heal. Sweet doth heal." She glanced over her shoulder to be sure she was still alone. "Gold doth heal. Silver doth heal. She shall be renewed this night. And through all others soon and late."

Laura ceased stirring and watched the soup, not certain

what would happen now. Clutching the spoon in her fist, she peered into the pot and waited. Steam rose and a slice of carrot bobbed to the surface, but nothing miraculous occurred.

"Laura!" Grandmother's voice and the bell over the entrance rang out simultaneously. "Where are you, dear?"

"In the kitchen!" Laura called out, scurrying away from the hearth.

Grandmother bustled into the kitchen, removing her bonnet, and glanced about the spotless kitchen. "Merciful heavens, what's all this?"

"I put dinner on about an hour ago," Laura explained, pleased by the older woman's delighted expression. "I also finished most of the orders waiting in the shop and put a pot of soup on for Mistress Tupper."

"And scrubbed the hearth and polished the furniture." Grandmother beamed as she admired the gleaming copper pots hanging in their rightful places. "I learned of Mistress Tupper's illness while up at the Hawkins place. Poor thing, she's had a time of it this year. I did so want to take something out to her."

"The soup is done," Laura declared, hefting the pot off the fire. "It will need to cool a bit before being carried."

"That will give me time to finish up those dresses for Mistress Brower."

"I've already done them."

Astonished, Grandmother asked, "The lace trim around the cuffs?"

"All done," Laura assured her. "And I'm all set to deliver them and the soup. You just take the afternoon and rest."

"Well, aren't you the sweetie." Grandmother chuckled as Laura led her to the ancient rocker waiting near the hearth. "Are you sure you can manage by yourself?"

"Of course. Is there anything I can get for you while I'm out?"

"Well, dear, if you have the time, could you run down to the docks?" The older woman sank into the chair, her weariness showing. "I heard talk in town that several ships were coming in today, and I do hope the material for Charity Wyatt's dress will be delivered.''

Laura hurried to fetch a shawl and tuck it securely about Grandmother's narrow shoulders. ''I'll make the inquiries while I'm out.''

By the time Laura had gathered the dresses to be delivered from the shop, Grandmother was nodding off peacefully in the rocker, and she hardly stirred as Laura picked up the pot of soup and slipped out the door.

Two

"Captain Power! You can't blame me for this misfortune!"

"When I send a man out with one of my ships, I hold him responsible for all that happens." Simon Power glared at the man cowering before him on the teeming wharf. "I certainly don't expect him to come back with an empty hull, sniveling about pirates."

"We were outnumbered!" Though the two men were shoulder to shoulder in height, fear and apprehension put the hapless sailor at a disadvantage. "They were armed to the teeth."

Simon let his gaze drop to the man's uninjured form, noting that his uniform missed not so much as a gleaming gold button. "You appear no worse for wear."

He turned away before Berkley could manage a reply. All he would get from the man were excuses, and excuses wouldn't return the fortune lost to pirates. He glanced back toward the *Tradewind* and contemplated going aboard to personally inspect the damage, reminding himself that he should be grateful the ship was not destroyed.

Growing tensions with England made seafaring more and more dangerous as well as lucrative. Goods such as rum, molasses, and sugar brought a high price in the colonies, but the risks ran high as well. At best, pirates would overtake the ship and transfer the cargo to their own vessel. At worst, they would kill the crew and take the ship along with its cargo.

"Captain Power!"

Simon turned to find yet another member of the crew scurrying toward him, no doubt with bad news.

"Captain, sir, we've docked the ship, but I'm afraid she'll need a bit of work before setting sail again."

"A bit of work, Chauncy?" Simon glanced back at the sagging sails and shook his head. "She'll never make the next run to Barbados before winter sets in, and you know what that will mean."

The man cast a sympathetic glance toward the ship. "Aye, sir, she'll be dry-docked for the winter. Can't sail in icy waters."

Simon didn't want to think about the *Tradewind* sitting empty and useless in the spring when the other ships returned with their hulls bursting with the exotic goods eagerly sought by the colonists. Trade in rum, molasses, and chocolate provided a lucrative enterprise for any man with a fleet of ships sailing for the islands.

The *Tradewind* was one of only three ships Simon had acquired through ruthless competition with established New England merchants. Though better equipped and financed, the wealthy traders couldn't match Simon's hunger for success. The last two years had yielded more profit than he could have hoped for in five. Enough to pay off the existing three ships and commission a fourth. Still, it was never far from his mind how easily a fortune could be lost.

Simon clapped Chauncy on the shoulder and tried to sound encouraging. "You keep a tight rein on the repairmen, and we'll see who spends this winter in the harbor."

The older man smiled and scurried down the dock toward the wounded ship. Simon's gaze followed, and he could already picture the *Tradewind* suspended above the icy water for the duration of the harsh New England winter. An idle winter would double the loss, and Simon could only hope his other ships could shoulder the burden.

• • •

The sounds of the teeming wharf reached Laura's ears before she even topped the hill leading down to the docks. The clang of bells, the screech of seagulls, and the shouts of seamen all imparted a sense of excitement and adventure. Her only experience with sea travel had been the voyage from Virginia to Salem, but she often dreamed of setting sail for far-off lands and exotic ports.

From the top of the hill, the scene was one from a painting—white sails rising against an azure sky. The gulls hovered above various fishing sloops, diving for scraps from the fishmonger, and merchants of every possible enterprise bustled to and fro to attend their patrons.

By the time she reached the docks, Laura was much less enchanted with the scene. Up close, the stench of fish and the sour smell of unwashed bodies assaulted her senses. She hurried to find the ship as Grandmother had instructed, anxious to be away from the thronging crowd. Nearing the end of the docks, she scanned the various ships, large and small, being unloaded. She caught sight of a burly man who seemed to be in charge of the army of men bearing cargo down from one of the ships and decided he would be as good a source of direction as any.

"Pardon me, sir." She struggled to be heard above the commotion. "I'm looking for a vessel called the *Tradewind*."

"This is her, miss." He jabbed his thumb over his shoulder in the direction of a ship.

Even with her limited acquaintance with ships, Laura found it hard to believe the vessel would stay afloat, let alone sail the high seas.

"I'm here to collect a parcel my grandmother was expecting," she offered, hoping for an explanation that she should seek another ship of the same name. "A bolt of fabric from the West Indies."

The man stroked his weathered jaw and eyed her with speculation. "I'm afraid there ain't to be no parcel for your grandmother or anyone else. The ship was looted by pirates on her way home."

"Pirates?" Laura was astonished.

"Yes, miss. The bloody bastards took everything they could carry. She's lucky to have returned at all."

She nodded sympathetically before asking, "How do I go about claiming my grandmother's reimbursement?"

The man was clearly startled. "You mean money, miss?"

"The fabric is very costly, and she was required to pay in advance to insure delivery," Laura explained. "No doubt, she is entitled to a refund since the fabric was in your possession and you are responsible."

"Not me, miss," he quickly replied with a vigorous shake of his head. "I've no claim to this ship."

"Who then?"

"Captain Simon Power owns the *Tradewind*."

Laura turned her gaze in the direction he pointed. It wasn't hard to determine which man was Captain Power. He was at the end of the wharf shouting orders. He stood head and shoulders above the men scurrying to obey his commands. Turning in her direction, he hurled his anger toward a man not ten feet from where she stood.

"You there!" he shouted, advancing toward the end of the wharf. "Get below and see that what cargo remains is unloaded without delay."

The man opened his mouth to argue but obviously thought better of it. Without a word, he made his way past Captain Power toward the *Tradewind*. Laura knew this would be her only chance to speak with the captain before he followed the man onto the ship, but she stood mute. He turned his gaze on her for a moment and she felt thunderstruck.

Towering above her, his eyes were the color of the sky before a storm. His dark hair hung loose about his broad shoulders. When she said nothing, he turned away

Steeling her determination, Laura hurried after him. "Captain Power! A word, please, sir."

He turned and glared down at her. "What is it, woman? Can't you see the men are busy? You'll have ample chance to tempt them out of their wages tonight at the tavern."

Laura felt color rise hot to her face. "I certainly intended nothing of the kind. I have business with you, sir."

A hint of a smile touched his lips. "What kind of business?"

"You owe me money, sir, and I intend to be reimbursed."

His gaze lingered on her face and the salty breeze rushed between them. "Surely, I would remember such pleasant business and would gladly have paid the price."

"Your lewd assumptions are an insult to yourself, sir, not to me. My grandmother was expecting a shipment of goods aboard your ship," Laura pressed. "A bolt of costly material. The goods were lost while in your possession; you are responsible."

All traces of humor left his face. "I haven't time for such foolishness. Get back to your kitchen, woman."

Laura could only stare at his retreating back, infuriated at the idea of being dismissed like a servant girl. She marched after him, and reached for his arm. Her fingers caught hold of his dark jacket and she held tight. "Do not walk away from me, sir. I will not be . . ."

The sound of tearing fabric rent the air, and Laura stood holding the sleeve of his coat in her clenched fist. Dumbfounded, she could only stare at the exposed fabric of his shirtsleeve. Laughter erupted from the men gathered on the dock, and Laura felt the color drain from her face. He turned to her, his anger barely contained.

"I beg your pardon, Captain," she stammered, fumbling to fold the dismembered sleeve before holding it out to him. "I had no idea it would rip so easily."

He stripped himself of the ruined jacket and thrust it toward her. "You have until tomorrow morning to have this repaired and returned to me, or I will have you thrown in the stocks."

Laura could only watch as he stormed off, the jacket clutched tightly in her arms.

"Chin up, sweeting," a man standing nearby called out to her. "Mayhap next time you'll catch the man and toss out the coat."

Another burst of raucous laughter spilled onto the docks,

and Laura turned and ran from their taunts, tears stinging her eyes.

Laura was still shaking as she ducked inside her tiny bedroom. Closing the door, she leaned against the heavy oak frame, willing her legs to support her weight. She had run all the way home, and her heart slammed hard against her breast. Thankfully, she had returned to an empty house and hadn't had to face her grandmother in such a state.

Tears of frustration burned her eyes as she threw the wretched coat onto her bed. She had wanted so badly to be a help to her grandmother, and now she must relay the news that the prized fabric was lost along with the money. The encounter with Simon Power only added to her misery.

She winced at the thought of the way he had eyed her with such arrogance, assuming that she was a strumpet vying for the attention of the men working on the docks. If only she could have rebuffed him with a haughty look and had him begging her pardon upon learning that she was the daughter of a wealthy planter or a powerful merchant. Instead, he had only become angry to learn that she was nothing more than a shop girl haggling over a lost bolt of material.

Laura glanced down at her drab woolen dress and thought of the exquisite silks and velvets she stitched for others. She had so wanted a beautiful gown of her own to wear to the Wyatt ball, but she couldn't ask Grandmother for anything now that they faced such a tremendous loss. She would have to attend the dance in her Sunday dress, and accept her station among the commoners.

Downstairs, she heard the bell sound over the entrance to the sewing shop, and she drew a ragged breath. Grandmother was home, and Laura had to face her with bad news.

"Laura, dear!" The cheery voice reached Laura's ears and she opened her bedroom door, preparing to meet the inevitable.

"Here I am." She pasted a smile on her face and ventured out into the hallway just as Grandmother topped the stairs. "I thought you'd be home resting."

"Bosh about resting, girl. I had a wee rest and then couldn't stand being idle. I decided to pay a call on Mistress Tupper, myself."

Grateful for the diversion, Laura asked, "She was sleeping when I delivered the soup. Is she any better?"

"Understandably weak." Grandmother shook her head. "The learned doctor was just leaving when I arrived. How a man of his education can't see that losing blood will not make a person stronger is beyond me."

"Did he put the leeches on her again?" Laura asked and shuddered at the thought.

"Thankfully, not today. He claims he has done all he can do and that her fate lies in God's hand. Fine thing, bleeding the poor woman to the point of death and then blaming the Almighty."

"She's dying?"

"There, there, child. I didn't mean to frighten you with my carrying on. After the doctor left, her husband asked if there was anything I might advise. I set about opening windows and fed the poor woman a bowl of that soup you made."

The spell.

Laura started. She'd nearly forgotten. In all the commotion of the afternoon, she'd completely forgotten the charm she'd repeated over the kettle. Reaching to help Grandmother remove her cloak, Laura dared ask, "Did it make her feel better?"

"Good food and fresh air always do a person good." Grandmother smoothed her palm alongside Laura's face. "You're peaked, child. Are you not feeling well?"

"Just a little tired," she admitted.

"Well, come on out to the kitchen with me." Grandmother took her hand and began leading her down the stairs. "I'll make some tea and have you right as rain in no time."

"A charm to secure the heart's desire."

Laura considered the page carefully, not certain she would know where to find a grove of cedar trees in which to cast such a spell. The charms were quite peculiar and detailed, and she wondered if the spell she'd repeated over the soup would really help Mistress Tupper. For the past hour, she had sat hunched over her tiny desk struggling to read the ancient book in the light of a single candle.

Forcing herself to put the book aside, she rose from the desk and stretched her aching muscles. Glancing toward her bed, she caught sight of Captain Power's jacket lying askew upon the coverlet. Settling on the bed, Laura examined the torn sleeve, grateful to find that only the seam had ripped and the material was unharmed. She would hate to ask Grandmother for new cloth and have to explain why she was repairing the jacket.

Taking up her tiny sewing basket, Laura chose a needle already threaded with stout black thread and her tiny scissors. She tied a tight knot at the end of the thread and turned the coat inside out, catching the faint masculine scent wafting from the dark lining. Closing her eyes, Laura could picture Simon Power staring down at her with those eyes.

He was handsome enough to easily steal a girl's heart and arrogant enough to know it.

The needle flashed silver in the lamplight as Laura carefully set the seam, her stitches quick and sure. She resented the attraction she felt toward Captain Power, and she hated knowing that he would be amused at the idea of her admiration.

"Pride cast down. Vainglory hurl below." She whispered the words from the charm book, wishing there were such a spell to humble an enemy. Indeed, she smiled at the notion of Simon Power being brought down a peg or two. Securing the final stitch, she mused, "Lest he sail another boat, let him be a billy goat."

She laughed aloud at the thought as much as at her own cleverness and stood to inspect the jacket. The sleeve looked as good as new, and she twirled about the room, holding the coat before her like a dance partner. She hummed a waltz and imagined dancing with the dashing Simon Power in a glittering ballroom. They would dance every dance and walk out into the moonlight and share a stolen kiss in the shadows.

She shivered at the thought and shook herself from such imaginings. She would return the coat in the morning and probably never see Simon Power again. Still, she couldn't help smoothing her hand over the rich fabric as she folded the coat and wondering what it would be like to steal those moments in the shadows with such a man.

"I'm here to see Captain Power, please."

Laura assumed the sour-faced woman peering out of the doorway was Captain Power's housekeeper.

"He's not in."

The door slammed shut and Laura stepped back, most unprepared for this rudeness. Incensed, she knocked on the door, forsaking the bell, and waited impatiently.

The door opened and the sour face peered out at her. "I told you, he isn't in."

"That, madam, suits me just fine." With a haughty tone, Laura managed to throw the woman off guard and force her way through the doorway into the foyer. "I merely came to deliver his coat. He was most insistent that it be repaired and returned by this morning."

"Repaired?"

"There was a rip in the sleeve."

"I normally see to the captain's wardrobe."

"Then you were the one who set these seams so poorly?" Laura raised an eyebrow in accusation. "My grandmother would take a razor strop to me if I made such careless stitches."

The woman's face grew even more sour, and Laura bit the inside of her jaw to keep from laughing. Grandmother didn't believe in spankings, but it was worth a lie to see the old crone's face pucker with annoyance.

"I don't *sew* for the captain," the housekeeper stated, her voice dripping with indignation. "His garments are made by one of the finest tailors in Boston. How did you come to be in possession of his coat?"

Before Laura could reply, the front door burst open and

Simon Power himself stormed into the house. The scowl on his face set both her and the housekeeper back a step.

"Captain Power," the housekeeper managed, clearly startled by his entrance. "You instructed me not to prepare a noon meal, and I assumed that you would not return before nightfall."

"I've no interest in the running of the kitchen," he all but growled. "Fetch a dram of whiskey to the study."

The housekeeper scurried toward the kitchen without another word. He turned to find Laura standing before him. She raised her chin a bit and said, "Good afternoon, Captain."

"I hadn't expected to see you again, Miss . . ."

"Stuart," she supplied. "Laura Stuart. I've brought your coat, as requested."

"Leave it with Mrs. Grundy," he said by way of dismissal. "I've more important concerns this day."

"I must insist that you try it on before I leave." She didn't flinch at his scowl. "I've more important matters than running back here should it not fit properly."

"Good day, Miss Stuart." He turned toward the study.

Laura followed after him, ducking inside the parlor just as he turned to close the door.

"Bloody hell, woman," he snarled. "Didn't I tell you to leave the coat with Mrs. Grundy?"

"You did, indeed," she snapped. "But I want to be done with you and your coat, and I'll not be running back here if you complain that it doesn't fit properly."

"Why wouldn't it fit? All you were to do was mend a rip in the sleeve."

"That coat was sewn improperly; I reinforced the seams and made an adjustment in the shoulder."

"Very well," he conceded, taking the jacket.

He slipped his arms into the sleeves, and, out of habit, Laura grasped the lapels to adjust the shoulders. Her thumbs skimmed the fabric of his shirt, damp from the harbor mist, and the heat of his body burned against her knuckles. She glanced up to find their faces mere inches apart, and his gray eyes glinted with the slightest hint of amusement.

"It seems you're quite capable of repairing your own damage." He raised his hands to the lapels, brushing her hands with his own. "And the fit does seem better."

"I let the seams out a bit across the shoulders," she confessed, startled by the feel of his fingers against hers. "It should be much more comfortable."

He nodded, gently grasping her hands when she moved to step away from him. "I was not much of a gentleman when we met yesterday. I pray you'll not hold that against me."

"Are you saying that you always behave as a gentleman?"

With exaggerated grace, he bowed elegantly and raised her hand to his lips. "Always in the company of one so lovely."

Despite his mocking manner, Laura's heart skipped a beat at the feel of his mouth grazing against her knuckles.

"The type of women who frequent the docks are not the sort a man minds his manners about."

"Yes, you made that quite clear." Laura withdrew her hands from his grasp and put much-needed distance between them. "Are they the kind you normally have thrown in the stocks?"

"Ah, you mean to make me pay for that, don't you?" He made no move to advance toward her; rather he stood still, eyeing her with a mixture of amusement and chagrin.

Like a loose thread on a shawl, Laura couldn't resist tugging at his remorse. She ducked her eyes and pretended to shrink from his gaze. " 'Tis not the sort of thing I'm accustomed to, sir. I must confess, you gave me quite a fright."

At that, he did advance toward her. "I assure you I had no intention of taking such severe measures all because of a ripped sleeve."

Her lip trembled. "B-but you said—"

"I'm afraid I've grown accustomed to the presence of rough-talking seamen who respond to nothing but threats and temper. I should never have spoken so crudely to you."

At her doubtful expression, he pressed, "Surely, I can prove myself and gain your trust."

Laura raised her eyes. "There is still the matter of the money you owe my grandmother."

"I am not in the business of selling dress goods." He retreated and began buttoning the coat. "I'm afraid your grandmother will have to deal with the person from whom she purchased the material."

"The material was in your possession," Laura reminded him. "And it was lost due to the incompetence of your crew. You are responsible."

"I will not discuss this with you any further."

"Fine. I will take the matter up with the magistrate and see if he feels differently." Laura raised her chin in exaggerated defiance. "After all, the material in question was for his daughter's wedding."

Captain Power's eyes narrowed, and it was all Laura could do not to shrink. "Do not make idle threats against me—"

Before he could finish, the front door burst open, and a frantic man stumbled inside. "Captain Power! We've just received word that the *Augusta* has been lost at sea."

"What?" he demanded, turning his fury on the messenger.

"There was a dreadful storm, sir. The entire crew may be lost as well."

"God's blood, that's two ships in as many days." He raked a hand through his dark hair and muttered a string of curses. "What devil has put a curse on me?"

Laura felt the color drain from her face, but neither man noticed her strangled gasp of alarm. She backed toward the parlor doorway, unwilling to believe she had caused the loss of the ship and possibly the lives of the crew. Horrified, Laura ran out of the house, desperate to search the charm book and assure herself that no spell had been cast.

Three

Laura scrambled up the stairs to her bedroom, heedless of her grandmother's startled expression, and quickly made her way inside the tiny room. She took care not to slam the door and drew a steadying breath. Merciful heavens, what had she done?

She knelt beside her narrow bed and dug the spell book from its hiding place under the quilts. Her fingers were trembling so that she could barely turn the delicate pages.

She scanned each page, but nothing sounded familiar. She had read the verses in no particular order, memorizing only snatches, and Laura couldn't recall the exact words she had spoken while stitching the coat. All she could be certain of was that she had been angry with Power and wished misfortune upon him. Misfortune that had quickly come to pass.

Truth be told, she had given no thought to the possible consequences of her halfhearted sorcery, taking lightly the power of something she didn't understand. Her insides quaked at the thought of what evil she might have unleashed, and she breathed a fervent prayer that she would be able to undo the harm she had caused.

At last she found a passage that spoke of reversing a spell. Relieved, she sank to the floor and began reading what she hoped would be the solution to her problem. Her relief, however, was short-lived as she read the stern reminder that no charm should ever be spoken in anger or jest. The warning was most explicit and she read on with a sense of dread.

"No charm shall be uttered without reverence and devotion, lest folly befall. Once cast, the charm may be broken only when remedied by another spell."

Reading on, she realized that the simplest thing to do would be to restitch the coat and recite a charm to drive away evil. How would she ever get her hands on that coat again?

Laura closed the book, willing herself to face the task before her. She had cursed Simon Power and already misfortune had befallen him. She was bound to set things to right, but how could she? She couldn't very well tell the man that she had put an evil spell on him.

She smoothed her hand over the buttery leather binding of the book, fearing that she had only garnered trouble for herself and danger for others. Guilt washed over her, and she wished she had never snooped through the attic. If only she'd asked Grandmother about the trunk, all of this might have been avoided. She considered asking the older woman what she should do now, but she couldn't risk involving anyone else in her mischief.

Indeed, the so-called harmless rumors regarding the seamstress's family dabbling in magic could easily flare into accusations of witchcraft. No one would believe that the older woman had no knowledge of Laura's use of the spell book, and Grandmother was too old to survive being jailed.

She crept downstairs. The sound of her grandmother's cheerful humming met her ears, and her guilt mounted. The spicy aroma of stewed apples filled the tiny home, and the rumbling of her stomach reminded Laura that she had missed dinner.

Grandmother was in the shop, bustling to and fro. Laura ventured inside to find the older woman hovering over the cutting table, humming to herself.

"Grandmother?" Laura called. "Why are you working so late?"

Startled, the older woman whirled at the sound of her granddaughter's voice. "Laura, dear, I didn't hear you come down. Are you feeling all right?"

"Yes, I'm fine."

"When you didn't come down to supper, I thought you might be asleep. Perhaps you should eat a bite. You look pale."

"I'm fine, really." Laura neared the cutting table. Her gaze drifted toward the material spread across the table. "Why, this is the material for Charity's dress! Where did it come from?"

"It arrived this afternoon." Smoothing a wrinkled hand along the material, Grandmother admired the way it gleamed in the soft lamplight. " 'Tis lovelier than I dared hope."

Laura gaped at the shimmering length of fabric. "Grandmother, this material was stolen from Captain Power's ship."

"Stolen?" The older woman's expression grew concerned. "You never said anything about it being stolen."

Abashed, Laura ducked her eyes. "Well, that's what I heard. That his ship was looted by pirates."

To her surprise, Grandmother only chuckled. "Pirates? Laura, dear, someone's been pulling your leg. Trying to up the price, I'll guess."

"No, 'tis true," she insisted. "I should have told you last night, but I didn't have the heart. I went to the docks and learned the ship had returned empty."

"Well, my fabric is here, safe and sound." Grandmother made her way to the end of the table. "Here, child, help me get this folded up. I've kept your supper warm."

Laura decided not to press the matter further, lest she divulge her true cause for concern. Her meddling with witchcraft had brought misfortune to Simon Power, and only witchcraft could set things to right. Now, the arrival of Grandmother's fabric complicated matters.

Laura had fervently wished she could replace the stolen

fabric and now here it was. Had she invoked the fabric's arrival? No, it couldn't be. Wishing wasn't the same as a spell.

She followed Grandmother into the kitchen and considered the possibility that she had been duped. Perhaps that would explain Simon Power's change in attitude toward her. Had he hoped to charm her into believing he had mysteriously located her fabric and charge her for the favor?

The tavern was crowded but unusually quiet this night; indeed, the mood of those gathered in the tavern matched Simon's own somber disposition. A tankard of ale, barely touched, sat before him, but he had no taste for the stout brew he normally enjoyed.

Word of the loss of the *Augusta* as well as several other supply ships had spread over the town. There would be a shortage of Jamaican rum served at taverns and inns, and without the barrels of fine molasses, the price of local sugar would double within a week. Even the British soldiers would suffer, with no tobacco or cotton from the southern colonies.

Surprisingly, Simon's thoughts were on Laura Stuart; he wondered how all of this would affect her. She had been so distressed over the loss of one bolt of cloth, and he feared having to do without sugar for her tea would send the poor girl into despair. He repented the thought as soon as it formed in his mind. She was obviously a woman of delicate sensibilities, and he had regretted not going after her when she ran from his home earlier.

"A good evening to you, Captain Power."

Glancing up, Simon found Elias Langford looming over his table. Ignoring the man's mocking expression of concern, Simon replied, "Good evening."

"I do hope you're not among those who have suffered loss." Elias seated himself across from Simon without invitation, motioning to a servant for a tankard. " 'Tis such a pity."

As one of the wealthiest merchants in all of Massachusetts, Elias had an abundance of much and was generous with nothing, least of all pity. Simon only shrugged, managing to sound indifferent. "It's a risk we all take."

The servant appeared with the tankard, and Elias quickly fished a coin from his pocket. "That should be ample payment for this and all that Captain Power has already consumed."

The servant gaped wide-eyed at the gold shilling gleaming against his dirty palm. "Indeed, sir, indeed."

Elias chuckled. "Good, and you may keep the difference, my boy. Buy yourself a bit of supper."

When the boy had scurried away, Simon couldn't resist observing, "Pity to waste such a charitable mood on the two people in Salem who will never prove useful to you."

Elias chuckled again, though more to himself. "What an arrogant bastard you are, Simon. I would have thought you man enough to take your losses with a little more dignity."

"I'm man enough not to be goaded by your insults," he retorted, hefting his own tankard of ale to his lips. He drank deeply before leveling his gaze on the older man and demanding, "What is it you want from me?"

Laughing aloud, Elias raised his own mug in salute. He drained half the tankard and mopped the foam from his mouth with the back of his hand. "Very well, I'll be blunt, if you like. I need a man to run cargo to Spain this winter, and I know you'll not be sailing your own vessels. I'd be willing to share the profits with you."

"Provided I'm not fed to the sharks by Spanish pirates?" Simon added and shook his head. "Why should I run your ships? I've only lost the *Augusta*."

"Everyone knows the *Tradewind* will never leave the harbor before winter, and you did lose her cargo." Elias rose to his feet and added, "A wise man knows when to cut his losses."

Before Simon could reply, a commotion near the tavern's entrance drew his attention.

"Be gone, woman," MacMillan, the innkeeper, bellowed at a tiny figure standing just inside the doorway. "I run a decent place, and I'll have no trollops sniffing around for a man."

"How dare you accuse me of indecency?" The female voice could be heard throughout the tavern as every voice fell silent. "Is this not a public place? I have as much right to be here as anyone."

Simon immediately recognized Laura Stuart's defiant tone and rose to his feet, not bothering to excuse himself to Elias Langdon. He crossed the common room just in time to spare the innkeeper from a futile argument.

"Good evening, Miss Stuart," he spoke casually, as if he had been expecting her.

MacMillan gaped at him in disbelief. "Captain Power? This young woman is in your company?"

"Only if you're willing to allow her into your tavern, MacMillan."

"Of course, Captain." Their host quickly stepped aside, though his expression remained doubtful. " 'Tis most unusual for a young lady to go about alone."

"Yes, Miss Stuart," Simon agreed. "You really should be more careful."

She glared up at him, fury simmering in her green eyes. Intrigued, he led her to a table in the far corner and motioned for her to be seated. Taking a place across from her, he demanded, "Now, what is this all about?"

Her eyes narrowed slightly. "I want to know why you lied to me."

"Lied to you? What about?"

"If your ship was looted by pirates, how did my grandmother's fabric come to be here in Salem?" She leaned forward and pinned him with a menacing gaze. "If you mean to cheat a helpless old woman, don't think I won't go to the magistrate."

"Go to the magistrate," he challenged. "Perhaps he might settle this once and for all. I've told you, I know nothing of any fabric."

"Then explain how stolen goods suddenly reappear."

Simon noticed several men at nearby tables straining to overhear their conversation, and he wanted no more attention drawn to the situation. "Miss Stuart, this is hardly an appropriate place to discuss such matters. Allow me to escort you home safely and we may talk further on the way.''

"I demand you explain—"

"Miss Stuart." He cut off her tirade with the tone he normally reserved for insubordinate first officers. He cut a warning glance toward a nearby table of men straining to overhear her. "Let us discuss this on the way to your home."

Laura shivered as much from fear as she did from the cool night air. She'd not wanted to risk going to the kitchen for her heavy cloak and have to explain her reasons for leaving the house, and her lacy shawl did nothing to shield her from the evening cold. The distance from her home to Captain Power's was not great, and she had thought to be home long before now.

Had she known that her search for Simon Power would lead to the rowdy tavern, she would never have ventured out, but she had to know the truth about the missing fabric that was no longer missing.

Simon's fingers cupped her elbow as he led her toward his waiting carriage, and the heat from his hand made her shudder with more than the cold. He was even more handsome than she had been willing to admit earlier, and she would have loved nothing more than to turn from the chill night air into his embrace.

Simon opened the carriage door and assisted her inside before climbing in himself and closing the door. She heard the driver call out to his team and the carriage lurched forward. Seated across from her, Simon leveled a demanding gaze on her. "Now, I want you to tell me what this is all about."

Unable to meet his stare, Laura focused her attention on her clasped hands. "You lied to me when you said the goods from your ship were stolen."

"What?"

"You said the ship was looted by pirates, but Grandmother's fabric arrived at our home this afternoon." Despite her anger, Laura was desperate for him to confirm her suspicions and free her of the worry that she had indeed conjured up the fabric. "You thought you could trick us into paying for the goods all over again."

"I wish that were true," he said with a halfhearted smile. "After losing the *Augusta*, I could stand to double my take on an entire shipload of cargo."

His reply cut her to the quick, and she cringed at the reminder of the consequences of her careless sorcery. Laura blinked at the sudden sting of tears, and bit down hard on her lip to stop the trembling. Fearing she might panic, Laura drew a steadying breath only to have a sob escape her throat.

"Shh, girl, don't cry." He moved beside her on the upholstered seat. "Be glad your grandmother regained her loss."

"I'm not crying," she managed, swallowing hard against the lump in her throat, but she felt the scalding of tears on her cheek.

His lips brushed softly against her face, teasing the corner of her mouth. She shivered as his fingers traced the sensitive flesh just below her ear, turning her face toward his. She hesitated only a moment, knowing she should push him away, but a flurry of longing unfurled within her and she raised her lips to his.

Shy at first, Laura gladly sank against him when he took control of the kiss. His mouth moved over hers, molding her lips like heated wax. She gasped slightly at the feel of his tongue, and he didn't hesitate to take advantage of her surprise.

Startled, Laura stiffened at the intrusion, but Simon gently coaxed her back into the dreamy state of desire. Gathering her close, his embrace was tender and reassuring, and her arms hung limp around his shoulders. He deepened the kiss, easing her back against the tufted seat of the carriage, and she whimpered against the onslaught.

"Captain Power," she gasped, tearing herself away from the kiss. "Please, we mustn't do this."

"Why not?" he murmured against her throat, not at all deterred by her protest. "Why not do this?"

Laura shuddered as the words feathered across her skin,

his lips finding the erratic pulse throbbing at the base of her throat. Her fingers knotted in the lapels of his coat, and his arms tightened around her.

"Laura, sweet, you enchant me."

Enchant. The word, like cold water, dashed over her and she froze in panic. "What?"

Unaware of her dismay, he trailed biting kisses across her throat. "I need you, more than I thought it possible for a man to want a woman."

The carriage slowed to a stop, and Laura scrambled away from him in hopes of dispelling the growing attraction that was clearly the result of a magic charm and not of any affection he felt for her. She grappled for the latch on the door. "You don't know what you're saying."

"Laura, wait!" He reached for her, but she dodged his touch and made her way down from the carriage. "I didn't mean to frighten you."

"This is all my fault, not yours," she assured him before closing the carriage door. "I'll make it right. I swear."

Simon hated being on the docks at night. The cold and the dampness were all too reminiscent of the London waterfront he'd escaped so many years before. He shuddered at the memory of rats scurrying down the alleys in search of scraps of food not claimed by the host of street urchins vying for survival.

Though he'd been born into that world, somehow he'd always known that there had to be something better; that children weren't supposed to eat out of rubbish bins, and mothers shouldn't reek of gin and urine. By the age of nine, Simon held no delusions about his circumstances, knowing that the only options before him were death or the work-houses.

So he fashioned his own alternative, running away to the sea. No matter how hard he was forced to work or how little he earned, he always had food in his belly and never again slept on cobblestones.

More unsettling than that memory was the thought that he could end up in the same wretched plight all over again.

With one ship looted and another lost at sea, everything he'd gained in the last ten years hovered on the brink of loss. Simon had never taken one comfort for granted, and he had no intention of standing by while all that he had worked for was plundered and sold out from under him.

He also had no intention of allowing Laura Stuart to be frightened away by the first fires of passion between them. He cursed himself as a rake, groping her like a randy teenager, but he had been quite unprepared for the desire that swept over him at the first taste of her sweet lips. The feel of her trembling in his arms had only served to stir his lust rather than cool his ardor. He would have a devil of a time proving to her that he was no blackguard.

Meanwhile, he'd been thinking about what Laura said about her missing fabric. If it was indeed stolen and had suddenly appeared, then someone here in Salem was disposing of cargo stolen from his ship and possibly others. He couldn't conceive of anyone being that brash or that foolish, but greed clouded wisdom often enough that he felt it worth his while to have a look around the docks for himself.

The wharfs that teemed with merchants and sailors during the day were eerily deserted after dark. Simon could hear the sound of men's voices coming from the tavern at the end of the row of wooden buildings, and a wedge of light spilled from the partially open doorway. He stood to learn much from the drunken conversation of sailors who might boast of their ill-gotten gains.

Before he could enter the tavern, he caught the unmistakable sound of hushed voices and shuffling boots further up the wharf. He gripped the carved handle of his pistol and silently approached the ship being unloaded without benefit of daylight or lanterns.

"I say, guv'nor, I wouldn't want to be unloading these goods here in me own backyard, if I was you," a hushed voice advised.

"Well, you are not me, and I won't turn away such a profit."

"Still, you'd be better selling off these goods in Boston or even Nantucket."

"Good evening, Elias," Simon called as he neared the huddled group. "Surely, you're not working late."

"Power, what on earth are you doing down here?"

The two men in Langdon's employ dropped their booty and turned to flee. Simon's pistol flashed in the dim moonlight, and he warned, "I wouldn't risk my life for another man's fortune."

Catching sight of the constable strolling by at the far end of the row of buildings, Simon called out, "Watch! Thieves on the dock!"

The constable quickly made his way to investigate, followed by a stream of curious gawkers from the tavern. The crowd of onlookers collected behind Simon, craning their necks for a better look.

"What's going on here?" a portly man demanded as he made his way through the crowd.

"A bit of midnight commerce, Magistrate," the constable explained. "Captain Power, here, claims these goods were stolen from his ship."

"A very serious charge, Captain." Henry Wyatt scanned the men congregated before him. "I hope you are prepared to prove that."

"Indeed, I am." Simon stepped forward and upended an overturned cask of molasses. "I can handily provide the bill of lading received by my first officer."

"That proves nothing!" Elias snarled. "We all deal in such goods."

"This keg still bears my seal."

Magistrate Wyatt bent to examine the crest burned into the wooden barrel and straightened with suspicion clear on his face. "Elias, what have you to say for yourself?"

"My reputation speaks for itself," he retorted in a haughty tone. "I have nothing to hide."

Wyatt nodded. "Then you won't object to having the ship searched."

Langdon paled visibly, but the magistrate did not wait for his answer. Instead, he turned to Simon. "Power, you and the constable go aboard with two other men and search the ship. Langdon and I will wait here.''

The search would only be a formality. Simon knew what he would find, and the seething anger in Langdon's eyes confirmed the conclusion.

Four

"A charm to secure the heart's desire."

Laura read the words over again, desperately trying to remember what exactly she had said while mending Simon's jacket. She had only meant to soothe her injured pride and dampen his arrogance with a harmless mishap such as a slip on the docks or a tumble into the water. She had also longed for a waltz and a chaste kiss.

If her wish for harm had manifested itself into tragedy, could her desire for admiration escalate into passion?

She closed the book and sank back against her pillow, tugging the covers more securely around her. Pale sunlight was peeking through the tiny window, and she could hear Grandmother bustling around downstairs. Laura's conscience stung at the thought of the sweet woman suffering the repercussions of having a granddaughter who dabbled in witchcraft.

She had never meant to harm anyone, and she wondered if it wouldn't be best to just destroy the book and pretend she had never discovered the trunk or its powerful contents. Running her fingers across the smooth leather binding, she decided against such action. The book was not evil, only dangerous in the hands of someone ignorant of its purpose. Since before dawn, she had carefully studied the verses, determined to learn the proper use of such magic.

Steeling herself against the morning chill, Laura threw back her blankets and rose from the bed. The floor was cold beneath her bare feet as she hurried to the washstand, and she gasped at the sting of cold water as she washed the sleep out of her eyes. The tiny mirror mounted over the washstand gave her a limited assessment of her appearance, and she wondered if it was vanity that made her long to believe that Simon might desire her without the benefit of witchcraft.

She combed and braided her sleep-tousled hair and smiled to herself at the memory of losing herself in his embrace. In his arms, she felt beautiful and alive, and she had to believe it was real and not the product of an incantation. Still, she couldn't go on deluding herself. If his attraction for her was not of his own choosing, she had to put an end to the magic.

Laura hurried through the task of getting dressed, trying to decide on a plausible excuse for leaving the shop this morning. She simply *had* to get her hands on that jacket. Once the seams were resewn and the curse undone, the spell on Captain Power would be lifted; perhaps his troubles would be reversed without the benefit of magic and his true feeling would also be revealed.

The thought gave her little comfort. What if cold indifference was all that remained? She wasn't certain she could dispose of her own feelings quite so easily. Not that she would have much choice. Laura had been most unprepared for the overwhelming rush of emotions for the handsome captain, and she had allowed them to take root in her heart. She smoothed her apron and searched out her shoes from under the bed.

If she didn't get that jacket and the spell went unchecked, the least of her troubles would be a broken heart.

"You'll have to take up the matter with Captain Power."

"Would you be his wife?"

"Certainly not." Mrs. Grundy glared at the troublesome peddler. "I am his housekeeper."

"Splendid! As this matter pertains to his household, you're just the person who can help." He lowered his voice, as though confiding a great secret. "You see, there's a little matter of a debt I owe the good captain. Twenty shillings, and I'm afraid I haven't the money."

"That is of no concern to me," she snapped. "I'm on my way for a holiday, and you are making me late."

"Beg your pardon, m'lady, but I was hoping Captain Power might accept goods rather than cash money."

Stepping out onto the back step, Mrs. Grundy closed the door behind her and pushed past the peddler. "You'll have to take the matter up with the captain. Now, step aside. I'll miss the stage to Boston."

Doffing his battered derby, the peddler bowed elegantly. "May I wish you Godspeed on your journey."

"Hmmph." Mrs. Grundy pushed her way down the steps and hurried toward the street.

The peddler smiled after her and replaced his well-worn hat upon his head. "I suppose this will be a matter for the captain, after all."

Binx began whistling a jolly tune as he returned from his cart with a young goat. The kid bleated in protest, straining against the rope, but he was soon tied to the iron railing. The old peddler gave the goat a fond chuck under the chin. "Now you wait right here for the captain, and maybe he'll learn not to be so demanding."

Laura smiled at one familiar face after another as she made her way through the streets of Salem. Friends and neighbors, one and all, they recognized her as the seamstress's granddaughter and accepted her as one of their own. What would they think if they knew she had stumbled into witchcraft?

She had heard whispered accounts from other girls about the witch trials. Old men and women recalled the spectacle from their childhood. Young girls had screamed in pain and cried out that a witch was pinching them or burning their hands, and on such accusations alone many were sent to the gallows.

Once, Laura had asked Grandmother about the witch hunts, but the older woman dismissed the happenings as a tragedy best forgotten.

If twenty-one possibly innocent people had been hung, what would happen if she was discovered to have cursed the fleets of Salem?

She rounded the corner toward Simon Power's home, more determined than ever to end the dreadful events she had set in motion. She had to get her hands on that coat, reset the sleeve, and reverse the spell. Her only challenge would be getting past the hateful housekeeper.

Laura decided that the more docile she appeared, the better chance she'd have of getting inside and acquiring the coat. Making her way to the delivery entrance, Laura froze at the sight waiting for her.

Tied to the railing, nibbling on a rosebush, a black and white spotted goat took no notice of her presence.

Lest he sail another boat, let him be a billy goat.

"Captain Power?" she finally managed in a strained whisper.

The goat looked up and gave an indignant bleat, quite irritated at being interrupted.

"Sweet merciful Lord," Laura breathed, her legs threatening to give way. She stumbled toward the steps and grasped the iron railing. The goat continued rooting through the withered rosebush, and Laura reached to touch the coarse hair along his back. "Oh, Captain Power, what have I done?"

Again, the goat only bleated, but Laura swore she saw accusation in his eyes. Wasting no time, Laura knew she had to get him inside before anyone saw and asked questions. With shaking fingers she struggled with the knotted rope and untied the poor creature.

Closing the door behind her, Laura looked about the dim kitchen. There was no sign of the housekeeper, and Laura prayed that she had not transformed the sour woman into a rat or worse. She tugged on the goat's lead, hurrying across the scoured floor, his cloven hooves clicking behind her.

"Mrs. Grundy?" she called out. "Mrs. Grundy?"

The house was empty.

"We must hurry, before Mrs. Grundy returns!" she whispered, urging the goat toward the stairs.

She couldn't worry about the housekeeper now. She had enough trouble as it was. She would hide Simon upstairs until she could return with the spell book. She shuddered to think what might have happened if someone other than herself had discovered the goat tied to the back steps.

Leading a goat up a narrow flight of stairs proved difficult, but she was more determined than he was stubborn.

"Get in here," she ordered, opening the door to the large bedroom at the end of the hall. The goat bleated in protest, but she shoved him inside and closed the door behind them. "I'm sorry, but no one can see you like this."

She took stock of the richly furnished room. Nothing ornate or pretentious, but the furniture was solid and polished to a high shine. She let the rope fall from her fingers and began searching desperately for the coat.

Laura glanced up to see the goat munching on the velvet draperies. "No, no," she scolded, catching the lead and gently turning him away from the window. "Oh, dear, Captain Power, how can I ever ask you to forgive me?"

A bowl and pitcher sat atop a marble stand and Laura poured a generous amount of water into the bowl. She dipped a cloth and found the water cool but not cold. Squeezing the excess liquid from the cloth, she turned to find the goat watching her warily.

"Do you understand what I'm saying?" Laura knelt before the creature, gazing into his striated eyes. She pressed the cloth against his brow. "Oh, Captain Power, I know this must be a terrible shock to you."

"Laura, I seriously doubt I should be surprised by anything you do."

At the sound of his voice, Laura scrambled to her feet and gaped at the captain, lounging in the doorway of his own bedroom. The goat bolted and charged for freedom, barely avoiding a collision with Simon in the process.

"What are you doing here?" she demanded.

To her surprise, he laughed. "I find you in my bedroom, nursing a goat you call by my name, and *you* ask for an explanation."

Downstairs, the sound of hooves clattering across the floor was quickly followed by the sound of breaking glass. Laura dashed past the bemused captain and hurried to round up the goat. The wayward creature stood at the bottom of the stairs, feasting on a scattered bouquet of flowers lying in a pool of water and broken china.

"You wicked beast," she hissed, taking up his lead before the goat could bolt again. She tugged on the rope, but the goat stood fast, refusing to be hauled away from his ill-gotten meal. With a firm swat on his rump, Laura persuaded him otherwise.

Laura led him through the kitchen, opened the back door, and shooed the goat out into the courtyard. Her entire body was trembling with anger and relief, and she would have bolted out the door herself if she hadn't remembered that she needed the jacket.

She peered inside the bedroom to find Simon leaning over the bowl of water, stripped to the waist. Her heart skipped at least two beats and then began a rapid tattoo beneath her breast. He splashed water on his face, and she watched in fascination as several rivulets escaped the towel and coursed down his throat, sluicing over his chest.

He glanced in her direction and smiled slightly. "Did he escape?"

"Escape?" she murmured. Then she remembered. "The goat! Oh, I put him outside."

At his doubtful expression, she merely offered, "He was here when I arrived."

He tossed the towel aside. "I'll speak to Mrs. Grundy about that."

Laura swallowed and breathed a prayer that he wouldn't ask her as to the housekeeper's whereabouts. On a chair in the corner, she noticed he had tossed the very jacket for which she was searching. Nonchalantly, she crossed the room and stood near the chair. "I came to apologize for making a scene last night. I should never have come to the tavern, and I can understand if you are angry with me.''

''On the contrary, Laura. I am deeply indebted to you.''
She stared up at him. ''I don't understand.''

''If you hadn't alerted me to the appearance of your grandmother's shipment, I would never have suspected that the goods stolen from the *Tradewind* were here in Salem.''

''How is that possible?''

''Elias Langdon has been running a very profitable smuggling ring. Selling stolen goods, sometimes to the very merchants from whose ships the goods were stolen.''

''And you're certain of this?''

''I went to the docks myself last night,'' he explained. ''There I caught him red-handed with cargo from my ship and others. The magistrate seized the lot of it, but I'll be able to claim what's mine after the proceedings.''

She forced a shaky smile and said, ''I'm happy you've had good fortune.''

''I certainly didn't expect to find you waiting for me.'' He closed the distance between them and took her hands in his.

Laura swallowed hard, not knowing how to answer. The truth, that she had come to search his home and steal the cursed jacket, was only complicated by the fact that she had feared he had been transformed into a billy goat.

''You don't have to explain,'' he whispered, drawing her gently against him. His lips hovered above hers.

This kiss was languid and warm, stealing all thought of escape from Laura's mind. She sank against him, welcoming the feel of his arms about her, and returned the embrace. Simon deepened the kiss, and she whimpered into his mouth, clinging to his broad shoulders.

The feel of his naked flesh beneath her hands sent shivers up her arms, and she breathed the scent of his skin. His hand rose to her breast, cupping the fullness in his palm, and Laura's resolve melted at the heat of his touch burning through her clothes.

Catching her limp body against his, Simon held her still while his fingers sought the laces of her bodice. Dazed with passion, Laura struggled to recall why she shouldn't allow

him the liberty, but all that filled her brain was the need
for his touch. His kiss.

Lifting her off the floor, Simon crossed the room and
placed her on the bed. He gathered her in his arms and
kissed her with a hunger that caused them both to shudder.
His fingers grew more intent in their quest to free her from
her garments, and Laura gasped at the feel of his lips trailing the expanse of her exposed flesh, her pulse quickening
beneath his fingertips. Her own hands smoothed over his
bare shoulders, and her fingers tangled in his dark hair to
hold him closer. The heat of his tongue on her flesh
wrenched a strangled cry from her lips, and she shuddered
as his lips closed over her nipple.

His hands continued their task of freeing her from her
remaining underclothes, and her belly quivered as his
roughened palm slid over her navel toward the juncture of
her thighs. Even as his fingers delved into the moist, hidden
recesses of her body, Simon transferred his attention to her
other breast, drowning her in an onslaught of passion.

Only when she began to move against his hand, straining
toward something she didn't understand, did he kiss her
once again, his tongue mating with hers. Slowly, he broke
the kiss, gazing into her eyes with a heated gaze, and drew
her hand to caress his throbbing flesh. Laura was awed by
the feel of his shaft pulsing against her palm, warm and
smooth, and was aroused by the desire that flickered in his
eyes at her inexperienced touch.

"Laura, sweet," he groaned, easing himself between her
thighs. She started at the feel of his manhood throbbing
against her aching flesh, and the first tentative thrust caused
her to gasp in alarm. He kissed her lightly, reassuring her,
"I've only given you a glimpse of ecstasy; let me show
you all there is between a man and a woman."

Simon took her lips in a kiss that claimed her body and
soul, opening her to his intrusion, and she clung to his
broad shoulders as their bodies joined in exquisite union.
He held himself still, allowing her tender virgin flesh to
adjust to his presence.

Laura dared not breathe, fearing her body would shatter

from the spasms of pain mingled with pleasure, a pleasure that rose swiftly and coursed within her. The sharp discomfort eased and heat pooled in her loins as Simon began to move within her. With a gentle and coaxing touch, he smoothed his palm down the length of her thigh and twined her limbs over his narrow hips.

He surged deeply within her, and Laura writhed beneath his weight even as she arched her body to receive him fully. His dark hair fell loose from its queue and feathered across her breast as he lowered his lips to the rosy peak. All she could do was cling to his broad shoulders and surrender to the growing tension that lifted her higher and higher.

His patience and control never wavered, and he moved within her with deliberate, tormenting ease. Her lower body tightened and strained against him, and still the ache worsened, wrenching a keening cry of need from her throat. He kissed her deeply and began moving with an urgency that matched her own.

Without warning, her body shattered as if from her very soul, and her arms fell limp at her sides. Her eyes blinked open to see his body gripped with the same excruciating pleasure, the muscles in his arms quivering as they bore his weight.

Ripples of pleasure passed over her, but Laura's heart sank when he whispered, "What spell have you cast over me, woman?"

A cry of dismay rose in her throat but was absorbed by a lingering kiss as he gathered her close in his embrace. She lay in uncertain stillness, not daring to speak or move, and listened to the steady rhythm of his heart. His lips nuzzled the tender flesh at her throat, and his breathing, at last, grew shallow as he gave way to sleep.

Laura studied the rugged lines of his features, softened by sleep and dark lashes that feathered against his face, and slipped from his arms when she was certain that he slept too soundly to notice. The temptation was great to remain in his arms, their bodies twined, and pretend that what they had shared was real and believe that it promised more.

That it wasn't witchcraft.

Laura hurried to gather her clothes and dress, moving silently about the room. Before turning to leave, she retrieved the cursed jacket from the corner chair and folded it over her arm. Pressing the garment close to her side, Laura knew this might be her only hope of undoing the spell and reversing Simon's misfortune. But his desire for her would also be reversed.

Tears threatened at the thought, but she refused to allow herself even an instant of self-pity. Simon would see her as a stranger, recalling nothing of the passion that had consumed them, but that would be a little more than she deserved for misusing a power she barely knew.

Laura's hands trembled so that she feared she would never thread her needle, let alone finish the mountain of tasks before her. Grandmother had declared that this would be the day that they would complete the work remaining for Charity Wyatt's wedding. Try as she might to concentrate on the delicate stitches, her mind wandered to Simon Power.

She shuddered at the memory of her wanton behavior, but nothing could have prepared her for the searing desire ignited by just one kiss. Admittedly, her experience in passion was limited to a few clumsy kisses from youthful suitors, but there was only one explanation for the fiery response that led to seduction.

Witchcraft.

The very thought caused her to pull so hard on the needle that the thread snapped. She hurried to tie off the broken thread and rethread the needle, but she glanced up to find Grandmother eyeing her curiously. Laura managed a bland smile and returned her attention to the lace cuff she was stitching.

She had enchanted him. Simon had said so himself, though she suspected the words had been more of passion than accusation. Still, the realization had struck her like a bolt from the blue. Her spell would bring Simon nothing but misfortune and all the while attract him to her, the very source of his calamity. She was beholden to undo the spell.

She would remove every stitch she had sewn into his coat, and remake the seams with thread from an unbroken skein and a new needle. With that the spell would be lifted, she prayed, and Simon would remember nothing of her.

Tears stung her eyes at the thought and her vision blurred.

"Laura, is something troubling you, dear?"

Grandmother's voice broke through the cloud of worry, and Laura glanced up, unsure how to answer. She swallowed hard against the knot at the back of her throat, and managed a raspy reply. "No, ma'am."

"I think I know what it is."

Laura's hands went still and she dared not look up from her work. "You do?"

Grandmother set aside the gown she was working on and crossed the room to stand before her granddaughter. Catching Laura's trembling chin in her hand, the older woman forced Laura's troubled gaze to meet her own reassuring one. "You're having misgivings about going to the dance at the Wyatts', aren't you?"

Laura nodded slightly, realizing that she had completely forgotten about the grand ball to be held in honor of Charity Wyatt's impending marriage. Had it really been only days since she was enthralled with the prospect of attending such a lavish affair?

"Perhaps I would be better off not attending," she suggested.

"Nonsense. You'll have a wonderful time." Grandmother smiled down at her. "Besides, Mistress Wyatt would be most offended if you declined her invitation."

With a sigh, Laura shrugged and let her hands fall limply to her lap. The lace dangled over her knees, and she was not at all cheered by the prospect of music and dancing.

"I have a surprise that might change your mind."

Laura watched her grandmother cross the sewing shop and lift the lid of a pine chest used for storage. She withdrew a bundle wrapped in brown paper and placed it on the cutting table, smiling to herself as she began to untie the string that held the bundle together.

"I remember when your mother was not much older than you are now," Grandmother spoke softly. "She was invited to a grand party, but she was such a shy thing I feared she wouldn't attend. I knew that with a little encouragement, she would be the loveliest young lady there."

Laying the paper aside, Grandmother held up a gown of midnight-blue silk, trimmed in exquisite gold stitches, and smiled at Laura. "The dress I made for her was just as lovely, but I do believe your beauty will outshine hers."

"Oh, my," Laura breathed, reaching for the dress. With trembling hands, she held it to her shoulders and peered into the mirror. " 'Tis so beautiful! How were you able to fit it without having me try it on?"

"My dear, I had only to copy the dress I made for you this spring." Grandmother chuckled at Laura's delight and smoothed the skirt over Laura's drab work dress. "I wanted to surprise you, but now I'll have you try it on for the final fitting."

"You're so good to me." Laura embraced the older woman, crushing the gown between them. She choked back a sob and held tight. "I never wanted to disappoint you."

Grandmother pulled back and studied her face. "Child, what's this talk of disappointing me?"

"I've done something awful," Laura confessed, before her courage could fail. Tears stung her eyes and spilled down her face before she could think to blink them away. "I'm so ashamed."

Grandmother laid the dress aside and led Laura to a chair and bid her to sit and calm herself. "Tell me what's happened, child."

Laura did, babbling like a child. She told of finding the trunk and the mysterious contents, of wanting to help Mistress Tupper, and of her encounter with Simon Power. At last she drew a ragged breath and said, "I never meant to cause such misfortune."

"Sounds to me the captain needed to learn a lesson."

Astonished, Laura gaped at her grandmother, who only smiled and patted her hand. "You're not angry with me?"

"No, child, I blame myself for not teaching you about

such things." She laced their fingers and squeezed Laura's hand. "The old ways are curious, and there's much I don't understand. The things in the trunk belonged to my mother, and she was reluctant to teach me more than I had to know."

"I should have asked you about the trunk." Laura accepted the handkerchief Grandmother held out to her and dried her eyes. "Now, I can only hope to undo the damage I've done."

"You can, my dear, if your heart is in the right place."

Five

"Would you like to have another look around, Captain?"

Simon scanned the stockpiled warehouse. "No, we've taken stock of everything and this is all that I can claim."

The magistrate nodded in approval as he read over the list of goods Simon was claiming for the *Tradewind*. "Most men in your position wouldn't feel obligated to be so . . . selective."

"I only want what's rightfully mine." Simon chose to appreciate Henry Wyatt's candor rather than glean an insult from the blunt remark. "I'm certain you'll find that to be the case with most people."

"I would have thought the same of Langdon up until yesterday." Wyatt shook his head at the unpleasantness. "I'm sure you're aware that Elias has enough clout to escape prosecution. He'll maintain that he had no knowledge of the goods being stolen, and no one can prove otherwise."

"Even though everyone knows better."

"A tarnished reputation is a severe punishment for a man like Langdon." He rolled up the sheet of parchment and tapped it against his palm. "Once word gets around that he was supplying the British army with goods stolen from our own ships, he won't find Salem a profitable place to do business."

Simon considered the statement and agreed that Langdon would indeed leave Salem. "Of course, that will mean his buyers will be in need of a new supplier."

Wyatt smiled. "A wise man sees opportunity in times of difficulty."

With a smile of his own, Simon shook the magistrate's hand. "I do appreciate your assistance in this matter."

"Indeed, many in Salem will be beholden to you for exposing this piracy." Wyatt turned and led the way out of the warehouse. "I should think there will be many anxious to do business with you. Perhaps, you would attend a party at my home tomorrow evening. My wife and I are honoring the upcoming marriage of our youngest daughter."

It went without saying that every prominent man of business and politics would be in attendance, and Simon's presence would clearly be seen as a nod of favor from Magistrate Wyatt. "I'd be delighted."

"Splendid."

Once again, they shook hands, and Simon turned toward the docks. His luck was definitely on the mend, and he scanned the crowd, hoping to catch sight of Chauncy. Nearing the wharf, he could hear the old sailor's gravelly voice grating the air with a myriad of obscenities, and Simon followed the stream of curses until he found Chauncy and the subject of his displeasure.

"I'll not listen to any more of your bloody lies!"

A hapless seaman stood before the old man, a coil of rope hoisted on each shoulder. "I swear to you, Chauncy, we're doing the best we can!"

Both men turned as Simon approached, and Chauncy was quick to involve Simon in the dispute. "We'll never have the *Tradewind* back in the water with no one willing to work on her, sir."

"We're breaking our backs on this bleedin' ship," the seaman insisted. "Nothing pleases this old bugger."

Chauncy's face turned purple, but Simon intervened before real damage could be done. "Carry on with what you're doing, sailor, but I expect you to follow orders.''

"Yes, sir," he replied before turning back toward the disabled ship.

"I never thought I'd see the day you turned soft on slackers.'' Chauncy's voice was thick with accusation. His eyes narrowed when Simon chuckled, and he demanded, "What's so funny?''

"Things are looking up, friend. I've recovered most of the cargo from the *Tradewind*.''

Chauncy was quick to point out, "That won't make up for losing the *Augusta*.''

Simon nodded. "No, but it will ease the blow. You have the *Reliant* ready to sail for Philadelphia by tomorrow. I want to have a look at the new ship and make sure the work is going on schedule.''

Chauncy made a face. He had been none to pleased by Simon's decision to have the new ship built in Philadelphia. "If you'd had the work done here in Salem you wouldn't have to be running back and forth to see after things.''

"It never hurts to broaden your horizons.''

Confident, Simon left the docks and headed home, unable to resist hoping that he might find Laura waiting for him once again. He cursed himself for the hundredth time for falling asleep and letting her leave without assurance that she would return. The house was dark and empty when he arrived, and disappointment caught him off guard.

He'd purchased the spacious town house within a year of settling in Salem, and it was by far the nicest home in which he'd ever lived. Much of the original furniture had remained in the house, and Mrs. Grundy saw to the upkeep. This was the first time he'd ever felt anything lacking, and he knew why.

Laura wasn't here.

He couldn't help but smile at the memory of finding her in his room and the image of her chasing after the rambunctious goat. The smile faded as he thought about the events that followed. She was sweet and innocent and he had taken her virtue with no consideration for the consequences she might face.

One thing was certain. He had to find her before leaving for Philadelphia.

"Good evening, Laura." Mistress Wyatt took her hands and beamed at the arrival of her new guest. "Don't you look lovely?"

"Thank you, Mistress Wyatt." Laura curtsied properly. "I'm honored to be here."

Henry Wyatt stood at his wife's side and also welcomed Laura to their home.

Laura caught sight of Charity Wyatt and her betrothed holding court at the far end of the room. Dutifully, she made her way toward them and hoped that she would be able to offer her sincere congratulations and escape with only a minimal account of how glorious their wedding would be.

"Laura, how sweet of you to come." Charity took her hands and beamed as Laura complimented her appearance. Taking the arm of her soon-to-be husband, she explained, "William, darling, this is Laura Stuart, our little seamstress."

He nodded awkwardly, as if he'd just been introduced to the maid. Charity tittered at his indifference and informed Laura, "Men just don't care about such matters. All they talk about is politics and farming."

Laura managed to keep the smile on her face, though her cheeks stung from the effort. She had promised Grandmother that she would enjoy the party, but she was already concocting an excuse to leave early. Thankfully, Prudence Rutherford appeared at her side and spared her further conversation with Charity.

They made their way across the room, Prudence leading Laura toward the long table laden with food. "Just look at this! There must be at least five different kinds of meat and a dozen desserts."

Laura accepted a cup of sweet apple cider and savored the taste. "I'm not very hungry."

"Well, I am," Prudence declared and began serving herself from the buffet. "I have to tell you, that dress is beautiful. Your grandmother made it, didn't she?''

"Of course." Laura smiled at her friend. "Thanks for rescuing me."

" 'Twas no trouble." Prudence bit into a tiny spice cake, and Laura caught the sweet scent of maple. "Charity can't enjoy being happy unless someone envies her for it."

They shared guilty smiles and Laura glanced back at Charity, who still held tight to William's arm. They would be happy, and Laura did envy them. Regret for what might have been stung unexpectedly; if only she'd not ruined things with Simon before they even had a chance to bloom.

In the corner, two fiddlers began a lively tune, and a few bold young couples began to dance. Others soon joined, and a dashing young man hurried to claim Prudence for his partner.

Laura looked on and smiled after her friend. Raising her glass to her lips, she let her gaze travel the room, skimming the whirling dancers and lighting on a group of men gathered near the doorway. Standing in the center of that circle was Simon Power, receiving a hero's welcome. Magistrate Wyatt himself clapped Simon on the back and made a great show of calling another man over to be introduced.

She swallowed hard, nearly choking on the cider, and began looking for a means of escape. She couldn't bear to have Simon see her here tonight. His rebuff would hurt enough without the added humiliation of a public rejection. The back door leading out into the garden had been propped open for ventilation, and she took the only route available.

The chill of the night air made her gasp, but she remained in the shadows. She would wait long enough for the men to assemble somewhere other than the entrance and then make her escape. She craned her neck to see them still standing there, hanging on Simon's every word. He glanced in the direction of the back door, and she skittered away from the light spilling out of the house.

The garden was bleak in late autumn, and Laura's spirits only dampened as she contemplated the mess she had gotten herself into. She had returned the charm book to the attic, promising herself and Grandmother that she would never again meddle with witchcraft, but curiosity lingered. If one was careful and selective, much good could be accomplished, and she wondered if she would ever have the courage to seek answers in the tiny book again.

"Laura?"

She started at the sound of his voice and turned to find Simon standing not two feet away from her.

He clasped her shoulders and brushed a kiss against her forehead. "I've been looking everywhere for you."

Her heart sank. The spell had not been broken, and danger still loomed before him. Laura knew she had to do something before the spell brought misfortune and ruin to the man she loved.

The need to feel his arms about her was great, but she dodged his embrace. "I didn't know that you knew the Wyatts."

"I met Henry Wyatt through business," he explained. Awkward silence fell between them, and he drew nearer. "Laura, you left before I had a chance—"

"Please, Captain Power." She turned away from him, her throat burning with misery. "We mustn't speak of what happened."

She stiffened at the feel of his hands on her arms and shuddered as he lowered his lips to her neck. "I'll not speak of it then. What words could say more than this?"

The feel of his mouth trailing along her throat drew a sigh of pleasure from her lips, and she winced, for she knew he heard. He turned her toward him, gathering her into the warmth of his embrace.

"'Tis a cold night," he murmured against her ear. "Let's go inside for a dance."

"No, please. I can't." She pushed herself out of his arms and tried to think what she should do. The spell had not been broken, and disaster surely loomed ahead. "I must go home."

"Let me drive you," he insisted. "I've plenty of time before leaving."

"Leaving?" The word made her breath catch.

"For Philadelphia," he explained. "I'm sailing out to-night."

"You can't!" she exclaimed, horrified by the thought of Simon sailing off with a witch's curse hanging over his head.

For the first time, she reached for him and clutched at the sleeves of his coat. It wasn't the same one she had resewn and secretly returned to his home earlier, and her brain seized upon the possibility that he would have to wear the coat before the spell would be broken.

"I must make inspection of a ship being built. I'll only be gone a week," he assured her, drawing her near. "Will you be waiting for me when I return?"

If you return . . .

The thought wouldn't form, and she shook her head fervently.

"I don't understand. You don't want me to go, but you won't be here for me when I return."

Passages from the charm book whirled in her head, and she desperately tried to think of someway to safeguard his journey. *"A charm to bind an enemy . . . a charm to recall the faithless . . . to secure the heart's desire—"*

That was it! Simon was her heart's desire and she could protect him with the spell. Surely, Grandmother would understand. She would need some personal object of his and she hadn't much time.

Laura grasped the front of his jacket and twisted fiercely at one of the gold buttons, ripping it loose in her hand. He stepped back and gaped at her, too astonished to speak. An explanation was warranted, but nothing plausible came to mind and the truth was unspeakable.

He seized her by the shoulders and drew her roughly against him. "Bloody hell, woman, are you daft?"

Laura twisted from his grasp and ran into the house and out the door, past the startled party guests and the magistrate himself. Heedless of appearances, she hurried home to the only hope she could claim.

•   •   •

Laura stole along the shadowed street, grateful for the clouds that dimmed the moonlight. She had changed into a heavy woolen dress, but the night air on the docks was biting cold. Her woolen cloak was soon weighted down with dampness, and she shuddered as the cold seeped into her bones.

If she had truly cursed anyone, she was beginning to believe it had been herself. Every time she touched the book of charms, she found herself mired deeper in the quandary than before. To her dismay, the book revealed that a charm cast to replace another charm required a lock of hair from the intended. Simon had thought her daft for ripping a button from his jacket; no doubt he would think her mad for wanting to cut his hair.

She hesitated outside the tavern entrance, remembering the unpleasant reception she had received from the man Simon called MacMillan. She also remembered the warmth of the room, and she longed to warm herself before the great stone fireplace, even if Simon wasn't there.

It would only be long enough to dry out her cloak, she reasoned, and then she could continue her search for Simon and try to explain everything to him. She slipped inside and closed the heavy door behind her, absorbing the heat that rushed to greet her.

Her respite, however, was short-lived. The burly tavern-keeper lumbered toward her, a scowl drawing his bushy eyebrows together.

"See here, woman. I've no tolerance for the likes of you."

Laura tossed the hood of her cloak from her head and glared at him. "I'm looking for Captain Power."

Recognition did nothing to soften the man's glare. "He hasn't been in. Be gone!"

She glanced toward the roaring fire. "May I wait for him?"

"Not in my place! I told you before—"

"MacMillan! How can you be so heartless?"

Laura and MacMillan turned in the direction of the voice. An older man made his way toward them, a kindly smile warming his face. "The poor child is half frozen. What harm will it do to let her wait by the fire?"

Laura smiled gratefully, and the tavernkeeper only grunted in reply. She sank to the bench and stretched her toes toward the fire. Tingles of warmth scampered up her limbs, and she already dreaded going back out into the cold.

"Here, child, this will warm you up."

She glanced up to see the man who had come to her defense holding out a pewter mug. She hesitated and he explained, "A wee drop of whiskey in a cup of tea."

Accepting the cup, she held it tightly with both hands before raising the steaming brew to her lips. The strong taste of liquor was a shock, but the warmth pooling in her belly was welcome. "Thank you, sir."

"Did I hear you say you were waiting for Captain Power?" he asked, joining her on the bench. "Simon Power?"

"Yes, I must find him before he sails for Philadelphia."

"Philadelphia?"

"He's going to inspect a ship that's being built there."

"I see." He paused thoughtfully. "Perhaps you'd do better to wait for him aboard his boat."

She hadn't thought of that. "I doubt I could find it at night."

"I'll wager he's taking the ketch, what with the *Tradewind* disabled and the *Augusta* lost at sea." He rose to his feet. "I'll be happy to take you to the *Reliant* myself."

The glaring reminder of the misfortune she'd brought Simon prompted her to her feet. She must either persuade him not to sail or take a lock of his hair. Neither task would be easy, but she wouldn't risk his life. The man offered his arm and she accepted. "Thank you for your help, sir. You're a friend of Captain Power?"

"Yes, an old friend," he replied, leading her out of the tavern. "Elias Langdon."

Laura was anxious to find Simon, but Mr. Langdon was in no hurry. He strolled casually down the dock, obviously familiar with the layout. At last, he halted before a small ketch and raised a finger to his lips.

"Perhaps you should wait here," he suggested in a hushed whisper. "I'll go aboard and see if the captain is there and then send him out to you. A ship is no place for a lady."

Without waiting for her answer, he turned and made his way aboard the ship, disappearing into the shadows. She paced the length of the wharf, huddling deeply inside her cloak. Voices rose from the *Reliant*, and she strained her ears to listen for Simon.

"I told you to get those crates below deck!"

"I can't store cargo and mend rigging at the same time!"

A stream of curses followed along with raucous laughter. Shadowed figures scurried along the deck, but she recognized neither Simon nor Mr. Langdon.

"All hands on deck!" a voice cried loudly. "Prepare to sail."

They were leaving! Mr. Langdon was still aboard and she had seen nothing of Simon. She hesitated only a second before racing down the gangplank. The hands were running to and fro and took no notice of her darting on board. She ducked behind a stack of wooden crates and prayed she would not be discovered before she could find Simon.

The ship groaned and heaved away from the dock, and Laura felt the deck sway beneath her. They were moving at a good clip, and the dock became farther and farther away. She had to find Simon before it was too late to turn back.

Slipping from her hiding place, Laura darted toward a narrow doorway she had seen men enter and went in search of the captain. She heard voices at the end of the dimly lit passageway and hurried in their direction.

"We've a good wind, Captain, and we'll make fine time."

"Good, Chauncy. The sooner we reach Philadelphia, the better."

"Simon," she called. "Simon, you mustn't go."

The two men gaped at her, and she rushed forward, offering no explanation. Simon was wearing the jacket she had mended and she prayed it was a good omen. " 'Tis dangerous," she insisted. "You must turn back."

"God's blood, a woman!" The older man called Chauncy took a step back. "She speaks the truth. I'll not sail with a female on board."

Simon glared at him and turned back to Laura. "I hope you can explain yourself."

"I can't let you go." She clasped her hands before her, unable to meet his gaze. "Please turn back and I'll explain everything."

Before he could answer, shouts came from up on deck. "Fire! Fire on deck!"

Simon grabbed her by the shoulders and demanded, "What have you done?"

"Nothing," she wailed, hoping it was the truth. A fire could consume the ship and leave them all for dead. "Believe me. I never meant for this to happen."

"There's not time for woman's talk!" Chauncy bellowed. "We'd best get on deck and put that fire out."

The men hurried up the narrow stairs, leaving Laura alone in the darkened passageway. Her insides were quaking and she rushed after Simon. The scene on deck was chaos, and she was nearly trampled by two sailors hauling buckets of water toward the flames climbing toward the billowing sails.

Smoke filled the night air and Laura choked on the odor of burning rope. A deckhand collided with her and knocked her to the plank flooring. She lay dazed for a moment, but she could breathe easier. Crawling out of the way, she huddled against a coil of wet rope and prayed for mercy.

The smoke began to clear and she caught sight of Simon throwing a bucketful of water on a dying flame. He tossed the bucket aside and rubbed the soot from his eyes. Laura breathed a sigh of relief that gave way to a cry of alarm.

Elias Langdon loomed behind Simon, wielding a club. Laura cried out, "Simon, behind you!"

He barely dodged the blow, and Langdon whirled to repeat the attack. Simon anticipated his move and ducked the swinging club but wasted no time in landing a fist in the man's belly. Langdon doubled over, dropping the club, and lunged toward Simon.

Laura rushed forward, her legs wobbly, and collided with Langdon. They fell to the deck, and Langdon's elbow made contact with Laura's forehead. She saw stars, and a fine mist whirled before her eyes.

"Laura!" Simon cried, and she tried to turn in the direction of his voice. She heard shouts and curses from every direction and the crack of a pistol split the air. The acrid smell of gunpowder burned her nostrils, and she strained to crawl to her knees.

"Laura."

His voice came again, soft and near. She felt his hands on her shoulders and blinked her eyes open to stare into his face. "Please don't leave. I don't want anything to happen to you."

"No, I'm not leaving," he assured her. "How did you know the ship was in danger?"

"I caused it," she confessed. "I caused everything."

"Nonsense," he whispered. He moved away from her long enough to remove his coat, and he gently slipped the garment around her shoulders. "Chauncy, fetch a blanket. She's in shock."

Grateful for the warmth, Laura dimly realized the coat was the very one that had held the spell. She hugged the garment around her, hoping to absorb any errant magic lest it cause Simon more misfortune.

As the ship slowly returned to the dock at Salem, Laura huddled beneath a coarse blanket, fighting off the chill that had nothing to do with the cold. Langdon was dead and Simon's ship was badly damaged. Spell or no spell, Simon would never want to see her again, and she struggled to remind herself that this was what she had set out to accomplish.

She looked up to see him approaching and her stomach knotted in apprehension. He stood before her, unsmiling, and said, "We're lucky to be alive. Even if the ship hadn't burned, the damage could have easily been worse, causing her to sink.''

When she said nothing, he pressed, ''Do you know what this means?''

She nodded miserably, unable to look at him.

''It will be at least a week before I can set sail for Philadelphia.''

Again, she nodded.

''Can you be ready to leave by then?''

Her head came up at that, startled. ''I don't understand.''

''I'm almost afraid to sail without you,'' he quipped, reaching out to tuck a damp lock of hair behind her ear. ''My luck is turning for the good, and I must have you to thank.''

Laura smiled weakly as his palm cupped her face. The spell was indeed broken, and he still loved her. Still, she needed confirmation. ''You want me to go with you?''

''You don't think I'll sail off and leave you behind where I can't keep an eye on you?''

She reached for him, her hands shaking. ''Simon, I promise. I'll never cause you another moment of worry.''

He gathered her close and smiled. ''Now, why don't I believe that?''

A Spell of
Mist and Roses

Amy Elizabeth Saunders

One

"For the sake of God, Kit . . . nay, for the sake of our friendship—just sign the damned paper!"

Christopher felt the tension behind his forehead tighten and pull. His eyes were hot and dry as they fastened on the king.

The famous Tudor temper was about to explode. He could see it in Henry's hard, glittering stare, in the tight way he held his mouth. He had seen it happen hundreds of times in his thirty-four years, but never before had the rage been directed at him.

He searched the face before him again, hoping for some trace of his friend, of golden Prince Hal, with whom he had ridden and laughed and sung innumerable ballads over innumerable tankards of ale.

But his friend was gone, and in his place was a king. The golden hair was streaked with gray, the face was hard, and bitter lines traced the once-happy eyes. Hal was forevermore gone, and in his place sat his most sovereign lord King Henry the Eighth, ruler of England and Ireland, defender of the faith . . . and if Kit signed the accursed paper before him, head of the church.

It was not so much the disavowal of the pope that rankled Christopher as the falseness of it. Henry wanted his divorce.

The pope, quite reasonably, had refused. And so there would be no pope, nor priests, nor monks, nor nuns in their convents. The church would be cast aside by the king in the same way he had cast aside his childhood toys. The way he had cast aside his wife and daughter.

He was no saint, Christopher Radbourne, and no martyr; but he was honest, and he was true. And he much misliked being bullied.

"May I remind you of the penalties, if you refuse, my lord?"

At the sound of the cloying voice, Kit shot a hard look at Cardinal Wolsey, who sat behind the king (as he ever did, these days) looking like nothing so much as a suet pudding in red velvet.

Kit didn't bother to restrain a sneer. "It is not so easy for some of us, my lord, to cast off loyalties of years." He deliberately turned away from the cardinal, back to the king. "I beg of you, Your Grace . . . for the sake of the years I have been your friend, and the truth I have always shown you . . . do not ask me to sign this thing."

The Tudor temper raged into the king's face with a crimson flood, and might have erupted if Wolsey had not spoken again.

"We need no more Thomas Moores, young man."

If the thought of Thomas Moore, sitting in his cell in the tower, awaiting death for refusing to sign the Oath of Supremacy, was intended to shake Christopher, Wolsey had overplayed his hand.

Instead, it shook the king. Bitterness and sorrow flooded the hard eyes, and for a moment, Kit caught a glimpse of the young man he had once known.

Wolsey started to speak again, but Henry silenced him with an upraised hand. He sat like that for a moment, sorrow on his face, the rings on his finger sparkling in the candlelight.

"No," he said. "We will have no more Thomas Moores."

He met Christopher's eyes for the first time in all that long night, fully and sadly. "A king," he said finally, "can ill afford enemies, Kit. But, by God, a king has only one friend, and that is his crown.''

And then, while Wolsey stood glowering and Kit stood silently, carefully devoid of expression and waiting for the blow to fall, Henry gestured to his secretary, whose scratching quill recorded the fateful words the king spoke next.

''I, Henry, king of England, Wales, and Ireland, by the grace of God, *et cetera*, do order the following. That having incurred the King's wrath, Christopher Radbourne shall remove himself from our presence at Hatfield, and furthermore remove himself from the city of London, and the county of Kent, not to return until the king's pleasure.''

Christopher's face began a slow burn, as the years of loyalty and friendship were cast aside.

Then the king spoke again, uttering the words that would change his life forever.

''And more, I strip you of all lands and titles I have heretofore granted you, including Earl of Sherborn and Lathrop, all your holdings and incomes thereof, and also your holdings in Radbourne Green, Langdon, and East Putnam.''

Everything, gone. Kit stood like a ship buffeted by a storm, hollow and floating.

''Out of our grace and mercy, we allow you to retain . . .'' The king hesitated, frowning, his plump jeweled fingers sorting through a stack of papers. Deeds and titles of holdings flashed before Kit's eyes.

''. . . your estate at North Farwindale and any incomes thereof. And may God have mercy on your soul.''

Christopher bowed with careful dignity, accepting the paper handed to him. He did not trust himself to speak.

He left the room with head high, not breathing until he heard the doors close softly behind him.

He had entered the room a rich man, a favorite confidant of the king, and left a veritable pauper. Except for this . . . this . . .

He squinted at the paper in his hand.

''God's nightgown!'' he bellowed. ''Walter!''

His manservant appeared, pale and tense with waiting. ''Sir?''

Kit handed him the deed with the same distaste with which he would have handled a dead rat.

"Where, in the name of God, is this *Farwindale*?" he asked, as if he were asking the way to the bowels of hell.

And when he saw it, three weeks later, he thought he might as well have.

TWO

"I should have gone to the tower."

Kit stared at the castle with stark horror. Actually, *castle* was the wrong word. It may have been a castle at one time, but the whole of it would not have contained the stables from his estates at Radbourne. The thick walls and crumbling stones of the watchtowers looked as if they hadn't been repaired since the days of the Norman Conquest. The small moat was choked with reeds and green muck.

The surrounding trees had grown up and over the mossy walls, so that any invader (though who would ever want to invade such a squalid place was beyond Kit's comprehension) need only have climbed through the forest brambles and up through the overhanging branches.

Rain poured from the gray northern skies, and over the crumbling towers of the keep and the heavy trees surrounding it. It streamed over Kit's head, soaking his heavy cape so that the fur collar smelled like a wet dog. He pulled his useless cap from his dark hair, regarded the pathetic strings that had once been a jaunty plume, and hurled it into the mud.

Walter, with his horse shifting impatiently beneath him, looked from his master to the castle, and then back again.

"I'm sure, sir, that there has been an error," he ventured

at last, wiping a raindrop from the end of his long nose.

"I daresay," Kit agreed. "A terrible error. And do you know who has wrought this error, Walter? God."

Walter turned his head quickly, his expression plainly saying that Kit had lost his reason. "Sir?" he quavered.

"Yes, Walter, the fault is the Almighty's. You see, on the seventh day, He rested, thinking his work well done. He had made man, and beast, and light to grow the trees and flowers. He had given us the earth, with all its beauties and abundance. But, Walter..." Kit drew a deep breath, and all his anger raged forth in a bellow. "*He forgot about the north country!*"

Walter's horse stepped back, and Walter himself wisely decided to keep silent.

"Damn the north, I say, and everyone in it. Of all the foul, despicable, Godforsaken places in this world, there is nothing as foul as the north. Damned rain and damned mud and damned useless cow paths they call roads—"

"Sir—" Walter ventured.

"And stupid moors and stinking bogs and Godforsaken forests that any man in his right mind would have hacked down years ago—"

"Sir—"

"But they didn't, did they? And do you know why? Because they're *northerners*, Walter. Stupid, sheep-eating, muck-raking, rain-pissing-down-on-their-thick-heads *northerners*. They'd probably still be running through the trees and painting themselves blue, but they're so stupid they've forgotten how. And do you know, Walter, what a northerner would say, if you told him this?"

Speechless at this tirade, Walter shook his head.

"It doesn't *matter,* Walter, because if he said anything, I couldn't understand a bloody word he said!"

Having vented his rage against the weather, fate, the north, and God in general, Kit slid from his horse, and promptly sank to his ankles in mud.

"Well," he said at last. "Shall we go in, and see what manner of hospitable greeting awaits us? You may want to lead your horse across the bridge; it looks none too steady.''

Kit led his shivering horse toward the decrepit wooden gates, and then stopped and looked back. ''Are you coming?''

Behind Walter, the few servants who had traveled north to share his banishment huddled together, like a herd of wet sheep. Seven servants, where there had once been hundreds, and all of them peering out from beneath their wet hoods with faces that accused him of betrayal.

He could hardly blame them.

''Come along,'' he called, trying to look confident. ''It cannot be as bad as it seems. Surely, there must be a steward within, and a warm fire. Some food and wine, perhaps, to raise our spirits.''

His false cheer began ebbing away as he walked beneath the arch of the gatehouse, and to the courtyard within.

Wild grasses and weeds grew between the broken cobblestones, and the windows of the keep were dark and empty. No stableboy came to take his horse, no welcoming torch appeared at the door.

An air of abandoned melancholy hung over the place, as dark and oppressive as the falling rain.

For a moment he stood there, beneath the skies that were as dark as twilight, even at midday, and then he drew a heavy breath and went to the huge wooden doors.

Thorns had grown up over the broad steps, brown brambles that snagged at his fine leather boots and woolen hose.

''God's teeth!'' he exclaimed, and drew his sword. He hacked viciously at the vines until he had cleared a path. ''Does no person tend to this? Where in the bloody hell are the servants?''

The idea that there were no servants had never occurred to him.

But it was undeniably so. The castle keep was abandoned. The hall was empty, with only a few broken pieces of furniture littering the cold floors. Cobwebs hung like dusty spirits from the timbered beams.

The castle had been empty for years.

"Sweet Mother of God," whispered Walter, behind him.

Christopher felt much the same. Melancholy and anger fought within him, and tiredness from the long, wet journey.

"Well," he said finally. "There is no help for it. Go get the others, and we will put as much to rights as we can before nightfall. Tomorrow, we will find the land's tenants, and roust them from their firesides. Their days of ease are done."

Walter walked briskly back to the door, where a square of gray light illuminated a path across the filth of the stone floor.

He stopped short just outside. "See here!" he called. "What do you think you are doing?"

The combination of anger and alarm in Walter's voice sent Kit hurrying across the floor. He stubbed his toe on a fallen beam, and swore viciously. Limping through the doorway, he came to stand on the stone step, rain streaming over him.

The seven servants who had made the perilous journey north with him had apparently decided against sharing his exile. They were busily unloading their meager possessions from the cart, bundling them onto each other's backs and under their arms, and preparing to leave.

Hodgkins, who had been Christopher's cook for almost fifteen years, was already through the gates, leaving his employer without so much as a fare-thee-well. Kit stared in disbelief at the man's broad back.

"Hodgkins! Come back, man!"

Hodgkins didn't look back.

Kit turned to his porter and scrubbing woman. "What do you mean by this? Stop this at once. 'Tis not so bad as it looks."

The scrubbing woman, whose name he couldn't remember if it meant his life (and at the moment, he felt as if it did) put her red hands on her ample hips, and rounded on him with fire in her eye. The scrawny girl who worked under her hid behind the woman's girth, peeking around at him with a pale but determined face.

"Not as bad as it looks!" the woman repeated. "Nay, I'm sure of that. No doubt worse than it looks, and it looks passing foul. And evil, as well. I heard a dog howl three times, and that's all the proof I need. I'm not going into that hellish place, me."

"Heard a dog howl three times," Christopher echoed, trying to keep his wits. He didn't succeed. "God's teeth, woman! What rot is that? I've heard one dog howl, I've heard a hundred dogs howl. That's what dogs do, you blessed fool! They howl!"

"You see?" the woman asked, as if that proved her point. "And just look where thee are, now. Not for me. I'm back to London, me. Come, Sal."

Scrawny Sal, carrying four bundles to her superior's one, followed her through the puddled courtyard, hurrying after the cook.

Christopher stared in mute appeal at his driver, his footman, and the stableboy.

They refused to meet his eyes, except for the stableboy, who offered him a weak smile.

"Sorry, your lordship," he said, and then they too scurried after the others, leaving Walter and Kit standing in the rain, abandoned in front of the dank castle.

Christopher drew a deep breath.

His two cartloads of possessions stood abandoned in the rain, water streaming over the leather chests and coffers filled with useless velvet and satin doublets, fine chests of ink and quills, silver plates and Venetian goblets that had no tables to rest upon. Thank God for the casks of wine, he thought, and the food they had purchased at the last inn.

He leaned against the wet wall, closing his eyes and praying for patience.

"God's nightgown," he muttered at last.

He stamped through the puddles and mounted his horse, pitying the poor dark beast who should have had a warm stable and bag of oats waiting for him.

"Sir?" Walter queried, huddled in the doorway, and looking near tears.

"Come along, Walter, and get your skinny arse back on

your horse." He wrapped his reins purposefully around his cold hands. "Let us go find our tenants, who care so little for their lord's holding. It's a situation that needs putting right."

Walter followed him with a doleful sigh. For a few minutes, they rode in silence along the muddy road beneath the canopy of autumn trees, rain spattering off the parchment-dry leaves of russet and gold.

"We've been cursed," Walter said, wiping the rain from his cold-blotched face. "Plain and simple."

"What rot," Kit answered.

At that moment, a distant howl sounded from deep within the wood—a lost dog, or perhaps a wolf. Despite himself, Kit glanced back at the dark, thorn-covered castle. A shiver raced along his back, and he had to resist the urge to cross himself.

"Cursed," he muttered contemptuously, "by northerners."

Three

The cottage was warm and bright with firelight, the stone floors free of dirt, and the wooden tables and chairs freshly shining beneath a coat of fragrant beeswax.

Isabelle bent over the newborn baby, sleeping peacefully in the wooden cradle near the fireplace, smiling as she laid her hand across his forehead.

Good. His temperature was comfortably warm, his breathing even and strong. She laid her fingers against his silken cheek, and waited.

After a moment, the familiar tingle raced through her like magic, and there it was: *the knowing*.

"He will live," she said confidently. "He is strong and perfect, and full of promise."

Relief showed on the face of the young father sitting at the trestle table, and he gathered his four-year-old daughter tightly against him. "God be praised," he said.

Isabelle smiled back. "God be praised," she agreed. She turned back to the corner of the room, where the new mother lay resting.

She bent over her and stroked her forehead. It was blessedly cool. "You've done well, Nan," she said. "You've a beautiful son, and strong. It was a good birth."

Nan's eyes shone up at Isabelle, with none of the dangerous cloudiness that preceded fever. Clear and happy eyes, tired, but too enthralled by the gift of the new child to sleep.

"Thank thee, Isabelle." she said. "Isn't he bonny faced? The prettiest baby ever?"

Isabelle personally thought he looked much like every other baby she had brought into the world, but nodded agreement. "He is. And you're not to worry about him. But rest, Nan. Until . . ." She made a quick calculation. Five days should do. "Until the new moon is a crescent. You must do nothing but tend to the baby."

She turned a stern face to James, Nan's husband, who was a good man, but selfish. "Do you hear, Jamie? Till the crescent moon. Otherwise, it will be very bad luck for the new one. And clean linens, every day, and the old ones boiled with sweet woodruff."

James nodded, looking properly awed.

Unable to resist, Isabelle threw in a little more, for effect.

"Only applewood is to be burned in the fire, and every day, you must sing three songs—three, mind you—to the babe."

"Three songs, and applewood," James repeated.

There. The applewood would smell lovely burning, and that would cheer Nan, and the singing would cheer the baby.

"And the cottage is to stay *clean*," Isabelle added, rising and smoothing the fine green wool of her skirts.

"Don't tha worry," James reassured her. "I will do. An' I thank thee, again."

He took a fine length of linen from the chest at the foot of the bed, well woven and a lovely cream color. "Your gift, if it suits thee."

Isabelle stroked the lovely cloth. "It suits me well, James."

She drew on her russet cape, tucking her dark hair beneath the large hood. She fondled the good linen with pleasure before tucking it in her leather bundle, next to the stoppered bottles of rosemary and gillyflower essence. Ah, the advantages of being the local witch!

She gave little Joan a sweetmeat of honey and nuts before she left, and admonished her to be kind to her mama and the new baby, and told James to send for her the *moment* Nan might run a fever, kissed the new baby, and went out into the cold.

Crispin, faithful as ever, rose up from where he had been patiently waiting, his long tail wagging. His white coat was damp and muddy, despite the shelter he had found beneath the overhang of the thatched roof. He stretched himself and regarded his mistress eagerly, his dark eyes bright.

"Aye, time for home, good dog."

Tail waving like a plume, Crispin started toward the path through the woods.

The skies were heavy and dark, and her breath showed smoky in the cold air. Isabelle cast one last glance at the warm cottage.

For a moment, envy caught at her. Oh, to be Nan! Simple and good, with two beautiful children, and a warm man holding her close each night.

"Rubbish," she said aloud, hurrying to catch up with Crispin, who was eager to be home. "Show your good sense, Isabelle."

It was all very easy to look at Nan, and envy her children and husband, but don't forget, she reminded herself, what else Nan has. Two shifts to her name, and not a moment to call her own. Backbreaking work, in her home all winter, then in the fields at the first sign of spring. Spinning and weaving late into the night, and then up at dawn. And always, always deferring to a man without half of her own sense. Not allowed to have a thought, a moment, a penny to call her own. Watching time and hard work fade her health and looks away.

"Envy that, Isabelle," she told herself sternly.

Instead she focused her thoughts on the beauty of the forest, the fire-bright scarlets and golds of the forest, the wood smoke and harvest smell in the cool air. She loved autumn, the mist-covered tapestry of colors that blanketed the land. It was a time of plenty, a time of settling into her beautiful cottage for the winter, a time for the weaving and

needlework that had been put aside for the summer. It was
a time for—

Change.

She stopped full in her steps. The word had come from
nowhere, but it had come clearly, as true and unmistakable
as a bell on a winter morning.

Her ears rang a little, and buzzed, and she had to breathe
deeply. *Think*, she told herself. *See.*

It was always like that, when the knowing came unexpectedly. A few moments of confusion, and then the sight,
pictures flashing across the darkness behind her eyes.

She closed her eyes tightly, willing the visions to come.

But they didn't. Instead, she heard voices.

Startled, she opened her eyes.

Crispin had heard it, too. He was waiting on the rise of
a low hill, looking over his shoulder at her, and he gave a
long howl, beckoning her to come.

"What is it, good boy?" she asked softly. Quietly,
quickly, she left the thin trail, and hurried to where her dog
waited, lifting her skirts from the ivy and leaves blanketing
the forest floor, bending her slender body beneath fallen
branches, until she crouched beside her dog.

From where they stood, they were looking down onto
the main road leading down into the valley, where the tiny
village of Farwindale lay.

Strangers.

She sat silently, watching. Two men, on horseback. Rich
men, judging by the cut and deep colors of their doublets
and sodden capes, and by the quality of their horses.

Change.

She narrowed her eyes, trying to see through the falling
rain. The word that came was not for the second man, thin
and slumped and miserable looking, she was sure of that.

It was for the dark one, sitting fierce and proud, letting
the rain fall over his coal-black curls as if it were beneath
his notice to cover his head. A tall man, broad of shoulder
and with sharp, almost elfin features; a high, proud brow,
and strong hands. She could feel the anger in the air around
him, and determination, and wounded pride.

And something else. Something wild and fiery, an element of his self that caused her heart to skip and tumble like a newly thawed brook. Something that made her breath weaken and her knees tremble. It was something she had seen happen to other women.

Yes, she had seen it happen to women, and she had seen what it did to them. It robbed them of their good sense and strength. It was a deceptive element, one that made their eyes and cheeks glow, and increased their grace, even as it ate away at their pride and power, at their very *selves*.

"It will not happen to me!" she whispered aloud, turning away.

Startled at her voice, Crispin regarded her with interest, and gave an uncertain whine. He looked back down at the two men on the road, asking with his wriggling body and anxious posture whether or not he should give chase.

Isabelle rose to her feet. "Home, Crispin," she said firmly.

With one last glance at the road, he obeyed, charging back to the path and waiting, while Isabelle followed, making her way carefully through the bracken.

"It seems we have a new lord in the castle again, Crispin," she said. "Not to worry about. This one shall go, like all the rest."

But even as she spoke, her words firm and resolute, a quiver of uncertainty trembled through her body.

Her sixth sense, the knowing that Gran had told her was a gift from God, had never been wrong before. And now it told her that this man, this dark nobleman clothed in velvet and pride, would not be as easily turned out as his predecessors had been.

Beyond that, she knew only two things—desire, and uncertainty. *Change* might be coming, but what change?

The desire she could cast aside. The uncertainty she would fight. She would bend it, forge it into reality. She would get rid of this man before the change could touch her.

"So be it," she told herself aloud, and hurried toward

home, where everything was orderly and safe and secure, as it always had been.

But for the first time in her life, Isabelle, the witch of the misty mountain, was frightened.

Four

The little village of Farwindale lay in a valley, sheltered by the forested hills. The scattered farms and cottages seemed all alike, built of gray stone and rough-hewn timbers and thatched roofs. The summer fields of barley and rye were barren and brown now. The village itself seemed to consist of a church, very old and in bad repair, and an inn, barely recognizable by the faded sign above the door.

It looked, to Kit, like a hundred other isolated farming communities, with hedgerows and thatched barns and low stone fences penning in a few sullen-looking cows and suspicious sheep.

"Except, of course," he pointed out to Walter, "that we have yet to meet a single soul who is not *mad*. A more surly, thickheaded bunch I have never seen!"

"They are, of course, northerners," Walter pointed out.

But that didn't explain the doors slammed and bolted in their faces, the children who ran from their muddy yards at their approach, the men who refused to even speak to them or acknowledge their words.

Kit glanced at Walter, now so wet that rain dripped off his nose like water from a duck's bill, save that no duck had ever been made so miserable by water.

"Even for northerners," Kit said, "they are passing peculiar. It is as if some disease has struck them all dumb.''

There was no stableboy at the inn to take their horses, so they tied them themselves in the long, low sheds and made their way through the muddy inn yard, hoping for a warming fire, and perhaps one inhabitant of the valley who could or would speak plain English.

The fire was there, blazing in the wide hearth, and a fine-looking piece of mutton roasting above it.

The man who might speak was there, too. Kit presumed him to be the innkeeper, since there was nobody else in sight.

He was an old man, with sparse hair that looked as if it needed a good comb, sticking out in all directions in comical tufts. His eyebrows, too, needed taming. His watery eyes regarded the newcomers with something less than welcome, and his bottom lip was pushed up so far that Kit thought it might reach the overhang of his large nose.

''Go 'way, youse.''

Walter raised a pleading glance heavenward, as though beseeching God to take him at that moment.

''At least he speaks,'' Kit muttered. This was something, at the least. Progress, of sorts, and he had no intention of ''going 'way.''

''Old man,'' he said, taking off his cloak and draping it across a scarred table, ''I can think of no reason for your rudeness. We have no argument with you, nor mean any ill. This is an inn, a public house, I believe, and we've traveled a long and tiresome way. May we not at least sit by your fire?''

''Oswin,'' was the sharp reply, and with much huffing and puffing, the old fellow turned his chair away so that Kit was left with the view of a stooped back and balding head.

''I beg your pardon?'' Kit and Walter exchanged puzzled glances.

''Oswin,'' repeated the surly fellow, without bothering to turn his head. ''That be my name. Not old man. I know I'm an old man. Any fool can see I'm an old man. Tha didn't have to come mucking in here to tell me I'm old. I know what I know.''

"I can hardly dispute that," Kit said, trying to be agreeable. He settled himself on a nearby bench, stretching his legs toward the welcoming fire. His boots of fine Spanish leather looked near ruin.

His ungracious host ignored him.

Kit glanced back at Walter, still standing, his clothes dripping a puddle onto the dried rushes that covered the floor.

Walter made a nervous "don't ask me" gesture.

Old Oswin gave Kit a suspicious look out of the corner of his eye, without bothering to turn his head.

"May I please have some wine? Or ale?" Kit tried his most charming, well-mannered tone.

Oswin turned his head at that, looking at Kit with as much outrage as if he had asked to rape his daughter and steal his sheep.

"Wine, is it?" he barked, so suddenly that Kit jumped back a little. "Ale, is it? Lord have mercy." But he got out of his chair, with a lot of sighing and labored breathing, as if the effort cost him greatly, and made his way across the room with a shuffling, slow progress, grumbling all the way, his rough smock swinging from his bony shoulders.

Kit had to strain to hear the muttered words. "Young folk," he heard, and "high and mighty," and "mucky boots," and "bothering old men," and in a particularly nasty tone, as the door swung shut behind him, "southerners."

"Good God," said Walter. "What was that?"

"That is Oswin, apparently," Kit retorted. "And as he's the first damned man that will speak to us, I advise you to tread carefully with him, before he sends us out into that accursed rain."

"Good God," Walter repeated, looking askance at the door through which the old man had exited.

After a very long time, he came back, bearing mugs of heavy crockery in each hand.

"Well-a-day!" he snapped, as they watched him. "D'

ye expect me to feed it to you? Big lads like you thinkin' an old man should fetch and carry to you.''

Walter hastened to take the mugs, and brought one to Kit, who sniffed it before drinking.

Thankfully, it was cider, warm and thick and potent. The finest wine could not have been more welcome.

"I thank you," Kit said, when he finished.

"That's good cider, that," Oswin said, as if they might challenge the fact.

"The finest," Kit agreed, trying hard to be patient.

He waited until the old man had settled himself into his chair, again with much huffing and effort, and made himself comfortable by his fire.

There they sat, a very uncomfortable-looking trio, until Kit could stand the silence not a second more.

"Oswin," he began.

The old man turned a disapproving eye upon him.

Kit took a deep breath. "I could not help but notice, as we made our way here, that the people of Farwindale seem . . . a mite unfriendly. That is, I seem to have given offense, and cannot think how. Why is it, Oswin, that we are turned away from every doorstep, and treated as if we had the plague?''

"Do you?"

"Have the plague? God's nightgown, no!''

"No need to swear," Oswin said, his lower lip creeping farther up to his nose. "The young lads, nowadays . . .''

"Why is it?" Kit repeated, trying to control his exasperation.

"It's not respectful, tha's all. Swearing to an old man.''

Kit buried his face in one hand and prayed for patience. "Not that. Why are we treated so? Do you know?''

"Everyone does." Oswin thought about it for an interminable length of time, and then decided to share. "It's because you're cursed, is what.''

Walter made a startled sound, and Kit choked a little on his cider.

"What in the hell do you mean?" he burst out.

Oswin took great offense to being sworn at again, and

said so, and Kit had to apologize, again, and Oswin said that the young were a loutish, mannerless lot these days, and Kit had to agree again, particularly southerners, Oswin thought, and Kit could barely contain himself, but agreed again, and eventually he smoothed the surly old rooster's feathers and steered him around (after many apologies) back to the curse.

"It's like this," Oswin said finally, in a tone that implied he half resented telling the tale, and half relished being the bearer of bad news. "There was a fine family up at the castle. And they was witches. Just the women, mind you. Good-looking lot. Witches, though."

The old man stared into the fire, lost in thought. After a time, he jumped a little. "Where was I?" he asked.

"Witches," Kit reminded him.

"Oh, tha's right. And the prettiest one, that was Bess. Just a little older than me. Of course, that wasn't old a'tall. We were young, then, though some may not believe it.

"As that may be, when Bess was just sixteen, and pretty—did I say she was lovely? She was. Her father died, and that king fellow in the south said she was to marry. A right foul old man he was, too."

"The king?" Walter asked, listening avidly.

"Don't know. Never met the fella, meself. And a good thing, too. Got no time for kings and that sort, me."

Kit could have kicked Walter for interrupting, but managed to content himself with a good glower. "So she didn't like her husband?"

"Husband? Hah! Tha's good, that is. Can't make a witch marry when she doesn't want to. No, by the time he got here, she were gone. Turned all the lands of the castle over to her people. And all legal-like, too. Papers with writing, and signed before the priest. Nobody was left to work the lands for the surly old barstard. Hah!" Oswin looked well pleased, and made a wheezing noise that could have been mistaken for a laugh. "He didn't much like that, I can tell you."

"I should imagine not," Kit agreed, but with a sinking heart. A castle with no tenants? A land with no income? It was unheard of! Why, it would leave you with—

Nothing. Just an empty, abandoned castle, with thorns growing over the walls, and spiders running through the rooms.

"And no matter what he offered to pay," Oswin went on, "he couldna buy the lands back, and none of his gold could buy him a servant. The castle fell to ruin, and his fields sat till the forest took them back. And there it is. Two other lords have come and gone, and the castle sits there like an empty piss pot."

Kit thought that a fine description of his new home.

"Good God," said Walter again.

"But surely," Kit said, after consideration, "the curse cannot be held against me. I've offended no witches, nor anyone else, for that matter."

"Hah!" Oswin said. "Too bad for you. That's the nature of the curse, you see. Not just agin' the lord of the castle, but anyone who bends to serve him, or moves to help him. It'd be bad luck for us if we did. Until the castle is returned to the witch's family, you see. Now, you be a good lad, an' take thaself back south where thee belong. We'm doing just grand, ourselves, without any lords and whatnot running about and getting in our way."

Oswin looked very pleased at himself for this clever suggestion.

"Jesu grant me patience," Kit said, and leaned forward to look at the old man.

Oswin granted him what might have been a smile, the lines on his face deepening like freshly plowed furrows in a field. "That's my best advice to thee, lad, and as good as thee might get. If thee was clever—and that I won't bet on—thee would heed it. Things could get bad for you, if thee were to stay. Now, me, I've said too much, and given too much a'ready. God help me if the witch found out."

Kit's belief in witches was marginal, at best, but Oswin's obviously was not. Still, it never hurt to try.

"Old—I mean, Oswin—suppose I were to offer you my protection, in return for your assistance. You might help to convince the local folk to work for me. I'd reward you well.''

"Your protection!'' Oswin's lower lip poked out like a shelf. "Don't be thick, lad. Lot of good that would do, did the witch find out. And find out she would.''

Kit's good nature was stretched beyond endurance. "God's nightgown, man! What would the crone do? Turn you into a sheep?''

Oswin glowered. "Eeeh,'' he said, a sound that spoke of his disapproval. "She might do.'' He leaned back in his chair and scratched at his tufted hair, as if considering. "Wha's the name of that great horse tha rode in on?'' he asked at length.

Kit drew a deep breath, exasperated. "What in the devil does that have to do with anything? It's a bloody horse. He doesn't even have a name!''

"Hah! I thought not.'' Oswin closed his eyes, and after a moment, looked as if he might be sleeping.

Kit and Walter exchanged frustrated glances.

"Looks a lot like my brother Sidney, that horse does,'' Oswin said, without bothering to open his eyes.

Walter clapped a hand to his forehead with a pained look, and Kit dropped his face into his hands.

Within seconds, Oswin gave a noisy snore, and then another.

The conversation was over.

Together, Walter and Kit cleared away as much debris as they could from the floor in the great hall, and swept a place clean before the vast fireplace, using makeshift brooms of leafy branches.

They managed to start a fire of what dry wood they could find in the keep, and the least-wet wood they could find fallen in the woods outside. It produced more smoke than heat, but was better than nothing.

They spread bundles of dry clothing before the fire, shared a cask of Sicilian wine, and lay down to sleep for their first night in Farwindale Keep.

Kit tried not to let his thoughts stray to his old bedchamber at Radbourne, his huge feather bed curtained in tawny velvets, the warming stove of glistening Dutch tiles, the clean and fragrant walls of carved walnut, the patterned carpets that blanketed the floors.

He was cold, and miserable, and disgusted with the ignorant villagers of Farwindale. He hated the north, and the king, and himself for his stupid ideas of honor and truth. He even hated Walter, and his annoying snuffling nose. And he hated the witch, the old crone living somewhere out in the wet forest, harboring a grudge for sixty years or better.

Tomorrow, he resolved, he would put this idiotic situation to rights. There was a church in the village, so there must be a priest. He would enlist his help, if possible, and confront the old crone and her curses.

Surely, no old woman in the woods would be a match for him. First thing in the morning, he would saddle up Sidney, and be on his way.

Five

The way to the crone's cottage was a small, twisting path through the forest. Kit regretted coming on horseback. Poor Sidney was being scratched by brambles, and several times he himself had to dismount to make his way under low branches.

It was almost as if Nature herself had contrived against him, he thought—the thorns, the fog, the uneven path that led up the steep hill. At least the rain had stopped.

He had wasted almost a full hour of morning convincing old Oswin to give him proper directions, and had to part with a full gold coin for the dubious privilege, only to have Oswin tell him that it was probably false, and then chastise him roundly for "mucking about and deceiving old men."

But Kit was determined. No old crone would interfere with his life, as pathetic as it might presently be.

He had dressed carefully that morning, hoping to dazzle and intimidate the ignorant old woman with the trappings of his wealth and power. He had combed his dark hair and beard, and chosen his favorite doublet of black velvet and silver thread, the sleeves slashed and puffed to show the fine linen beneath. Jewels glittered on his fingers, and his cape was lined with priceless black sable from Russia. He knew that he looked rich and powerful, and hopefully intimidating. He would have the ignorant hag begging for his mercy—if he could ever find her.

Just when he had decided that Oswin had purposely misled him, and that he was lost in the accursed forest, he came to a stream with a narrow but sturdy plank bridge across it.

On the other side of the bridge, the trees opened into a clearing, and there stood the witch's hovel.

But it was not a hovel.

It was amazing, really. The land surrounding the house was clear of trees. Orderly gardens, as carefully tended as any noblewoman's, surrounded the lovely house. Herbs and autumn flowers grew in designs of knots and circles, and a careful path of stones led to the door.

The house itself was a surprise. It was small, certainly, but at least twice the size of the cottages dotting the countryside. It was built of sturdy stone and dark timbers. The thatched roof looked new and thick, the door was well built, with heavy hinges and a fine lock. Most amazing of all, the shutters were open, showing glass windows, something he had never seen in a peasant's cottage, and they glowed through the fog with the warm light of a fire.

It gave him pause. What manner of crone was this, to have amassed such wealth and comfort? His own stewards and gatekeepers did not boast such fine houses!

"Be damned," he muttered aloud. Perhaps this wouldn't be as simple as he had imagined. Obviously, the hag had convinced enough people of her power to amass a certain amount of wealth.

Little mind, though. Whoever she might be, she would be no match for him. He started forward, tugging on Sidney's reins to guide him over the bridge.

For the first time in six years, the horse balked. Kit pulled again sharply.

"Come, horse," he ordered, in sharp tones.

Sidney shook his head, and pulled back furiously, huffing great clouds of breath into the cold air, and struggling against his master's pull.

Kit engaged in a furious struggle for several minutes,

swearing at the balking beast, but Sidney refused to cross the bridge, and at last settled the matter by ramming his head squarely against Kit's chest.

The blow knocked Kit's breath from his chest and his feet from the bridge, and he barely managed to catch his balance as he landed knee-deep in the stream.

He looked down with fury as icy water filled his boots and autumn leaves swirled past his knees, floating downstream. To add insult to injury, his velvet cap fell off, ruby and gold clip sparkling, and followed the leaves like a mighty warship chasing a small armada.

He drew a deep breath and glowered at his rebellious horse, who had retreated from the bridge and was contentedly eating leaves.

"You motherless son of a pox-ridden whore," Kit said. "Devil take you."

Sidney raised his head, gave his master a contemptous look, and turned his backside to view. His black tail twitched as if in dismissal.

Kit climbed from the water and back to the bridge, water squelching between his toes. He started toward the horse again, and the animal pulled back in alarm. An astounding thing, almost as if the animal were . . .

Bewitched.

The word came to him with such a clarity that he froze in his footsteps and lifted his hand to cross himself.

"What superstitious dung!" he exclaimed aloud, annoyed with himself as much as his horse.

Sidney cast a long look over his flank, his ears twitching.

"Ballocks," Kit muttered at the traitorous animal, and he turned to face the witch's house. He hesitated, then grew angry at himself for doing so, and strode up the flagstone path, shoulders squared and chin thrust forward.

He hammered at the door with his leather-gloved fist, and waited.

There was no answer.

He looked around. The tidy gardens and surrounding forest lay silent. Only the sound of the brook, tumbling over the rocks, sparkled in the foggy wood.

He felt wary, uneasy . . . almost as if he were being watched.

"Rot," he muttered aloud, and banged at the door again. "Old crone," he shouted. "Show yourself."

He waited, and looked around again. Across the bridge, Sidney watched with great interest, his mouth full of leaves.

Kit banged again. "Old hag!" he shouted. "I am being reasonable. Come out and speak to me, or I shall enter unwelcomed. It is no good hiding yourself. I can wait all day and night, if needs must."

He heaved a sigh, and tried again. "Right, then. You try my patience, witch! You'll not play me for a fool. I'm a patient man, and a reasonable man—"

"Then why are you shouting at an empty house, pray tell?"

He whirled about, one hand flying to the dagger at his waist, and confronted the hag.

But she was no hag.

More like a fairy queen, or the legendary green lady of the wood. She stood, straight and slender as a young willow, a basket of greens under one arm.

Her eyes were bright and sparkling with mirth, a tawny golden brown, set in a face of silken smooth texture, with a sheen to her rounded cheeks like the blush on a fresh apricot. A few freckles sprinkled her nose like cinnamon on cream.

Her hair was confined beneath a fine white cap, the strings untied and hanging over her shoulders, and a riot of deep brown curls hung from beneath, clean and with an autumn red gloss.

Her dress was of fine green wool, tucked up at the sides to keep it from the wet grass, showing an underskirt of butter yellow beneath, trimmed with gay ribbons of red and green. The bodice of her gown was likewise laced with shining ribbons, showing the clean white of her smocked chemise and sleeves, and a healthy swell of bosom above.

Her cape of russet was tossed back over her shoulders, and at her side stood a large white dog, watching him with narrowed eyes.

"Will you not speak, sir?"

Flustered and shaken by the sudden appearance of this glowing creature, Kit stammered for a moment before he found his tongue.

"Ah, yes. I thought—that is—I'm here to speak to the witch."

The dark brows rose over the merry eyes. "Are you? Then you are in luck, for I am she."

"You aren't. That is, I was given to understand that you were much older. The lady of the castle, that was turned out, that is . . ." Damn! He was stammering like a fool, caught by surprise and feeling at a distinct disadvantage.

"I see." She tipped her head, and cast a knowing look at him. "You were expecting my grandmother, I think. And she was not 'turned out' of the castle; she left, freely and of her own accord. She married her own true love, and together they built this house upon his land, and it is now mine, and you, sir, are trespassing. I bid you good day."

Having delivered this incredible and haughty speech, she pushed past Kit as if he were nothing, and took a great ring of keys from her belt, fitting one to the lock on the heavy door.

"Witch—" he began, and she whirled about, one eyebrow lifted.

He felt like a schoolboy caught in a breech of manners.

"I do not know your name," he explained, feeling rebuked by her affronted look.

" 'Tis not 'witch,' that I can tell you, any more than Oswin is called 'old man' or Crispin here is called 'dog.' We are backwards here in the north, but not that much, Christopher Radbourne."

Again, she had him rattled. She tossed a haughty look over her slender shoulder, turned the key in the door, and went into the house, her basket swinging on her arm. Behind him, the white dog made a low noise in his throat.

"Crispin! Come in!" she called.

Kit stood awkwardly, trying to collect himself, and then she popped her head out the open door.

"You may come in, too, Christopher Radbourne, for a

moment or two. But I advise thee to be on good behavior, or Crispin shall take offense.''

He stepped in after her. This was not how he had intended this scene to be played. He was to have ridden up on his fearsome mount, dazzling the old and ignorant peasant woman with a show of strength and wealth, and have her groveling at his feet within moments.

And instead, he stood humbly by the door, uncertain of how to proceed, dazzled by this sharp-tongued, enchanting young woman, who was as lithe and lovely as any woman of wealth.

''Things don't always happen as we might like,'' she said.

Christopher had the uncanny feeling she had read his thoughts. He simply stood in the doorway, silent, looking around.

It was a large room, as cottages go, and startling.

To begin with, there were no rushes covering the floor, for fleas to live in or mice to eat at the bits of food that fell from the table. Only smooth stone, clean and shining.

A fire burned briskly in the stone fireplace, reflecting gold and red off the shining floor. A few good pieces of silver—a bowl, a large cup, and a few plates—were displayed on the mantel.

There was a cozy chair, of fine woodwork with a high back, bearing cushions of faded but clean blue brocade. It looked as if it had come from a better place. A lute leaned against it, a rosette of ribbons streaming from the neck. The trestle table was of plain but highly polished oak, with a single silver bowl upon its worn surface.

Shelves lined the wall, and a great cupboard, its doors open to reveal many jars and bottles and flasks of both glass and crockery. Dried herbs hung in abundance from the beams, filling the cottage with a spicy, delicate perfume.

It was, without doubt, the cleanest, most fragrant room he had ever been in. No odors of sweat, or rotten meat, or smoke. No mold upon the plastered walls, or insects buzzing about. Just the smell of rosemary and lavender, and fresh bread.

"Sit down, and break your fast, if you like."

He watched as she moved about the room, her motions quick and efficient as she left her basket of herbs on the table, untied her cape, and laid it neatly across the narrow bed by the wall, smoothed her hair, and went to the fire.

She used an iron hook to drag a large kettle from the coals, and uncovered it. She lifted small loaves of bread from the kettle with a long fork, and deposited them on a clean slab of polished wood.

"Sit," she said, without turning to look at him.

Silently, Kit obeyed, and watched her as she unlocked her pantry. She spoke not a word as she filled the table before him with fresh, crumbling cheese and hot bread, a wooden bowl of cooked apples, and a pewter mug of ale.

It was amazing. She paid no more attention to him than she would have paid to a visiting cottager. Her calm and confident air verged on arrogance, as if she was completely unconcerned with what he might be doing there. He had never seen a peasant behave so in his presence.

She sat down opposite him while he ate, and began tying the herbs from her basket into neat bundles, wrapping twine around their stems with expert fingers.

He ate quickly, feeling indebted for the good food. It was filling and warming and excellent. There were no bits of stone in the bread, and the apples were cooked with a generous amount of sugar, and seasoned with nutmeg.

He finished quickly, and started to speak, hesitating when he realized he didn't know her name, even though she had learned his.

"Isabelle," she said, without looking up from her herbs.

Damn! How did she do that? Was she truly a witch, or simply observant and clever?

"Isabelle," he repeated. It suited her. It was fey and pretty, but had a brisk sound. It was a name that meant business. "Isabelle, we seem to be at odds, and it must needs be put to rights."

"I'm very happy, thank you," she said, looking up long enough to offer him a short, mirthless smile. "I can think of nothing in my life that needs tending to. You, on the other hand, seem to be quite distressed. My advice to you is to go back where you've come from, and leave well enough alone. Farwindale Keep cannot possibly hold any attraction for you. It would take an army of workers to make it comfortable, and those you have not, nor will you have. Give up, go home, and don't bother me again.''

She spoke to him as if she were his equal, or even worse, his better. As if she had the right to give orders!

He had been polite long enough. It was time to switch back to his original plan.

He drew himself up to his full height, and looked sternly at her.

''Are you aware, woman, that it is against the law of England to practice witchcraft or sorcery?''

Her eyes met his gaze squarely, tawny and clear and unafraid. ''To the word of the law,'' she retorted, ''it is illegal to attempt to do or wish harm to the king's person by sorcery. It is not illegal to practice healing, or astrology, or to study herbs and their medicines. I've broken no laws, nor caused any ills, nor committed any heresy against the church, nor offended the king's person in any way. Which, by the by, you must have, or you wouldn't be at Farwindale.''

''Damn!'' The wench was too clever by half. ''How did you know that?''

''I watch and I listen. And sometimes, I just know. 'Tis a gift I have.'' Again her eyes flickered briefly to him, bright and clear.

''I don't believe you. You might keep the villagers in thrall with your tales of witchery and claims of power, but I don't believe it. I'm no ignorant country boy to be bullied and frightened.''

''Good.'' She scooped up her herbs, climbed to stand on the bench, and began hanging them from the rafters in orderly lines. ''Then we understand each other. I am no ignorant country girl, to be bullied and frightened. That was what you had intended, was it not?''

Half admiring and half infuriated, Kit watched her as she worked, her slender body and shining curls dipping and swaying as she hung her herbs to dry from the dark beams. "Aye," he finally admitted, "that was my plan."

"You've failed," she observed.

"See here." Kit straightened his posture. "Why be difficult? Why make me to suffer? What cause could you possibly have to mislike me so?"

She stopped and looked down at him, and he was struck again by her pretty, intelligent face, and the clean glow of her skin. Her cap had slipped back as she worked, and a dark curl had fallen to caress her cheek. He wondered what she was thinking.

At length, she shrugged. "What do you think I might do? 'Twas not my curse that bedevils you, 'twas my grandmother's."

"That stupid curse," Kit muttered. "What good is it to you?"

"A lot," she retorted, climbing down at last. She placed her hands on her slender hips and seemed to consider her words before she spoke. "Very well, Christopher Radbourne. I shall speak honestly to you. I am no more witch than you. The only magic I possess is my education in the ways of herbs and people, a belief in that which cannot be proven, and an occasional gift of second sight. And the most powerful magic I possess is this: the belief of the people of Farwindale."

He nodded, accepting what she had said, even though he doubted the second sight business.

"The curse my lady grandmother leveled against the new lords of the keep has held true over three generations' time. If you were to move in, and begin leading a merry and comfortable life, do you know what the people would say?"

"I wouldn't care, really," Christopher answered, "as long as I had a good bed to sleep in and food to eat."

"That's all well for you. They would say I had lost my powers, that the witches of the misty grove were no more able to change the course of time and nature than they themselves. They would lose their belief, and I would be nobody. Just another woman."

"And what if they did?" Kit demanded. "What would be so terrible about that?"

Her eyebrows shot up, and she looked at him with something like contempt. "You're just like all the other stupid rich, aren't you? Cannot see anything past your own desires and comforts, can you? Have you ever considered, my lord, the life of a poor woman without defenses?"

"They marry, don't they? Like all women?"

"Aye, they do," she retorted, and began clearing away his empty mug and trencher with quick, sharp movements. "And when they do, they sign their own death warrants. They have nothing. A woman may not call her shift her own, 'tis the property of her husband. And he can take it from her, and beat her for complaining if he likes. And the children, sir! Ten and more, one after the other, and most dying before they can walk. The grief of it! But no time to mourn, she! Up at the next dawn, scrubbing and planting and weaving and sewing, and waiting on the great lout that rules her life, and working late into every night. Mayhap a day of peace, if you call it that, while she whelps another pup, and mayhap one more day to bury it. Marriage! Speak not of marriage to me!" She dipped the pewter mug into a pail of water, and polished it furiously on her apron.

"God's nightgown." Kit was shocked by the fury in her voice. "It cannot be as bad as all that."

"Can it not? Would you swallow your pride and soul to become slave to another's wishes? Renounce your beliefs?"

She stopped and drew breath, and then stared at him with a queer, curious look on her face. The ripe color in her cheeks deepened, and her tawny eyes clouded, and then brightened.

"Of course you would not," she said softly. "After all, that is why you were sent away, is it not? You would not be false, either to yourself, or to that you believe in."

He could not answer. He simply sat, stunned at her perception, or knowledge, or whatever it was. He could do nothing but stare at her.

And for several moments, he believed in her power. She

was magic. She knew. She was beautiful, and sharp as a sword, and fiercely true to her own honor. She was like no other woman he had ever met.

At that moment, the sun outside broke through the fog, and flooded through the heavy glass of her windows, lighting her hair and face with a glow that seemed almost mystical, framing her slender body like a gilt frame. And Kit felt an answering spark within himself, one that was more earthly than mystical.

It shocked him, the sudden desire, the heat of it. And it disturbed him that it was not just her pretty face and glowing skin that caused it, but also her quicksilver mind and quick wit.

"By the saints!" he exclaimed, turning impatiently from the sight of her, and struggling to regain what was left of his wits. "You try me sorely. None of this has to do with me. 'Tis foolish prattle, this bemoaning of a woman's lot."

The dog, who had stretched his long body out for a good nap before the fire, raised his head with a low growl at the harsh tones.

"Foolish to you. To me, it is my very life. Should I give all this up, then, so that a rich man can have one more castle?"

"Give what up?" Kit demanded, looking around. "A peasant's hovel in the forest? A garden? Are you mad, woman? It's not worth the smallest ring on my finger."

His contempt didn't move her. She simply walked to her chair by the fire, and pulled the tapestry frame toward herself. She took the needle in her fingers, and turned to give him a proud, knowing smile.

"How wise you are. How foolish of me. I have nothing, and you are a rich and powerful man. That having been set straight, I advise you to leave me to my squalid cottage, and go back to your fine castle. Oh, and see if that ring you mentioned will feed you and warm you."

Infuriated, Kit could not speak.

"And close the door behind you," she added, her eyes intent on the needlework before her. "Or Crispin might take offense."

At the sound of his name, the great dog rose to his feet, and turned his dark eyes on Kit.

"God's teeth," Kit muttered, unwilling to admit defeat. "This is not finished, madam."

He did not look back as he left, though he did close the door tightly out of deference to Crispin's formidable jaws.

Sidney was standing where Kit had left him, having finished his breakfast of leaves, and now appeared to be enjoying the rare autumn sunlight.

"Traitor," Kit said, climbing none too gently onto the sturdy back. The sunlight glittered off his rings as he took the reins, and he glanced at the jewels with disgust, thinking of the cold ruin of a castle that awaited him.

Worthless. His jewels were worthless, and his gold would not buy him one decent working man, because of Isabelle.

"I am not giving up, Madam Witch," he said, turning and looking back at the stone cottage. "We shall see which of us bows first."

Somewhere in the glowing gold and crimson leaves of the forest, a bird chattered, and it seemed to Kit that it was mocking him.

Six

He swore that he would find some way to defeat Isabelle, and bend her to his will. He swore that he would not give up.

He rode to the inn, and tried again to bribe old Oswin into becoming his ally. He parted with three silver pence, and in return received nothing more than a mealy bowl of porridge, a decent mug of cider, and a running monologue of the old man's complaints about the young, the weather, his chilblains, and the misery of life in general.

He located the village priest, and found Father Timothy to be a personable if useless man. The rumors of witchcraft, according to the good father, were just that—silly rumors; he spoke with great respect of Isabelle's skill with herbs, her diligent care of the villagers, and her high moral character, and gave a very lengthy discourse on the quality of her cowslip wine, which he did not offer to share.

Disgusted, Kit returned to the castle to find Walter huddled in the dust before the dying fire, sniffling and composing poems to a lass he had known in London—maudlin verses about her sterling qualities.

Kit was feeling nasty enough to point out that her most obvious quality was the length of her nose, the only one he had ever seen that surpassed Walter's. He then added insult to injury by bullying Walter into helping him dung out the stables, a foul job made worse by the lack of shovels.

Tired and filthy, they returned to the great hall to find that rats had helped themselves to the meager remnants of their foodstuffs, with the exception of some particularly foul cheese.

"Beg the witch," Walter suggested. "Offer her anything. Everyone has their price, Kit."

"Do they?" Kit retorted. "As to begging, I'd rather have my teeth removed with broken glass. She's an arrogant and vain wench, and I'll not beg anything of a superstitious peasant girl. I'd rather starve."

"We may well do," Walter grumbled. " 'Tis a sorry shame we cannot dine on pride, Kit. You'd have enough for a feast."

Disgusted, Kit left Walter huddled in his cape before the fire and went off in search of firewood. He had never before thought of what a passing amount of work it took just to keep a fire going.

When he lay on his makeshift pallet that night, huddled before the fire and listening to the wind howl through the empty castle, he tried not to think of Isabelle, who was probably asleep in her warm bed, on lavender-scented sheets beneath blankets of soft wool. He wondered what she had dined on, sitting before the fire in her sweet-scented cottage. A mutton pie, perhaps. Maybe some of the cowslip wine Father Timothy had mentioned. The thought made his stomach grumble.

"Damn!" he exclaimed, and pulled his cape tighter around him. Outside, he heard a distant rumble of thunder, and soon the rain started again, slapping against the trees and trickling down the walls.

"I'll not beg her," he muttered, and Walter made a sad sound in his sleep from the other side of the hearth, and then commenced snoring, an irritating pattern of a long, broken snort followed by a series of whimpering sniffles.

Kit cursed again, pulled his cloak over his head, and tried

to sleep, swearing that he would never beg the witch.

His resolve lasted only two more days.

Isabelle looked closely at old Oswin's eyes. They looked cloudy. She rested her fingers briefly at the base of his throat, and frowned at the pulse. It seemed slower, and every now and then skipped a beat completely.

"You've not taken your physick, have you?" she asked.

Oswin glowered, looking more like a sulky child than a man of almost eighty years. "Nasty stuff, that."

"I know. But if you put it in your cider, you will scarcely know."

"And ruin a good mug of cider," Oswin grumbled. "And for what? I'm old, and that's that. No need for me to keep hanging on. No wife, nor children. Who'd miss me?"

"Why, I should, Oswin." Isabelle carefully measured an amount of the medicine into the old man's mug. "And the fine lord of the castle would. He'd be starving, if not for you."

"Eeeh," Oswin said. "That wouldn't be right, that. He's not a bad fellow. Big mouth, but not all bad. For a southerner," he qualified, taking the mug from Isabelle and drinking. "Trying to kill me, you," he added with a grimace.

Isabelle smiled, and turned back to her willow basket. "Here. I've brought you some of this morning's baking, and some pies. Chicken."

"Chicken's not bad," Oswin admitted.

It was his favorite, Isabelle knew. "It will do," she agreed.

The old man sighed, and leaned back in his chair. He tired more easily these days.

"Have you chosen a husband yet?" he asked suddenly, opening his eyes. He liked to argue, and this was one of his favorite topics when Isabelle dropped by.

"No, indeed," she said, laughing. "I'm still waiting for you to speak, Oswin. If I can't have you, why, who else would I marry?"

"I'll be dead and gone before long," he said, which was his second favorite topic. "And then what will thee do, lass? Don't want to end up like me, all alone and none to care."

"There are worse fates." She glanced out the window. The sun was breaking through the fog, and the morning was already spent. "Have you heard aught of Atwell's Betsy? Is her cough better?"

"Don't know. All I've seen for a fortnight is that poor young lord from the castle. Pity, that. He's not looking too spry."

"Then he should go home." Isabelle checked her basket, and began drawing on her gloves.

"Eeeh, tha are a hard one! Did thee think he would not, if he had somewhere to go to?"

"He's a rich man," Isabelle said, picking up her cape and shaking it. She didn't trust the rushes on Oswin's floor; they were riddled with fleas, but nothing could convince him that they were unhealthy. "These rushes are filthy. You should have them replaced."

"And who'd do that, eh? I'm an old man."

"I'll find someone," Isabelle promised. "Now, I've got to see to young Betsy. Promise you will take your physick. Every morning, Oswin."

"There's no point to it," he complained. "It's a terrible thing, being a lonely old man. I'd be just as happy in my grave. Nobody telling me what to do there."

Isabelle smiled, tossing her cape over her shoulders. "Just St. Peter. I should think he's bossier than I am."

"Not likely."

"I'll be back in a few days," she told him. "God keep you, Oswin."

"Rather he didn't," was the mournful reply as she went out the door.

She drew in a deep breath of the cool air, and called to Crispin, who was chasing something in a pile of brush, and started up the muddy road. First to Atwells', to check on Betsy's cough, and then to Jamie and Nan's, to see after the new baby, who would be christened on Friday. Then the village would have a merry celebration—outside, weather permitting, or at Oswin's inn, if not.

Isabelle loved to dance, and looked forward to the days that work was set aside. A new baby, a good harvest, May time—there were not enough such days in Farwindale, and she treasured them.

She was humming a ballad and swinging her basket when she saw Christopher Radbourne coming toward her, looking as doleful as she was happy.

His forest-green doublet was looking stained and wrinkled, and his thick dark hair needed a comb. His hose had a tear in one leg and his boots were muddy. As she drew closer, she saw that he had dark circles under his eyes. From worry, or lack of sleep?

"God's greetings, sir," she called. Again, she felt the unfamiliar nervousness in her breast. What was it about him? True, he had a handsome face, but not the first she had seen. But there was something about him that made her suddenly self-conscious, and the irritating, feminine thought crossed her mind that she was glad to be wearing her new yellow skirt, as gay and light as an autumn leaf.

He didn't return her greeting, but stopped in the road and waited for her.

"Isabelle," he said, "we must speak."

His voice saying her name made her shiver. She straightened her spine and ignored it. "Must we? And why?"

"Pray, Isabelle, don't be so haughty." His blue eyes looked weary, almost sorrowful. "I don't deserve such treatment."

"Very well. What do you want?" She stopped walking, crossed her arms, and waited. Crispin barked a greeting, running around them in circles.

Christopher, she noticed, kept a wary eye on the dog as he spoke. "I want to ask something of you. A favor, if you will."

She waited, saying nothing.

"Lift the curse, Isabelle. For mercy's sake."

He looked excessively pitiful as he spoke, as if the words

pained him. "I thought you didn't believe in spells, Christopher Radbourne."

"I don't, but that's naught to do with it. The villagers believe."

"They do," she agreed. "And that's to my advantage."

"I understand that, believe me. But there must be some way to convince them that the curse can be lifted. And if I must stay, Isabelle, I must have help. A boy to tend the horses, and keep the fire going. A cook, for mercy's sake."

"What? The great superior man from the south, where all people are so much more clever than we backward folk, and he cannot feed himself? For shame!" She shifted her basket on her arm, and began walking toward Atwells'. "Why not go home," she suggested, "where you belong?"

"Mercy sake, Isabelle." He grabbed her arm. "I cannot."

There was an urgency in his voice that caught her attention. She looked up at him, and saw the desperation in his eyes. Clear blue eyes, reddened and dark-ringed from lack of sleep, but still beautiful. And while she looked at him, she felt that dangerous shiver, that quivering heat.

They were linked in fate together, she and this proud man. Somehow, he would change her life, irrevocably.

She turned her head away, fighting the feeling. But how could she? The knowing was there, it had never been wrong.

And what would happen, if she decided to fight her own fate, whatever it might be? She had seen others try. It was a waste of strength, ending in defeat.

His hand on her arm was warm. She looked at it, at the long, strong fingers. It struck her as a singularly beautiful hand, strong and graceful. It made her wrist look very frail. Frailty was not a quality she cared for.

She drew her arm back, quickly. "I will lift the curse."

The words were out before she knew what she was saying, and it seemed to her that they carried a terrible weight.

He let out a delighted whoop, and when he laughed, she saw that his teeth were strong and white, a mark of good health. "I knew you would see reason," he said. "There's a clever wench."

His smug words rankled.

"It's not that easy," she snapped, irritated at her own weakening. "Do you think I have only to wave my hand, and say it to make it so? You'll be asking the villagers to cast off a belief that most of them have accepted all their lives, and one that serves them well. They're a proud people, Christopher Radbourne, and likely won't want to come running to do your bidding. We must make them believe that the curse is gone, firstly. 'Twill not be simple, for them or you."

"What do you mean?" She saw the wary look of suspicion in his eye, and it pleased her.

"Why, a curse cannot be lifted overnight, can it? There is always a price to pay."

"What price?"

She laughed at the suspicion and uncertainty in his voice. Good, it made her feel more sure of herself. "A price that will absolve you of the past wrongs done my family, and allow me to keep my power. That's all you need know, for now."

He was obviously a man used to getting things when he wanted them. His impatience showed in the narrowing of his eyes, in the tense muscle that twitched in his cheek.

"When, then?"

"Friday," she said quickly. "There will be a festival in the village for the birth of a baby, and I ask you to come, as my guest. Bring a gift, for the child, and I will tell you then."

"Friday! God's teeth, Isabelle, you try my patience! What am I to do till Friday?"

She shrugged. "Stay warm. A frost is coming." She continued on her way, her basket swinging, Crispin running at her heels and wagging his great white plume of a tail.

She didn't need to look back to know that he was watching her. She could feel his eyes on her back, angry and resentful. And her awareness was more than her knowledge of human behavior, more, even, than her gift of sixth sense.

It was as if she had some knowledge of Christopher Radbourne that was unique to her alone, as if she had known him for a hundred years. She was sure, if she looked back now, that she would see him glowering, raking his ringed fingers through his tousled dark hair. She could feel the heat from his eyes upon her back.

She liked the feeling, and that frightened her.

Kit stood in the road, staring after Isabelle. He marveled at her fearless arrogance. Obviously, she had never been trained to respect her betters.

But then, how could she have been? No lord had stayed in the castle long enough to gain any control in the area. And she was, after all, descended from the original lords of the keep. It must be, he decided, that breeding that gave her that particular air of grace and beauty.

He watched her as she made her way down the lane, quick and nimble, her skirt swaying like the yellow leaves that arched above her, her dark hair tumbling unbound from beneath her cap, proclaiming her status as a maiden as proudly as a banner in the breeze.

He wondered that she dared to travel the roads thus, with no fear of being accosted. But then, travelers were a rare thing in these parts, and no local would dare assault the witch.

No wonder she was loath to relinquish her power. He couldn't help but admire her cunning, even as he resented it.

He wondered what she had planned for him on Friday. He hoped it wouldn't involve drinking or eating anything particularly nasty. He had heard stories of these country witches with their concoctions of frogs and newts.

Though given a few more days on his meager diet, a newt might not look too bad. He reached for his pocket and felt the few silver shillings there. His purse was low, and showed no sign that it might be replenished in the near future.

Oh, well. He'd best go see that old robber Oswin, and see what it would cost for a meal today. The old man would have him a pauper in no time, he knew, but there was little help for it.

Until Isabelle lifted the curse. He should be grateful, he knew, for her agreement, but all he felt was a strong premonition of mistrust.

Seven

"Good Lord help us," Walter said, staring. "It looks more like a pack of Druids preparing for a sacrifice, than a christening festival."

Kit was inclined to agree. But there was something about this country, the wooded glens and wild moors and foggy hills, that made one inclined to superstitious thought. And tonight was no exception. The moon was full and golden, hanging low over the dark hills, and the village green between Oswin's inn and Father Timothy's church was lit with a huge bonfire. The cool night was scented with smoke and roasting meat.

The entire village seemed to be assembled there, all in their holiday finest, and the raucous laughter and chatter that rose from the crowd told Kit that their spirits were high.

Kit slid from his horse's back and tied him to a low hanging branch, his eyes searching the crowd for Isabelle.

All day he had been torn between relief that the curse would be lifted, and dread at the payment that would be demanded. True, he still had much coin, but it would not last a year at this rate, with Oswin charging him for every mouthful of coarse bread.

His misgivings temporarily fled at the scent of the varied

foods wafting in the cool air, and then vanished altogether when he stepped onto the green and saw Isabelle dancing in the light of the bonfire.

The country musicians were playing a quick and spritely air, the flutes and bells and drums sounding pagan and enchanting in the frosty air, and Isabelle was dancing as if she had been lured by a fairy spell.

She moved as gracefully as any noblewoman of the court—more so, really, not being weighed down by fashionable brocades and velvets and furs. She looked like a fairy queen, with a garland of ivy woven in her dark hair, and ribbons streaming from the gathered puffs of her sleeves. Her bodice was carefully made of velvet, and it perfectly fit the curves of her slender body.

He stood and watched as she moved with perfect ease through the steps of the country dance—three steps forward, and then three back, and then a half turn to her right where a new partner waited to spin her in three circles, to begin again.

He watched her like a man enchanted, missing nothing—the way she laughed at a passing remark, the way her arm lifted as gracefully as a willow branch, the show of brilliant white underskirts and slender ankles when she spun, and the way her rainbow-hued ribbons fluttered from her slender arms.

He was so intent on watching her that he didn't notice the attention he was receiving—the silence that descended over the crowd near him, and then spread, and the suspicious eyes watching him, until the musicians lay aside their pennywhistles and drums and bells, and the dancers stopped, all eventually turning to stare at him, the unwelcome stranger in their midst.

It seemed to him that he stood there a very long time, the focus of a hundred sets of wary eyes.

They were a strange bunch, these Farwindale folk, with their beliefs in witches and long-ago curses; what might have been an ordinary village festival did look strange and pagan: the young men gathered round the bonfire, the musicians with their flutes and drums, the young girls with flowers and ivy in their hair, the old men perched on benches like birds on a fence.

They all sat, still and silent under the pale moonlight, with the flames of the bonfire dancing across their closed and hostile faces.

Behind him, Walter cleared his throat and plucked at the sleeve of his doublet.

And then Isabelle stepped forward from the crowd of revelers, the color high in her cheekbones and her amber eyes alight. A low murmur ran through the crowd as she approached him.

"Welcome, Christopher Radbourne," she said clearly.

The whispers in the crowd grew louder, and then dwindled as all leaned in to hear what she would say next.

Kit stood as tall as he could, hoping that his unease didn't show on his face.

Isabelle was enjoying this, he could tell. The entire village was waiting for her to speak, to pass judgment upon him, at which time they would welcome him in or cast him out, as she saw fit. He had no doubt that if she ordered them to cut his throat, they would.

He was as much a victim of her power as he had ever been of the king's, and he hated it.

She smiled at him, and held out a wooden mug.

"Will you share my drink, sir?" she asked softly, and the crowd stared and whispered in a rising swell of disbelief as he reached out.

For a moment their hands touched, and he wondered briefly at the soft warmth of her hand before he took the mug and drank deeply of the spiced wine.

He offered it back, and couldn't help but feel relief as she put her lips to the cup where his had been, and drank. At least she wasn't poisoning him.

"Have you brought a gift, for the new baby?" she asked, lowering the cup.

He had been watching the line of her slender throat as she drank, and thinking what an incredibly intimate thing it seemed, that both their mouths had touched the same vessel. The question caught him unaware, and he jumped a little.

"Oh, yes. Of course. Walter . . ."

Walter offered him the silver cup he had chosen from his household goods, chased all over with a pattern of vines.

"This. It's good luck, you know . . . silver, for a christening . . ."

She tossed her head with a pretty gesture toward the fire, where a young mother, a wreath of marigolds crowning her hair, sat with a newborn baby. The motion set a loose curl bobbing against her cheek.

"Give it to Nan, then, with your wishes."

He walked over to the young woman, and murmured something stupid about how comely the child was, and offered her good luck. It annoyed him that the woman looked to Isabelle before accepting his gift.

But at Isabelle's nod, she accepted the cup in her work-roughened hand, staring in disbelief at the costly silver. Her husband, a tall, lanky-looking fellow, regarded the gift with distaste, and then spoke.

"See here—that's wrong, that. Bad luck, accepting something from the castle, I thought. We don't need bad luck."

The villagers murmured assent. Isabelle raised her hand with a graceful motion, and they fell silent.

"It was on this night, exactly sixty years ago, that my grandmother left Farwindale Keep, and spoke her words against those who dwelled there."

"More like fifty-some years, and 'twas June, I thought," murmured a voice near Kit's ear, and he glanced at old Oswin, who stood near his elbow, a mug in his hand and a sprig of ivy tucked in his wispy white hair.

"There have been signs, of late," Isabelle continued, "that the curse should be lifted. The last sign I saw in a dream. I saw the Lord of Farwindale bearing a gift of great value to a newborn child of the village. And you have seen it come to pass."

The villagers crowded closer, fascinated.

The father of the infant looked from his child to Isabelle, and then to Kit with wonder. "What else was in the dream, Mistress Isabelle?" he asked, his voice more respectful than it had been before.

"My lady grandmother, Bess of Farwindale, spoke to me. She said that a worthy lord would come, banished unjustly from the south because of his honesty and honor; a man who loved truth more than wealth."

"And cider, too, I reckon," muttered Oswin, but if he appeared unimpressed by Isabelle's speech, the others did not. They gazed at Kit with new respect.

Kit began to relax. This was going jolly well. Bless pretty Isabelle, she wasn't such a bad sort after all.

"And my grandmother said," Isabelle announced, "that the new lord would prove himself, and lift the curse. And he would do that by acting as serving man to any villager who might need his service, from the time he gave the gift until St. Crispin's day. That he would willingly bend his back to help the people of our village as much as he would ask it of them. And on that day, the curse will be lifted."

She turned to face Kit, and her amber eyes sparkled with secret mirth.

"Are you this man, my lord?"

Kit stood, silent and stunned and furious. Several replies came to mind, the mildest of which was "in a pig's ass." Damn her, and her glowing skin and pretty curls and vicious heart. How dare she?

He was Christopher Radbourne, lately one of the wealthiest and powerful men in the kingdom, and now being brought so low that he was expected to work as jack-of-all-trades to a village of ignorant peasants, in return for the services that had been his all of his life.

She smiled at him, as if she had read his thoughts.

He was trapped like a rat.

He doffed his hat, and made an elegant bow to her, keeping his eyes on her face and lowering one hand to his hip where his dagger rested. Though the bow was graceful, the deliberate stance of head and hand was an insult that would not have been lost on any courtier. It was not lost on Isabelle, either, though the villagers noticed nothing amiss.

And she seemed more amused than insulted.

"By the whim of fate, I indeed seem to be your man," he replied, hoping that his smile seemed less like a grimace than it felt.

The whispers around them rose, and became a chorus of exclamations and oaths and expressions of wonder. Such a thing was unheard of; it was amazing! It was a story that would be repeated around firesides for sixty years, he was sure.

The musicians took up their instruments, the villagers drank and chattered, and went to regard Nan's baby Jonathan with new interest, predicting an auspicious future for one whose christening day had been so eventful.

Old Oswin peered up at Kit, and took a healthy swallow from his horn cup. "Eeeh. Any man's servant, are thee?"

"Apparently so." Kit stared after Isabelle, blending into a circle of dancers.

"That's something, that."

"It is something," Kit agreed, his words short and bitten-sounding.

"Till St. Crispin's day," Oswin mused, scratching his balding head. "That be ... what? Nineteen days? Twenty?"

"I believe so." Kit watched as Isabelle spun past, her dark hair shining in the firelight. He wished he could grab her and throttle her.

"I need my rushes cleaned."

"I beg your pardon?" Kit stopped staring at Isabelle and turned to the old man at his side.

"The rushes. They be dirty, and want changing. Roof's leaking, too."

The old man's watery eyes were sparkling, as if he'd heard a splendid joke.

He had, Kit realized; and he was the butt of it.

"That's a good lad," Oswin said. "Come round tomorrow. Not too early, mind. I'm an old man."

"I've heard," Kit said. He turned his back. Walter was nowhere to be seen. Kit stalked through the crowd, scarcely noticing the smiles and welcoming looks that came his way, where a few days before he'd have paid his last crown for one.

At last he spied his manservant, dancing with a village maiden who was as robust as Walter was thin. "You ass," he muttered, venting his anger on poor Walter, who had already endured enough of his temper to earn a place in heaven.

"Out of sorts, my lord?"

He whirled to face her—Isabelle, the contrary, arrogant sham of a witch who had brought him lower than he ever could have dreamed.

"This hand is yours, madam," he said, glowering, "but the game is not yet done."

She raised a single brow, and smiled.

There was something particularly infuriating about that brow. He left the village green without another word, toward the horse that had also seemed to betray him. Behind him, the music and laughter of the revelers floated in the frosty night.

"Christopher!"

He ignored her until she came running up behind him and caught his sleeve.

"Please, my lord, a word."

"I should think you've spoken enough words tonight. Or do you plan to turn me into a dog, to beg for bones at cottage doors?"

At least she didn't laugh out loud.

"Please, sir. It wasn't my intention to humiliate you."

"In truth, Isabelle? 'Tis hard to believe."

Her fingers plucked at his velvet sleeve, and her clear eyes looked up at him, dark and earnest. "I swear. But it was the best way I could think of. You see, if I had just said, 'The curse is gone,' some would have believed, and some would not. But none would trust you. And they might have said that I was afraid of you. And if they have no faith in my power . . . why, I would be no better off than poor Nan."

He looked where she gestured, to the young woman with

the baby. At that moment, her young husband was bending to admire his new son, and he stopped to give his wife a tender kiss.

"Poor Nan," Kit said. "She certainly looks to be sorely suffering." He glanced impatiently at Isabelle, and to his surprise, he caught a look of sorrow in her eyes as she regarded the tender familial scene.

"God's nightgown, woman! What a fool you are. If you want a husband and child, go get them, and quit playing at being the mighty sorceress of the forest."

She whirled around, her eyes narrowing, a furious darkness in her cheeks. "It's not my fate," she said, lifting her chin proudly. "I would not give up my power."

"Ballocks," Kit retorted, pleased to have found a chink in her armor. "You and your piddling 'power.' It won't make love to you at night, or kiss your pretty mouth. Any common village wench is happier than you."

"Than we're even," she snapped. "Because all your noble birth and arrogance will never buy you the same. But you will miss it, and I will not. I'm not a stupid, wooden-headed girl, sighing for kisses. I don't need them."

Beneath the proud words, he heard a slight quiver in her voice. Uncertainty? Sorrow? Whatever it was, it gave lie to her statement.

What possessed him, he didn't stop to analyze. But her fierce denial struck him as a challenge.

Without hesitating, he pulled her to him. She started to speak, but had time only to exhale one indignant breath before his mouth covered hers.

He had meant to startle her, and mock her for it. But the second their lips met, all coherent thought left him.

Her mouth was soft and warm, like rose petals warmed by the sun. Her skin gave off an indescribable scent, like clean grass and spring flowers. And her body—at first she stood stiffly, her hands pushing against his chest, and then slowly, sweetly, she began to melt against him.

He had kissed a hundred women before, but he never remembered a feeling like this. He forgot who she was, who he was, why he was kissing her. There was only the indescribable sensation of those lips against his, and the warmth of her back, supple and smooth beneath the velvet bodice, and the feeling of her breasts tight against his chest, and his hand sought the silk of her hair, pulling her mouth more tightly against his own.

She tasted of apples and honey and spice. He felt as if he could live off the sweetness of it, and the breath that mingled with his own.

We are perfectly fit together, you and I.

The thought came so clearly to him that he thought he had spoken aloud. It startled him, so sure and clear did he hear the words.

He released her so abruptly that she stumbled a little, and then stood back, her slender hand rising to cover her mouth, as if her own lips had betrayed her.

He felt a surge of triumph, joyful and intoxicating, at the sight of her.

Her eyes were brilliant and dazed in her pale face, her dark curls tumbling from the ivy wreath that crowned her. Her bosom, soft and white in the moonlight, rose and fell rapidly with her breathing.

For a moment they were perfectly silent, staring at each other. An autumn breeze, cold and smoky, whispered past them, rustling leaves.

"It seems, Isabelle, that at last we have found something we can agree on." His own voice didn't sound too steady. No matter, he didn't care. He reached for her, already missing the feeling of her in his arms.

It was a powerful hunger, dark and insistent. He had never been the type of man to tumble peasant girls at his leisure; he had always considered it beneath him. But Isabelle—ah, this was different.

"Don't!"

Her cry was almost wild, and she stepped quickly away from him. Her eyes were huge, blazing with as much passion as fear, he was sure.

But he stopped, and lifted his hands back. "Isabelle?"

She was stunningly beautiful in the moonlight, her pale

face alight with a hundred emotions, none of which he was certain of.

"I'm no whore, sir." She was regaining her self-control, though her voice trembled. She turned and began walking away, her hair and skirt swaying.

"I didn't think you were! Damn, Isabelle . . ."

He wouldn't chase her. Damned if he would. He simply stood, his heartbeat thudding and his blood racing with a savage, hungry rhythm, watching her as she made her way back to the village green, the ribbons fluttering from her sleeves.

He watched as she took a few deep drinks from a mug someone handed her, and straightened the ivy garland in her hair with an uncertain hand.

Around her, people talked and laughed and raised their cups and danced. And she stood there, silent and somehow apart from them, looking very alone.

Like me, he realized. We two are much alike.

What utter rot. What was he doing, standing on a muddy road, thinking melancholy tripe about some wench? She was nothing, nothing at all to him but a very large thorn in his side.

Mind that thorn stays in your side, and doesn't reach your heart, Kit, he thought, and that struck him as so ludicrous, such melancholy schoolboy rubbish, that he swore out loud at himself.

The fire had gone out when he returned to the castle, and he was too disgusted to even bother with it. He fumbled around in the dark until he found extra blankets, and lay down to sleep on the cold hearth.

He spent a restless night, tossing and turning. Inevitably, his thoughts kept wandering toward Isabelle, imagining her body wrapped with his inside his fur-lined cloak, silken and warm against his skin.

Isabelle couldn't sleep. Restless and shaken by the depth of her own passion, she paced the floor of her cottage, filling the sleepless night with a hundred small tasks.

She blended anise with honey, laying in a good supply

for the colds and sore throats that would come with winter, and she thought of Christopher. Kit, his manservant Walter called him. It suited him. It made it easy to imagine him as he had been before he came to Farwindale, careless and merry and always laughing.

She strained the sediment from some elderberry wine she was fermenting, and wondered if Kit would like it. She imagined him sitting before her fire, complimenting her on her skill as he drank it, and then reaching for her . . .

"Stop it, Isabelle," she warned herself. She busied herself with her wine, and cleaned her table again.

In a rare moment of self-indulgence, she lit no fewer than eight beeswax candles, and settled herself before her tapestry frame, carefully unwinding the colored silks she had bought at last year's Michaelmas fair.

She looked at her tapestry thoughtfully. She had finished a fair rendition of the main keep of the castle, the steps surrounded by the dark brambles that had grown there as long as she could remember, brambles that managed to put off a few pale and spindly shoots of roses each spring. Suddenly, the image displeased her.

She threaded two needles, one with deep green and one with brilliant rose, and with painstaking stitches began adding leaves and roses to the brambles.

The process distracted her from the restless hunger of her body. While the forest and countryside slept, Isabelle worked until the gray hours of dawn, while Crispin slept at her feet.

Not since her grandmother had died did she remember her cottage ever seeming so lonely.

Eight

Christopher woke in the gray light of dawn, as had become his new habit. He huddled beneath his blankets, thinking, as he did every morning, of the days when he could loll in his feather bed, drinking warm cups of mulled wine, basking in the glow of a warm fire. Well, those days were gone. There was only the cold, the never-ending work, and Walter, with his sniffling and snoring.

"Good damned day," he muttered, and threw off his blankets all at once, braving the cold.

Walter, a snoring huddle of blankets, didn't stir, and Kit thought how strange it was that his servant lay abed while he built up the fire each morning. But Walter was damned useless at fire building, and he himself had acquired considerable skill at the chore. In fact, he was surprisingly proud of it.

The fire had burned down to a few coals, and the kindling was slow to catch. He puffed at it, and then, impatient, reached for a piece of paper that Walter had discarded. More of his maudlin, homesick poetry, he supposed.

He was crumpling the paper when his own name caught his eye, written in Walter's meticulous hand. Puzzled, he stopped and straightened the crumpled sheet.

A few lines into it, he hurled the paper to the floor, and whirled toward Walter, kicking the blanket in the area that looked most like Walter's skinny rump.

"Wake up, you Judas! You bloody turncoat! You half-arsed, sniveling ballocks . . ."

Walter leapt to his feet, scurrying away from Kit, clutching his blanket.

Kit gave chase, stumbling over an open chest, which gave Walter time to catch up a large silver goblet from the table, which he waved ineffectually at Kit as he sought refuge behind the table.

Panting, Kit stopped, trying to recover his dignity. "Stop waving that stupid goblet. What do you mean to do with it? Clout me on the head before you abandon me?"

Walter looked wildly about, as if searching for the explanation that might explain the predawn attack.

Kit pointed to the crumpled letter on the floor.

"What is that, pray tell?"

Walter paled, then took a deep breath and set the goblet down upon the rough trestle table. He lifted his chin with an attempt at dignity.

"My letter of resignation, sir."

"I read that much. So, it has come to that, Walter. After all these long years, and all the trials we have suffered together, you leave me like the others. Back to London, and a new position, and that long-nosed wench you left behind?"

"No, sir."

"No?" Confused, Kit waited.

"That is, yes, sir, but no, sir. I am leaving, sir, but I am not going back to London. I will stay here, in Farwindale."

Baffled, Kit said nothing.

"I am to be married," Walter confessed, and his gaunt face flushed with rosy pride. "I have never understood love before, but it has broken upon me with the same golden splendor as dawn herself, touching the cold and dreary hours of night, before which a mere man—"

"Your poetry is bad enough upon paper. I beg of you not to hurt my ears with it, at least not at this ungodly hour.

So, you have fallen in love. And who is this paragon of womanly perfection who has inspired you to such dazzling heights?'' Kit knew he sounded snappish and sarcastic, but he didn't care. He felt as abandoned as a lost puppy.

"Edythe," Walter said proudly, uttering the name in dulcet tones of delight.

"What, Edythe the brewer's widow?"

"The same."

"Good Lord, man! Are you joking?"

Walter drew himself up with affront. "Pray, sir, what can you mean? She is a delight and comfort, a very model of womanhood; a rare and precious gem worth any two women I have ever met."

"And the size of any two women," Kit muttered unkindly, but when he looked up and saw the joy in Walter's weasel-thin face, the pride in his pale eyes, something deep inside him was touched by the man's sincerity.

"God's blessings be upon you, my friend," he said softly. "It is a happy thing to find love in this uncertain world, and I wish you nothing but the best. You have been a good and loyal friend, above and beyond your duty, and I happily release you from your service."

Walter smiled and bowed, looking ridiculous in his long shirt, with his hair standing on end and his spindly, pale legs exposed.

"I thank you, my lord. You are as much or more of a gentleman in your reduced circumstances as ever you were in your wealth."

Embarrassed, Kit turned away and began pulling on his boots. "Thank you, Walter. Now, the great lord of the manor is off to shovel sheep dung from the fold at Farmer Higgenbottom's."

Walter gave an understanding nod. "My sympathies, sir. But take heart—the days are passing quickly, and soon the witch will lift her cursed spell."

"Not soon enough," Kit grumbled, and set off to his days tasks, feeling abandoned, mistreated, and, to his surprise, envious of Walter and his happiness.

· · ·

St. Crispin's day was fast approaching. The leaves were darkening and falling from the trees, and Isabelle had harvested the last roots and herbs from her garden before the frosts set in.

The days were darker now, swathed in fog or shrouded with rain, and she blamed her melancholy on the weather, and made excuses not to go into the village.

But always, she thought of Kit. The bits of gossip she heard from her infrequent visitors were not enough. She knew that Walter had abandoned him, and was living with Edythe the brewer's widow, and that a few days later Kit had quit the castle, and was sleeping at Oswin's inn.

She heard that he had been cutting reeds from the marshes for Edwin the thatcher, and having a miserable time of it, and had been hauling sacks of flour from the mill for the baker, and that he had even undertaken the foul job of cleaning the flea-ridden rushes from Oswin's floor, and a thousand other homely tasks that were part of daily village life.

But she didn't ask for details, not wanting to betray herself. The questions that she wanted to ask were kept closely to heart.

Does he think of me? Does he hate me? Does he wake up at night, remembering the way our mouths felt together?

She did. Though she never saw him, he was as much a part of her life as if he were there in the cottage with her. He intruded into her thoughts a hundred times a day, while she was spinning, while she was baking, while she was tying ropes of garlic to hang in her kitchen.

And she counted the days until October twenty-fifth, St. Crispin's day, when she knew she would see him again.

"I dread it as much as I long for it," she confessed to herself.

She was seated by the fire, sewing a new shift of fine lawn while the light was still good. The fabric was too soft and fine for an ordinary rail, so she was adding smocking at the neck and cuffs, and tiny vines and rose patterns in heavy white silk thread. It would be beautiful.

Her mind wandered, as it did too often these days, and

she imagined herself in the shift, with her hair loose, and Kit seeing her. The firelight would show through the fabric, and he would see her body through the gossamer folds, and take her into his arms . . .

Out in the garden, Crispin began barking, and she jumped, blushing. Usually, she could sense when someone was coming, but her thoughts had been so distracted lately.

She hurried to the door, smoothing her skirts. She glanced quickly out the window and saw that it was a man, clad in loose smock and heavy cape. Likely Martin Smithing, whose wife was near her birthing time. But it was early. She hoped there would be no trouble. Early babies frightened her—such fragile creatures, who took cold so easily and had trouble nursing.

She lifted the latch, and swung the door open, and her anxious greeting died on her lips.

It was Kit, stomping up the garden walk with a miserable look on his face. He was dressed in the homespun smock and rough woolen cape of a village man. He carried a large basket over one arm, like a woman going to market. Two of Isabelle's geese followed him, nipping at the heels of his worn boots, and Crispin followed the geese, occasionally chasing one a few feet away, but more interested in the visitor.

Isabelle was so startled at the sight of him, and relieved that Martin's child was not coming, that she burst into startled laughter.

Kit stopped, kicked at a goose, and glowered. "I'll thank thee not to mock me. I'm in a foul mood already."

"I beg your pardon, sir." Isabelle pressed a hand against her smile. "Pray come in."

He accepted her offer with a sour look, and stomped past her, shaking the raindrops from his hair. It had grown over his collar, she noticed.

"Here," he said with little grace, shoving the basket at her. "From the Atwoods. They bid me tell you that Betsy's cough is cured, and send thanks."

Isabelle looked into the basket, and found two hares, skinned and cleaned. "Give them my thanks."

"Tomorrow. My afternoon is full."

Even sulking, she found him delightfully handsome. The cold had stained his proud cheekbones with a red flush, and his eyes echoed the blue of the rough cape, dyed with common wood.

"Come sit by the fire, and warm yourself," she offered. "That is, if you have the time. What are you doing, that your time is so dear?"

He took off his cape, and sank into her chair. "If you must know, I'm watching the children while the women make sausages."

Isabelle choked back a laugh, trying to picture it. "Whose children?"

He cast a sharp glance at her, and hesitated, as if it hurt him to reveal more. "All of them. Or rather, a lot of them. An army of them. I can't remember the damned names. Young Tom, and young Bess, and a couple of Janes, and an uncommon number of little Henrys. And Bevin the beard puller."

She couldn't help it; she had to laugh again. "That would be Fenwick's Bevin."

He held his hands out to the fire. "Or Satan's. He's a scamp."

For a moment Isabelle stood quietly, just enjoying the sight of him, with his dark hair curling and damp from the rain, and his long legs stretched out as he warmed himself by her fire. Somehow, the peasant clothing made him seem more handsome than his velvet doublets and slashed sleeves. He looked thus in her daydreams, she realized. Not like a rich lord, but like an ordinary man. One that might love her, and ask her for her hand. A man that was not out of her reach.

He looked up at her, and she felt her cheeks warm, as if he had been able to read her thoughts.

"Would you like some wine? Some apple beer?" she asked quickly, turning away.

"Wine, if you please. My hours of leisure are small enough."

She hurried to get it, polishing the pewter mug on her

apron and choosing some of her best cowslip wine. When she returned with it, she found him looking at her tapestry.

"A fine rendition of that hellhole I own," he remarked. "Who are the people?"

"That," she said, pointing, "is my grandmother. And there is my grandfather. He was a fine carpenter. He built this house, and all the cupboards and chests. And over here . . ." She pointed beneath a blossoming apple tree. "That is my mother, feeding the doe. She died when I was very young."

"And your father?"

She shrugged. "Nobody ever mentioned him. I suppose that makes me a bastard. Though grandmother used kinder words. 'Love child,' and such."

"So you've no idea at all who fathered you?"

"I have an idea." She straightened. "I think he was one of the lords who came to live in the castle. He took what he wanted from my mother, and left. A common enough story. It's what happens to young women who let their hearts rule their heads."

"Ah," he said, sounding very knowing. "So you take your revenge against me, for the wrong done your mother. How very unjust, Isabelle."

The idea startled her. She considered it, and then shook her head. "No, I did not. Truly. I knew that you wanted the spell lifted, and I had no idea how. So I came here, and I sat, and . . . thought—" No need to tell him about the knowing, and that she had sat gazing into a bowl of water, as her grandmother had taught her. "—and that is how the answer just came to me. It seemed to make sense."

She turned away, and changed the subject abruptly. "How is Oswin?"

"How do you think? Miserable, bad-tempered, and demanding. Though he's delighted to have a servant to fetch and carry and cook and clean for him. Not that I do any of it well enough, mind you. Just ask him." Kit took a deep swallow of his wine, and drained the cup. "Very good," he told her. "Speaking of Oswin, he asked me to tell you that his hips are hurting, and will you send him something for the pain. And he demands to know why have you been keeping yourself away. Shall I tell him that you're avoiding me, because I heated your blood to such a frenzy that you're afraid of me?''

His frankness caught her by surprise, and the accuracy of his statement caused her face to flush with heat. Even her ears burned. For a moment she couldn't speak.

"That's a lie," she managed, finally. "I've been very busy, getting ready for winter." It sounded false, even to her own ears.

"Oh, come, Isabelle." He leaned back, looking truly pleased for the first time that day. "You know that it's so."

"I know that you're a pompous ass." She was still blushing, and her snappish reply only made him laugh.

"I've touched a sore spot, it seems." He reached out, rising from the chair, and caught her wrist. "Pray, Isabelle, is it so hard to admit? You're a young woman, and your blood is as warm as mine. I felt it."

"You didn't." She turned her head away, but he touched her chin with a warm hand, and gently turned her face toward him. "Look me in the eye, and deny it. Don't you remember? Standing in the trees, and the way your lips opened beneath mine? The way you pressed your breasts against me, and your hands against my neck?"

His voice was low and soft, and she had to close her eyes against the heat of his gaze, clear and blue and seductive. Oh, yes, she remembered. She had been unable to think of much else.

"Would it be so bad?" he whispered, and his lips brushed across her cheek, as softly as a swan's down. She shivered, and tried to ignore the rush of heat she felt moving to the very depths of her body. "Would it be so wrong?"

His breath was intoxicating, moving through her hair.

She pushed him away, and took a steadying breath. "Aye. It would be that bad. I'm not one of your serving wenches, for you to tumble at your will. And it would bring me nothing but grief, in the end."

He stood silently for a moment, and his eyes upon her

were as hot as his touch had been. "Would it? What is the worst that could happen, pray tell?"

"A child," she answered immediately. Even as the words left her mouth, she felt a quiver run through her body, and her vision blurred and darkened. *A child. Her own child. A child that she and Kit would make together, sharing their hearts and breath and bodies. A beautiful, strong baby, nursing at her breast, reaching his perfect dimpled hand to grasp his father's finger.*

The passion of the vision, the hunger for it, shook her. And it was not just the simple natural urge to bear a child, she knew. She wanted all of it. She wanted the man, as well. She wanted Kit to be there, to love her, to watch their child grow.

She had never wanted anything so fiercely, and she knew it was impossible. She was a peasant wench to him, and a bastard one at that.

"Go away, Christopher Radbourne." She couldn't look at him as she spoke, and the words were painful to say. "Go away, and don't come back with your lusty words and pretty face. I'll set my dog on you, if I see your face."

She sensed rather than saw him stiffen.

He was silent for a long time. "Very well," he said at last. "You've humbled me enough. I'll not ask anything of you again."

She didn't look up until she heard the door close behind him.

She stood there for what seemed a long time, her face hot and her eyes burning, until tears began rolling down her face. She dashed them away, calling herself fool and idiot and all manner of names, and ordered herself to be strong.

But her pretty cottage seemed emptier than ever. She had never felt so alone in her life.

Nine

Isabelle marked the days till St. Crispin's day, dreading it. She told herself to be strong. She need only see him at the feast, and pronounce the curse lifted, and be on her way. She need not see him or speak to him again.

The thought left her bereft and melancholy. She tried to empty her mind, and let the knowing visions come, with the inevitable sense of peace they brought, but she felt nothing, saw nothing.

It was as if Christopher Radbourne had moved into her mind, and left her nothing of herself. His kiss had depleted her energy, her power.

For the first time in her life, she had the feeling that she was fighting against her true fate, and she began to doubt the certainty of her visions.

But what she had told him was true. The twenty days' tasks she had set for him *had* come in a vision, she was sure.

Or was she? Was what he had said true? Was she simply deluding herself, taking revenge upon him for the wrongs done to her mother, and her grandmother before her?

She had never doubted herself before. She had always tried to act for the good of others, and it was that, she was sure, that made her strong.

She prayed for answers, but none came. When the village girls came to her, begging love potions and cures for troubled skin, when young mothers came for tinctures of mint and hops to cure the colicky stomachs of their babies, she dispensed her cures and advice as usual, but felt like a sham.

And at no time did her visions come to her with the certain, sure clarity they always had.

She had lost her power, she was positive of it.

The night before the feast of St. Crispin, she finished her fine new shift. She washed every inch of her skin carefully before putting the garment on and making ready for bed.

She blew out the candles and patted her dog, remembering the day that she had found him, exactly eight years before, a hungry and shivering puppy by the side of the road. She had been on her way to the feast in the village, and named him Crispin in honor of the day.

The dog gave a happy whine, and thumped his tail against the floor.

Funny, that his companionship had seemed enough for so many years.

She climbed into the clean linens and blankets of her bed, pulling the covers tightly under her chin and watching her cottage in the dim light from the fire.

Outside, the rain poured down in sheets, and the wind blew against a loose shutter.

She could not sleep.

She rose from her bed. A strong drink might help, she thought, and was on her way to find one when she stopped.

Her ears began to hum, and her vision darkened.

Knowing.

She stopped and waited, her eyes closed.

It came suddenly, strong and clear, invading her senses until she lost all sense of herself.

She was sitting in a chair before a fire, and yet she was not herself. She was seeing through somebody else's eyes, thinking another's thoughts.

Somebody was speaking to her, or to the person in the chair. A pleasant conversation. A young man, speaking of

*an especially harsh scolding he had received for not fetch-
ing water quickly enough. He was doing a wickedly funny
impersonation of Edythe, the brewer's widow.*

Isabelle tried to rise above the vision, to view it with
detachment, but could not. She took a deep breath, murmured, "So be it," and allowed her spirit to become one
with the man in the chair.

*It was good to laugh. So good, to have a young face at
the inn. God bless young Kit. What would it have been like,
to have a son like this?*

*If only I had not been so damned proud of my indepen-
dence. Should have got a wife while I was young.*

Oswin, Isabelle realized, in some far-off part of her mind.
She was listening to Oswin's thought, seeing through his
eyes.

He was watching Kit, and laughing at his stories. They
had fallen into a happy friendship.

Tomorrow, Oswin was thinking, *tomorrow that young
man's days of work shall be at an end, and I will be alone
again. Terrible thing, that. Not natural, for an old man to
be alone. He should have a wife, a house of fine sons,
someone to sit by the fire with him in his last days.*

Oswin's grief was so real to Isabelle that it hurt. His
loneliness made her heart ache. She tried to will herself
away from it, but could not.

She could only stand, her chest aching, trying to smile
as Oswin was smiling at Kit's chatter.

*The ache grew, and spread through his heart. It twisted
and burned. Young Kit's voice sounded as if it were growing farther and farther away, and the terrible pain was
pulling him down.*

*He tried to speak, tried to get Kit's attention, but the
pain was too mighty.*

"I'm going down, Kit," he thought, the only words in
his mind. *"I'm going down. Don't let me die alone."*

As clearly as if she were in the room, Isabelle heard Kit's
sudden shout of alarm, heard his boots rushing across the
room to the fallen man.

She could feel Kit's arms as he lifted Oswin, and she

could hear Oswin, now beyond words, begging silently for the pain to stop.

She could hear Kit's fear, and the panic in his voice, and heard him making soothing sounds, promising help.

And then suddenly she was standing in her kitchen, clutching her table for support, shaking.

Crispin stood before her, his anxious doggy eyes fastened on her face, wagging his tail.

"God grant me speed," Isabelle gasped, when at last she could speak.

Old Oswin was dying, and in terrible pain, and she must help him, if she could.

She flew across the floor, grabbing her basket with a trembling hand, and dumping the walnuts from it with a great clatter as she threw open her cupboard door.

Belladonna to relieve the heart, and the syrup of poppies to ease the pain. A dried sea sponge that had been soaked in mandragora, ivy, and hemlock. When wet, she could place it beneath a patient's nose, and the fumes would render him unconscious. She used it only in the most terrible cases of pain.

She dressed quickly, throwing her green woolen bodice and skirt on over her shift, pulling on her thick hose and leather boots. She threw her heaviest cape over it all, and grabbed her keys as she rushed to the door, Crispin following at her heels.

The darkness of the forest didn't bother her. She knew the hills and trails of the wood and countryside as well as she knew her own cottage, and with her dog at her side she had no fear of predators, human or animal.

Her only fear was that she might not reach the old man in time, and he might have to cross to the next world in pain, or without the words of reassurance and love that are every being's right, both when they enter the world, and when they depart.

It seemed that she could not hurry fast enough, even though she was almost running, her basket banging against her hip. She wished that she had the speed and endurance of her dog. Crispin ran happily at her side, his breath panting, his tail swishing like a white plume in the dark night. The rain didn't bother him.

Suddenly Crispin lifted his ears and gave a happy, welcoming bark. Isabelle peered ahead into the dark rain, down the road that led to the village. If someone was there, it was someone the dog knew, and liked.

"Isabelle! Is that you?"

It was Kit, running toward her, his white shirt soaked with rain, his dark hair plastered flat to his head. He reached out as he approached, and she didn't hesitate, but stretched her own hand out in return.

Their hands met, and they stood there in the darkness, trying to catch their breath, unable to speak.

"I was coming to get you," Kit said at last between hard breaths. " 'Tis Oswin—"

"I know." She breathed the cold air deeply into her lungs. "I'm on my way. Is he worse?"

Crispin circled them, barking happily, impatient to continue his run.

"Worse? I don't know what worse is. He is dying, Isabelle."

There was real grief in Kit's voice, and it touched her heart.

"Then let us hurry. He is a good man, and doesn't deserve to die alone."

He didn't let go of her hand as they hurried toward the old inn, and she was grateful for the warmth and comfort of it.

He was a good man, she thought. He had hurried out into the night without even stopping for his cloak, out of concern for an old man he had only known a little while.

She wondered briefly that Kit had come for her. He had never shown any respect or faith in her abilities before.

She glanced up at his face, but his expression showed nothing in the darkness. Only his hand over hers, strong and warm, seemed to offer her a promise of his strength and help.

They hurried down the road, the October wind blowing around them, and the rain dripping through the dying leaves as if the very sky were weeping.

Ten

Father Timothy was coming down the stairs of the inn as they entered, his aging face resigned. He greeted Isabelle and Kit with a resigned sigh.

"I have read his last prayers," he said simply. "It is in God's hands now. If you will ease his pain, Isabelle, it is all we can do, I think."

She nodded, removing her wet cape and draping it on the chair by the fire to dry. "I thank you, Father." It was not the first time they had been through this together, she and Father Timothy, working together to ease the dying into the next world.

She climbed the narrow stairs, holding her wet skirts so she didn't stumble.

Kit followed her. "I didn't know what to do," he explained softly. "I didn't want to leave him alone."

"You've done the right things, bless you," Isabelle reassured him. "There's no need to fret yourself."

She drew a deep breath before she went into Oswin's chamber.

"It was very small and empty. There was nothing in there that told anything of Oswin, or who he had been in his life. Just a very old man, lying in a bed, with his breath coming in slow, labored gasps.

Kit hung near the door, and watched as Isabelle approached the bed. She warmed her hands briefly over the flame of the candle, before touching Oswin's head.

She moved so calmly, with perfect ease, as she smoothed the sparse hair, and touched her slender fingers quickly to the old man's throat and chest, and then laid her hand across his forehead. She stood that way for a while, her eyes closed.

"Oh, Oswin," she murmured at last. "Don't be afraid. Here. I'm going to give you something to ease your pain."

"Can he hear?" Kit asked, staring at the closed eyes, and the gaunt face.

She nodded, reaching in her basket. She drew out a stoppered vial, and carefully placed a few drops against the old man's tongue.

"Only a minute or two," she said softly, "till the pain eases."

Kit watched, and after a minute saw Oswin's face relax and his breathing steady.

"Kit, will you bring me a chair, please?" she asked.

Anxious to feel useful, he hurried down the stairs and returned with a chair for Isabelle and a three-legged stool for himself.

Oswin looked better by the time he came in. His eyes were still closed, but his breathing seemed easier and his wrinkled face more peaceful.

"Is he going to get better?" he whispered.

Isabelle shook her dark head and smoothed her damp hair back from her face. "Nay. But he is not in pain. That is all I can do. And sit with him. He does not want to be alone."

Kit regarded the motionless figure in the bed. *We all come to this,* he thought, and he wondered, when his day came, who would smooth his hair and make sure that he suffered no pain.

He pulled the stool close to the bed. "Has he nobody we should send for?" he asked. "No family, no friends?"

Isabelle shook her head, her dark eyes sorrowful and soft

in the candlelight. "Oswin preferred to live alone. There's nobody."

Kit reached out and covered one of the old man's hands with his own, trying to warm the dry, cold fingers.

"There's us," he corrected. "You and I, Isabelle." He wondered if Oswin could hear him, and decided to trust Isabelle's word on the matter. "Don't worry, old friend," he whispered, leaning over the dying man. "I'll stay with you, as long as you need."

Isabelle stroked the old man's brow, as if he were a sick child. "It could be hours," she warned Kit.

Kit shrugged. "No matter. He fed me and helped me when no one else would. It's the least I can do for him."

Isabelle looked at him with gentle surprise, and then smiled; the grace and beauty of her eyes made Kit bend his head, awkward with the feeling.

They sat together through the long night, talking softly together, wiping the cool sweat from Oswin's brow and touching his hands with reassuring fingers.

It was a marvel to Kit, how calmly Isabelle spoke to the dying man, how efficiently she measured medicines to ease his pain or lighten his labored breaths.

He asked her once, how she had known to come.

She looked a little surprised, that he had asked. "I told thee before, Kit Radbourne. Sometimes I just *know*. The rest of it—the medicines and herbs—that is learned. The spells and charms—that is . . . well, not so much trickery, as it is an exercise in thought. But knowing . . . that is a gift. I thought I had lost it, for a time; but now I see I have not."

"And when you set me to my twenty days of work, Isabelle? Which was that? Trickery, or a true message, for a purpose?"

She smiled softly. "You know, I had begun to doubt myself. I began to wonder. But it was right, Kit. If I had not, up to the very day, asked for twenty days of labor from you, would you have been here tonight, when Oswin fell?"

Kit sat still, gazing at her across the bed where old Oswin

lay, seeming to sleep. "Nay, I would not have been here."

"And he might have died alone," she said. "It was what he feared most. It is an unnatural thing. He took much pleasure in your company, Kit. I thank thee for it."

Kit cleared his throat, and looked away to hide the sudden sheen in his eyes. "It was little enough," he said.

They sat together in silence for a very long time, while the candle grew shorter and the rain drummed on the roof. Oswin's breathing would sometimes falter, and then grow stronger. Isabelle sat beside him, her eyes closed, her slender hand covering his. She almost looked as if she might be sleeping, but Kit was sure that she was not. Her face was beautiful in its tranquillity.

He was admiring the gentle curve of her jaw, and the smooth curve of her cheek, when something in the air changed.

He wasn't exactly sure what it was, but suddenly the very air of the room seemed full. It felt like the waiting air before a storm breaks, or the silence in a room before somebody speaks, or the moments before the birds begin singing at dawn. It felt like all of these things, and not really any of them at all.

Kit straightened his aching back, and looked toward the bed at the same moment that Isabelle's eyes opened.

"It's time now," she said softly. "Can you feel it?"

She stood, and bent to kiss the forehead of the old man in the bed. Kit had to lean forward to hear her whisper above the sound of the rain on the roof.

"Don't be afraid, Oswin. I thank you for your friendship, and wish you well, with all my heart. Go with God, my friend."

Unable to speak, Kit leaned forward and took the old wrinkled hand that lay still on the bedcovers, and gave it a silent squeeze of farewell.

Oswin's chest rose and fell in a soft sigh. For a moment he was still, and then sighed again.

Isabelle laid her hand across his forehead, and closed her eyes. She looked as if she were praying.

Oswin exhaled softly, and then was still. He was simply gone.

Isabelle brushed her hand softly across the wrinkled cheek, and stood. She let out a deep, quivering breath.

"It is always hard," she said in a strained voice, "to bid farewell to a friend." She pushed her fingertips tightly against her eyes to stop the tears, and then gave Kit a shaky smile. "Thank you. He was grateful to you."

Kit released the old man's hand. He felt stunned. Of course, old men died; he knew that. But it seemed so strange that a human being could slip away so easily. One moment you were here, and the next gone, and so little to show for your life.

"It doesn't seem right, somehow," he said, his voice hoarse. "There's just nothing left, is there? A year from now, nobody will ever know that he lived. It seems so . . . wrong."

Isabelle nodded. "Thank God that he was not alone, and not in pain, Kit." She took the candle and went to the door. Kit followed, glancing back at the silent figure in the bed.

"I know," Isabelle said. "It always feels wrong to leave them, doesn't it?"

"It does feel wrong. There's just . . . nothing. Nothing left."

"That," Isabelle said softly, "is why people have children. So that there is always someone left to remember, to show that they were alive. Since Oswin has none, let that be our task. To remember him, and tell funny stories of him, and laugh."

Kit followed her down the narrow stairs, into the silent great room of the inn. Oswin's chair by the fire looked empty and lonely. The old man's mug lay where it had fallen on the hearth. He was surprised at the sting of tears in his eyes, the sorrow he felt for the cantankerous old fellow he had known so briefly.

Isabelle began moving with her usual quick, efficient steps, picking up the fallen cup and bearing it off to the kitchen, clearing away the trenchers from the table where Kit and Oswin had eaten.

What a wonder she was, Kit thought. Even now, sorrowful and with tears dropping from her dark eyes, she kept moving, always maintaining her air of tranquillity and purpose.

She brought him a cup of warm cider, and built up the logs in the fire, and fed the scraps of dinner to her dog.

She was scrubbing the long trestle table when Kit fell asleep in his chair by the fire. His last thought was how odd it was, that he took such comfort in her presence, and that if she ever did marry, her husband and children would be blessed.

Eleven

He stayed at the inn for a week, melancholy and alone. Father Timothy had suggested he do so, until the matter of what to do with the building was settled. It was more comfortable than the cold emptiness of the castle, so he agreed.

He sat, and brooded, and thought of what would become of his life.

Walter came to visit one night, and Kit got roaringly drunk on apple beer, and heaped abuse on his former servant, and, offended, Walter went back to his newly found bliss with the brewer's widow.

When he awoke the next day, Isabelle had been there and gone, leaving a gift of bread and mutton pies, and he sulked that she had not awakened him.

On the day after All Saints' Day, he awakened to a tremendous noise. There were dogs barking, and people laughing. It sounded as if the common room of the inn was full.

He hurried down the stairs, pulling on his breeches, his boots in hand.

The entire village seemed to be assembled there, down to the youngest child, and all buzzing with excitement. His eyes found Isabelle immediately, gowned in the soft green she favored, her hair freshly combed and streaming from beneath her cap.

"I give you good morning, sir," she called, laughing up at him.

The villagers echoed the greeting. Kit, running a hand through his tangled hair and still dazed from sleep, replied awkwardly.

"Is it a feast day?" he asked, confused by the activity. " 'Tis barely dawn."

"Of sorts," Isabelle replied, a mysterious smile playing on her lips. "Come, Kit Radbourne. Had thee forgotten, this past week? The curse upon Farwindale Keep is lifted, and we have all come to offer our congratulations."

"Oh." Kit was unsure what response was called for, and stood uncertainly.

"Isn't that just like 'im?" he heard a woman say. "So sorrowful over our Oswin he'd no time to think of himself."

There was a general consensus to this, and the men said what a good fellow he was, and the women clucked and said things like "poor lamb," and other silly things.

"Hurry, Kit Radbourne," Isabelle cried, "and dress yourself. We've a gift for you."

"A gift? Oh, no, really . . ." His protest was shouted down by the crowd, and Kit found himself pulled to the door, where Sidney waited, a village boy holding his reins. His saddle was freshly cleaned, the silver trappings sparkling.

Wondering, Kit climbed upon the horse's back, and waited.

"Go on," Isabelle said. "Your gift waits at your castle."

Confused, Kit looked at the crowd. Everywhere he looked he saw encouraging smiles, and suppressed secrecy.

"Alone?" he asked. "Pray, come with me, Isabelle." He offered his hand to her, and after a slight hesitation, she climbed up behind him, holding tightly to his waist.

"Let us be off, then," she said, and perplexed, Kit started down the lane, the shouts and good wishes of the villagers following them through the fog and darkness of the early morning.

Kit stopped abruptly on the road, staring in disbelief at the castle.

The trees had been cleared from the walls, and the brambles pulled away. The drawbridge had been repaired, and the fallen logs and weeds dragged away from the moat. Fresh torches blazed on either side of the gatehouse, creating glowing halos of light in the mist.

The haunted, decrepit look was gone. Garlands of ivy and autumn flowers hung from the gate.

Isabelle laughed with delight. "Go in," she urged.

Sidney carried them over the drawbridge as if he knew his way home, and to Kit's surprise, one of the village boys came running from the stables to take the reins.

The weeds and thorns that had climbed over the steps were cleared, and as Kit mounted the steps, Isabelle behind him, the great doors swung open.

"Welcome home, sir," Walter said, bowing. Behind him, Edythe the brewer's widow, neatly gowned, bent her plump body in a curtsy before coming to take his cape.

Speechless, Kit stepped into the great hall. The dust and cobwebs were gone. Torches lined the walls, and a hundred candles of fragrant beeswax sparkled, reflecting off the polished and waxed stone floors.

A fire burned in the great fireplace, and where the hall had been empty, there were now tables and benches and chairs of new oak, plain, but clean and shining.

The carpets and tapestries he had brought from London lay on the floor and covered the walls, and more fresh garlands hung everywhere, lending a festival air.

The smell of baking bread and roasting meat wafted from the kitchens.

"God's nightgown," Kit exclaimed, staring at the transformed room.

He turned to see Isabelle smiling. "Do you like it?" she asked. "True, 'tis not what you are used to, I'm sure—"

"It's amazing. How did this happen?"

"Oh, everyone helped. The whole village. Work goes quickly when everyone turns their hand."

He moved through the rooms, dazed. He climbed the staircase of ancient stone and found a bedchamber clean and fragrant with herbs, a mattress of goose down, clean linens, a fire blazing in the fireplace. On the wall there, he found Isabelle's gift to him—the tapestry she had been working.

He stopped before it, admiring the work. There was her grandmother, Bess of Farwindale, and her mother, feeding a graceful doe. There was the castle gate, garlanded in roses.

He was grateful. It was part of Isabelle, of the long and lonely nights she had spent in her cottage, and the memories of those she loved. It was a priceless gift.

His favorite goblets of brilliant Venetian glass stood on the bedside table, and a decanter of dark Corsican wine.

He filled two glasses and went downstairs, where Isabelle waited by the fire, seated on a cushioned bench.

"What think you, my lord?" she asked.

Kit paused, looking at her. Her eyes of amber and mahogany sparkled at him; the apricot blush on her cheek was bright with pleasure.

"The truth?"

"Aye, the truth."

Kit coughed, and offered her one of the glasses before he answered.

"It does not please me."

Her dark brows rose, and her mouth dropped with indignation. She stared at him, fury rising in her eyes.

"It doesn't please you?" she echoed, her voice incredulous.

"Nay. Do you expect me to live like this?" He waved his hand around the clean and glowing hall. "Truth, Isabelle, it . . . lacks."

Her eyes were sparkling with rage, and he hoped she wouldn't bash him with the wineglass.

"And what exactly is it that you lack, my lord?" Her words were short and sharp.

"A woman," he said simply. "I would rather have liked to find one in my bedchamber. A beauty, to grace the down of that mattress. If it wouldn't be any trouble."

She was incoherent with anger and began sputtering. Kit couldn't recall ever having seen her speechless before.

"Let me be more specific," he said, trying not to laugh. "You see, I've had a lot of time this week past, sitting by the fire and thinking . . ."

"Whilst we were breaking our backs to please you!" she spat.

"And," Kit went on, as if he hadn't heard her, "I've come to certain conclusions about my life here."

"Oh, pray, enlighten me," she said, her words cold and dripping with sarcasm.

"Well, I must first make a liar of myself," Kit said. "For I promised you I would never humble myself to you, and now I needs must. I doubted much about you, Isabelle, and learned that I was wrong. And you say the curse is lifted, but it was said that the curse would hold till the castle was restored to your family.

"So, I propose that we solve all problems at once, with your grace. Woman, curse, my life, all of it."

She stood, wary and uncertain, her eyes fastened unblinking on his face, her fingers tight around the stem of her goblet.

Kit allowed himself to smile at last, and dropped to his knee. "Isabelle Lathrope of Farwindale, witch of the misty forest—I would beg a final favor of you. And then, I swear, this really *is* the last time I will humble myself before thee, so enjoy this."

She stood frozen, her eyes baffled.

"I beg of you to have pity on me, and marry me, and in doing so, I return this castle and what lands are left to it to your family, who lost it unjustly because their honor was so dear to them. I beg you to be my wife, and stay by my side always, and carry my children beneath your heart; for I can think of no safer or precious place to be. And when I am as old as Oswin, let your kiss be the one that I last feel, and let your words of love see me safely to the next world. And I will wait for you there, forever if I must.''

She dropped to her knees, and her face was pale and stunned. She stared at him as if she could not trust her ears. Tears filled her eyes, and trembled like stars on her lashes.

''Truth?'' she asked, so softly that he could hardly hear it.

''Truth,'' he replied, and raised his glass in pledge to her.

She exhaled quietly, and raised her glass to his, and they each took a sip of the dark, sweet wine.

Kit threw his glass into the fireplace, where the precious glass splintered into a million sparkling shards.

''There. No less wish can ever be made upon that.''

She stared at him, and slowly shook her head, and her smile shone on him like spring sunlight. ''You mean it.''

He bent forward in answer, and their lips met. The rest of the world fell away as their souls touched in the magic of their mingled breath, and the curse of Farwindale fell away into the mists of time.

It was a favorite story of the villagers, told time and time again, repeated always at the feast of St. Crispin, and around a hundred hearths throughout the rest of the year. It was irresistible: the young and handsome lord who had been enchanted by the village witch. Old Oswin's grave became something of a shrine, and it was said that if you were very polite to him, he would grant favors to young lovers.

And it was told over and over again, how the morning after Isabelle had first risen from Christopher's bed, and gone out the castle doors to wash her face in the dew (for everyone knew that was how she stayed beautiful), the thorns that had grown around the castle door had burst into a hundred roses—in November, no less! More cynical folk thought that they had bloomed because of the first vigorous pruning they had suffered in sixty years.

But it seemed a good sign; and must have been, for Isabelle bore no fewer than four sons and two daughters, and all of them lived, and were strong until old age.

Isabelle and Christopher lived to see sixty years together, and shared every day together, until the day that the old man passed over. And it was said that he did so with a smile, with his wife's kiss of love upon his lips, and her promise that she would join him.

The roses that grow on the wall of the castle bloom every November, in defiance of the winter, showing brilliant scarlet in the mist. They are considered to bring great fortune to lovers whose hearts are true.